Praise for Ward Larsen
and
THE PERFECT ASSASSIN

"... plenty of action ... technical detail that would do Tom Clancy proud ..."
— *Publishers Weekly*

"a top-notch international spy thriller. ... exciting ... entertaining ... intriguing ... this book has it all ..."
— **Military Writers Society of America**

"... a high-octane thriller that brings back memories of Robert Ludlum. Larsen knows how to keep the pages turning."
— **James Swain, bestselling author of** *Midnight Rambler*

"A spy novel with heart and emotion. *The Perfect Assassin* is as intriguing as it is exciting."
— **James O. Born, author of** *Escape Clause*

"... a solid spy novel ..."
— *Midwest Book Review*

"Ward Larsen delivers a thriller ... a dynamic new voice in espionage and intrigue."
— **Debbie Stowell, Circle Books**

"A thriller that slowly weaves the threads of various events together to create a tapestry of intrigue of the highest order ..."
— *ForeWord* Magazine

THE
PERFECT
ASSASSIN

THE
PERFECT
ASSASSIN

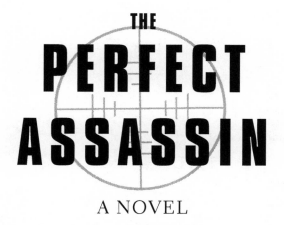

A NOVEL

WARD LARSEN

OCEANVIEW PUBLISHING
SARASOTA, FLORIDA

FIRST OCEANVIEW PAPERBACK EDITION 2007

ISBN 978-1-933515-15-1

Published in the United States by Oceanview Publishing
Sarasota, Florida

www.oceanviewpub.com

10 9 8 7 6 5 4 3

PRINTED IN THE UNITED STATES OF AMERICA

With apologies to LvB

Für Elise

THE PERFECT ASSASSIN

Prologue

CAPE TOWN, SOUTH AFRICA

The longshoremen scrambled across the pier to finish their task. Lured to work by an offer of triple-time wages, the few who had shown up were getting anxious. The cargo had arrived late, and tonight everyone had more important things to do. Tall floodlights presided over the operation, their sulfuric glow staining the night sky an obscure yellowish hue, and calm winds were no help in flushing away the noxious haze that had settled over the city. Mostly it came from the fires outside town, but now mobs were adding to the conflagration, looting and burning in the city itself as the last viable corner of the Republic of South Africa slid to oblivion.

At 2,000 tons, and 150 feet along the waterline, *Polaris Venture* was not among the largest ships to have visited the Port of Cape Town in the last week. She was, however, the only vessel berthed there now, and that singular presence managed to enhance her stature. A converted trawler built by Sterkoder of Norway, her lines were decidedly square, as if to attest to the solid vessel she was. *Polaris Venture* had been in port for eight hours, which was about as long as anyone had stayed lately, but having taken on her cargo it was time to go. The loading crane and gangways backed away, and dockhands on the pier tossed heavy mooring lines into the water. *Polaris Venture*'s crew scurried around deck to hoist up the lines, then her single screw was engaged and she began to crawl up the channel.

The ship moved slowly toward the jetties and open ocean. A

leviathan in the narrow waterway, she'd soon become a speck on the vast ocean ahead. Sliding beyond the lights of the pier, *Polaris Venture's* profile fell to a vague silhouette. By the time she'd cleared the jetties and picked up speed, her running lights and a dim glow of white light from the bridge were all that punctuated an otherwise black ocean. Minutes later these extinguished, a nicely symbolic end to the entire affair, as the port would likely not see traffic again for a very long time.

The ugly noose of apartheid had been lifted over a decade ago, but those expecting quick rise of a new and just South Africa had been roundly disappointed. Like a failing dam, the cracks had started slowly. Festering land disputes and tribal arguments seeped out. Corrupt politics added pressure until, seemingly overnight, the madness burst through. The authorities were little help, they having already begun to split and polarize to the different camps. It was a textbook civil war left behind in *Polaris Venture's* wake, one whose course to an end would be anything but a predictable, straight line.

Back along an empty pier the dockhands dispersed, many silently wondering if they'd ever see work here again. A second group of men, those who had delivered *Polaris Venture's* cargo to the docks, gathered uncertainly around their leader. With the final seams of order shredding in a country that had been undone by racial bitterness, it was an odd counterpoint that the two dozen soldiers were equally divided — twelve black and twelve white. Their uniforms were sanitized, displaying rank, but no regimental patches or other insignia. This much had been a firm directive, related to the night's work. But it was also an appropriate terminus for a unit whose sole mission had just departed on the high tide.

The detail's leader, a colonel, had little to offer. With a few words of congratulation on a job well done, he awkwardly dismissed his troops — to what or where nobody was sure. The men milled about for a few minutes to say their own good-byes, then disbanded in groups of two or three, knowing they would likely never see each other again.

The colonel was the last to leave. He paused on the pier, his thoughts still resting with his troops. He was an honorable sort who, while not particularly religious, did find comfort in the occasional divine request. The colonel stood at water's edge, closed his eyes, and offered a prayer for his men, a simple plea that their treason might be lost in the chaos.

Chapter One

Christine Palmer saw it right on schedule, a waxing three-quarters moon on the horizon. Bright and beautiful in its own right, the moon began lifting up toward the stars for what would certainly be another celestial master-piece over the eastern Atlantic. She'd always been amazed by the number of stars you could see out here, away from the usual lights and pollution. Gentle swells made a rhythmic, hollow slapping noise against *Windsom's* fiberglass hull. The only other sounds were those of the boat's rigging, which creaked and groaned in proportion to the strength of the wind.

Christine raised her chin into a crisp southeasterly breeze, finding it remarkable that conditions on the open ocean could vary so greatly. The first night of her trip had been like this one, calm seas and a gentle breeze. The second night had been a singularly miserable experience. A strong weather system had rolled in, pounding *Windsom* with vicious winds and towering waves. Christine could do no more than keep the boat on course and the sails trimmed, all under a constant lashing of rain and frigid ocean spray. She'd spent most of that night on deck, wet and chilled to the bone. When the storm finally broke, late the next morning, she had col-lapsed onto her bunk, without even the energy to remove the foul weather gear that had done so little to keep her dry.

That had been four nights ago. Since then, the weather had largely cooperated and Christine convinced herself, perhaps with reaching opti-mism, that such trying times were necessary to find true appreciation of life's more placid moments. It was a satisfying concept, and one she sus-pected would be quickly discarded in the next squall.

Sitting at the helm, she twisted her shoulder-length hair into a pony-tail and poked it through the back of her baseball cap. The luminescent hands on her watch told her it was five-thirty in the morning. The sun wouldn't be up for an hour. Christine tended to be an early riser, but sail-ing somehow magnified the trait. In the four days since the storm her rou-tine had taken shape. She went to bed an hour or two after sunset, set the alarm to wake up once at midnight to check the sails, the autopilot, and the weather, then slept again until four or five. Aside from the one wake-up call, it was a natural fit for her body's circadian rhythm. And it allowed her to enjoy her favorite time of day.

Christine went below to the galley. When she crawled out of the bunk each morning, coffee was always the first order of business. It had to be brewing before she could go topside to face the day's other issues, such as whether or not *Windsom* was still pointed west. She poured her fix into a big ceramic mug, the one her father had given her last Christmas. It was an oddly shaped thing, similar to the Pyrex flasks she'd used so often in chemistry lab, wide at the bottom and tapering to a narrow, round open-ing at the top. The mug had drawings of famous schooners all around and a rubbery non-skid coating on the base. It was, in fact, the very same cup she had picked out for her father that Christmas. Mom had instantly seen the humor — the two sailors thinking alike again, probably even ordering from the same catalogue.

The pain returned as Christine thought of her father. It had been three months since Dad had died, and the hurt still came, only not as of-ten, and it dissipated more readily. Being on *Windsom* seemed the best tonic. It had been a place of great happiness for their entire family this last year. She and Dad had crossed east to Europe last summer. On arriving in England, Christine flew back to Maine to finish her third year of medical residency. Then Dad had somehow coaxed Mom to England to spend a month cruising Europe and the Mediterranean. This was a terrific coup, since Mom normally kept herself a great distance from all large bodies of water. Christine had no idea what persuasions her father might have used to get Mom aboard until the answer slowly presented itself — a constant stream of postcards from the ports of Europe. It was a second honeymoon, Christine thought, much deserved after having spent twenty-eight years raising a family.

Christine smiled as the pain subsided. Making this westbound re-turn was a catharsis of sorts. It was the first time she'd ever tried the cross-

ing alone, her two previous runs having been with him. She had been trying to talk Dad into it only weeks before the stroke — a solo retrieval of
Windsom from France during her winter break. He hadn't gone for the
idea, and initially Christine was angry, thinking his reservations had to do
with her sailing ability. That didn't wash, though. Christine had been sailing since she was a kid, and they'd both spent countless hours on *Windsom*. She decided he was only disappointed that she hadn't invited him
along. Or perhaps he saw it as a final sign that his fledglings were all truly
gone from the nest. Christine was the oldest, but her two younger sisters
had recently ventured off on their own, one to college and one to the al-
tar. Yet even after they were gone, Ben Palmer continued to dote on his
girls. The fact that "little Christi" had been out of the house for nine years,
and was more often addressed as Dr. Palmer, didn't diminish that she was
still his girl. And only now did Dr. Palmer realize how much she'd actually liked it.

Christine went back up top, making sure to reconnect the safety line
to her harness. It was a fast rule to never be on deck without it. Even the
most sure-footed sailors could be sent overboard by a snapped line or a
freak wave, and it was a sealed fate for a solo driver to go over in the open
ocean without being attached to the boat.

She estimated her speed at four knots, about right for the untended
graveyard shift. Now that she could keep watch on things, though, Christine let out more sail and was soon making closer to six. She clambered
around the perimeter of the boat, checking *Windsom*'s rigging up close. A
halyard needed adjusting on the mainsail. A tie-down was loose on the
eight-foot fiberglass dinghy that lay overturned and lashed to
the portside deck. Her only other discovery was a small flying fish that
had come aboard — recently, judging by the fact that its gills were still la-
boring slowly. Christine gently picked up the fish and dropped him back
into his element, trying to see if he swam off under his own power. She
couldn't tell.

It took half an hour for Christine to finish her morning rounds. Afterwards, she settled into the cockpit with her second cup of coffee. She
held it close with both hands, not wanting to let any of the heat escape. It
would still be a couple of weeks before the latitude and trade winds took
the chill from the air. She looked to the horizon astern, brushing away
strands of hair the breeze had swept across her face. Christine could just
make out the subtle glow that announced the entrance of a new day. She

watched, mesmerized, as the eastern sky slowly fell awash in rays of light. Then *Windsom* shuddered along its entire length.

Coffee went flying as Christine's hand shot instinctively to the tiller. "Christ!" she sputtered. The boat had hit something. Something big. Christine stood and looked ahead, but there was only ocean. A heavy scraping sound drew her attention to the port side, close in, where a huge timber slid by. It was half the length of her boat and as big around as a telephone pole. With another hollow clunk, it fell behind, rolling heavily in *Windsom's* wake.

Christine disengaged the autopilot and turned into the wind. The sails flapped loosely as she scanned all around. There was more flotsam. An empty gallon jug and some smaller bits of wood, but nothing like the first monster she'd hit. She eased the boat back on course and pulled in much of the sail to keep her speed down.

Reaching into the cabin, Christine found the binoculars. The sun broke the horizon to provide light as she scanned the surrounding seas, giving particular attention to what lay ahead. She spotted more debris, but nothing worrisome. It had probably come from one of the big ships, either thrown off as trash, or washed over in a storm. In any event, she'd keep her speed down for awhile until she was sure it was all behind.

Christine re-engaged the autopilot, figuring she'd better go up front to check for damage. She moved forward along the port rail, still scanning the waves ahead suspiciously. Nearing the bow she spotted something, bright red and squarish, bobbing in the distance to starboard. It looked like a big plastic cooler, and there was something lying over the top of it. She brought up the binoculars, focused, and was stunned by what she saw. It was an *arm* hooked over the cooler. There was actually someone out there!

Christine dropped the binoculars, but kept her eyes locked on the cooler as she backed toward the cockpit. She averted her gaze just long enough to open the hatch to the engine controls and start *Windsom's* small diesel. It sprang to life and Christine swung the boat straight at the bobbing red dot — she knew how hard it was to find something out here once you lost sight of it. Looking again with the binoculars, she could make out a head and shoulders above the water. Once she was closer, and certain she couldn't lose contact, Christine pulled in the sails to better maneuver.

As *Windsom* closed in she saw the person, a man, turn his head and wave weakly. Christine slowed the boat to a crawl, idling the engine ten yards away. She wouldn't venture any closer in the small but rolling seas.

"I'll throw a line and pull you in!" she shouted.

The man waved again.

Christine coiled a rope and heaved it across the divide, but the line fell away as he snatched at it. She gathered it in and tried again, this time laying the line right across his shoulder. He grabbed on and was barely able to wrap it once around his wrist. Christine pulled the man slowly toward *Windsom*'s stern, but halfway there he lost his grip — first went the cooler, then the rope. He disappeared underwater, but came right back up. Without the cooler for support, the man seemed barely able to tread water. When he went under a second time, Christine had no choice. She checked that her harness was secure and dove in.

The shock of the cold was piercing. The man resurfaced as she swam over, and Christine approached him from the rear. "I'm behind you!" she shouted. "Just relax and let me pull you in!"

He went limp so suddenly that Christine wondered if he was even still conscious. She threw an arm across his chest and started pulling herself back toward *Windsom* by the line, praying he was alert and strong enough to get up the boarding ladder. She approached it with care, as the stern rose and fell heavily on the waves. Christine grabbed the bottom rung and was relieved to see him do the same.

"Okay, you first. Try to get a foot on the bottom step," she said. It dawned on her that the man might not speak a word of English. He got a leg on and she tried to shove him upward, but then he lost his grip. The man tumbled back in a graceless flop and disappeared. Christine lunged out, snatching with her hand, and was rewarded with a fistful of shirt. Pulling with all her strength, she got him back up, coughing and spewing.

Christine had only been in the icy water for a few frantic minutes but she already felt her strength beginning to ebb. She wasn't strong enough to pull him up from above. *It was such a damned simple problem!*

They both latched onto the ladder again and she yelled, "This time when the boat falls with the swell, try to get both feet on the ladder and stand. Let it pull you out as it rises, okay?" She pointed to the bottom of the ladder and the man gave a nod as if he understood.

With all the leverage she could manage, Christine pushed him up as the stern fell. He stood on the ladder and rose with the next upward swing. The wave crested, and at the high-point he wobbled for a moment, like a child's top losing its spin, then tumbled forward into *Windsom*'s cockpit. "Yes!" she shrieked, right before getting slapped in the face by a breaker.

Putting a leg on the ladder, she came out with the next swell and crumpled to the floor of the cockpit next to him, frozen and completely out of breath. She could only imagine how he must feel. The man lay still as Christine collected herself. She knelt next to him, checking his pulse. It was weak, too slow for all the exertion. His skin was deathly pale, almost white. Then she noticed the blood stain on his shirt. She unbuttoned it far enough to reveal a four-inch gash running between the bottom two left ribs. He'd obviously lost some blood. Christine wondered how long he'd been out here. With that kind of injury, and with the water so cold, it couldn't have been long.

The man stirred and looked around blankly, a dazed expression on his face. He tried to sit up, but *Windsom* took a wave broadside and the jolt sent him back down to the deck, grimacing. Adding insult, both were doused with a sheet of salty spray.

Christine looked across the water and wondered if there could be any others. If so, would he even know?

"Do you speak English?" she asked.

The man didn't respond. His eyes drifted shut, and Christine knew what had to be next. She pulled her best drill sergeant's tone — he might not understand the words but at least she'd get his attention. "We've got to get you down below, into a bunk!" His eyes cracked open and she motioned to the cabin. He seemed to comprehend.

She helped him stand, and he leaned on her heavily, in obvious pain. They made their way to the steps, which he negotiated with the wobbling precision of a drunkard, Christine doing her best to stabilize his wandering inertia. Once in *Windsom*'s main cabin, he collapsed onto the bunk. She propped his head on a pillow and figured the wet clothes were next. Gently, she pulled off the tattered shirt. His upper body was lean and muscular, and judging by the number of scars, Christine decided he must have found himself in the company of strange doctors on a regular basis. There was one particularly nasty-looking scar near the fresh wound on his ribcage. She took a good look at the new damage, hoping it was superficial.

"Any pain when you breathe?"

Again, no response. His eyes were closed and he was still pale, but at least the man's respiration had slowed now that he was lying down. To top it all off, he had what looked like a terrible sunburn, his face and arms blistered from exposure to the elements. She dug out her first-aid kit and dressed the wound, then checked for other injuries — any cuts, swelling or bruises. Christine gently palpated his rib cage and abdomen, finding no obvious complications. He wore no shoes, but she noticed when she took off his wet socks that the bottom cuffs of his pants were bound tightly around the ankles, tied with shoelaces. How strange, she thought. Christine untied them and removed his sodden trousers, leaving the man in his briefs. Next she got a towel, dried him off, and finally covered her patient with two heavy blankets. He stirred for a moment and his eyes opened, but they were void any semblance of coherence.

Christine went to the galley and poured a glass of water. She pressed it gently to his lips, "Try to drink. You must be dehydrated."

He managed a few swallows, but then coughed roughly.

"Take your time."

His eyes focused more clearly and he scanned the cabin, obviously trying to comprehend his surroundings. He finished the water, then drifted off again.

Christine was weighing what else she could do for the man when it dawned on her. *Damn!* She had never checked *Windsom* for damage. She wouldn't be much help to anyone if the boat was sinking.

Christine hurried up the stairs, refastened her harness, and went to the bow. There, she leaned over and saw where the big timber had first struck. The paint was gouged, and there was a noticeable scrape back along the port waterline. She looked closely, but didn't see any structural damage. Thank God for the resiliency of fiberglass, she thought. Just to be sure, Christine decided to check the hull from the inside. She looked over the railing and tried to gauge just how far down the damage was from deck level. That picture in mind, Christine headed back aft. She was approaching the companionway when she heard the crash from below.

She rushed down to find her stranger sprawled across the map table, an empty water glass in hand. Then she saw the smoke, billowing from a wet, buzzing rack of radios. Christine whipped around and opened up the fuse box on the bulkhead behind her. She tripped the breaker labeled NAV/COM and a couple of others for good measure. The equipment powered down, and seconds later the smoke began to taper off.

"That's all I need!" she said with a scowl. "An electrical fire to top off my morning." She picked the man up and guided him back to the bunk. He seemed weaker than ever.

"If you need more water, ask!" she chided. Her admonishing tone was sure to circumvent any language barrier. "You shouldn't get up for anything!"

He raised the palm of one hand, an obvious apology.

Christine sighed. "All right, all right," she softened, "just let me do the work."

She refilled his glass and gave him another drink. This time he took half, then settled back and closed his eyes.

Turning to the radio rack, she eyed it dejectedly. Later she'd have to dismantle everything and dry off the components. Questions began to turn in her mind. Were any others still in the water? How could she summon help with all communications temporarily out? Christine wiped the table dry and spread out a map. They were at least two day's sail from the Madeira Islands. Lisbon was slightly farther in the other direction. Even if she could reach someone by radio in the next few hours, Christine doubted a real search could be mounted before tomorrow morning. By then it would be pointless. Nobody could live for two days in water so cold. Within these constraints, Christine set her plan.

She would search all day for any other survivors. After dark, she'd set course for Lisbon and try to get the radios working. Lisbon was slightly farther, but the course would take her right across the shipping lanes that led to the Straits of Gibraltar — there was a chance she could flag down help along the way. She took a good look at her patient. He was resting quietly now and seemed stable, but very weak. She'd have to watch him closely. If there was any turn for the worse, she'd abandon her search and get him straight to a proper hospital.

Christine went forward in the cabin, finished her damage check, then moved up top and planned the search in her mind. Once established in a pattern, she picked up the binoculars again and began to scour an endless expanse of blue. Early this morning, the Atlantic had been her own private refuge. Now, she thought, it just seemed big.

Chapter Two

Benjamin Jacobs was nearing the end of his tether. He'd been elected Prime Minister of Israel nearly two years ago. His platform for regional peace was the bastion of a winning campaign, but forging promise into reality, as is so often the case in politics, was another matter altogether. It had taken twenty months — twenty months of painful, partisan negotiations — to be finally perched on this brink of success. Unfortunately, the accord he would sign in Greenwich, England, was still two weeks off, and in this part of the world two weeks could be an eternity. Jacobs' economic stimulus package had long ago been put on the back burner, hostage to the peace process. But that would be next in line. No peace would ever stand against fourteen percent unemployment, higher in the Palestinian areas. Too many idle hands and minds on both sides.

Then there was the American problem. Israel's staunchest ally, and her staunchest pain in the ass. They'd only sell more F-15Es if the West Bank settlements were halted. So much opportunity. So much important work to be done. And Benjamin Jacobs found himself mired in shit — ankle deep, in fact, or at least that had been the case an hour ago during his morning constitutional to the first-floor men's room.

Jacobs sat in a wide leather chair behind his weighty desk, listening with determined patience.

"Portable toilets, sir," Lowens said with stiff seriousness.

Jacobs was glad that Lowens was here. He doubted anyone else in his government could present the issue with such dignity, or for that matter, with a straight face. Lowens was the assistant deputy council of something-or-other, but after today, Jacobs mused, he would always associate the man with toilets. Special Assistant to the Prime Minister for Toilets — perhaps a new cabinet-level position.

"It's a temporary solution, sir, but our only option at present. Last night some men were working on a water main across the street and they tangled into a sewer pipe. There was backflow, which the older plumbing in this building didn't prevent as it should. We have cleaning crews working overtime, but it will take a couple of days to straighten out. Our only option for the time being is to bring in portable toilets. Unfortunately, setting up these facilities will be problematic. If we put them in back of the building there are security concerns, and that leaves only one other option."

"I can't imagine," Jacobs deadpanned.

"We can put them on the roof. Lift them up with a crane, or maybe a helicopter."

The Prime Minister's eyes closed, visualizing the spectacle, and a tortured look fell across his naturally photogenic, politician's face.

Lowens pressed on. "I realize it might look silly getting them up there, but if we do it at night . . . well, once they're in place no one will be able to see them. We can hide them between the stairwell and the air conditioning equipment. That would be optimal. For appearances."

Jacobs remained silent at the pause.

"Ms. Weiss thought I should run it by you before we did anything," Lowens finally added, an obvious disclaimer from a career civil service man. Betty Weiss was Jacobs' Chief of Staff.

"Put the toilets on the roof, Mr. Lowens," Jacobs said, exasperated. "Anything else I should know about?"

"No, Mr. Prime Minister." On that, Lowens, having spent twelve years serving politicians at various levels, clearly recognized the chance to retreat. "I'll keep you informed," he promised. The staffer got up and left the room with exemplary decorum, no doubt hoping he'd done nothing to endanger his prospects.

Jacobs mumbled to himself, "Keep me informed. Please."

His secretary knocked once on the open door.

"Yes, Moira?"

"It's Anton Bloch, sir. He says it's quite important."

Jacobs considered a quip about the importance of his last meeting, but held his tongue. "Send him in."

Anton Bloch was Director of Mossad, Israel's vaunted foreign intelligence arm. When he entered the room the look on his face was grim. But then it always was. He was a solid man whose large, square mug gave a decidedly blunt appearance. His hair was cut high and tight on the sides. On top it was gone.

Without waiting for an invitation, Bloch took the seat Lowens had just vacated.

"*Polaris Venture*," he said.

The name got Jacobs' attention, and the Prime Minister braced himself as Bloch shuffled through a stack of papers in his lap.

"We've lost her."

Jacobs spoke slowly, wanting to be clear, "You mean you don't know where she is? Or has she sunk?"

"Definitely the first, maybe both . . . we think."

Jacobs deflated in his chair as Bloch found the paper he wanted and began inflicting details.

"The ship had two satellite systems, a main and a backup. They were supposed to transmit encoded coordinates hourly. Late yesterday we stopped getting the signal. She was off the west coast of Africa the last time we heard from her."

"And you don't think it's a technical problem?"

"That's what we hoped, at first. We spent all last night trying to raise her, but no luck. The communications links are independent, with batteries to back up their power supplies. The odds of everything failing are slim, but if that's what happened, our man on board had instructions to use the ship's normal radio gear to send a message — in the clear if necessary." Bloch descended into grim certainty, "No, I have a feeling there's more to this than communications problems."

The Prime Minister put his elbows on the desk and buried his face in his hands. He took a deep breath as he recalled the previous week's meeting. "Anton, when we debated this mission we came up with a worst case scenario. Is that where we are?"

"It's going to take some time to find out, but yes, she may have sunk. Or been hijacked."

The Prime Minister slouched lower. His political instincts had told him this was a risky venture. But Bloch and the rest had made it sound so easy. Of course, in the end, the decision had been his.

"How many of our people were on board?"

"Only one, from my section. And a crew of fifteen, all South African Navy."

"What about a rescue? If she sank there would be survivors, right?"

"There's a good chance. The British and French have aircraft, and of course they'd be willing to help. Morocco is closer, but I doubt it has much capability for search and rescue that far out. The problem is—"

Jacobs waved him off with both hands, "I know what the problem is. If we ask for help, a lot of questions will come up. What kind of ship? Where was it going? What was on board? Everything could come out." The thought made Jacobs' stomach lurch. "What would *our* capabilities be?"

"For a search? I'd have to ask Defense to be sure, but we're awfully far away. It's not the kind of thing our Navy and Air Force are built to do. We probably have a half-dozen airplanes that could get out that far. And our ships, the few real ocean-going ones we have, are all here. It would take days to get them to the Atlantic."

"How do we find out what's happened?"

Bloch was out ahead for once. "We have to send a reconnaissance aircraft, our EC-130. I'll get right with Defense and have it sent to the area. My team arrived in South Africa the day before *Polaris Venture* sailed. They installed, among other things, two emergency beacons. If the beacons come into contact with salt water, or are turned on manually, they'll emit a signal once every hour on a certain frequency. Our EC-130 is instrumented to pinpoint these kinds of beacons. It'll take a day or so to get the airplane overhead, but if the ship is there we can get a good fix and find out exactly where she went down."

"And if she's not there?"

"Then she's been taken. And we'll find her."

Bloch spoke with a certainty the Prime Minister knew was optimistic.

"All right, call Defense and have them send out everything they can for a search. I'll convene the Cabinet in two hours," Jacobs said with a look at his watch.

Bloch scribbled notes onto the mess of papers in his lap, then strode to the door, a locomotive gathering steam. Jacobs yelled for Moira and she appeared almost instantly.

"Cancel the rest of my day. The Cabinet will meet in two hours."

"The French Foreign Minister just arrived downstairs," she warned. "He'll be here any minute."

Jacobs sighed. He noticed that nasty smell again. One of his security detail had tried to clean Jacobs' shoes after the sorry affair earlier in the men's room, but the stench was hanging tight.

"All right. Stall him for a few minutes. And get Lowens back up here right away," he added.

"Lowens, sir?"

"Yes, he's about my size, and a sharp dresser. Tell him I want his shoes."

A blue BMW. It had only taken a matter of minutes for Yosef Meier to distinguish the tail behind his taxi as they snaked their way through heavy traffic in London's West End. Meier felt good about spotting it. He was no longer a field operative, having taken a headquarters job back in Tel Aviv, so that he might finally get to know his two young children. Evie was seven and Max eight. After missing the greater part of their first five years, he'd put in for the transfer. Now, in spite of two years on the sidelines, Meier was glad to see he hadn't lost his touch.

The initial satisfaction of spotting his pursuer faded briskly as Meier considered why anyone would be following him to begin with. Try as he might, he always came back to the same, unsettling answer.

Meier saw the familiar facade of the Israeli Embassy just ahead. Behind, in the distance, he caught glimpses of the brooding structure that was Kensington Palace. He half-turned to see the BMW a few cars back, as it had been all the way from Heathrow. The cab stopped directly in front of the embassy and Meier gave the driver a healthy tip, asking him to wait. He avoided an urge to look again for his escort. It was around somewhere.

Meier approached the front gate, fishing for the expired embassy ID card in his pocket. It sported an uncomplimentary mug shot of Yassir Arafat, a gag he used to run with the old crew at security. Back then they all recognized him anyway, so nobody ever checked his ID. He'd brought it along on this trip intending to keep the ruse running, but one look at the unfamiliar, serious faces that were now standing at the embassy gate forced him to reconsider. Somehow the idea had lost its appeal. Meier presented his headquarters ID, took a hard stare from the sentries, and signed into the building. He just wanted to see David Slaton and get this over with.

Meier went to the receptionist's table and finally found a familiar face.

"Hello, Emma."

"Yosy!"

Emma Schroeder got up and moved around her table with arms spread wide. She was a heavy, bosomy woman whose penchant for large, shapeless dresses did nothing to minimize her presence. Yosy took a crushing hug, something Emma reserved for those few embassy staffers who were able to stay out of her personal debit column. Meier smiled through it all.

"Emma, you're the one thing that will never change around here."

She gave a throaty laugh. "Of course I change. I get bigger all the time. And smarter too," she added in a devious whisper.

"Are you still going to write that book?"

She chortled again but didn't answer, leaving the mischievous question open. Emma was a career civil servant and had been on the first floor desk in London longer than anyone could remember. She had a mental library of facts, rumors, and gossip about the place that was unsurpassed, and for years she'd threatened to write a tell-all book and retire on the proceeds. Meier sometimes wondered whether she actually might do it.

"So what brings you here from headquarters? Nobody told me you were coming." She was obviously concerned that her networks might have failed.

"Don't worry Emma, nobody snuck anything by you. I'm on holiday. I came to see David Slaton. He and I were going to do some hunting out at the lodge."

She looked doubtful. "David's not here. He got slammed four days ago. *I* don't even know where he is."

Meier felt his stomach tighten. "Four days ago?" He did the math. He had talked to Slaton on Sunday, six days ago. It was a casual conversation, and he'd learned in a roundabout way that Slaton had no intention of leaving soon. Then, it had taken nearly a week for Meier to arrange his leave and get here without arousing suspicion. In that time, Slaton had been slammed, Mossad slang for an immediate assignment — don't pack, don't kiss the wife, just grab your passport and get to the airport.

"Have you heard from him since then?"

She shook her head. "No. And I don't know when he'll be back."

Meier's mind raced as he considered what to do.

His look of concentration wasn't lost on Emma Schroeder. "What was it you'd be hunting for?"

It was a loaded question that Meier ignored. He suddenly wished he'd called first. "All right Emma, thanks anyway. If you hear from David, tell him I've been looking for him."

"Where are you staying?"

"I'm not sure yet," he sidestepped, "but I'll let you know."

Meier left with Emma eyeing him suspiciously. He walked slowly to his cab, still lost in thought. When he got in, the driver asked, "Where to next, guv?"

"I'm going to rent a car. There's an Avis agency over in Whitechapel."

The driver tried to be helpful, no doubt in light of the generous tip Meier had already provided, "There's an Avis just up the road 'ere. Save you twenty pounds from goin' all across town."

"No," Meier lied, "I have a certain car reserved there, thanks."

"As you like," the driver said, pulling out into traffic.

It took half an hour to get there. The BMW was still in trail.

Meier was particular in renting a car, selecting a small red Fiat — slow and easy to see. He fell in with the heavy traffic and headed west, all the way back across town. His pursuers picked him up right away and they negotiated the traffic well, having no trouble keeping up in the powerful German sedan.

Twenty miles later, Meier was on the M3, leaving behind the western outskirts of London. The traffic thinned and he saw his trailer was still there, farther back now, a dot in the rearview mirror. They were doing a respectable job of keeping back and masking behind other cars, but they never lost visual. This told him two things. First, there were no other vehicles involved. If that had been the case, the BMW would have backed out of sight occasionally for a tag team. Second, there were no other means of reconnaissance involved. No aircraft, satellites, or tracking devices. He was being followed the old-fashioned way, by a couple of guys who had to keep him in sight while trying not to be seen themselves. This made his tactical problem easier, but it also confirmed his fears about who might be in the car.

Meier sped up to seventy miles an hour. The little Fiat's engine whined at a high pitch. He took out the detailed map he'd purchased at the car hire agency and set it on the passenger seat. Yosy Meier looked at his watch.

It took another two and a half hours. Meier saw the BMW fall back and take an exit. He looked at his own gas gauge and saw slightly over a quarter tank. After all the stop and go city driving, followed by hours on the M3 and A303, the big car had to be on fumes. Meier had also seen the gas station just off the exit ramp, and he suspected it might be where they'd take their chance. He pushed the Fiat's accelerator to the floor. It hit eighty-eight miles an hour and stuck, the little engine revved to a screaming pace. He didn't bother to look at the map yet. Right now he needed one thing — to get out of sight. He reached the next exit in five minutes. Meier took it, then made a quick series of turns onto smaller roads. Finally satisfied, he eased off the accelerator and referenced the map. There was no one behind him now.

Christine was at the stove, tending to a pot of chicken soup, when she glanced over to find her patient awake.

"Well, hello," she said cheerily. "Glad you're back. I thought you might sleep all the way to Portugal."

The man seemed bewildered. Christine sat next to him on the bunk, showing both a smile and an interest that were completely genuine. "How are you feeling?" she asked.

He propped himself on his elbows, grimacing at the slow, tentative effort.

"Easy." She held out a hand and introduced herself, "Christine."

He took her hand and responded in a raspy voice, "Nils."

"Nils? Swedish?"

He nodded, "*Ja, Svensk.*"

Christine gestured toward herself and said, "American." Christine was surprised that he apparently spoke no English. The few Scandinavians she'd met before had all had a working grasp on her own language. As he eased himself into a sitting position on the bunk, she went to the galley and drew a glass of water.

"You'll need a lot of this," she said, holding it out.

He took it and emptied the glass in a matter of seconds. Christine quickly offered a refill as she studied her patient. There were a lot of questions to ask, but she had no idea how to go about it.

"I'm a doctor," she offered.

He showed no trace of understanding. She slowly pulled back the sheet that covered his chest. "Doctor," she said again.

He seemed unbothered as she began her examination. First she checked the wound on his ribcage. It looked no worse, but a new dressing was in order. Christine found herself talking out loud in her best hospital voice. "Lie still." He might not understand English, but all the world's health professionals spoke with the same antiseptic, no-nonsense tone. That much he'd recognize.

"It doesn't look infected, which is good because this hospital's pharmacy is not very well stocked."

Christine removed the old tape and gauze, and replaced it with new, wishing she had better supplies. She wondered how he'd gotten such a nasty cut. After changing the dressing, she looked at the blistered skin on his arms and face. She wanted to clean the worst areas, but without the right sterile conditions she might do more harm than good. Christine tried to imagine how painful it must have been — salt water constantly washing over wounds like that. His face was shadowed by a few day's growth of beard, but shaving would be out of the question for some time. Aside from the exposure, he still presented pale and drawn.

As she studied him, Christine couldn't help noticing his eyes. They were a stark blue-gray, and something about them broke her concentration. They held a strength, an intensity that was not at all consistent with his physical condition. Christine found herself locked to his gaze and was suddenly unnerved. She turned away abruptly, trying to think of something to say to this strange person with whom she shared no common language.

"All in all, I think you'll be in good shape after a couple weeks of R and R."

He handed her the empty glass and Christine decided to wait fifteen minutes before the next refill. She went to the galley, poured a short cup of chicken soup from the pot on the stove, and gave it to him. He took a cautious sip, smiled gratefully, then went at it with relish. The doctor was encouraged. Recuperation was under way. The only thing to temper her satisfaction was the nagging possibility that he might not have been alone. She decided to try again.

"Any others on *Polaris Venture?*"

He gave her a quizzical look and tried to mimic the words, "Polars Venure?"

She sighed. She had assumed that was the name of his ship — it was stenciled on the cooler he'd been hanging onto. But wouldn't he recognize the name, in any language? Christine threw a frustrated glance at her communications panel. Right now it didn't matter what the ship's name was, since there was no way of reporting it. She needed a radio, but with one glass of water he'd shorted out half the rack. Incredible. The two-way was dead, so no talking on the ship-to-ship bands. The SAT-COM was out. The only radio that worked was the little battery-operated weather receiver. She wasn't great with electronics, but tonight she'd make an effort to get one of the transceivers operational. It crossed her mind that his ship might have put out a distress signal itself before going down. Christine had seen no evidence of a search, though. No boats, no planes. They were out here by themselves.

He finished his soup and handed her the cup. She considered offering more, but before she knew it he'd fallen back and closed his eyes. Christine poured a bowl for herself and studied her patient. Within a few minutes he was motionless, his breathing rhythmic. Over the course of the day she had checked on him hourly. He'd been in serious shape when he first came aboard, and Christine was worried he might take a turn for the worse. Now she had him eating and taking in liquids. The blisters on his face and arms still looked raw and painful, but, all in all, he seemed to be doing remarkably well. Christine pulled the blanket up over his chest. He seemed peaceful now, but she remembered the look that had been in his eyes only minutes ago. What had been so strange about it?

You're a curious one, she thought. The most curious man I've ever plucked out of the ocean.

The hastily convened session of Israel's Cabinet brought twenty people into place around a big mahogany meeting table. They were a keen mix of the Prime Minister's staunchest political allies and enemies. Most were members of the Knesset who had been elevated, by way of partisan jousting, to Ministerial status. The only person not to have a regular seat at the table was the Director of Mossad. Anton Bloch sat in the chair of the absent Minister of Communications, who was in Argentina and completely irretrievable. There was also a stranger seated against the back wall, flanked by two empty chairs, which served to emphasize his isolation.

When Benjamin Jacobs came into the room, they all remained seated. His predecessor would have expected everyone to rise, but this

Prime Minister wasn't one for formalities. He took a seat between Sonja Franks, the Foreign Minister, and Ehud Zak, the Minister of Finance.

"Good afternoon ladies and gentlemen," Jacobs said, his tone implying otherwise. He spoke in English. Customarily such meetings were conducted in Hebrew, but English was understood all around the table, and most guessed, correctly, that it was chosen for the benefit of their guest. Jacobs decided with a quiet survey that about half of those present had not been here for the previous meeting on the day's subject. The Prime Minister knew he'd have hell to pay for that, but he was ready.

"I'm sure you've all recognized one stranger to this Cabinet," Jacobs said, gesturing toward the man against the far wall who wore an unfamiliar military uniform.

"Ladies and gentlemen, I present General Wilm Van Ruut of the South African National Defense Force."

The South African stood to attention and nodded formally. He was a tall, gaunt man with bony features and a handlebar mustache. Van Ruut sat back down without speaking.

Jacobs pressed ahead, "I recognize the irregularity of having someone like General Van Ruut at a Cabinet meeting, but I think the reasons for his being here will soon be clear. One week ago, the Director of Mossad approached me for the approval of a mission, an irregular operation, to say the least, and one that had a brief window of opportunity. There was risk involved. However, in my opinion, inaction carried even greater risk. I called an immediate Cabinet meeting and, after some discussion, the mission was given a green light. Since a number of you were not here that day, I'll let Anton fill you in."

The burly Director of Mossad went to the opposite end of the table and everyone rotated their attention. Anton Bloch, having always been an operational type, bore a healthy dislike of politicians. He looked like a man headed to the dentist's chair.

"As you know, South Africa is in extreme turmoil right now, and the standing government may not survive. General Van Ruut contacted us last week. He told us that military command and control was disintegrating and, in particular, he expressed doubts about the security of his country's nuclear capability." Around the room there were a mixture of reactions, disinterest not among them.

"I thought South Africa had disarmed," Sonya Franks remarked.

Bloch explained, "The South African government began a very public project to dismantle its nuclear arsenal about ten years ago. Six weapons, all of a moderate tactical yield, were involved. Under international supervision, the critical components were destroyed, and the fissionable materials placed under care of the International Atomic Energy Agency. There were, however, two . . . exceptions."

The Cabinet members who had not been present at the first briefing stiffened in their chairs.

"At the last moment, orders were given to keep two weapons intact. General Van Ruut knows nothing about the reasoning for this, but it goes without saying that it became a closely held national secret."

Van Ruut gave a distinct nod and said, "A small cadre of special troops has been guarding these things for over a decade. They are a legacy, and our politicians can't decide whether to keep them, destroy them, or . . . well, lately there has been talk of using them."

General Gabriel, Chief of Staff of the Israeli Defense Forces, broke in. "Weapons like that wouldn't have any impact on such a widespread civil war. We're not talking about battling tank armies here, were talking about a half-dozen rebellious factions, some of them armed with nothing more than spears and machetes. Setting off a nuclear device would only give the opposition a cause to unite behind."

Van Ruut said, "I agree sir, from a tactical standpoint. But our leadership is fracturing. They might not act in a militarily rational way if things truly collapse."

Someone else asked, "So you think these weapons are a danger?"

"Yes," Van Ruut said. "I originally wanted to find some way to dismantle them, but the assets to do that weren't under my control. I discussed the problem with some of my closest peers in the military command structure, and they all agreed that these two weapons were a serious threat. Then, ten days ago, the answer fell into my lap. I was ordered to move them from a storage facility in the Kalahari to a weapons complex outside Cape Town. It occurred to me that we could give them to another country, a neutral third party, to be held. The only country that made sense was Israel."

Jacobs watched the varied reactions around the table. Some appeared to relax, intrigued but no longer concerned. Others squirmed, sensing more to come.

Bloch said, "Nine days ago, General Van Ruut contacted us, explained the situation, and asked for our help. He did this at great personal risk, I should add, and knowing that his career in the South African Defense Forces would be at an end. Time was of the essence. This was put to us the day before the weapons were to be moved. We had a matter of hours to decide. The Prime Minister called an emergency session of this Cabinet, and the decision was made to go ahead."

Ariel Steiner, leader of Jacobs' archrival Labor party, interrupted and volleyed his comments straight at the Prime Minister. "I'd like to see the minutes of that meeting, since I was out of the country."

Jacobs was ready. He slid a copy of the minutes over to Steiner who eyed it suspiciously. "Read it later," Jacobs said. "We'll go over the highlights now so that everyone has the picture."

Not put off, Steiner tried a different tack. "With respect to the General here, how do we know he's not just working to disarm the South African government in favor of the rebel forces?"

"You don't," Van Ruut said, glaring at the politician but maintaining his bearing.

General Gabriel intervened. "Mr. Steiner, I've known General Van Ruut for nearly twenty years. He is an honorable officer with genuine concern for his country."

"Seems to me he's stabbing his country in the back. If the rebels win this thing he'll be a hero to them. They'll probably make him Chief of Staff of the new military!"

Van Ruut bristled.

Ehud Zak, Jacobs' right-hand man who often became a buffer at such meetings, pleaded, "Gentlemen, please!"

Jacobs had heard enough. "We weighed these issues last week and decided he was on the level. Some people in positions of power can put aside self-interest." The remark was leveled squarely at Steiner, and Jacobs let it hang in the air for a moment. "In any event, there was a more compelling reason for us to get involved."

Bloch said, "You've all heard of Project Majik. It brought us our own nuclear capabilities, back in the 1960s. Some details of that project are still closely held, and they are relevant to this discussion. Mordechai should explain."

Bloch relinquished the head of the table to Paul Mordechai, officially the Special Assistant to the Minister of Energy. He was a thin, bespectacled man who, at thirty-one, was fifteen years junior to anyone else in the room. His curly hair was much longer than it should have been and he exuded a gleeful energy. Wearing khaki pants, a striped button-down shirt, and a miserably knotted tie, he could have been a graduate student about to lecture a university class, which had indeed been the case ten years earlier. Mordechai stood and bounced a bit at the head of the table, then grinned at an impressively somber collection of faces. His less than professional appearance annoyed some, but everyone knew Mordechai's level of job security was likely higher than that of anyone else in the room. He had an uncanny knack for connecting the technical to the practical, an attribute that would make him a fixture in many Cabinets to come.

He began the lesson. "A great many things are necessary in order to develop nuclear weapons. Some of those things we had in 1960. We had the theoretical and scientific know-how. We had the engineering capacity. There was, however, one crucial element we lacked, that being a large supply of high quality uranium ore." The engineer scanned for any reaction, but his pun had fallen flat on the dour group. He forged ahead. "During this time, South Africa was also after the bomb. She had a strong base of theoretical scientists and plenty of uranium ore, but was struggling with the engineering. In particular, the design and construction of a re-processing plant."

Steiner blurted, "So they gave us ore and we built them a reprocessing plant."

Mordechai was clearly intrigued by this rushed display of flawed logic. He looked curiously at Steiner, as a botanist might study a four-leafed clover.

"No. This came at a time of high tension for Israel. We were consistently at war with our Arab neighbors, and we knew the first time we lost would be the last. Building a plant in South Africa would have taken time. The solution was simply this — they sent us the ore, and we sent back a percentage of what we processed."

The Minister of Public Works weighed in, "This is all interesting, but are you saying these things that happened over forty years ago affected your decision to take these weapons?" A Labor man, he emphasized the word "your" while looking at Jacobs.

Mordechai answered, coming nicely into form. "Absolutely, so try to follow. At the time, many countries were working on the bomb. The established nuclear powers put a lot of effort into finding out what everyone was up to. Reprocessing uranium is not a sterile business. Various radioactive isotopes are inevitably released into the environment. They can be found in soil samples taken from around the facility, and also in upper atmospheric air samples downwind of the plant. At the time, we were in a hurry, and not concerned with the environment or who knew what we were up to."

Zak said, "I'll bet we made it intentionally dirty, just to scare the crap out of the Arabs."

"Perhaps. The Arabs themselves did not have the technology to detect this sort of thing. But the Russians did, and of course they were aligned with our Arab enemies."

"Who else would have known what we were doing?" General Gabriel inquired.

"The Americans of course, maybe Great Britain or France. But there is one other salient point to be made. These nuclear residues provide a unique signature for any given batch. Essentially this means that any U-232 we've ever processed can be traced to us." The Special Assistant to the Minister of Energy let that one sink in.

"Even after it . . . blows up?" Steiner asked.

"Fission would not deny identification."

The group went silent and Jacobs stepped in. "Thank you, Mr. Mordechai."

Mordechai smiled and loped casually back to his chair, the weight of matters seeming to have no effect. The rest of the room churned in widely angled thought.

"So, ladies and gentlemen," the Prime Minister said, "these two particular weapons were part of this legacy. They could theoretically be linked to us. Of course, if they were used in South Africa, we could tell this whole story about how they got there. Our enemies would call it a lie and accuse us of selling weapons of mass destruction. Most of the world would probably believe our version, but we'd be admitting violation of every nuclear non-proliferation agreement ever known. For these reasons, I decided the prudent thing would be to take the weapons back, to safeguard them until things have stabilized in the region."

Steiner added, "And we'll have a big bargaining chip with whoever comes out on top."

Jacobs fixed a seething glare on the Labor clod. "I gave my word to General Van Ruut that the weapons would be returned with no strings attached. This is simply a security issue, for both our countries."

Steiner sat back, humbled for the moment, and the Prime Minister addressed the others. "Now that you all understand the background of this matter . . . Anton?"

Bloch stood next to a video screen that was built into the wall. "Five days ago a cargo ship named *Polaris Venture* left Cape Town with the weapons. The crew was South African Navy, and one of my people was on board to help with security. After three days at sea, somewhere off the coast of western Africa, *Polaris Venture* disappeared."

A map came into view on the screen. Mostly blue, it depicted the Atlantic Ocean and the northwest coast of Africa. A red course line came up from the bottom of the map, paralleling the coast well offshore. Halfway to the Straits of Gibraltar, it changed from a solid to a dashed line, and a large red box was drawn around the transition point.

"We were supposed to get hourly position updates by a secure satellite link." Bloch pointed to the red box, "Somewhere in this area we lost contact."

"You're saying this ship has sunk?" Steiner asked in amazement.

"Or was hijacked?" General Gabriel suggested.

"Hijacked?" Steiner was incredulous. "Good God! By who? Our enemies?"

Zak said, "Calm down, Ariel. Let's get the facts first." He looked at the map. "What are we doing to locate this ship?"

"Our EC-130 took off an hour ago. *Polaris Venture* was equipped with two locator beacons, and if she's gone down, the EC-130 will be able to pinpoint them."

General Gabriel prodded, "What about the crew?"

Bloch said, "Search and rescue in the middle of the Atlantic isn't something our country is really equipped for. We could ask for help, of course. The French and British are fairly close, but if we do that—"

Steiner pounced, "If we ask for help this whole fiasco will blow up in our face!"

General Van Ruut spoke up, "Mr. Prime Minister, there are sixteen men out there. We must consider them first and foremost."

Jacobs said, "General, I understand your position. I have been a field commander myself, and I promise that we will take all reasonable steps to find these men."

The "all reasonable steps" clause signaled a shifting tide.

Van Ruut pleaded, "Those men could still be out there! We have to act now!"

"Mr. Prime Minister, with all due respect to General Van Ruut," Steiner said in a manner that held none, "this is now a security issue for our government. We all appreciate his help, but I think the General should no longer be present at this Cabinet meeting."

Jacobs sighed. Even the Prime Minister had to choose his battles, and this was not one of them. "Mr. Steiner is correct, General Van Ruut. I'll have to ask you to leave. You have my word that we will try to find your men. One of ours is out there too."

Van Ruut glared at Steiner, and his reply was clipped, "I understand." Dignified in defeat, the South African stood straight and did a sharp about-face toward the door.

As soon as he was gone, Jacobs made the phone call to security. There was no point in trying to be discreet. "General Van Ruut is on level three. Please escort him to the executive lounge. Give him every courtesy, but do not let him leave the complex."

The Prime Minister frowned and scribbled down a note to give Van Ruut the use of his personal suite. He then refocused on the task at hand. "Your thoughts?"

Sonja Franks, the ever diplomatic Foreign Minister said, "How long must we detain him?"

"At least until we find out what's happened," said Jacobs. "But let's not forget, he's on our side. Who knows what might have happened if we hadn't taken those weapons out of South Africa."

Zak said, "I agree. We owe him, and he seems a decent man. But it brings something else to mind. I don't think the loss of this ship is a random maritime accident. I don't know if it was hijacked or sunk, but security was obviously breached. Aside from Van Ruut and half the people in this room, who knew about the mission?"

Bloch said, "There were sixteen men on the ship. Another two dozen South African soldiers were involved in the transportation and loading."

"But how many knew the nature of the cargo?" Zak wondered aloud.

"This mission was a scramble from the start, and I can't speak for security on the South African end. According to General Van Ruut, only *Polaris Venture*'s captain and our two men were fully briefed, but any of the others might have figured it out."

"Two?" General Gabriel inquired. "I thought we had just one on board, Anton."

"I sent two to Cape Town. One oversaw the loading process and actually went along when she sailed. The second man was only there to install the communications gear and some scuttling charges."

"Some what?" a voice asked.

Bloch finally put forward a scrap of good news. "Explosives, big charges placed below the waterline. They could be set off intentionally, to sink *Polaris Venture* fast. It was meant as a precaution against hijacking."

"What would have triggered these explosives?" Zak asked.

"Who, actually," Bloch said. "My man on board had the ability to set them off."

Steiner asked, "What if hijackers got to him first?"

"Nothing's impossible, but boarding a large ship that's under way on the open ocean — it's no easy thing. Even harder to do it and not be heard or seen by lookouts or radar. I know because we've tried."

Jacobs said, "So someone might have tried to take *Polaris Venture*, but then our man sank her intentionally."

Bloch agreed, "That would fit most of what we know. It's also remotely possible that one of the scuttling charges might have gone off by accident."

Sonja Franks said, "So, in either case, the ship went down, and as soon as we find it we can get to work retrieving these weapons."

"Retrieving the weapons would not be an option," Bloch said.

"Why not?"

Bloch turned again to the map. "We pre-programmed a course for the ship that kept her in very deep water. The area where she's down has a minimum depth of nine thousand feet. A salvage there would be a major undertaking. Only a few countries in the world have the technology to do it, and none of them would have any interest in weapons of this type — they're dinosaurs."

"All right, so what now, Anton?" Jacobs asked, wanting to wrap things up.

"The EC-130 should report back tomorrow. Hopefully they will have found the ELTs and we can pinpoint where the ship is."

"And then?" Steiner asked.

"And then nothing, if we're lucky," Bloch said. "We just let it sit on the bottom of the ocean and keep our secret as best we can."

Some around the table seemed relieved, but General Gabriel looked concerned. "What about searching for survivors?"

"We can't ask for help and expect to keep this quiet," Steiner insisted.

"I'm afraid he's right," Sonja Franks agreed.

Jacobs nodded reluctantly. He looked to General Gabriel. "Let's put everything we have into a search. Planes, ships, whatever we can do."

"Yes sir," Gabriel responded.

It was a feeble gesture and everyone knew it. The room was quiet until someone asked, "What if somebody else picks up survivors, or finds the wreckage floating around?"

Bloch said, "I've been told there are no shipping lanes where she went down. Just a lot of ocean."

Zak concurred, "It would really be a long shot."

"Yes . . ." Jacobs hedged, "but not out of the question."

Zak said, "Anton, why don't we send a message out to all our stations in North Africa and Europe. Let's listen for anything on this — discreetly." Heads nodded around the table.

"All right."

Jacobs rose from his chair. "We'll meet again tomorrow morning, or sooner if anything breaks. Everyone's on a half-hour call-back until further notice."

Yosy Meier walked out of Harrods with one of the newest Barbie dolls and a model airplane kit tucked under his arm. In the other hand he carried his small suitcase. He'd always been able to find something for Evie and Max at Harrods. In the old days, it was more an effort to ease his guilt at having been gone so much. Today he did it just to see the smiles on their faces — that and to kill some time, since his flight didn't leave for another three hours. He had turned in the rental car at a different location from where he'd gotten it, telling the agent he was in a hurry. From here, Meier would take the tube to Heathrow, only he didn't want to be early.

He wondered if he was getting paranoid. He hadn't seen anything of the BMW or its occupants since ditching them yesterday. That much was good. But he still couldn't find Slaton. He'd called the embassy twice and talked to Emma. Still nothing. Meier finally decided it was too risky to stay on, and he booked the first flight home.

Traffic ran heavy along Brompton Road in the midday rush. Meier looked at his watch and figured he had about an hour to lose before getting on the tube. He paused at the curb of a busy intersection. Businessmen, tourists, and shoppers jammed the sidewalk around him, none venturing to jaywalk as cars, taxis, and scooters shot past. Meier spotted a Thai restaurant across the street. What better place to kill an hour? he thought.

A car alarm suddenly went off somewhere behind. People turned to look. Meier was struggling with his packages when a heavy forearm shoved him in the back. It caught him completely off-guard and he pitched forward into the street. As he fell, everything seemed to revert to slow motion. He saw the Barbie falling. He saw the street, with its painted crosswalk coming toward his face. And he saw the grill of the huge red bus that was barreling straight at him. Yosy Meier realized he was about to die, and the last instant of his life was spent thinking about the family he would never see again.

The sound, a muffled thud, was what most people noticed first. Next was the screeching of brakes and an image of what looked like a big rag doll rolling into the intersection. Once they realized what had happened, the bystanders reacted, a cacophony of hysterical screams, shocked "Good Gods!" and the wailing chant of an old Indian man.

Someone yelled to call an ambulance, although everyone could see it was no use. A hundred feet back on the sidestreet, no one noticed the owner of a big blue BMW as he calmly walked to his car, disabled the alarm, and drove off.

Chapter Three

Christine looked at the telltales on the shrouds and trimmed in the main sheet. A brisk early morning breeze was pressing *Windsom* along at nearly seven knots, but it was rough going. The seas were four to five feet, and choppy. Fortunately, it didn't seem to bother her patient. He'd been asleep since the previous afternoon. His vital signs were strong and the wound across his ribs showed no signs of infection. Even the blistering on his face and arms had begun to improve, but she still wished she had antibiotics and an IV to give him fluids. Best of all, Christine had calculated that with these winds she'd make Lisbon by noon the next day. One week in a proper hospital and he ought to be as good as new.

She'd spent two hours the previous night toying with her recalcitrant radios. The SAT-COM, the one she really could have used, was still down — she couldn't even get it to take power. The marine two-way had dried out and seemed to be working, but she hadn't been able to raise anyone. After one last check on the autopilot, she decided to go below to check on her patient and try the VHF again.

Christine had just reached the companionway steps when she saw it, slightly off the port bow. *A ship!* A big freighter of some kind, probably ten miles off, and on a crossing path that wouldn't bring it any closer. But definitely within radio range.

She ducked down into the cabin, turned on the VHF and grabbed the microphone. The radio was already set to the emergency frequency, 121.5 MHz. Christine stretched the spiral cord tight and poked her head back through the hatch, somehow not wanting to lose sight of the ship as she spoke.

"*Mayday! Mayday! This is* Windsom *calling any ship this frequency.*"

Nothing.

"*Mayday! Mayday! This is* Windsom, *over.*"

More silence, and then finally a deep voice with a thick German accent. "*Calling mayday, this is the* Breisen. *Say again your call sign and what is nature of your problem.*"

"Yes!" Christine shrieked. "Breisen, *this is the sailboat* Windsom. *I am a civilian vessel of United States registry. I have to report the sinking of another vessel in this area and my* SAT-COM *is out. Can you relay information for me?*"

The silence returned. "Breisen, *this is* Windsom, *over.*"

Something wasn't right. Christine hadn't heard the clicks from the radio sidetone on her last transmission. She looked down into the cabin and was stunned to see her patient standing next to the radio. He had his finger on the power switch — and it was off.

"What are you doing?" she asked incredulously.

The man simply stared at her, a direct, riveting look in his eyes. Christine lowered the microphone from her lips.

"Your shipmates might still be out there. Shipmates," she insisted, wishing to God she knew the Swedish word. "We must start a search. Search!"

The man shook his head, his gaze level and strong. "There's no one else out there," he said. "They're all dead." He reached out, gently pulled the microphone from her hand and unplugged its cord from the back of the radio. The man then tossed the handset out the hatch, its arcing path ending with a plop in the cold blue Atlantic.

Christine took a step back, stunned. Stunned that he was not letting her start a rescue. Stunned that he had just spoken perfectly clear, concise English. As she backed away, he moved toward her.

"What do you want?" Christine asked.

He began climbing the stairs out of the cabin, no longer looking tired and weak. Christine kept backing slowly. She spotted a big brass winch handle lying on the seat next to her. She grabbed it, putting on her most determined face.

Reaching the deck, he stopped his advance. The man seemed bigger now, taller. She realized she'd never seen him when he wasn't hunched over. His expression was noncommittal as she brandished the heavy brass bar.

"Put that down," he said calmly.

Christine stood her ground.

"I'm not going to hurt you. You'll have to do what I ask for a few days, that's all. We're not going to Portugal. We're going to England."

"We'll go wherever I say! This is *my* boat."

He sighed, looking at her with the regard one might hold for a petulant child. The man moved again, slowly and deliberately toward her.

Christine raised the brass handle over her head. "Stay back! I warn you!"

She swung with all her might. Her arm came to a painful stop midway through its arc, and his hand clamped around her wrist like a vice. She kicked out, but he parried every blow, still holding her arm tight. Christine lost her balance and fell onto the railing, one leg dangling over the side before he pulled her back up. She wrenched away and fell to the deck, her heart pounding.

"I've done nothing but help you!" she spat. "I saved your life!"

The blistered, unshaven face remained a blank.

"You have no right to do this!"

He pried the winch handle from her grip and dropped it casually into the ocean.

"I've got more of those!"

"And the next time you try to use one on me I'll keep the handle and toss *you* overboard."

Christine glared at him. She knew she was in good shape and could put up a fight, but they both understood. He could have easily put her overboard moments ago. He hadn't.

"Please don't think I'm not grateful. I know I'd be dead right now if it wasn't for you. I've got to get to England, though."

"Why not just ask? Why play the pirate? If you'd explain everything and—"

"And what?" he cut in. "Ask you to sail three days out of your way? Would you have done it?"

They stared at one another — she with suspicion and anger, he with nothing more than blunt awareness of the new chain of command. In a matter of moments they had become adversaries. Now that the line was drawn, however, his bearing seemed to ease.

"I have to get to England. I won't ask anything more."

It sounded nearly apologetic, Christine thought, and laughable in the face of his mutiny.

"I won't harm you," he repeated. As if to emphasize the point, he slowly turned away. A calculated retreat. "I'll go below and plot the new course."

He dropped down into the cabin and bent over the navigation table.

Christine took a deep breath. She tried to concentrate. Who on earth was this man? And what did he want? He was tackling charts now as though nothing had happened. But for how long? Christine looked out over the water and saw *Breisen* still on the horizon. They had heard her first distress call. The crew would be searching, but at this distance *Windsom* was too small. They'd never spot her.

Christine looked down into the cabin. Again, he seemed different. Was he leaning over the navigation table — or *on* it? The man had overpowered her, but she suspected he was using all his strength to prove the point. He could not have fully recovered from what he'd been through.

"Come to heading zero one five until we reprogram the autopilot." It was an order.

Her instinct was to refuse, but as *Breisen* shrank on the horizon she hesitated. Maybe there was one more chance. "All right," she conceded with clear distaste, "zero one five." She took the tiller in her hand and steered the new course. Then, while he was still hunched over the map, she inched her way aft. Christine began to play a line with one hand while the other opened the hatch to a small storage compartment. Keeping her eyes on the rope, she groped around inside the bin. It was empty.

"Looking for these?"

She turned to see him holding up a half-dozen emergency flares and the gun that fired them. He threw them over the rail.

"If you can learn to behave I'll stop throwing bits and pieces of your boat into the ocean. Course zero one five." He went back below.

Christine slumped over the tiller. She watched *Breisen* fading from sight. When had he taken the flares? He hadn't been out of the bunk until just now — unless he'd done it while she'd managed two hours sleep in the forward compartment last night. Then there was the radio. The man had clearly sabotaged it during his first moments on board. He'd been in terrible shape, badly injured and weak. Christine honestly had doubts as to whether he'd pull through that first day. Yet, even in that condition, he had been hatching a plan and acting on it.

Who was this outlaw she'd plucked from the ocean? Certainly no ordinary sailor trying to get back to his home port. She wondered what he could be after. It had been a one-in-a-million chance she'd even found him. Did he want *Windsom?* Was he kidnapping her for money? She doubted even the most opportunistic of criminals would have had the presence of mind to start acting out a scheme like his within moments of staggering aboard. None of it made sense.

Christine watched him as he worked on the charts. His big hands smoothed out the paper and drew an even line across it. He seemed to know what he was doing. Christine fought her frustration and tried to think logically. He wasn't going to kill her. Not now, or he would have thrown her overboard already. That meant one of two things. Either he had no intention of harming her, or he needed her, perhaps to sail the boat. In either case, she was safe for the time being.

She steeled herself and went down into the cabin where he was still hovering over a chart. She stood firmly and waited until he looked up.

"All right. I will take you to England. It is a serious inconvenience to me, but I'm sure you don't care. What's the nearest port? The sooner I'm rid of you, the better."

He stared at her for a moment with something in his expression she couldn't place.

"Good," he said finally. "Let's get to work. Oh, and my name's not really Nils." He held out his hand, "It's David."

"Christine Palmer," she replied, crossing her arms over her chest. "Charmed, I'm sure."

The Bertram 45 crashed roughly through choppy, four-foot seas. She was a steady boat, wide for her class, and the twin Cat diesels pushed her along at twelve knots. She could have done more had the conditions been better, but they were taking a beating as it was.

"Reel in those damned fishing lines," the man at the helm ordered.

The mate frowned, but didn't argue. The fishing gear was purely for show — two deep-sea trolling rigs jammed into rod holders. The boat was going so fast that the lures skipped from wavecrest to wavecrest, spending as much time out of the water as in. Amazingly enough, they'd actually gotten a hit a few hours ago, a big Wahoo that had somehow latched onto the port rig and ran. Unfortunately, the skipper never considered slowing down to land the brute, and the mate's vision of a fresh fish dinner had disappeared when the line snapped on his first turn of the reel.

The man at the wheel pulled back on the throttles and the big boat settled to a stop. He double-checked his navigation readouts. "All right. Anywhere in here," he growled.

The mate went into the cabin, then came back out struggling with two metal boxes, one under each arm. They were painted yellow, each about the size and weight of a car battery. He lumbered to the stern of the boat and, with a final nod of approval from the bridge, heaved the boxes unceremoniously over the transom. They disappeared instantly into the inky blue water, the mate silently wondering how long it would take them to sink two miles.

The skipper put the diesels back in gear, and with a sweeping right turn they were soon battering through the ocean again, now on a reciprocal course to that which had brought them here.

"How long back to Morocco?" the mate shouted over the roar of the engines.

"Sixteen hours."

"Then what?"

"Then we wait."

With *Windsom* gliding purposefully on her new, northward route, the tension eased considerably, and Christine was confident her situation had improved. She and this stranger had become two sailors — certainly not friends, but a crew with a common goal. They worked together to navigate and tune *Windsom*'s rigging for the new run. Still, Christine had the sense he was always watching her.

And she, in turn, watched him. He wasn't a seasoned sailor, of that Christine was sure. He moved around steadily, though, and seemed to have a rough idea of what to do around a boat. To his credit, he never made any major changes without asking first. She also noticed he was tiring rapidly. Recovery from his ordeal was far from over. Presently he was up top, seated by the tiller, and engrossed in the navigation control panel.

Christine was getting tired herself, having not gotten much sleep the night before. And she felt grubby after wearing the same clothes for two days. She went into the forward cabin and closed the door that separated the boat's only two compartments, making a point of engaging the metal hook that latched it closed.

She picked out some fresh clothes. A pair of cotton khaki pants, a T-shirt and a heavy cotton sweatshirt. It would get colder soon as they made their way north. She grabbed a washcloth and doused it with cold water from the small sink, then stripped down and rubbed the cloth over her face and arms, finally leaving it to cling soddenly at the back of her neck. It felt cool and wonderful. She was completely naked when the door burst open.

Christine gasped and her heart seemed to stop. She nearly screamed, but was stilled by fear as they stood facing one another an arm's length apart. His eyes fell to her body — only for an instant, but it seemed like an eternity — before he turned away.

Christine ripped a towel from the rack and desperately tried to cover herself.

"Get dressed," he said.

She held the towel with her chin as she fumbled to pull on her underwear, pants, and finally the sweatshirt.

He stood facing away and spoke over his shoulder. "Tell me when you're decent."

"Decent?" she said contemptibly. "You should ask that before you go smashing through doors. All right. I'm dressed now."

He turned. His expression was contrite, but the tone authoritative, a headmaster setting the rules. "You closed the door and locked it. I can't let you do that. I can't trust you that much."

Christine looked at the remains of the door as it hung limp and crooked on its hinges. The metal latch was torn away, lying on the floor among splinters of wood.

"Well, as far as locked doors go, that won't be a problem anymore. There was only one on this boat and you've taken care of it nicely."

"I'll fix the door. But no locks. If you need to be alone, ask first."

Christine wanted to protest, but relented. Now was not the time. "All right."

He looked at her appraisingly for a moment and she tried to gauge what he was thinking, but the man gave nothing away. Apparently satisfied, he turned and made his way back up on deck. Like nothing had happened.

Christine slumped against the bulkhead and took a deep breath. Calm, she thought. If she was calm and reasonable, he would respond in kind. Christine needed something to get both their minds off what had just happened. Looking around the cabin, her gaze settled on the galley. Food! That was it! The way to a man's heart. Remembering the emptiness of his stare, she wondered if this brute even had one.

Christine was rummaging through the pantry minutes later when he came below.

"We're not going to eat now," he said.

She thought he looked pale as he leaned heavily against the stairwell. His gaze, however, was sharp. Christine acquired her "doctor's orders" tone.

"Look at you. You need food. I'll fix something for both —"

"Lie down," he commanded, pointing to the bunk.

Those two words shattered whatever fragile confidence Christine had been able to build. "I'm not tired," she said, her voice cracking.

"I am, so lie down."

Her hands instinctively balled into fists and every muscle in Christine's body tensed. She was steeled to fight if it came to that.

Her posture was obvious enough, and he clarified his motives. "Look, don't misunderstand. I apologize for my bad manners. I'm very tired." He busied himself spreading out the sheets on the bed. "It will take us three days to get to England and I'm still recovering. I need sleep." He found an extra pillow and tossed it on the big double bunk. "Since I am hijacking your boat, I can't trust you out of my sight. If I doze off with you running around, doctor, I imagine I'd wake up lashed to an anchor."

"No, I'm not the keelhauling type."

"Neither am I." He gestured again to the bed, this time with overt politeness. "When I sleep, you sleep. That's all."

Christine searched his eyes. Somehow what he was saying made sense, at least from his point of view. If he had wanted to molest her he wouldn't ask. He'd just do it. Still, the mere idea of sleeping next to this thug repulsed her. She eased warily toward the bunk and sat down.

"You're on the inside," he said.

She scooted to the far side of the mattress, not taking her eyes off him.

"I told you. Behave and I won't harm you."

He laid down close beside her and she half-rolled away. She felt him come to rest against her back, felt the warmth of his body through their clothing — and she hated it. Christine wished to God she had never come across this person. Why couldn't she have been asleep when he drifted by? Why couldn't that storm a few nights ago have blown *Windsom* a little farther south?

"I'm going to put my arm over you." He did so slowly. "If you move, I'll know it."

"You expect me to get rest like this?"

"No, I expect to get rest like this. You can get yours now, later, whenever you like. It's almost noon. Don't get up until three."

Christine closed her eyes, her heart racing. His arm lay draped across her waist, heavy, like the lead weight belt she used for diving. She tried not to move as she lay facing the little digital alarm clock. The minutes advanced with glacial speed. Gradually, she felt his body relax, his breathing become more rhythmic. After ten minutes, she was quite sure he was asleep.

Sleep. It was the farthest thing from her mind. Christine wondered if she might somehow lift his arm and get up. But deep down she knew it was pointless. He would know. He probably knew what she was thinking right now. She looked at the clock. 11:55. Three hours would be an eternity. Try as she might, Christine could not hold back. Her diaphragm tightened, and small convulsions welled up from deep within. She was glad he was asleep and couldn't feel it. Christine did her best to hold still as tears began to trickle from her tightly closed eyes.

The EC-130 lumbered northward at twenty-two thousand feet. It was a version of the U.S. built C-130 Hercules, a tactical transport aircraft designed in the 1950s. Rugged and overbuilt, its ungainly appearance drew constant jibes from fighter pilots who mused about the large number of moving parts associated with four big turboprop engines. And then there was the Herc's slow speed. They'd say the aircraft didn't need an airspeed indicator, just a calendar. The Israeli Air Force had modified this particular aircraft with a number of large, bulbous antennae, which only heightened its decidedly non-aerodynamic appearance.

In spite of it all, the Herc was one of the most effective military aircraft ever built. The same basic design had been in production for fifty years, far longer than any other current military aircraft. It was used for airlift, airdrop, intelligence gathering, search and rescue, disaster relief,

Arctic supply, command and control, and a plethora of black and gray special operations. The C-130 did it all, and it was hard to find a pilot who didn't enjoy flying it.

Major Lev Schoen banked the airplane into a steep left turn on a command from the electronic warfare officer. They were in the clouds, as had been the case for the last two hours, but the conditions were irrelevant. This search was electronic, not visual.

"Roll out heading one niner zero," came the scratchy instruction over the intercom.

"I'm glad we found it right away," Schoen's co-pilot commented.

"Right where they said it would be," said Schoen.

The crew had been rousted out of bed, straight into a nine-hour flight from Israel to Rota Air Base in Spain. After a short rest and refueling, they continued southwest over the open ocean. All had hoped it wouldn't be an extended search and, luckily, after twenty minutes on station the faint signal had begun to register.

Schoen said, "Two more passes and we'll head back to Torrejon."

The loadmaster's voice came up on the intercom, sounding sleepy — no surprise since the only cargo today was a single pallet of electronic gear. "How long did you say we'll have in Madrid, skipper?"

"Twenty hours, unless someone changes their mind. Then we head back home."

"Twenty hours!" Schoen's co-pilot remarked to the loadie. "You'll have time to get drunk twice, Kroner." The two pilots laughed. Sergeant Kroner had a reputation for getting out of hand on layovers.

Kroner replied crustily, "And it'll take more than that candy-ass *veen rooge* you sip on lieutenant."

Ten minutes later the EWO made the announcement they'd all been waiting for. "Fourth pass confirms. We've got it down to a gnat's ass."

"Good, let's go home," Schoen declared. "Rudi," he said, addressing the EWO, "fire up the SAT-COM secure. Send in the position you plotted."

"Roger."

As the plane sped northward, albeit a relative term for the big Hercules, it was still enveloped in layer after layer of high stratus clouds. It took another hour before they began to break out of the weather. Late afternoon sun filtered onto the flight deck, warming bodies and spirits all around.

Soon after finding clear skies, Kroner's husky voice came excitedly over the intercom. "Hey skipper! I see a boat down low on the port side. Maybe we could go down for a titty check?"

Schoen looked out his side window and spotted a small sailboat three or four miles off, headed north. Kroner always pressed for a low pass on pleasure craft to get a look at any unsuspecting, partially clad females who might be frolicking around. He claimed a success rate of one in four. While Schoen doubted that statistic, Kroner carried a camera with a tele-photo lens to document any triumphs, and some of his more well-endowed targets had their pictures plastered on the squadron bulletin board.

"Sorry Kroner. Even if there were vixens aboard, it'd be way too cold for what you have in mind."

"But skipper, I've seen 'em tanning their—"

"*Not today*, Sergeant." Schoen's voice gave no room for argument.

The loadmaster went silent, no doubt fuming.

Major Schoen looked over at his co-pilot and smiled. "He's such a pervert."

Christine's body ached from the stillness she'd forced. Laying with him, their torsos remained meshed — his relaxed, hers rigid. There was no way she could ever sleep under these conditions. Her rest would have to come later.

He had stirred periodically over the last three hours, though never actually waking. At one point she'd heard an aircraft, and Christine wondered if it might be searching for survivors from his ship. Since the course *Windsom* was running backtracked the currents, they might be near where it had gone down.

His arm was still draped across her waist like a huge tentacle. How long would he be out? So far the weather had held, but sooner or later she'd have to go topside to check things over and — *and what?* One part of her wanted to keep *Windsom's* sails taut to reach England as quickly as possible and get this nightmare over with. But what would he do when they arrived? He might only be keeping her around because he had doubts about sailing *Windsom* solo. Perhaps he'd toss her over when they approached port, as easily as he'd discarded the winch handle and flares.

The thoughts rattled around endlessly in Christine's head as she lay next to her captor. Her emotions tracked the ocean's depths, from shallow hope to abysmal despair. Still, she always came back to the same thing in the end. He'd said he wouldn't hurt her, and he hadn't. Christine would wait. She'd look for everything and anything to get out of this fix, but she had to wait.

He stirred an hour later. His body stiffened, but she sensed he was still asleep. She could feel his warm breath on her neck, more rapid and shallow than it had been. Suddenly the arm lying across her waist jerked outward, and his legs moved as he began to mumble. He was having a nightmare.

More than ever, she wanted to get away. Christine willed herself to lie still as he muttered through his semi-conscious state. She tried to make out what he was saying. Numbers. *Five? Something seven?* Then it sounded like he said *doctor.* Christine wondered if he was dreaming about her. His body began to twist violently and it was all she could do to keep still. She felt his damp sweat. She smelled him and it made her afraid. The convulsions reached a peak and Christine could take it no more. She threw his arm off and scrambled away from the bed.

He woke instantly, bolting to a sitting position. Beads of perspiration covered the man's face. His clothes were soaked. He gasped for air and Christine saw something new in his wide-open eyes. Was it fear? Or perhaps pain? Some kind of terrible pain. It only lasted a moment, then the blank mask returned. Whatever had been there was gone, like a lone wave crashing into a seawall in an explosion of energy, then receding anonymously into the surrounding sea. Christine was pressed against the far wall, alert and ready, not knowing what to expect. The man laid back down and fell still, to a Zen-like tranquility.

Christine began breathing again. "Are you okay?"

"I'm fine."

His reply was too quick.

"Bad dream?"

He made no attempt to deny the obvious. "Everyone has their share."

"You've been through a lot in the last few days. Would it help to talk about it?"

He frowned, "Did you specialize in psychiatry, doctor? Because I suddenly feel like I'm on your couch."

"I did a rotation there, but no, I'm just a general practice kind of doctor."

"Then let's leave the psychoanalysis to the professionals, shall we?"

"I wasn't asking in a professional capacity. I just thought you might like to talk about it."

He sat up and swung his legs over the side of the bunk. "And if you can get me to bare my soul and give you my inner thoughts, then perhaps you can make me your friend. Friends don't harm friends."

Christine tried to look hurt. Was she that transparent, or was he that omniscient? Or perhaps he'd been in situations like this before.

"Forget I asked. I was just trying to help."

He had no reply, but looked at her appraisingly.

"What?" she asked.

If Christine had gone to the mirror she would have seen it as well. Deep lines of worry creased into her forehead and dark shadows were set under two bloodshot eyes.

"Didn't you get any sleep at all? You look awful."

"Of course I look awful. I just spent my afternoon in the arms of a foul pirate."

"Don't take it to heart." He stood up and stretched gingerly. "It's not a date, you know. It's a kidnapping."

A flippant remark. Christine remembered his frantic wake-up only minutes ago. He could certainly slap right through the gears.

He said, "I need you rested and healthy, so you can take care of me. Speaking of which, I'm famished. How about something to eat?"

She thought he was already looking better. In fact, amazingly so given the shape he was in yesterday morning. His color was good, and he showed no ill effects from the wound on his belly. The doctor in her wanted to check it, to make sure the gash was healing. On the other hand, where was gangrene when you needed it?

"You seem well enough," she said. "You won't need me around to take care of you much longer." Christine suddenly realized what a stupid thing that was to say, but he seemed to ignore it as he busied himself looking through the two cupboards where provisions were kept. Next, he rooted around in the refrigerator.

"Listen," he said, "I'm feeling better for the moment. Let's say I do something to earn my keep. I'll make breakfast."

Grudgingly, she accommodated. "All right. I'll go up top and check on things."

Christine climbed above to find a crisp breeze whipping across the deck. She paused at the sight of the water and the stunning blue sky. It was so incredibly open and unconfined. She took deep breaths, overwhelmed with relief. Only now did Christine realize the tension she'd been under. She went as far aft as she could go to the transom and made perfunctory checks of the rigging, knowing she was really just trying to get as far away from him as she could. The air below had seemed stifling, but now her thoughts cleared. That was good, because a sharp mind was her best weapon.

The next twenty minutes were spent on deck taking care of *Windsom*, and as she made her way around, Christine caught traces of the unmistakable scent of bacon frying. A carnivore. No surprises there. On her rounds, she discovered a reefing line on the jib that had frayed and was tending to jam. She made a mental note to fix it soon. Her last stop was to check the autopilot, which still held a tight, true course. Blessing or curse? she wondered.

He called from below, "Soup's on!"

Christine charged her lungs with a few last breaths of fresh air, then went below. He had set up the table between the two bunks, complete with placemats and the appropriate silverware. It looked as if he were entertaining, the only thing missing, a pair of candles in the center.

"Have a seat." He made it sound more an invitation than a command.

Christine sat, and he dropped a plate in front of her. A big cheese omelet, the bacon she had smelled, toast, and the last of the fresh fruit. Christine tried to remember when she'd last eaten. She ought to be hungry, but her appetite was nonexistent.

He, on the other hand, slid in across the table with a plate of his own and attacked it with purpose. He shoveled in everything, quickly and mechanically, the knife and fork in constant motion. Nothing was held to the palate, no attempt to measure subtleties of taste or texture — it was instead the elementary process of adding fuel to a furnace nearing empty. He was practically done when he noticed she hadn't touched her meal.

"What's the matter? Am I that bad of a cook? Or are you afraid I've poisoned it?"

Christine looked at her plate. "No. It's fine." She nibbled on a strip of bacon. Perhaps taking the meal he'd prepared would add to whatever tenuous union she could form with this person — breaking the bread, one of those ancient human bonding things. Wasn't that what the police al-

ways did in hostage situations? Order pizza for the terrorists? More importantly, Christine knew her body might need the energy. She didn't know
when or for what, but she had to be ready.

She finished ten minutes later. He took up her plate and replaced it
with a cup of hot coffee.

"So," he said, obviously with things on his mind, "I figure it's about
three days to Land's End. Sound right?"

Christine had taken a good look at the chart earlier. "I'd say so.
Where exactly will you be getting off?"

"I haven't quite decided, but you'll be the first to know. In a hurry to
be rid of me?"

There was a hint of playfulness in the question. She went along.
"Oh, no. Stay as long as you like. And next time bring some friends. I'm
sure they're a fun bunch."

"Indeed they are."

"If you brought enough of them, next time you could commandeer
a freighter. Maybe even a cruise ship."

Christine thought she actually saw his rough, chapped lips crack at
the corners.

"Of the two, definitely the cruise ship," he said.

"Why?"

"Because I'd hate to be forced into sleeping with my arm around
some smelly old sea dog."

"That *would* be disgusting."

"Your protest is duly noted. But nothing changes."

She sighed, and the man looked at her with something bordering on
concern. "You know, you really look like you could use some sleep."

Christine had to agree. Physically and emotionally she was drained.
He started to clean up the galley.

"Go ahead. Lie down. I think I can handle the boat for now."

She suspected he could handle it in a typhoon if he had to.

He finished cleaning and climbed up the stairs. "I'll wake you if anything comes up."

Christine looked longingly at her bunk and decided it was worth a
try. She stretched out and her body was immediately grateful. Knotted,
aching muscles began to loosen and relax. As wonderful as it felt, though,
her thoughts were still a scramble of worrisome questions, as they'd been
all day. How had she gotten into this mess, and when would it end? Three

days from now in England? And *how* would it end? What would he really do with her? The only realistic answers were frightful. Christine pulled a blanket up to her chest, finding warmth and even a thin, laughable sense of security. The bunk was soft and she closed her eyes. Three days to England. Would she ever be able to sleep with him lurking around? That question danced lightly in her mind for a few moments, then was answered.

Chapter Four

It was called the War Room, the name an obvious choice for a place designed with exactly that in mind. The Israeli government had seen more than its share, and after the invasion of Lebanon in 1982, it commissioned the nation's best and brightest structural engineers to design a complex that would harbor the country's leadership through whatever dark days might lay ahead.

The engineers took to the task with relish and quickly identified an ideal site for the fortress, one which at the time, unfortunately, was occupied by the Ministry of Agriculture and Rural Development. The engineers made a compelling case for the location, based on geological stability, advantages of the existing structure and, most importantly, proximity to the Knesset. So it was announced, with great public fanfare, that a new headquarters would be built for the Ministry of Agriculture. The Ministry's employees cheered the announcement, although some thought it suspicious since the old building had been renovated at great expense only a year earlier.

These doubts were quickly erased by way of a spreading rumor that the real reason for the move involved the original building's foundation — it was suspect, and might collapse at any time. An engineering report surfaced, confirming that the rickety structure was indeed doomed to ruin. The place was boarded up and notices of condemnation were posted all around at street level. Ministry employees were given notice to clear out their personal possessions, and an entire department of government was temporarily relocated to a rented building on the outskirts of town.

Another engineering survey soon declared that the original structure was perhaps salvageable, but not without extensive modifications. Heavy equipment began to appear, ushering in a period of constant activity. Endless trains of vehicles passed through the lone construction entrance and disappeared into what used to be the basement parking garage. Huge earthmoving and digging machines crawled down into the bowels of the structure. Cement was brought in, dirt hauled out. It was nearly two years before the heavy equipment gave way to a procession of smaller vans and trucks. Contractors of all sorts set to work on plumbing, electrical, and ventilation jobs.

If anyone had been keeping track, a number of things would have been strangely obvious from the start — such as the fact that the volume of dirt hauled out could have filled a stadium. Or that more concrete was used in the "shore-up" than had been used to construct the entire building in the first place. Employees of the adjacent buildings were among the first to note these discrepancies. Six months into the project, at least one office, the claims department for a large insurance company whose third floor suite had a bird's-eye view of the proceedings, had begun a pool to guess what was going on across the street. Among the speculative answers to the mystery were an underground military base, a bomb shelter, a gold mine, and a secret archaeological dig. An official winner of the pool was never declared, a fair result really, since all those answers held a fraction of the truth.

The War Room was on the lowest level of the refuge. Situated under a full two hundred feet of dirt and reinforced concrete, it could withstand any burrowing conventional weapon ever designed, and at least one direct hit from an air or ground burst nuclear device. Six independent air intakes were filtered for chemical, biological, and radiological contaminants. Three wells drew water directly from deep aquifers. Electrical power was taken from the grid above, backed up by two 1,750 kilowatt diesel generators. Fully staffed and provisioned, the fortress could be sealed off to operate independently for over a month.

Presently, the Prime Minister sat at the head of the War Room's long meeting table. Directly behind him, a large Israeli flag sagged from its staff. It was 6:00 in the morning, and the thick smell of coffee permeated the air. Most of the men and women around the table looked sleep deprived, with the exception of Paul Mordechai who was trying to balance a pencil on his finger, and probably calculating the physical forces involved.

"We've found her," Anton Bloch said.

He fiddled with a remote control until the large map of West Africa and the adjacent Atlantic Ocean was projected onto the wall behind him. It was the same map the Cabinet had been presented yesterday, only now the course lines were gone, replaced by a bold black X to mark *Polaris Venture*'s final resting place, a convention that made Jacobs feel as if he was looking at a pirate's treasure map.

"We found her late yesterday. The EC-130 made four passes to confirm the location. It's accurate to within a hundred meters."

"Just how far off the coast is that?" General Gabriel asked.

"Two hundred and thirty miles west of Gibraltar."

"That's good at least," Gabriel said. "Some of those crazies in North Africa think they can claim sovereignty all the way out to two hundred."

Bloch continued, "The other good news is that she's in over ten thousand feet of water. Unsalvageable, as we said yesterday, to all but a few major countries. And they'd have no interest."

Zak asked, "What about survivors?"

"No one in the water could still be alive, it's too cold. All the life rafts on board were equipped with radios. The EC-130 monitored 121.5 megahertz the whole time it was in the search area — that's the international VHF distress frequency. Unfortunately, there were no contacts." Bloch looked to General Gabriel for help.

"*Moledt* is on the way. She's our fastest ship available, a Reshef class corvette," Gabriel said. "*Moledt* cruises at thirty knots, so she should be on station the day after tomorrow. *Hanit* will be a half-day behind." Heads around the room nodded, approving of the pointless formality. Jacobs listened grimly.

"They'll keep a search running until we call it off," Gabriel added in his confident, soldier's voice.

Deputy Prime Minister Sonja Franks addressed the Director of Mossad. "Anton, what about the possibility of someone else finding survivors? Have our stations picked up anything?"

"No. But then, as we agreed, we're not asking questions. It's a passive order, listen only. Radio traffic, newspaper articles, gossip in the bars. It might take a few days for anything to turn up."

Ariel Steiner picked up where he'd left off, shooting straight at the Prime Minister. "This is a fine mess. We've found the ship, but can't be sure the weapons haven't been hijacked."

Jacobs was in no mood for it. "Ariel, you know damn well—"

"Gentlemen, please," Zak interjected, becoming a referee between the two most powerful men in his country. Jacobs exchanged glares with the Labor Party man as he receded into his chair.

"Paul and I have given this some thought," Bloch said. "We know the ship has gone down, so the only question is whether the weapons are still intact. We can find out."

"I thought salvage was out of the question," Sonja Franks remarked.

Paul Mordechai piped in, "We're not talking about salvage. We're talking about reconnaissance. I spent an hour with our Naval Systems people last night. What we need is a deep-water surveyor — a small robotic sub. It can go down to the wreck and determine if the weapons are still there."

"Do we have something like that?" Steiner asked.

"No," said Mordechai. "They're used primarily for oceanographic research and working on oil rigs, that kind of thing. These machines aren't cheap, but they are commercially available."

"One of these gadgets can tell us whether the weapons have been hijacked?" Zak asked.

Bloch said, "Probably. When ships go down at the depths we're talking about, it's hard to say exactly what will happen. They can break apart, scatter over miles and miles of ocean floor. But if *Polaris Venture* was scuttled as we suspect, the charges were placed so she'd go down fast and in one piece. I think there's a good chance we'll find the weapons."

"How long will this take?" Zak asked.

"Three or four days. Possibly longer if we can't find the right equipment."

Steiner threw his arms up in exasperation. "And in the meantime, two nukes might be on their way to our doorstep."

"He's right," General Gabriel said. "If one of our enemies has taken them, could they be used right away? Aren't there codes or something to arm them?"

Mordechai answered. "There *are* codes, and we have good reason to believe they're secure. To use one of the weapons without them, the current arming and fusing system would have to be reprogrammed, or the whole device rebuilt. Either case would require highly skilled scientists. To reprogram you would also need the bomb's technical design specifications. Without that, it would be easier to just take the thing apart and rebuild it with your own triggering device."

"How can we be sure these codes are secure, given how things are in South Africa?" someone asked.

Mordechai grinned. "Because they're not in South Africa. They're on the bottom floor of this complex."

The room was silent and nobody asked the obvious question. Bloch was compelled to explain, "As soon as *Polaris Venture* left Cape Town, General Van Ruut personally handed the codes over to my man, who brought them straight to us. We needed them to prepare the weapons for storage."

The Prime Minister summed it up. "So it's likely that these two weapons are sitting on the bottom of the ocean. If someone has taken them, but doesn't have the codes, they'd need three or four weeks to make them usable — worst case. More likely months. We have enough time to take a look without going on high alert."

"And if they are on the bottom of the ocean?" Deputy Prime Minister Franks asked.

"We leave them there," Mordechai replied happily.

"Let's get on it," Jacobs said. He directed Paul Mordechai to quietly find an appropriate submersible, then turned to Bloch.

"Keep up the passive monitoring for any intelligence about the sinking or, God forbid, hijacking of *Polaris Venture*."

The Prime Minister then reminded everyone of the extreme sensitivity of the situation. If they kept a tight lid, the whole thing would probably be a nonevent in a few weeks. The members of the Cabinet concurred.

Jacobs inquired about any other business. General Gabriel said there had been a grenade attack on a troop convoy near the Lebanese border. He also reported that the Syrians had launched an SA-6 surface-to-air missile the previous night. There were no Israeli aircraft in the area and the missile seemed unguided, so it was likely a technical glitch. "One less they have to fire at us," he reasoned. Anton Bloch said a headquarters Mossad man had been killed while on vacation in London, but that it appeared to be an accident. All in all, a quiet day aside from *Polaris Venture*. The Cabinet adjourned and its members filed out of the War Room.

After all had left, the Prime Minister sat alone and directed a circumspect gaze at the map with a big black **X** on the far wall. A "nonevent," he'd said. To everyone except those sixteen people who'd been on board. And their families. Jacobs knew why he had lost his temper with Steiner. One of his own men was out there. Bloch had told him the name — David Slaton. A man gone off to do his duty. No one had expected it to be a dangerous mission, but those were the ones that always stung you. Jacobs had commanded an IDF infantry company in the '73 war. His unit took thirty percent casualties, but he was proud that he'd never left any dead or wounded behind. Looking at a map full of ocean he knew General Van Ruut must be having similar thoughts. Van Ruut had fifteen men out there.

Jacobs got up, walked to Bloch's seat and picked up the remote control. He'd never met David Slaton. Hadn't selected him for the mission. All the same, as Slaton's commander, he'd made the final decision to leave him out in the ocean, with no real attempt made at a rescue. At the time, there seemed to be sound, practical reasons for doing so. But now they escaped the Prime Minister. Jacobs pressed the button that turned off the projector and the screen went blank.

Windsom crashed along at eight knots. The sky was dark, and strong southwesterly winds drove a following sea. Christine looked to port and saw the Isles of Scilly passing ten miles abeam. The craggy islands of rock jutted up defiantly, sentries locked in a perpetual battle against the crashing swells. It was the same sight that had been seen for centuries, ever since sailors began venturing into the open ocean southwest of England. To see it on the return voyage was traditionally a good thing, a transitional signal that the hardships of sea were behind and the comforts of port ahead. Christine saw nothing hopeful in it.

She watched her tormentor at the bow. He had just changed out the jib, going with a smaller, heavier canvas in the strengthening wind. Now he was stowing the bigger sail into the forward hatch. His movement was sure and confident, no relation to the broken creature she'd dragged aboard four days ago. She was quite sure he'd never done any serious sailing before, yet Christine was amazed at how fast he picked it all up. The new sail was up, the old one stowed, and now he was on his way back, no doubt to ask what he should do next.

The last days had been a strange, awkward experience. At times they were a crew, tending to chores on the boat, taking meals together. Then uncertainty would prevail over the sleeping arrangements or a clipped conversation. When they did talk it was always about her, never giving Christine insight to the man or his intentions.

Christine looked again at the sky. A line of clouds, almost black, was immediately to the west and bearing down fast. The weather forecast, taken from the one radio he allowed her to use, had been right. It was going to be a serious blow.

She had wanted to outrun it, hoping to make a case for ducking into the first port, which happened to be Penzance. But now it was clear they were going to get caught, and maybe that was for the better. Christine still didn't know where he planned to pull in, or what he would do with her. She had tried to obliquely broach the subject a number of times, but neither his answers nor his expressions gave anything away. In the distance, Christine could just make out Land's End.

England. Freedom. It seemed so very far away.

The gust hit suddenly twenty minutes later. *Windsom* heeled over so far that her side cabin windows went under for a moment. Christine stayed at the tiller and reefed in the main, leaving out just enough sail to keep up steerage. She decided to roll in the jib, but the line wouldn't move when she pulled it. The seas were still following, and *Windsom* surfed ahead awkwardly on huge twelve-foot swells. Sheets of cold rain lashed across the ocean, making undulating patterns on a crazy, uneven surface. Christine had to get more sail in. She gave a few sharp tugs on the line that controlled the mechanism at the base of the sail. Nothing. It was jammed.

"Great," she fretted. Christine looked below and saw him at the charts. His legs bent in concert with the boat's wild gyrations, and he showed no interest whatsoever in nature's display above deck.

"I need your help!" she shouted over the static noise of wind-driven rain slapping against the fiberglass deck.

He poked his head out. "What?"

"The reefing mechanism on the bow is jammed," she said, holding up the offending slack line. "I need you to go up front and take a look."

He looked at the sky, the unpleasantness of which was momentarily accentuated by a close-in bolt of lightning and the associated *crack*! He frowned.

"Either that or come steer and I'll go up. The autopilot doesn't work well in seas like this."

"All right, all right. I'll go," he shouted. "Have you got another rain coat?"

She shook her head. "Sorry." Christine had already donned the only set of foul weather gear.

He took off the sweatshirt he was wearing, an oversized one that said U CONN on front. Being the only thing on board that fit, he'd had no reservations about commandeering it. Underneath were the same clothes he'd been wearing for probably a week.

He bolted up and began winding a path through rigging toward the bow pulpit. Christine suddenly realized he wasn't wearing a lifeline, but again, there was only one — it was, after all, supposed to be a solo voyage. He reached the bow, bent down over the reefing mechanism and had it free in a matter of seconds. She pulled the line and took in the sail.

"That's good," she yelled, adding a thumbs-up in case he couldn't hear over the wind and rain.

As he started back aft, a big wave hit *Windsom* awkwardly and she lurched hard. He lost his balance for a moment before grabbing a stanchion to steady himself. Christine suddenly looked at the main sheet, the line that held the boom in place. If she released it, the boom would swing free. In this wind it would waylay anything in its path — and in a matter of seconds *he* would be in that path. This was the chance she'd been hoping for! She needed time to think, but there wasn't any. Another big wave crashed into *Windsom*, sending a sheet of spray over everything.

Christine reached for the rope and undid the hitch that held it secure. Now one turn around the cleat and her hand were the only things holding it in place. She could see his legs as he moved behind the sail. *One more step . . .*

Her hand seemed to act on its own. Christine let go. It only took a second for the free line to rip through a series of pulleys as *Windsom's* big metal boom flew outward. It struck him squarely in the chest. There was a sickening thud and she heard a guttural sound as air expelled from his lungs. He flipped clear over the side, the sound of his splash lost in a storm-driven sea.

Christine jumped up and looked over the side. He surfaced just behind the boat and instinctively made a grasping lunge for the stern, but at the speed *Windsom* was traveling there was no chance. After a few moments of stunned inaction, Christine turned the boat hard to port and into the wind. *Windsom's* momentum slowed and she came to a gradual stop, her loose sail snapping wildly in the heavy squall. Christine saw him clearly a hundred feet back, a picture strikingly similar to the one she'd seen four days ago. It seemed like a lifetime.

He made no attempt to swim to the boat, no wave or shout, and so he already knew it had been no accident. He just sat there treading water in a freezing ocean. Rain continued to sweep down and they stared at one another in a surreal standoff, the victor and the vanquished.

Christine could hardly believe it. She had done it! Her captor was in the water and she was free, having beaten the thug at his own game. With one pull on a rope, *Windsom* would be under way, and he would never threaten anyone again.

Then her moment of elation ebbed. The water here was so cold that no one could last more than an hour or two. And the coast was at least ten miles off — he could never swim it, even if he knew which way to go. No, she thought, pull the sheet on the mainsail and I'd be killing him, as surely as putting a gun to his head and pulling the trigger. Christine had acted instinctively, when there was no time to think about consequences. But now there was time, and she knew what she had to do.

She went aft and unlashed a yellow horseshoe life ring. It was stenciled with *Windsom's* name in an arc of big black letters. She attached the life ring to a line and heaved it out to him.

"Can't say I don't take care of my patients," Christine mumbled in frustration. "Hypocrites, I hope you're proud."

He swam slowly to the ring and pulled himself in, taking more than one breaking wave in the face as he made his way back. She kicked the boarding ladder down into the water, but made no attempt to help him up as *Windsom's* stern rose and fell severely on the big waves. She knew he'd make it. This guy was indestructible.

True to form, after being thrown off the ladder twice, he managed to boost himself up. Slowly, like a mountaineer at the summit, he reached the top and clambered over the transom to face her.

He said nothing. His lips were already blue, his breathing rapid from the exertion of getting back aboard. He simply stood in a driving rain and

stared at her with an odd, quizzical look, as if he was completely confounded by what she'd just done.

Christine wondered what amazed him so. That she had put him
over the side? Or that she had let him back aboard? Not sure what to expect, she simply held her ground and stared back, defiant in the victory. It
was as though the tables were turned from that other day, when he had
burst in as she was changing clothes; this time she was seeing *him* naked,
seeing something human behind the cloak that always obscured his
thoughts and feelings. He searched her eyes, desperate for some explanation. Christine wasn't going to offer any. She turned away and began tending to the boat.

"Go below and get dried off," she said.

Without a word, he did.

Viktor Wysinski sat in a lounge chair and squinted against the bright tropical sun. Morocco's white sand and water were merciless in their reflec-
tive properties, and the stocky ex-commando put a hand over his eyes to
shield them as the young girl approached. Her long brown legs carried
her effortlessly through loose sand. She carried two tall, tropical drinks,
one of which she handed to him before sprawling her lithe figure onto the
lounge next to his.

"*No salt, Veektor,*" she said with a thick French accent and a smile.

Wysinski said nothing as he took the drink. He was a short, thickly
built barrel of a man. His meaty face was topped by a standard flattop haircut, the same "style" he'd been sporting for twenty years with the Israeli
Defense Forces.

He had retired two years ago with the rank of captain, much farther
down the ladder than he'd once hoped for. Those traits that had served
him well early in his career had eventually stunted his advancement.
Wysinski's manner was as brutish as his appearance — fine qualities for a
lieutenant, but not field-grade material. He had never understood how his
peers, the ones who took desk jobs and went to all the goddamn commander's cocktail receptions, had managed to get promoted over a warrior like
himself. In his book, soldiers killed the enemy. But it was the rear echelon
pussies who made full-bird colonel while they sat on their fat arses in
command centers writing "mission statements" and "contingency plans."
If nothing else, Wysinski was proud of the fact that he'd spent his entire
career in the field, always in the fight. Even in retirement.

He picked up his newspaper and shook off the sand. The Moroccan dailies were all in French, and a two-day old *New York Times*, discarded on a table in the hotel's lobby, had been the only thing he could find that wouldn't require an interpreter. He scanned for a few minutes, found nothing, and wondered if that was good or bad. Who cares? he decided.

Wysinski crumpled the paper and looked out at the beach. The sun was at its equatorial apex. Behind him, in the dusty maze of alleys and low sandstone buildings that made up Rabat, the natives had enough sense to huddle in whatever shade they could find. But here, along that narrow strip where cool water met land, it was the opposite. People were everywhere. People from other places. The young and beautiful frolicking, the old and rich watching from the shade of umbrellas. Wysinski eyed them all contemptuously. He had never been the first, but —

"*Sweem?*"

The thin voice shattered his concentration.

"*Sweem?*" the girl repeated, gesturing hopefully toward the water.

"No," he waved her off. "No, later."

The girl pouted and flipped onto her stomach, a well-designed act that not only expressed dissatisfaction, but also added an element of symmetry to her vulcanizing process. She was a beautiful thing, and spirited. But very young — sixteen, seventeen perhaps. Of all the girls available at the bar last night, she had been the prize. Her worthless brother had negotiated a steep price, but she'd been worth every dirham. Now there was a bastard, Wysinski thought. If I had a sister like her I'd cut the throat of any man who looked at her the wrong way. Maybe I should do her a favor before I leave and — again, his thought process was interrupted, this time by a steward.

"*Monsieur Weeseeski, non?*" The man presented a shiny silver tray with a cordless telephone on it.

"*Oui,*" Wysinski said noncommittally. He was used to people butchering his name. Especially peons.

"*Pour vous, monsieur.*"

Wysinski had never been given a phone on a silver tray before and he thought it looked stupid. He grabbed it, got up, and slogged off through the hot sand. He didn't start talking until his feet hit the water.

"Hello?"

The voice was familiar.

"You were not at the primary number."

"You found me," Wysinski grumped.

"The timetable for your next meeting has been moved ahead."

"To when?"

"Now."

"*What?*" Wysinski shot back. They had only gotten back yesterday, after pounding through the ocean for thirty hours. "Why the hell didn't we just stay and—"

"Stop!" the man on the phone insisted.

Wysinski backed down, "All right, all right. What's the rush?"

"I can't explain, but it is vital you go right away. Contact me as soon as it is done."

The line went dead and Wysinski, unable to think of anything more clever, hissed a stream of expletives under his breath. He hit the off button and stood sneering at an ocean of turquoise water. He didn't mind getting it over with. In fact, it would drive him crazy to sit around this place, aware of the task that lay ahead. But it ticked him off to not know what was going on, to not be in on the planning. In the old days he had been a tactician, a decision maker. Now he answered a phone, and was ordered to do the bidding of his distant superior. In a fit of anger, Wysinski wound up and threw the little handset far into the Atlantic. It splashed and disappeared.

The stakes were getting higher, but Wysinski knew this would be the last time. After this there would be no more need. He and the others could do as they wished — legitimately. Wysinski turned back to the beach and trudged up to his chair. Next to it, the steward stood staring at him, a statue with an empty silver tray in its hand.

"Put it on my bill!" Wysinski barked.

The steward, void any remnants of decorum, stumbled and retreated toward the pool.

The girl had clearly noticed his fit as well. "*Quelle est?*" she inquired in a particularly nubile voice.

Wysinski ignored her and headed straight for his room. He would call the marina and tell Joacham to ready the boat. Trudging through deep sand, Wysinski passed the little thatched hut that was the bar. On top he saw a Moroccan flag hanging flaccidly — no wind. That was good. The sooner they got this done, the better.

Jerusalem had been at the other end of the line. There, the caller dialed a second number, the purpose to give confirmation that the words for

Wysinski had been sent and received. The caller mentally reviewed a careful script. Here, there would be no discussion, no room for error. The second number was, in fact, a local call. In a plush corner of the Knesset Office Building a seldom used phone rang. It was answered immediately.

The storm had subsided, the torrential rain now a light drizzle, the wind and seas fallen calm. Christine sat at the helm, steering by his instructions. They had been close to shore for an hour, holding about three miles out, but occasionally ducking in closer. In spots, the steady drizzle transformed into mist. Dusk, still about five hours off, might bring the visibility down fast.

"Come thirty left," he commanded from his station next to the mast.

Christine turned the tiller while he scanned the shoreline with the binoculars. She wondered what he could possibly be looking for. Penzance was still twenty miles ahead, Plymouth fifty. There were no harbors of any kind here and the coastline was rocky, unapproachable as far as *Windsom* was concerned.

"Hold this course," he said.

He'd been quiet since the storm, only speaking when it came to the business of maneuvering the boat. Christine wished she knew what he was up to, but, predictably, he wasn't letting on.

With *Windsom* about two miles offshore, he began shifting the binoculars sharply between points along the rocky coast. Christine looked, but saw nothing remarkable. Steep cliffs as far as she could see, with boulders dominating the tide line, then a lighter color above on the near-vertical incline, probably some kind of coarse vegetation.

"All right, that's it," he said suddenly. "Turn her into the wind."

Christine complied and the sails flapped loosely as *Windsom*'s momentum gradually slowed. He went below, rattled a few things around, then came back on deck. Christine tensed immediately when she saw what was in his hand. It was her father's old diving knife. Eight inches long with a serrated edge on one side, it was rusty and lethal-looking. God, where had he found that? she wondered. Still, he wore the same serious, intense expression that had been there all along, which was comforting in a strange way. This man was no berserk killer. There was purpose in everything he did, and Christine knew the knife was not intended for her. He did, however, point it casually in her direction for emphasis.

"Keep her into the wind," he said, obviously not wanting a repeat of the day's earlier incident.

Christine watched in amazement as he went to the mainsail. Holding the knife over his head, he jabbed viciously into it. Yanking and pulling, he ripped the canvas through its entire length. He made another cut and another, until the sail was shredded into a half-dozen loosely connected pieces. Next, he went up front and gave five minute's treatment to the jib. Then he cut the halyards and sheets. He went all around the boat cutting and slicing.

Christine watched in silence, trying to understand. He was disabling *Windsom,* but why? Was he going to motor into Penzance and say, "Look at what the storm did!" How would that help him? Perhaps if he was alone? Christine forced the ideas from her mind. She'd know soon enough.

Her captor went below and for two minutes she heard metallic, banging noises. He came back up with a few critical pieces of the engine — the plugs and some wiring. He threw them over the side and they disappeared.

With a thoughtful look around the boat, he nodded, apparently satisfied with his destruction. Again the man went below, this time emerging with a pair of oars. He went forward along the port side and began to unlash the dinghy.

The dinghy! That was it!

Christine was overwhelmed with relief. He had disabled *Windsom,* and now he was going to row himself ashore. In a matter of moments she'd be free!

She watched as he tied a short painter onto the little boat's bow and slid it into the water. He bent down and held the dinghy close with one leg, then turned.

"I'm sorry," he said evenly.

Giddy with relief, she nearly laughed out loud. Sorry? For what? she wondered, anger creeping in. For kidnapping me? For keeping me in constant fear over the last four days and nights? Or for tearing my poor father's boat to shreds? She wanted to scream it all at the top of her lungs. But Christine held back, because more than anything else, she just wanted him to go.

He stepped into the dinghy and used one of the oars to push off. Then, locking the oars in their gimbals, he began rowing toward the shoreline. Christine scanned the rocky coast. It looked impenetrable from where she stood, two miles away, but she had no doubt he'd make it. She watched him go, rowing strongly. Again she thought about how quickly he had recovered from his injuries. Christine was thankful for that. Thankful because the strength was taking him away, stroke by stroke, out of her life for good.

"Keep going," she said. "Keep going so that I'll never see you again."

A hundred yards away, David Slaton faced aft as he rowed ashore. He saw *Windsom* bobbing aimlessly, her torn sails and cut lines flopping uselessly in the breeze. And she was there, watching him.

He could hear the faint sound of waves breaking along the coast. The sound would gradually become a roar, but he would deal with that later. He pulled the oars hard through the cold water. Slaton felt beads of perspiration already forming on his face, and the muscles in his back and legs began to feel warm and full.

The physical labor was good. He needed the exercise. But more importantly, Slaton finally felt like he was doing something. For days he'd taken it easy, letting his body recover. He had used the time to think, to try and make sense out of what had happened to *Polaris Venture*. She'd been sabotaged — of that, he was sure. But by whom? And why? There had been fifteen others on that ship, good soldiers one and all. The whole operation had been tightly held, known to only a few people in South Africa and those at the highest level of his own government. Yet it had been compromised all the same.

Then there was Yosy's phone call, right before Slaton had departed England for the mission. It had seemed harmless enough at first, but then Yosy dropped the name Sheena into the conversation, a fictitious character they'd devised years ago while working together in southern Italy. The name was a flag, their personal warning code. It had never gotten used in Italy, but last week Yosy brought up the name during an otherwise casual conversation — twice. Extreme danger. Slaton had been thrown quickly into the *Polaris Venture* mission, and was unable to contact Yosy by a more secure means. Once briefed on *Polaris Venture*, he never considered that it might be the subject of Yosy's warning, given the level of secrecy around the project. Now he saw that was clearly a mistake.

Yosy might not have known specifically about *Polaris Venture*, but he'd seen a danger and tried to give warning. Slaton decided that as soon as he was safe, the first order of business would be to get in touch with

Yosy. He could be trusted. Everywhere else there were doubts. Slaton had
to be careful, because somewhere there was a traitor, and he had a bad
feeling it was on the Israeli side of the fence. At the moment, however, he
held one distinct advantage. Only one person in the world even knew he
was alive, and she didn't know who he was.

Slaton took one last look at the small sailboat. She was standing
astern with an arm raised, holding onto a stanchion. At this distance her
figure was nothing more than a silhouette. A strange corollary flowed into
his mind as he decided she was an exceptionally attractive woman, from
any distance. It was a plain beauty, simple and unadorned by cosmetics or
trappings. She was average in height and build, with a distinctly athletic
carriage, fluid and steady, never bothered by the movement of the boat.
The hair was straight and brown, with lighter streaks from the sun, the
skin clear and tan. His mind held a vivid image.

It was, however, an impression that could not be permitted to linger.
It bothered him and he pushed it away. There was no place for it. There
had not been for a very long time. Slaton looked again over his shoulder
to evaluate the task at hand. He spied the small house atop the bluff, the
one that undoubtedly commanded a breathtaking view of this craggy
coastline. He had spotted it with the binoculars from *Windsom*. A vacation home, with any luck abandoned this time of year. That was where he
was headed. David Slaton reestablished his grip on the oars and pulled
hard. Now it was time to work.

Chapter Five

He dragged the dinghy up a steep pathway, thankful it wasn't any heavier. Slaton's bare feet slipped now and again on loose stones, and he had to grab at the bases of the sturdier shrubs for leverage as he lugged his load uphill. The path rose from a tiny patch of sand and pebbles — what must have passed for a beach along this rugged stretch of coastline — which had fortunately been accessible during the low tide. If he had arrived six hours later he might still be rowing up the coast, looking for a place to put in. Even better, the footpath eventually led to the very house that had piqued his interest. Slaton had already been up the path once to do his reconnaissance. The house was vacant, as he'd hoped.

Finally reaching the top with the dinghy in tow, he stopped for a moment to catch his breath. The house lay in front of him. It was a boxy, two-story structure with a small shed off to one side, the type of quaint summer residence common to the area, and probably used only a few months of the year.

He grabbed the dinghy again and dragged it to the shed. There, he tipped it up on one side and leaned it against the wooden building. No better place to hide something than right out in the open. Slaton went around to the front of the shed and swung open its squeaky door. The padlock had been a problem, but then his lock-picking tools were less than professional grade. The tensioner was a tiny, flat-bladed screwdriver, the rake a thin metal rod, both scavenged from the sailboat's toolbox. Old and rusted, the lock on the shed had taken five minutes. Fortunately, the back door of the main house had been far more accommodating, giving up in a matter of seconds.

The shed was dark inside, light only coming by way of the open door and a few cracks that had evolved between the old wooden wall planks. There was a single bulb mounted up on the ceiling with a pull-cord, but it would be no use since the power had been disconnected for the season. Slaton's eyes gradually adjusted. He could make out an old lawn mower that looked like it hadn't been used in years, a scattered assortment of gardening tools, a tireless rim from a bicycle wheel, and an old rusted wheelbarrow. The place had an oily, musty odor. Some gnarled driftwood lay in a pile in one corner, and Slaton heard an animal scratching and scurrying underneath.

He spotted a bulky tarp covering something large in one corner. Slaton maneuvered through the junk and yanked the tarp away, revealing an ancient Brough motorcycle. He shoved aside a rake and a few old boards to get a closer look. There was a helmet, the tires were up, and he saw no obvious parts missing. It was a relic, but might be serviceable. He shoved more junk aside and eventually made a path wide enough to walk the machine outside. There, the first thing he noticed was a current license plate. That was a good sign — probably a toy of the owner's. He checked for fuel and found less than half a tank. Slaton got on and began to kick the starter, still not hoping for much. After ten tries, the machine coughed, spit, and eventually held a tenuous grip on idle power. Slaton added some throttle and it clunked to a stop.

He got off, put his hands on his hips, and sized up the tired old contraption. Other than walking, it was his only mode of transportation at the moment. Slaton cast a glance up the coastline. Earlier, from the top floor of the house, he'd seen that the nearest neighbors were a half-mile away on either side. The house to the west looked vacant, though he couldn't say for sure. The house to the east was definitely occupied — there were lights on, and a thin wisp of smoke emanated from the chimney.

He considered how much time he might have. The neighbors were far enough away that they wouldn't notice him anytime soon. More pressing was the good Dr. Palmer. She was a capable sailor. He had no doubt she'd have some kind of sail rigged up by now. Even so, it would be at least nightfall before she could make any port. What worried him more was the chance she might flag down another boat. If she could contact the authorities by radio, things would go a lot faster. Sometime in the next twenty-four hours the police would start searching this stretch of coastline for a man — six-foot-one, sandy hair, and recovering from a nasty sunburn. They'd start by looking for the boat he'd come ashore in, the one that was now tucked neatly against the woodshed.

Gasoline dripped slowly off the bottom of the Brough's engine. Slaton scratched his chin and decided he'd give it an hour. There were a few rudimentary tools strewn about the shed. If he couldn't get it up and running by then, he'd move by some other means. Jump into a truck, steal a bicycle, or walk if necessary. He had to distance himself from this place in order to get safe. Only then could he begin the real work that lay ahead.

It took forty minutes. A loose clamp on the fuel hose and a badly adjusted carburetor were the main problems. Slaton had also cleaned the spark plugs and found some oil to add. That done, the thing ran. It would never be the cutting-edge racing machine it had been sixty years before, but he figured it would hold together long enough to get him out of Cornwall.

Slaton went into the house and climbed to the second floor. The lone room there was arranged as a library or den of sorts. He edged up to a window, keeping his own profile in the shadows, and looked out across the treeless, heathered landscape.

A thin column of smoke still wafted up from the chimney of the house to the east. Slaton studied the meandering road that loosely connected the properties along the coast. So far, there had been no traffic. He surveyed the lay of the land and tried to recall the coastal features he'd seen from his approach to shore earlier; that in mind, he guessed the quickest way to a main road would be east.

Downstairs were two bedrooms and he started with the smaller. He found linens and boxes of needlepoint, but nothing of use. Slaton wasn't particularly careful about fingerprints. That would only slow things down and he didn't have the time. Eventually the authorities would match some of the prints around the house to some of those on the sloop *Windsom*. It didn't matter. His prints were not on file. Not with Scotland Yard, not with Interpol. It would be another dead end.

He moved to the other bedroom and was quickly rewarded. A small wooden box on the dresser held three twenty-pound notes and another five or so in loose change. In the closet he found what he really needed — clothing. The rags he had on were disintegrating fast, except for the U CONN sweatshirt he'd stolen. More importantly, tomorrow all of it would be included in the police description of a man on the loose, a mad kid-napper who'd been plucked from the ocean. This quiet little hamlet would be in an uproar by midday. Fortunately, the house seemed to have at least one seasonal occupant who was roughly Slaton's height. Unfortu-nately, he was also about fifty pounds heavier. It would have to do.

He chose a pair of dark work pants and a cotton pullover shirt. A belt from the dresser, cinched to its smallest circumference, kept the pants in the vicinity of his waistline. He found two sweaters and put both on, the heavier, a wool pullover, on the outside. The brisk temperatures outside would turn downright bone-chilling in a seventy mile an hour breeze, or whatever the old machine could muster. Slaton went back to the closet and rummaged further. The selection of shoes was limited, but happened to be a good fit, and he chose a newer pair of leather hiking boots. Finally, Slaton took a few more items of clothing and stuffed them into an old can-vas backpack.

Dressed and packed, he positioned himself in front of a full-length mirror and evaluated the effect. The thick, bulky clothing made him look stockier. He was still dirty and greasy from working on the motorcycle. Slaton wiped his filthy hands on the trousers, then, for good measure, smudged the sleeve of his sweater. It was good. The scraggly, half-grown beard helped, and the blisters on his face, not completely healed, gave his complexion a ruddy appearance. It was quite good. *A working man. Just finished an honest day's work and on his way home, or maybe to the pub for a pint.*

Satisfied, he pocketed the money he'd found and went outside. Sla-ton closed the door to the shed and looked around to see if anything else was obviously out of place. Other than a new boat leaning against the shed, the exterior was just as he'd found it.

He climbed on the Brough and kicked it to life. The thing spewed heavy blue smoke before chugging itself into a rhythm. He gave the throt-tle a turn and the old bike scampered up the dirt and gravel driveway, churning a cloud of dust along the way. Slaton hit the road at speed and turned east.

A surly Anton Bloch was putting on his coat to head home when Paul Mordechai came bounding energetically into his office. One hand held a piece of paper, which he shook wildly over his head, the other a can of

Coke, the sugar and caffeine elixir that Bloch suspected was partly responsible for the engineer's constant state of motion.

"We've found an ROV in France. It's owned by a non-profit environmental group and they want to sell it so they can upgrade to a deeper model. This one will work just fine for us, though. I even talked them down to a great price."

Bloch couldn't have cared less. "When can we get it?"

"As soon as we transfer the funds. It's in Marseille right now."

"Which ship have you decided to use?"

"Of those we have enroute, I think *Hanit* is the best choice."

Bloch put his coat back on the rack. "All right. I'll have her diverted to Marseille."

"Don't you want to know how much?" Mordechai asked cheerily.

Bloch ignored him, picked up the phone and arranged for a secure line to Defense. Waiting for the connection to be run, he was naked to Mordechai's stare. "All right, give me the account information and I'll arrange payment," he said impatiently.

Mordechai grabbed a notepad from Bloch's desk and scribbled the account numbers from memory, talking at the same time, "Six hundred and fifty thousand. It's a steal! I'll bet they paid one-three, maybe one-five last year. We got the controller, cables, displays, and all the spares."

Bloch glowered. "Go pack your bags. You're going to Marseille. I'll have a jet waiting for you at Palmachim within the hour."

The engineer smiled, clearly pleased he'd be able to play with his new toy.

"You'd better hurry," Bloch said pointedly.

Mordechai shrugged, took the last swig of his Coke, then wheeled around and launched the empty can basketball style at a trash bin across the room. Missing badly, he scurried over, scooped up the rebound and performed an exceptionally awkward slam-dunk. The engineer then zoomed out of the room, completely oblivious to the Director's seething expression, a look that would have shriveled any other employee in the building.

"If he wasn't a goddamn genius . . ." Bloch muttered through clenched teeth.

Clive Batty had been around the docks in Penzance for all his sixty years but he'd never seen anything like it. The harbormaster stared at the little sloop that had just crawled in out of the mist. It was propelled by a few strips of loosely sewn canvas and what looked like a flower-print bed sheet. The boat eased closer to where he stood on the dock and a young woman moved to the bow with a coiled rope. She tossed the line and it fell across the planks right next to him. Batty secured it to a cleat and she threw him another line, this one attached to the stern of the crippled little boat. Together they pulled and pushed *Windsom* alongside the dock and tied her on.

"Must've been a bad blow you went through there, missy. We had some of it 'ere, but it didn't hit us hard." Batty kept looking up at the rigging. Damnedest thing he'd ever seen. Broken lines everywhere. A bunch of spaghetti, like you'd expect if the mast had gone down — only the mast was up.

The woman jumped onto the dock and her gait turned wobbly. Batty knew sea legs when he saw them. He thought she looked tired, too.

"Been out for a while, 'ave ye?"

She walked up and offered a hand. "Christine Palmer."

"Clive Batty. They just call me Bats." He scratched the gray stubble of whiskers on his chin. "Looks like you'll be in the market for a good sailmaker. Me cousin Colin just happens to run a shop up the street. He does quality work and charges a lot for it." Batty leaned toward Christine and whispered conspiratorially, "But I think you could get a more reasonable deal than most. He's got a soft spot for the ladies, he does."

Christine laughed. "Now I know I'm back in the real world."

The harbormaster was puzzled.

"I'm sure your cousin is a terrific sail-maker and an honest man. I'll be sure to see him."

Batty grinned amiably, but the young lady's features tightened.

"Before I can talk to him, though, I'll need to see the police."

He stood back and eyed her curiously. "Police, is it? And what might you be needin' them for?"

"It's a long story, I'm afraid. But I should talk to them right away."

"Aye, then." He pointed ashore. "Up that street and take the second right. Hester Street. Number 6."

"Thanks." She pointed toward her boat. "Can you look after her for now?"

"Like a child o' me own."

Christine smiled. "Thank you, Bats."

He nodded. "Good luck, missy." Batty watched her walk up the dock and then took another look at the ripped apart sailboat in front of him. He wondered what a nice young lass like that might have gotten into.

It took Slaton three hours to reach Exeter on the Brough. The machine was running rough by then and seemed to be overheating. He left it among a group of motorcycles parked together in a hospital parking lot, a few blocks from the train station. He walked the remaining distance and arrived, by the station clock, at 4:21. Slaton had been without a timepiece since *Polaris Venture* had gone down, but he estimated it had been roughly five hours since he'd left *Windsom*. He wondered if Dr. Palmer had gotten her boat to Penzance yet. Probably not, he decided, but it shouldn't matter now. He had put a lot of distance between himself and West Cornwall, and the next step would take him even farther out of reach.

He'd hoped to acquire his ticket from an automated machine, but the only one he could find was out of service. With two sales booths to choose from, Slaton studied the respective clerks. One was an officious older woman, the other a young man, not much more than a teenager, with spiked hair and a bored, lethargic manner. An easy choice, even though the young man's line was a little longer. Slaton purchased his ticket with cash, the agent barely looking up at the scruffy bloke who wanted a one-way for the 4:50 to Reading, with a connection to Oxford.

Slaton went to the men's restroom. He cleaned up his face and hands in a washbasin while another man stood at a urinal, humming while he went about his business. When the hummer finally left, Slaton was alone. He moved into a toilet stall and shut the door. Five minutes later, he emerged in a pair of jeans, a collared knit shirt, and a red windbreaker. All of it fit badly and the beard still promoted a rough texture, yet it was an altogether different impression versus the ruffian who had gone into the loo — still working class, but a few rungs higher up the ladder. Slaton spotted a *London Times* in the trash can. He pulled it out, gave one neat fold to display the sports section, and slid it into the pocket of his canvas backpack, a picture of footballer David Beckham protruding obviously.

He boarded the train twenty minutes later, selecting an open seat next to a nicely dressed older woman. She had an expensive, well-tended appearance, and sported a tremendous diamond wedding ring. Like a good snob, she avoided eye contact with Slaton, no doubt put off by his pointedly proletariat showing. He doubted she'd find a word for him the entire way to Reading.

With doors sealed, the train started off, slowly picking up speed. Slaton settled back and closed his eyes. He'd be in Oxford in five hours. Five hours to get some rest, and to concentrate on his next step.

The Penzance police station, a remote outpost of the Devon and Cornwall Constabulary, was a small affair. Nothing more had been necessary when it was built two hundred years ago. After the First World War, one of the original stone walls had been taken down to allow for the construction of three holding cells adjacent to the main room. The police chief at the time had been an ambitious man, but aside from the occasional brawl at the Three Sisters pub, the cells went largely vacant and had evolved over the years. One remained a holding cell, one was redone as the chief's office, and the last had taken plumbing to become a water closet — at least that was what the sign on the door said. Virtually all business was undertaken in the main room, where a hodgepodge of desks and chairs served as foundation for a hodgepodge of books and papers. Altogether, it afforded the station a compact, yet very busy appearance, decidedly at odds with the sleepy hamlet outside.

Christine sat in an uncomfortable wooden chair, her clenched hands resting on a rickety folding table. She had just finished her story for the third time and the man across the table was methodically going back over the details.

"And when he tore apart your boat and took the dinghy . . . how far from shore did you say you were?" the man asked.

"Two miles, I guess. Plus or minus a half mile."

Chief Walter Bickerstaff nodded. He was a broad-chested man whose round face was fronted by a broad, flattened nose that looked like it might have been broken any number of times. Presently, his jowls were darkened by the shadow of a coarse beard — the type that would yield to nothing but the sharpest of razors — and his brow set furrowed in deep concentration.

"So let's see," Bickerstaff said, thinking aloud, "if a man can row at three . . . let's give him four miles an hour, he might have been ashore in half an hour. And you said he left at roughly noon today. That would put him ashore just before one o'clock this afternoon. Of course that's if he went straight in. He might have had a time finding a place to land along the coast. Pretty rocky in those parts."

Christine tried to look interested in Bickerstaff's thoughts, but she was tired. She'd been rehashing the facts for three hours. Once for Constable Edwards, and now twice for the chief. Bickerstaff had gauged her closely the first time, in the way one might size up a person thought to have stayed out a pint too long. The second time through, her answers got terse, enough to make him realize that she was serious and not the least bit inebriated. Still, Christine couldn't really blame the man for being skeptical. It was a pretty incredible story.

Bickerstaff tapped a pencil on the table. "You said you thought this man had been on a ship named *Polaris Venture*. Is that what he told you?"

"No. He never used that name. I saw it stenciled on the cooler, the one he was hanging onto when I found him."

Bickerstaff was about to ask something else when the phone rang. As far as Christine could see it was the only one in the station. Bickerstaff picked it up and began nodding as the caller went on about something. Eventually, Bickerstaff responded with a few quiet remarks that were out of earshot for Christine, then hung up.

"That was Edwards. He's been looking out along the shoreline at Mounts Bay. Nothing yet, but it's getting dark now. I'll have him press on in the morning."

"In the morning?" Christine shot back. "This man could be long gone by then. Chief, I tell you, he's a menace. You've got to find him. Have you sent this up to higher authorities?"

Bickerstaff responded sharply to her accusative tone, "Now see here, miss. Everything that can be done is being done. We'll investigate this as I see fit. There's no need getting emotional about these things—"

"I am emotional about it!" Christine snapped. "He hijacked my boat! He threatened me! By now he could be halfway to France!"

Bickerstaff's beefy figure bristled and he sucked in a full chest of air, as if ready to lash back. But then he deflated, got up, and paced around the room. After a few moments his manner softened. "I think that's about all we can do this evening, Miss Palmer. Do you have a place to stay?"

She sighed. "Yes, my boat."

"No, I'm sorry. There may be evidence aboard and we haven't had time for a proper search. There's a good hotel right up the coast road, near enough that you can walk. Chessman's. I'll call to make sure they give you a good, quiet room. You must be exhausted after your ordeal."

Christine had to agree there. She could never remember having been so tired. "Can I at least go back to *Windsom* and get a fresh change of clothes?"

"Yes, of course. Get what you need. Just try not to disturb things any more than necessary. We'll go over it first thing in the morning. I trust you plan on staying for a few days while we sort through all this?"

The question took Christine by surprise. For the first time since she'd pulled that man out of the sea, she could plan ahead. She could think about the next day, the next week.

"I suppose I'll be here long enough to get *Windsom* back in shape. That'll probably take a couple of weeks." She felt like she could sleep at least that long.

Bickerstaff made the call to Chessman's. He raised an obvious fuss about reserving the best room in the place, not letting on that his uncle Sid was the owner, or that this time of year she'd likely be Sid's only guest. That done, he showed her to the door.

"Come by 'round ten tomorrow morning, Miss Palmer. From here we can go down to your boat. I'd like you to show me around."

"All right."

He walked her out to the street. She paused for a moment as if unsure of which way to go, then turned downhill toward the docks.

Bickerstaff went back inside, sat down at the station's lone computer terminal, and began pecking slowly with two index fingers. It was a laborious process, but in time he got what he expected. Police data, naval reports, news articles — nothing anywhere about a ship having gone down off the coast of Africa. The only maritime accident he could spot over the last ten days was a helicopter that had crashed into a North Sea oil rig.

Just to make sure, he made a phone call to Lloyd's of London. They insured practically every big ship in the world, as far as he knew. If something had gone down, they'd know about it. The clerk there was quite helpful — it was police business, after all — and Bickerstaff started by asking for any information on a ship named *Polaris Venture*.

The clerk explained. That particular name was quite popular among big ships. In fact, at least nineteen vessels on file matched. He suggested that Bickerstaff add the owner's name, or at least the country of registry, and things would go a lot faster. Not knowing either, Bickerstaff told the man that he could easily narrow his search to ships that had gone down in the eastern Atlantic within the last two weeks.

To that, the Lloyd's man had an immediately knowledgeable and simple reply. In the last two weeks there had been three ships reported lost in the entire world. Two small freighters had sunk from a collision in Malaysia, and an ice breaker in Antarctica had ingloriously not lived up to its calling — the ice had won. Nothing at all in the Atlantic for over two months. It was just as Bickerstaff had suspected. He thanked the Lloyd's man and dialed a more familiar number. A woman answered.

"Hello, luv."

"There you are," Margaret Bickerstaff declared. "I've been doing my best to keep your supper warm but if you can't be home by nine, I'll not be responsible."

"Sorry, luv. We had this bird come in today, had a story to beat them all, she did. I'll tell you about it later, over some tea. I don't know how they think them up."

"Touched, was she?"

"To say the least. American."

"Ahh," Margaret Bickerstaff replied.

"Says she's a doctor. Shouldn't be hard to put some holes in her story. A few calls to the states and I'll find out where she's escaped from."

"That means you'll be workin' a bit later, then?"

"I'll get on as fast as I can. It won't take long." Bickerstaff checked his watch. "The places I need to call in the states will still be open a few more hours. If I don't get hold of them now, we'll be into tomorrow afternoon. And I've got to send a quick report to the Yard."

"Then I'll be giving your chop to the cat," she chided. "No sense in good food going to waste."

"You know best, luv. I'll be home as soon as I can." Chief Bickerstaff frowned and rang off as Constable Edwards walked in.

"Blast!" Bickerstaff fumed.

"What's the matter, Chief? Cat got your supper again?"

Slaton walked up St. John Street a few strokes after one in the morning. The lateness of the hour was by design. His train had arrived in Oxford hours ago and he'd stopped at a pub near the station to eat, taking his time. Slaton wanted no chance of running into any neighbors on the way up to his apartment. He was, after all, a dead man, and there was no telling who might be aware of his demise.

The building was Number 12, a block of eight flats, his on the third floor, in front and facing the street. Slaton looked over the familiar structure as he approached. There was only one light on in the building, emanating from the caretaker's flat. That was as it should be. Mrs. Peabody was a seventy-two-year-old widow, always in bed by ten, who drew comfort from leaving a light on. Slaton figured the only tenant he might possibly run into at this hour was Paddy Cross, a retired machinist and right solid alcoholic who kept a schedule for no man. Fortunately, when Paddy did find his way home, he could usually be heard singing ribald songs in full voice long before he was seen.

Slaton moved quietly up to the third floor landing. He stopped outside his flat and took a good look at the brass number six on the door. Two things were missing, one being the top screw that was supposed to keep the number in place. Invariably, every time the door opened, it fell and hung upside-down on the bottom screw, making a number nine. Also missing was the trace of sawdust he'd placed in the crook of the six. He'd had visitors. That was also as it should be. No doubt his government had decided he was missing and probably dead. They'd have sent a team from the embassy to go over his flat, to make sure he hadn't left anything embarrassing lying around.

Since his keys were in a bag on a ship at the bottom of the ocean, Slaton again made use of the lock-picking tools he'd pilfered from *Windsom's* toolbox. As he worked the tumbler, he realized that the few bits of normalcy he'd been able to acquire in his life were now completely gone. He was a dead man breaking into his own home.

The lock on the door handle was old and stiff, but soon gave way. There was another, more solid lock, but it was of the type that could only be engaged from inside the dwelling. Good for personal safety while you were home, but useless for protecting your things while you were out. Yosy had always insisted it to be of communist design.

Once inside, Slaton saw the flat largely unchanged. The appearance was decidedly spartan. A few basic pieces of furniture, a couple of cheap paintings on one wall. All of it had come with the lease. There were no photographs or travel trinkets. A small bookshelf offered a generic selection of classics and some well-worn popular novels of various themes. These too had come with the flat.

He looked around and concluded that things were more or less as he'd left them. The place had been searched, but not torn apart. He walked quickly to the bedroom, wanting to make it fast. A few clothes went into a canvas backpack, and he was happy to find four ten-pound notes stashed amongst his socks. Slaton looked for his Israeli passport, but was not surprised to find it gone, along with his British driver's license.

He headed back to the living room. There, he went straight to the bookshelf and selected an aged, leather-bound edition of *Treasure Island*. He ran his hand along the spine and, content, stuffed it into the backpack with the clothing. At the telephone stand he noted that his personal register of addresses and telephone numbers was missing. Again, no surprise. He looked at the answering machine and saw a steady light. No messages.

He took a last look around the room — more to inventory than reminisce — then started to leave. Slaton paused halfway to the door. He turned and looked again at the answering machine. The little red light held steady. *Steady.* No *new* messages. His pals from the embassy would surely have listened to the tape. Anything noteworthy and they would have taken it. Empty, the machine's green light would flash, so they had either taken the original and put in a blank tape, or decided that any messages on the existing tape were harmless. Slaton went back to the machine and hit the play button. It whirred, clicked and finally produced a voice he recognized as Ismael, an administrative clerk from the embassy.

"*Mr. Slaton*," the voice said officiously, "*Ismael Pellman. You haven't filed a travel voucher for your trip to Paris on August three through five. Please do so, or call me to straighten it out before this Tuesday.*" Then a beep, followed by a thickly accented voice. "*Hello. This is Rangish Malwev at Rangal's Fine Clothing. The leather jacket you have given us to repair is done. The charge is seventy-seven pounds, three. You may pick it up at your leisure.*"

That one would have gotten the boys moving, Slaton thought. Of course all they'd find was that he really had sent in an old jacket to be repaired. For seventy-seven pounds he could have gotten a new one, but he was partial to the one he had. Or used to have.

Another beep and a dial tone.

A fourth beep and another message, the caller strangely familiar, but he didn't recognize her right away. "*David. Oh, David. I'm sorry but I didn't know who else to call. They've been here all day but . . . I can't believe what they tell me.*" It was Ingrid Meier, Yosy's wife. He'd known her for twelve years, yet Slaton barely recognized the quavering, broken voice that crackled from the recorder. Ingrid was one of the most rock-solid people he'd ever known, but here she sounded a shattered, babbling mess. Slaton's blood went cold. *"What happened, David? What happened?"* She was crying. *"Please call. I don't know these people who came to see me today. They took his papers, his things. I want to hear it from you. He was coming to see you, to go hunting. Were you with him? What happened to my Yosy . . . please David . . ."* She broke down, sobbing, and then a dial tone.

Slaton stared blankly at the machine as it stopped and then spun in the methodical process of rewinding. *What happened? What happened to Yosy?* Slaton felt ill. He could think of only one thing that would put Ingrid Meier in a state like that. His thoughts accelerated. *He was coming to see you . . .* London? Yosy had called with a warning, then tried to come see him. To explain the danger in person? But then what?

He checked the clock in the kitchen. 1:15 in the morning. How could he find out anything now? If something had happened to Yosy in England, anyone at the embassy could explain. But who could he trust? No one. Not now. Slaton picked up the phone, planning as he dialed. He had to know. The number he chose was not listed in any directory. It was low priority and non-secure, but unless someone had tinkered with it lately, this particular line would not be recorded or traced.

A tired woman answered, "Israeli Embassy."

Fortunately, Slaton didn't recognize the duty officer's voice. A newby must have been socked with the late shift.

"Good morning," Slaton said, gaining an octave. "This is Irving Weisen at Headquarters Personnel."

"It's morning here, but not by much," the woman answered, yawning.

"Oh, of course." Slaton said awkwardly. "We're having a records inspection here, and I'm missing one of my files. I thought you might be able to help."

The duty officer didn't try to hide her disdain for the headquarters paper-pusher. "Look, this is the London station. We don't keep hard copies of personnel records."

"I realize that, but whoever checked it out was sloppy. Very sloppy. The only part of the checkout slip I can read has something scribbled on it about the London station. It might be one of your people, and if it is, perhaps we can figure out who would have wanted the folder here at headquarters — something like that."

"Okay, okay. What's the name?"

"Yosef Meier."

"Shit!" the duty officer spat indignantly. "Don't you guys have any idea what's going on out here in the real world? Put a window in that building. Yosy Meier was killed in an accident here in London last week."

The woman in the London embassy communications room heard nothing at the other end of the line. "Does that solve your mystery?" she finally asked with annoyance.

"Yes, I'm sorry. How did it happen?"

"He was hit by a bus, or a truck or something. Ask somebody at the Western Europe Desk. They ought to have a clue."

Quietly, Slaton finished what he started. "All right. I know where that file would be. I'm sorry to have bothered you." He heard the click as the embassy woman hung up.

Slaton stood motionless. His best friend was dead. An accident, the woman had said. For Slaton there could no longer be any doubt. Someone had tried to kill him. Someone had sunk *Polaris Venture* with her entire crew. His body tensed. They were on him again, the feelings he had faced for so long. The horror he'd battled until there was nothing at all — only numbness. Now, in a moment, that pain returned. Or maybe it had never really gone. He wondered what Yosy could have known. If he'd only come to London a few days sooner, Slaton would have been around to find out. And maybe Yosy would be home now, and his wife wouldn't be a basket case, and his children — God, his children —

There was an audible *crack* and Slaton looked down. The plastic telephone receiver, still in his grip, had fractured. Small shards of white plastic lay on the floor at his feet. He looked at his hand for a moment as if it were not part of him, not under his control, while his heart continued to pound. Then Slaton saw his reflection in a mirror on the far wall. There was a sudden urge to throw the phone, or something, anything, at the image. He remembered how much he hated what he saw. Slaton closed his eyes.

It took a full two minutes. He stood without moving. Slowly, his breathing came under control, his hold on the broken phone eased. Slaton opened his eyes and carefully, almost delicately, placed the shattered receiver next to its cradle. He pulled the phone jack from the wall, then picked up his canvas backpack and went to the front door, not making a sound. At the door he stopped and listened patiently. The only sound to register, a car engine off in the distance. He opened the door a crack and saw the hall was empty.

Slaton left the building quickly and quietly. He made no attempt to right the upside-down six.

Thirty minutes later Slaton was on the outskirts of Oxford, one of the more industrial quarters that generally escaped the paths of most tourists. The city's blue collar underpinnings ran deep, however the situation was played down for most intents and purposes. Car parks, walking paths, and public transportation were arranged to emphasize a more marketable image — that of a city of universities, an everlasting academic nirvana where the world's best and brightest, strolling around in caps, gowns and white bow ties, designed solutions for a troubled planet. The big Rover car factory, vital as it might be to local dinner tables, was not an "image enhancer."

Slaton stood across the street from a storage facility, an open-air design with a small office at the front, then four narrow rows of storage sheds surrounded by a three-meter metal fence. The only way in was through an electronic gate next to the office, where access was granted at all hours, seven days a week.

The place was owned by a chubby, nearly bald, pink-skinned fellow whom Slaton had met when renting his unit. The man lived in a flat above the office, allowing him to advertise "24-hour on-premises security and surveillance." Of course, he probably slept for eight to ten of those twenty-four hours. Then, and on his days off, a single camera at the entrance supposedly recorded all activity to and from the rows of storage sheds, thereby rendering the advertisement correct in its most literal sense.

Slaton watched for ten minutes. No one else approached the place, and the proprietor's flat over the office was still dark. He crossed the street and went straight to the gate. There, he entered the dubious access code — 1–2–3–4. The lock on the wire gate made a click, and he was in.

Slaton had rented the smallest compartment offered, 10-foot by 5, and those units happened to be right up front. The lock was his own, a simple key padlock, and distinctly less hefty than those on many of the other sheds — sure to emphasize the insignificance of what lay inside. He took out the key he'd retrieved from the spine of *Treasure Island* — the boys from the embassy had been sloppy — and opened the roll-up metal door.

Happily, everything was as he'd left it. There were a couple of beat-up old chairs, an apparently virgin stereo receiver (which actually hadn't worked for years), and a few boxes containing books, magazines, and some old clothing. There was also a small, skewed table, and next to it, on the floor, an old television. The television's picture screen had a severe diagonal crack and its plastic case was damaged on two corners. It looked for all the world like it had probably fallen off the crooked table, an effect Slaton had only been able to manufacture by dropping it to the concrete floor three times. Anyone raiding the cubicle would have immediately written off the television as junk and settled for the stereo. The rest was sure to disappoint all but the most desperate of thieves.

Slaton checked outside to make sure he was still alone, then went to work. He dug out a screwdriver from the bottom of a box of clothing and picked up the battered television, setting it on the table that, in spite of its asymmetrical appearance, was in fact quite sturdy. Slaton worked the back panel, pulling screws until the plastic cover that concealed the picture tube came loose. He removed the panel, revealing the usual array of circuit boards and wires, along with a small black pouch.

The pouch, that type of "fanny pack" often worn by tourists, was encased in a large zip-lock plastic bag. Slaton removed the plastic bag, opened the nylon carrier and quickly took inventory. There were five thousand British pounds and three thousand U.S. dollars, all in various small and medium denominations. Two Mossad-produced identification packages provided passports, driver's licenses, and other associated documents, one even including a valid credit card. Of the identities, one was Danish and one British, chosen, quite simply, because those were his two most proficient languages. There was also a time-worn wallet.

This was Slaton's get-well kit. He had set it up many years ago, mainly to recover if he ever became compromised as an "illegal." Certain missions could have no ties to Israel. If he had to run in such a case, Slaton would be on his own to get safe, with no help from the embassies and their more legitimate staff. Because of this, he had built the kit and was meticulous about keeping it current and available. In the beginning, he'd used bank safe-deposit boxes, but the advent of self-storage enterprises provided a much more anonymous opportunity to squirrel his things

away. Few cameras, fewer signatures and, best of all, no nosy bank offi-
cials.

There was one problem. The kit was missing the thing he needed
most — a weapon. He'd taken the Glock semi-automatic to his flat for
some upkeep. Earlier, he found it had been taken from his room, no
doubt removed by the embassy cleaning crew.

He studied the two sets of identification. Every time he passed
through Tel Aviv, Slaton would stop in Documents Section and switch
out at least one of the packages. His special status in Mossad came with
the label AUTONOMOUS — all records of the identities he chose were ex-
punged, and no one in Mossad was supposed to keep track of them. He
now wondered if that was truly the case.

Slaton opened the wallet and began stuffing it with documents that
presented him as Henrik Edmundsen, along with some cash. The old
leather wallet was one he hadn't used in years, and had been with the kit
as long as he could remember.

As he came to the small plastic pockets where he was going to put
the driver's license, he found an old photograph, one he had mistakenly
left inside. Slaton stopped and stared at the picture, not able to help himself. The confluence of emotions immediately swept in and churned, like
a half-dozen rivers meeting in one spot, but with nowhere to go. Abruptly,
Slaton shoved the picture back behind a leather sleeve in the wallet
where it couldn't be seen. He cursed himself for his carelessness. It *had*
been carelessness. He snatched up the remainder of his documents and
cash, shoving everything back inside the nylon pack, all except the wallet,
which he pocketed.

He closed up the shed and locked it for the last time. It was paid for
through the end of the month. A month or two after that, the owner would
rip the lock from the past due shed and toss out Slaton's little collection of
junk. Leaving the facility, he dropped the key down a storm drain and
walked east toward the train station. On the way he passed a cab, two bus
stops, and a car rental agency. The storage shed had been a good choice.

Slaton suppressed the urge to check six. No one would be following
him. Not yet. The world thought he was dead. Everyone except a young
American doctor, who was probably in a police station in Penzance. And
she had no idea who he was. All the same, he stayed alert.

The first train to Reading left at four in the morning. He boarded a
nearly empty car at the far end of the platform and took a seat. Slaton

closed his eyes as the train lurched ahead. He knew where he had to start. Ingrid Meier had told him, the anguished voice echoing in his head. *What happened, David? He was coming to see you, to go hunting.* There was such pain in her voice. The kind of pain that would never go away. Not without answers.

Slaton vowed to find out what happened to Yosy. When he did, he would go to Ingrid and tell her everything. Then, perhaps she could heal. Perhaps she could recover as he never had.

Chapter Six

At that same early morning hour, in the basement of the Israeli Embassy, the watch officer on duty opened his second can of Coke. He needed the caffeine to stay awake during another graveyard shift, which he, being the most junior person assigned to the station, was awarded three nights each week.

The windowless room was dimly lit, regardless of the time of day, and the duty officer sat surrounded by a forest of radios, cipher machines, computers, and telephones. There were also two televisions, tuned respectively to BBC News 24 and CNN, Mossad's reluctant admission that even the world's best intelligence networks were often scooped by some unrelenting newshound.

The duty man scraped for crumbs at the bottom of a bag of potato chips — he needed the salt to make him thirsty — then went to a computer station and began searching the newswires. There was a Reuters dispatch about a French arms sale to Iran. Nothing new there. As he continued searching, he remembered the dead-drop letter. It had come in just before the shift change, and the woman he'd relieved suggested he decipher it sometime during the night.

He found it, simply enough, in the IN basket. The letter originated from a source inside Scotland Yard, a mid-level man who worked in the Operations Center. He was an agent whose information was supposed to be delivered each Thursday, taped to the underside lid of a toilet reservoir in the men's room at the Shady Larch Pub in Knightsbridge. It actually came with great irregularity — once a month at best. Nobody at the station could decide whether the agent's skittish nature was due to fear of being found out, or a randomly active conscience. The man was a British citizen and apparently had no ill will against the Crown. He was, however, also a Jew whose maternal grandparents had both perished in Bergen-Belsen, and he confessed to his control officer a nagging urge to aid the ancestral homeland. There were millions of people who could trace their lineage to victims of the Holocaust, and the Mossad made a living out of recruiting them.

Unfortunately, this particular agent was a ragged, sweaty bundle of nerves. He actually vomited on his control during their first meeting. The good news was that the information he *did* provide had always proven authentic and accurate. The Israelis decided it best to give him a dead-drop location and let him produce whatever he could, quietly hoping he might eventually move up to a higher position at the Yard.

The duty officer yawned as he labored to decipher the coded letter. It used a cumbersome one-time pad. Time consuming, but very secure. It was the ship's name that raised his eyebrows. *Polaris Venture*. He tried to remember the Watch Order headquarters had put out a few days back. Was that the name? He was shuffling through papers when he heard someone in an adjacent office. He walked over and found a familiar face.

"Hey, Itzaak. What are you doing here at this hour?"

The more senior man frowned sufferingly, "Dumb-ass reports, due yesterday."

The duty officer nodded sympathetically.

"Do you remember that Watch Order headquarters just put out? They were looking for a ship in the eastern Atlantic."

"I guess. Why?"

"Well, our boy at Scotland Yard came through today. I just deciphered it and he's got something in here about a woman who says she rescued some guy from the middle of the ocean. Then this guy commandeers her sailboat and they end up in England. She thinks the name of the ship that went down was . . ." the duty officer looked at the deciphered message in his hand, "*Polaris Venture*. Wasn't that the name?"

Itzaak answered right away, "Nah. I saw the message. I don't think that was it."

The duty officer shrugged and walked back to his station. After all, it was a crazy story, which was probably why the agent at Scotland Yard had tacked it onto a few other more relevant bits of information — that odd English sense of humor. He'd ask his relief about it at six. In the meantime, he considered getting a sandwich from the snack machine, but one glance down at his newly expanded waistline quashed that idea. He didn't need it.

Three hours later, Emma Shroeder came into the embassy basement to visit the coffee maker.

"Morning, Emma," the duty man offered.

"Morning," she replied in her raspy, deep voice.

"Listen," he said, "I know it's not your area, but do you know where they keep the current Watch Orders?"

Emma eyed the new guy, clearly not having decided about this one yet. She sighed, went to the file cabinet by his knee and pulled out a file, nicely labeled WATCH ORDERS.

"No," she said, retreating to the stairwell, "I'm not cleared for stuff like that."

The duty officer's smile lasted until he found the order in question. Itzaak had been out to lunch. The name *Polaris Venture* was highlighted in yellow and seemed to jump off the page. Worried that he'd screwed up, the duty man immediately condensed the agent's report and transmitted it to headquarters in Tel Aviv. He had no idea what a hornet's nest it would stir.

The message arrived at Mossad headquarters just after 5:00 GMT. It was quickly routed up, and Bloch got the news over breakfast. He called to check the Prime Minister's schedule, then arranged for a secure message to be sent to London.

> TO:LND:COS
> FROM: HDQ #002 30NOV0552Z
> RE PREVIOUS MESSAGE 0510Z. SEND TEAM TO
> INVESTIGATE DISCRETELY. NO, REPEAT, NO
> CONTACT. FURTHER INSTRUCTIONS BY
> NOON ZULU. ACKNOWLEDGE.

Ninety seconds later the reply came.

TO: HDQ
FROM: LND:COM
RECEIVED HDQ #002 30NOV0552Z. WILL COMPLY.

Chief Bickerstaff had gone back to the Penzance station at five-thirty in the morning. He didn't normally start so early, but his phone calls to the States the previous evening had been troubling. By six this morning, he was uncomfortable, and now at six-thirty Bickerstaff was quite sure he'd blown it.

He had fully expected to find that this Christine Palmer woman was going through a messy divorce, a bankruptcy, or maybe she was just a loon. Unfortunately, his phone calls had proven quite the opposite. She had indeed graduated, with honors, three years ago from the University of Connecticut Medical School. Having completed the first part of her residency at the Maine Medical Center in Portland, she was on a temporary leave of absence to retrieve her late father's sailboat from Europe. The faculty and staff at the medical center held Dr. Palmer in the highest regard, both as a physician and a person. The more Bickerstaff found out about her, the more she seemed a perfectly normal, intelligent twenty-eight year-old woman.

The phone rang and Bickerstaff eyed it warily before picking up.

"Edwards here, sir. I think we've found something."

Bickerstaff grimaced.

"I'm at the Tewksbury house, two down from your aunt Margaret's place. We've found a dinghy up against the shed that seems to be the one we're looking for. I called Mr. Tewksbury in Manchester — woke him up, I'm afraid. He said he doesn't even own one. He told me where to find a key and I let myself in the house. Looks as though somebody's been through it."

"Didn't you check out that area last night?"

"I did."

"And you didn't see the boat then?"

"That's the funny thing," Edwards said. "I was looking down along the shoreline last night. This shed, it's not one of those that are down on the beach. It's up right next to the house. He must have lugged the thing all the way up the cliff."

Bickerstaff tensed. "Right. Because we wouldn't be looking for it there, would we?"

"One other thing you should know about, Chief. Tewksbury and I tried to figure if anything was missing. The only thing that's gone for sure is an old motorcycle he kept in the shed. Tewksbury says he hasn't used it in over a year. He didn't think the thing would run, but it's definitely gone."

"All right," Bickerstaff said. "Anything else I should know?"

"Tewksbury's coming down tonight on the 6:10 from Manchester. He wants to go over the place and make an insurance claim. I think that's all, Chief. I thought I should give you a call right off."

"All right. Stay there and see what else you can find. Tonight I want you to meet Tewksbury when he gets off that train. Get him to his house and find out exactly what's missing."

"Right."

"Call me if you find anything else." Bickerstaff hung up, realizing he should have added in a "well done" for Edwards.

"Now what?" he muttered to himself. Bickerstaff knew he'd botched it. Christine Palmer's story had seemed so far-fetched that he hadn't given it much credence. The man at Lloyd's had been so sure. *No ships lost in the Atlantic*, he'd said. *Not for over two months now.* The phone calls to the States last night hadn't fit in, but still . . .

Bickerstaff realized he was setting his excuses. He had no choice but to call in help. If there was a dangerous man out there, Bickerstaff had given him a big head start. He might as well go straight to the top with it. Bickerstaff dialed Scotland Yard.

The call took ten minutes. It led to two hours of shuffling from one department to another, no one at the Yard seeming eager to handle the matter. There was kidnapping and destruction of property, all with foreign nationals involved, and then the business of a sunken vessel. First it was routed to Special Branch, which recommended the Foreign Office. The Foreign Office, in turn, thought the Royal Navy should handle it. The Navy, of course, wanted no part, and it finally ended up back with Special Branch. They all reacted as they had on Bickerstaff's initial report last night. It was incredible, probably some kind of silly hoax. A sergeant from Special Branch finally got with Bickerstaff and asked for more details. He assured the chief that a thorough investigation would commence. Possibly today, but more likely tomorrow.

Slaton hired a car at an all night agency in Reading, a Peugeot. He used the Danish identity since it was the one associated with the credit card. From Reading, he traveled south on the A33, then southeast on the M3 to Hampshire. As he arrived in New Forest, dawn's light began to spread its warmth across the countryside. The land seemed to open up, deep un-fenced fields, interspersed with plots of thick foliage. The topography re-tained an unspoiled, medieval aura, a concept accentuated by the early morning mist.

It was shortly after sunrise when Slaton arrived at his destination. A series of small dirt roads edged away from the main highway, meandering through stands of trees that grew more and more dense as he went. Nar-row drives occasionally branched off left and right, and small shacks — a few could almost be called houses — were just visible through the walls of fir and oak.

He went past the familiar turnoff, then pulled over to the side. Leav-ing the car running, he got out and walked slightly ahead. Slaton stomped on the shoulder of the gravel road, making sure the ground was firm, then got back in and coaxed the car slowly into a gap in the brush. It wasn't completely hidden from the road, but it would do. He'd go the rest of the way on foot.

Slaton had no way of knowing if there would be anyone at "The Lodge," as it was commonly referred to. The small hunting cottage had been used many years ago as a Mossad safe house. It was actually owned by a businessman in Newcastle, a *sayan* — the Hebrew term for "helper." The place had been considered compromised as a true safe house years ago, but a few of the embassy staff still used it now and again as a getaway to hunt or shoot targets, that being something you couldn't do just any-where in England without drawing notice. Rumor had it that some even used the place for more amorous pursuits.

Slaton moved quietly through the thick underbrush. The forest was damp and silent, the result of a light rain the night before. Instead of look-ing ahead, Slaton looked down to watch where he stepped, avoiding twigs and branches, and allowing the wet leaves to cushion his steps. In such dense vegetation, sound was far more important than sight. Every twenty paces, he stopped to listen.

When the lodge finally came into view, he saw there were no vehi-cles in front. Slaton moved laterally through the forest and did a quarter-circle around the perimeter, alert to register any motion or sound. He waited and watched. There was no smoke from the chimney, but that meant nothing. The lodge had electricity and was equipped with a small space heater, thanks to an owner who had no enthusiasm for the manual labor involved in splitting and hauling firewood.

After a full ten minutes, Slaton decided it was safe. He moved quickly out of the brush and backed up against the side of the house, near a window. He reached out and touched the back of his hand to the glass pane. It was cold. With one look inside he was finally convinced. There was nobody home.

He retrieved the key from under one side of a small log pile near the front door — it had been a long time since any effort was made to keep the place secure. Slaton went in and found it just as he remembered. One room, some comfortable old furniture and a fireplace on one side, a big lumpy bed on the other. Next to the bed, tucked into a corner, was a small kitchenette. Throw rugs covered most of the wood floor and there were cheap, drab curtains pulled back from the windows. A slight musty odor made him think the place had probably not been used in many weeks. He checked the fireplace and found a small pile of cold ashes. Slaton went to the back window and tried to open it. The lock was stiff, but he finally pried it aside and lifted the wooden frame up. A cool breeze wafted in, but that wasn't the point. If anyone came up the driveway, he'd hear it a lot sooner with the window open. It was also an extra way out.

Slaton looked around the place. He could almost see Yosy lolling on the couch, a beer in his hand and maybe throwing at the dartboard across the room, just as many darts ending up in the wall as on the board. They had come here a half-dozen times together, sometimes with others from the embassy. It was a getaway, a place to relax, to forget the constraints of the bizarre world in which they existed. Occasionally they'd go off into the forest to shoot targets, or even bag a couple of pheasant for dinner. Mostly, though, they'd relax, drink, and discuss what things would be like if they were king. All in all, light relief for the heavy reality of their day-to-day ops. A reality that had never seemed more suffocating than now, Slaton thought.

He'd first met Yosy at the "schoolhouse," nearly twenty years ago. Slaton remembered the smiling, gregarious young man with whom he'd had so much in common. Their days were spent in classrooms, buildings, and fields, going over strange, sometimes unimaginable lessons — things that would supposedly save their lives, or perhaps even their country someday. With the idealism of youth, Slaton, Yosy, and their classmates played the game during business hours, then escaped nightly for food, drink, and revelry.

To talk about their training outside the schoolhouse was strictly forbidden. More than one cadet had been eliminated from the program for lack of discretion, and they were sure the instructors had sources in every watering hole in Israel. Still, the student-spies found ways to escape, and the order of the day was to find humor in the inane, seemingly ridiculous things they were learning.

Slaton remembered one particularly libatious evening. As they sat at an outdoor café in a large square, Yosy had posed what seemed an insurmountable challenge. In the center of the square stood a statue, full-body and to scale, of a male lion. The statue was surrounded by a knee-deep reflecting pool. Yosy had guided Slaton's attention to a rather prim, frail young woman who was dining in the company of a thick paperback novel at the adjacent café. Yosy had recognized her as a librarian from the nearby university (in fact, the institution from which he'd graduated two years prior). Slaton was tasked to somehow have the woman sitting atop the lion within the next ten minutes, a gin and tonic raised in her left hand, offering a toast in the general direction of the judges. Upon issuing those instructions, Yosy called a time hack and the race was on.

Slaton's ale-induced haze had not helped, but he began improvising. He took a camera from Yosy's backpack, then went to the bar and ordered a gin and tonic. From there he walked halfway to the statue, then made a beeline to the woman's table.

"Irena! Where have you been?" he admonished when he was nearly on top of her, with a hard look at his watch.

The woman glanced up from her romance novel, perplexed. "I beg your pardon?" she said meekly.

Slaton was masterful, oblivious to the giggling and taunting going on three tables away. He tilted his sunglasses up over his eyes, mixing surprise with awe. "I'm sorry to bother you, miss. Only . . . it's just that you bear a striking resemblance to Irena, the model who was supposed to meet me here half an hour ago. She's late, and I am losing the light . . ."

After a pause, Slaton asked the woman, if it wasn't too much trouble, to remove the reading glasses that were perched low on her nose. Yosy and the others fell quiet as they strained to hear the performance.

"Yes, a remarkable resemblance. The project today? It will be for the cover of *Leisure Travel* magazine. It might seem unusual, but you see that statue over there . . ."

On it had gone until, as attested to by five witnesses, the woman had sat atop the great stone beast, smiling mechanically as she raised her glass in salutation. One minute and ten seconds to spare. Slaton even used Yosy's camera, and an entire roll of film, to record the triumph.

At the time it all seemed so innocent, a game with no harm. Slaton had learned his lessons well, the arts of deception and destruction. As had Yosy. Only now Slaton sat here alone, and it seemed anything but a game. Yosy had come to see him, to warn him, and now he was gone. Why had Yosy told his wife he was going hunting, when in fact he was the one being hunted? Slaton held one hope for the answer.

He went to the couch and gave it a shove across the floor, then rolled up one side of the rug underneath. If Yosy had come, this would be the place. There was a single loose floorboard, the one he and Yosy had heard creak under their feet so many years ago. Then, they had found two bottles of wine stuffed underneath, a soothing Cabernet. Now Slaton pulled up the short plank hoping to find something, anything to explain what was happening. The hole beneath the strip of wood was only six inches deep, but it extended far along the length of the floor to one side.

Slaton curled his arm into the nook and instantly latched onto something. He pulled out a heavy manila envelope, then groped once more in the dusty hole to make sure there wasn't anything else.

He brushed the envelope off, opened it, and sank onto the displaced couch. Inside was a two page, handwritten letter. Stunning, it answered many of the questions that had been tormenting him. But it raised even more.

Well, partner, if you've found this, I guess you know something's up. I was hoping to explain it in person, but here's what you should know.

A few weeks ago I got a phone call from a fellow named Leon Uriste. I worked with him once, when he was in military intelligence. We were never great buddies, but I think he looked me up because I was the only Mossad guy he knew. Uriste was dying of cancer, and he asked me to come see him in the hospital. I could hardly say no.

When I got there, a nurse confirmed that Uriste only had a couple of weeks left. I barely recognized him. He was fifty-one, but looked twenty years older. As soon as he saw me he got frantic and started babbling some really crazy stuff. As the proverb goes, "None brings conscience like the face of Death."

Uriste drifted in and out, and part of me said it had to be the drugs. But David, he laid out an incredible story. He said there's an organization of traitors within our service, attacking Israel. Mossad and Aman people bombing our own markets, shooting our own soldiers and policemen. Sound crazy? That's what I thought at first. Uriste talked as fast as he could draw breath. There were so many details — meetings, targets, casualty figures. He told me who was in the organization — names, but more code names. Everything was run by someone called Savior, and Uriste swore it had been going on for over twenty years.

It sounded absurd. Yet something about it bothered me. Here was a dying man trying to cleanse his shame. I played along and asked him who was behind it. The Palestinians? Hamas? Syria? Uriste broke up. He fell back on his bed, sobbing and babbling. He kept saying, "We had to do it. No other way." About that time, a nurse came in. She saw that Uriste was disturbed and kicked me out. I decided to go back the next day to talk again, and maybe bring a video camera. Uriste never made it through the night.

I was tempted to write it off as a dying man's drug-induced hallucination, but instead I followed old Lesson #1 — It's Good to be Paranoid. Sure enough, Uriste had another visitor after me that day. Whoever it was didn't sign into the hospital log, and none of the staff remembered much. One big dead end. That did it. I spent a few hours in Archives, checking and cross-checking. Those hours turned into days and the days into weeks. David, the more I looked, the more I saw. Not much hard evidence, but lots of shoddy investigations and inconsistent reports. Certain names kept popping up again and again. Worst of all, there's someone near the very top involved.

I copied some documents, made notes of others. It's mostly circumstantial, but a few hard facts. Enough to convince me, *old friend. These vermin really exist, they have for a long time. I don't know how many are involved, or which of our enemies they're associated with, but it's got to be a small operation. Otherwise, they'd never have been able to keep it quiet for so long. I was able to identify six people who are almost certainly involved, and another three who are probable. But I still don't know who runs it. One other thing — they seem to be launching fewer attacks now than in years past, but the things they've done lately have been bigger, real newsgrabbers. And for the last six months it's been especially quiet. I think they're looking for something really big.*

I'm going to take it all to Anton Bloch. I think he's clean, but for insurance I wanted somebody else to know. That would be you, buddy. I decided to come to London to lay this all out, but first I called to warn you with that "double Sheena" bit last week. When I got here, you were gone, so I came to the lodge and wrote this. We need to meet soon. I've had company lately. I'll show you what I've found, and hopefully you can add something. Maybe enough to hang these guys. I'm headed back home now, before anyone at the office gets suspicious. (Or even worse, Ingrid!) Call me.

Oh, and be careful. From what I've seen, these scum have a strong presence in England at the moment. At least four or five in the London station. I was followed from the airport, but made a clean break on my way here to the lodge. If things get rough, do try to remember everything I taught you.

Cheers.

Yosef.

Slaton sat with the letter in his lap, staring blankly at the wall. He knew it was true. It was all true. Ingrid said they'd taken Yosy's papers. The documents? It didn't matter. Slaton didn't need that kind of proof. Someone named Uriste was dead. Yosy was dead. And they had tried to kill him. Proof. *Polaris Venture's* crew. More proof. Then there was *Polaris Venture's* cargo. There was surely more to that. His mind swirled. How many others had there been? Twenty years of innocent victims. Israelis killing Israelis. How could it have gone on for so long?

Slaton snapped. He jumped up and kicked over a table, sending it flying across the room. The act broke his concentration and took him away from where he knew his questions were leading — that precipice from which he might not be able to turn back.

Slaton went to the kitchen and drew a glass of water from the faucet. It was cold and clear. He held the glass to his forehead and its coldness was a mild shock, unraveling the mental snarls. He stood still, thinking and agonizing until it suddenly came to him. For all the questions and possibilities, Slaton realized exactly where to go next. Even without knowing *who* they were, he knew *where they would be.*

The revelation gave clarity. It gave purpose. Carefully, Slaton washed and dried the glass, then placed it back in the cupboard exactly where it had been. Ten minutes later, the rest of the lodge was as he'd found it. He hurried back to his car, hoping it wasn't already too late.

A rap on the door brought rude end to the deepest sleep Christine had managed in years. She rustled groggily in the sheets and tried to focus on the clock next to her bed. The red digital lights read 10:24. Another knock. It had to be the maid.

"I don't need any service," she said in the loudest voice she could muster. Christine rolled over, hoping for a few more minutes rest, but consciousness was unavoidable as the events of the last days invaded once again.

Another knock, this one louder and more insistent, rattled away her sleep-induced fog. It was hopeless. She got up slowly and stumbled to the door, vaguely trying to remember what time she had told Chief Bicker-staff she'd be in today.

"Who is it?"

"Miss Palmer," a muffled voice called in a clipped British accent. "I'm Inspector Bennett, Maritime Investigations Branch. My partner, Inspector Harding, and I would like a word with you."

Christine put a bleary eye to the peephole and saw two men looking expectantly at her door. They both wore suits, ties, and professional smiles. Behind them, a nearly empty parking lot basked in the mid-morning sun. She unbolted the door and opened it a crack, peering her head around the corner.

"Maritime Investigations?" she queried, squinting against the light of day.

The nearer man thrust out an identification card with his photograph on it. The other nodded politely. "Yes, Maritime Investigations, Scotland Yard. We've been called in to assist the local police on this matter of your abduction."

The word "abduction" sounded peculiar, but she supposed it fit. She nearly let them in before remembering that all she had on was a T-shirt and panties.

"Can you give me a moment to dress?"

"Yes. Yes, of course. We'll wait right here."

Christine hadn't expected company. She rummaged through the few clothes she'd retrieved from *Windsom* and found a pair of Levis to slip on. She took a quick look in the mirror, then wished she hadn't. Her hair was a frightful mess — she'd taken a shower last night and gone straight to bed. Christine decided the policemen wouldn't care. She let the two Scotland Yard men in.

"I *am* sorry," Bennett said. "It looks as though we've rousted you out of a sound sleep."

"Oh, that's all right," she lied. "It's time I got up anyway."

Christine plucked two used towels off the couch and threw them on the bed. The two men smiled amiably and took a seat.

"We won't take much of your time. Perhaps you could tell us your story, just in a general sort of way. Then we might have a few questions. The more we find out about this devil, the better chance we'll have of catching him."

"So you're searching for him now?"

"Absolutely."

Christine was relieved. "Have you already talked to Chief Bickerstaff?"

"Oh, yes, of course. But we'd like to hear it straight from you as well."

Christine sighed. She'd already gone over it so many times. It was becoming tedious. She started from the beginning and went over everything, or at least most of it. She omitted the parts about him crashing in while she was getting dressed, and that she had to lay with him while he slept. She didn't want anyone jumping to the wrong conclusions. It took ten minutes. Bennett and his sidekick listened attentively. They didn't interrupt to ask questions, but Christine could see them both mentally storing up for later. When she finished, Bennett was clearly struck to compassion.

"You've had quite an ordeal."

"I came out all right. My boat's another story, but that can be repaired."

"Of course," Bennett said. "Tell me, do you have an accurate position for where you came across this man?"

"Sure. I didn't record it right away when I found him. I had a lot of other things on my mind. But I did eventually make the plot and mark it on a chart, probably good to within a mile or two. I figured somebody would need the fix to start a search."

"Do you remember the coordinates?"

"No. But it was roughly halfway on a line between Gibraltar and the Madeiras. Chief Bickerstaff was supposed to go over to my boat this morning, so he probably has the actual numbers."

"I'll get the coordinates from him, then. Tell me again, what did this man look like?"

"About six feet tall, maybe a little more. Thin build, but very strong. His hair was sort of a light, sandy color, blue eyes. He looked a bit gaunt in the face, but that was probably from going without food and water for so long."

"You say you examined him when he first came aboard?"

"Yes. He had a wound on his abdomen, a shallow cut. I cleaned and dressed it."

"Did he have other scars? In particular, a large one right here?" Bennett pointed to a spot on his ribs exactly where the nasty scar had been on her abductor.

"Yes! You know who he is?"

Both the men nodded knowingly.

"He told me his name was David."

The policemen exchanged a look and Bennett said, "We don't know his name, mind you. Not his real one. He goes by any number of aliases. The man's a terrorist of sorts, a mercenary, and every bit a killer. In all honesty, I'm surprised he's let you off alive."

Christine tried to comprehend. "How did he end up in the middle of the ocean?"

"No telling right now," Bennett mused. "Perhaps he was hired to sink the ship, this *Polaris Venture*, and then botched up his escape."

"He told me there were no other survivors. I thought that was odd."

"Nothing odd about it. All his doing, I suspect. Now, you said that he made you turn your boat around and take him here, to England. Did he mention why?"

Christine considered that and was about to answer when the telephone rang. She went to the nightstand to pick it up when Harding spoke for the first time.

"Let it go, Dr. Palmer. They'll leave a message at the front desk."

"No," Christine said, "I think it might be Chief Bickerstaff. I told him —" Her line of thought derailed. Something was wrong. What was it? Harding had spoken for the first time, and his voice — no his accent — it was anything but British. She turned to see both men moving toward her.

"What—"

She reached for the phone but Harding's hand came down firmly on top of hers. When the phone stopped ringing, he reached around behind the nightstand and unplugged the wire.

Chapter Seven

Christine sat quietly on the couch, stunned. Her stomach was knotted, her muscles rigid. Harding sat next to her, a gun in his far hand. She wanted to cry out, to scream for help, but they'd warned her against it. That warning was reinforced by the ominously calm expressions of her new captors. It had happened again. Ever since she'd pulled that miserable, half-dead wretch from the ocean, her life had gone mad, a nightmare with no end.

They had spent the last few minutes asking questions, many of the same ones they'd already asked her. She could see them mentally compare her answers to the previous ones. The two men exchanged looks and nods as she talked. Christine couldn't imagine what they wanted from her.

Bennett performed the questioning, "And what were the actual coordinates where you found this man?"

Christine tried, but it was hopeless. "I told you, I don't remember the exact latitude and longitude. I marked the spot and recorded the coordinates on a chart, but I didn't memorize them. I do remember plotting it to be 280 miles on a zero-five-zero bearing from the Madeiras."

More looks. Harding got up, and the two men retreated out of earshot for a hushed conversation. Christine didn't like it. They were standing right by the big window at the rear of the room. The only other way out was the front door, but she'd never make it if they were serious about using that gun, and she suspected they were. For some reason, these two scared her even more than the other madman.

Bennett and Harding, or whoever they were, broke their huddle. Harding's gun was gone, but she figured he could make it reappear fast.

"You'll need to come with us."

"I'm not going anywhere. All I did was pull some poor soul out of the ocean, and ever since people are pushing me around. I'd like to know why!"

"The man you found is very dangerous. We're trying to find him."

"Well, that still doesn't tell me who you are. You're certainly not the police."

There was no reply to that. Bennett went to the front door. He opened it, looked in both directions, then left while Harding closed the door and stood in front of it, a guard with his eyes locked on a prisoner. Christine heard a car pull up outside, and moments later, a single knock on the door.

"Time to go," Harding said.

Christine stood fast.

"No harm will come to you." His accent was hard on the consonants. He put a hand obviously into his jacket without showing the gun. "Now!"

Christine knew she had to find a way out, and find it now. She walked slowly to the door and Harding reached out, obviously intending to lock an arm around her before going outside. Christine was passing the small alcove that served as the closet when she saw what she needed, up on the shelf above her clothes. When Harding turned his head to find the door handle, Christine lunged up for the clothes iron on the shelf.

Harding, alerted by her quick movement, reached into his jacket for the gun. He arced it up toward Christine, but before he could level, she smacked the iron down onto his arm. Harding screamed in pain as he lost his grip on the weapon. The gun hit the floor along with the iron. Christine went for the gun, as she thought he would. But Harding surprised her by lowering his shoulder and charging, using his bulk to drive her crashing into the wall. The blow stunned Christine and she collapsed, gasping for breath, her vision blurred.

When she finally looked up, she saw Harding holding his gun gingerly with the arm she'd just whacked, a thoroughly angry look on his face. He grabbed Christine and yanked her violently to her feet. She stumbled, still woozy from the blow she'd taken. Her head, her shoulder — everything hurt. Harding propped her up, opened the door, and was about to shove her outside when they both froze at the sight. Bennett was lying face down in a planter, groaning weakly.

Harding never had time to react as a hand swung around from the right and caught him in the throat. The big man fell back into the room, pulling a stumbling Christine with him until she fell to the side. Harding recovered his balance but had no time to raise the gun before another strong blow, this one a heel kick, crashed into his face just below the nose. It snapped his head violently up and back, the motion ending with an audible crack. Harding crumbled heavily to the floor and lay motionless, his head twisted at an impossible angle.

"Damn!" she heard her rescuer say. It was a voice she knew. Christine looked up in disbelief.

"*You!*"

David Slaton ignored the girl and charged the other man who was stumbling toward the open driver's door of a big BMW. He collared him and threw him headlong into the car's fender. The man groaned and rolled onto his side. Slaton picked him up roughly and sat him against the front tire. He didn't bother searching for a weapon — if there had been one, he'd have already used it.

"Who is Savior, Itzaak?" Slaton demanded.

The man gave no response.

"How many are in the group?"

No response again. Slaton looked to his left and saw someone scurrying in the window of the motel office. There wasn't much time. The girl was still sitting beside the dead man. Slaton moved toward her.

When she saw him coming, she scrambled on her hands and knees, searching frantically for the dead man's gun. She found it under his hip, but before she could do anything more, Slaton was on her. They struggled with the weapon, grabbing and twisting, her finger near the trigger. A shot rang out and she let go reflexively as bits of plaster rained down from the ceiling above.

Slaton took the gun, a 9mm Beretta, and stood over Christine and the dead man. He looked back and addressed the man who was still leaning against the car. "Who, Itzaak?" he yelled.

"I don't know," came the weak reply.

Slaton pointed the gun at the man's partner and let go a round. The girl jerked away involuntarily at the shot, and a small hole erupted in the wood floor right next to the body. Slaton walked purposefully to the man he knew as Itzaak, leveled the gun at his head and said, "That's it for him. Last chance for you."

The man's eyes went wide as he recognized the fate of his comrade. He broke, his expression disintegrating into raw fear, and Slaton knew he'd get the truth.

"I don't know! I *swear* I don't know who controls. I take my instructions by phone."

"Who are the others?"

The man babbled a half-dozen names. The two Slaton recognized had to be small fish.

"There's more, but I don't know who they all are."

"How many in all?"

"I . . . I don't know . . . fifteen, maybe twenty."

Slaton heard a siren in the distance. It was time to go. He pointed the pistol squarely between the man's eyes and spoke slowly. "Itzaak, tell them the *kidon* is going to find them. I will find them all!" Slaton safed the Beretta, dragged the man to his feet, and threw him into a neat row of shrubbery. He was about to get in the car when he remembered the girl. He looked at her directly.

It was a stare that instantly mobilized Christine. She got up and broke into a run toward the office.

Slaton bolted, taking an angle to cut her off. She slid to a stop in front of him as Slaton put his hands out, palms forward, trying to appear less threatening.

"You have to come with me," he said.

She shook her head violently, "No!" she pleaded, "No more!"

Slaton saw she wasn't going to go easily. "I don't have time to negotiate here."

He grabbed an arm and pulled her roughly over to the BMW, shoving her inside and across to the passenger seat. Slaton got in, slammed the car into gear, and flew out of the parking lot. Cocking his head to the mirror, he saw blue pulsating lights. He had half a mile to work with.

Slaton drove wildly for two blocks, took a right turn, two lefts, then stopped abruptly. He got out, pulling Christine along, and hurried ahead to the next street where the Peugeot was parked. He put her in and started driving again, this time moving quickly, but with more control. Ten minutes later, the small town of Penzance faded away behind them. Slaton eased to a normal speed and began thinking about his next step.

They drove for an hour, winding across deserted country roads. Slaton made turns without ever referencing a map. He had come up with three preplanned avenues of egress. The first ran east on the A30 — fast, but highly visible. The second took him east along a series of less traveled secondary roads. The last was a westerly route, to the isolation of Land's End. It was something no one would expect, and definitely reserved as a last-ditch jink to get clear, since doing so would severely limit his subsequent options.

Leaving Penzance, Slaton decided the police would find the BMW quickly. But he was reasonably confident that no one had seen them switch to the rented Peugeot. They had managed an anonymous departure from the chaos, and so he'd selected the second route, hoping to avoid detection while still heading in the right direction.

Slaton eyed his passenger. She seemed to be in shock, curled up against the door with a distant, glazed expression. It was a look he'd seen before, in many different scenarios — battlefields, prisons, hospitals. All the places where trauma tore at the human mind and body. It usually didn't bother him.

"I'm sorry about shoving you around back there," he offered. "I didn't have time to explain things."

She didn't move or speak.

"I said I'm sorry," he repeated.

She looked at him this time. "Sorry?" she whispered. "Again, you're sorry?" Without warning she lunged at him and started swinging, a flurry of fists that nearly caused Slaton to veer off the road. He struggled to stop the car while being beaten about the head and shoulders. Her swings were wild, but a blow landed painfully on his jaw and he recognized the salty tang of blood in his mouth. She continued to lash out as the car came to rest on the shoulder of the road. Slaton did his best to fend off the barrage but did nothing to stop her. Eventually she slowed, then finally stopped, the tantrum having run its course.

"Sorry for what?" she yelled. "For killing that man back there? Or the others you've killed? How many have there been?"

He said nothing.

"Why can't you just stay away from me?" She flung out another fist that glanced off his shoulder.

He looked at her impassively, a trickle of blood at the corner of his mouth.

"Are you done yet?"

"No!" She shouted, tears now streaming down her cheeks.

"I came back because I realized those two men, or someone like them, would come after you."

Christine laughed, "Oh right, you came to rescue me."

"No. I came to find *them*. I knew they'd track you down, so I found out where you were staying, and then waited."

Her eyes narrowed as she tried to understand. "What would they want with me? Who are they? Or perhaps I should say, who were they?"

"I only killed one of them," he said distractedly, studying the rearview mirror, "and that was an accident."

"Oh, it was an accident that you kicked him in the face so hard you broke his neck. I suppose it's okay then."

"It happens."

"Not where I live it doesn't!"

He shot back, "And what do you suppose they had in mind for you if I hadn't come along?"

Christine had no reply. She drew back to her corner, pressing against the door.

"This is crazy," she finally said. "Two men I've never seen before in my life, asking me questions and trying to pass themselves off as police. When I figure out that they're lying, they want to kill me. Only then I'm saved by . . . by yet another recurring lunatic."

She looked at him, her eyes pleading for some simple explanation. Slaton offered nothing.

"So now you're my hero?" she said. "Returning the favor from when I pulled you out of the Atlantic? Somehow I don't feel like we're even. If I hadn't found you, I'd be a thousand miles from here, halfway to New Haven by now. My biggest worry would be whether I wanted a can of beans or a can of hash for lunch. Instead, I've got strangers chasing me around a foreign country, threatening me. And the local police think I'm psychotic."

"Look, you saved my life and I am grateful. I wish you hadn't been pulled into all this. But I can't change it now."

"You wish I hadn't been pulled into it?" she asked incredulously. "You hijacked my boat! You . . . you killed someone and then forced me into a car at gunpoint!"

"There was no time to explain back at the hotel. I had to get you out of there. It wasn't safe."

"And now I'm safe?"

"No, you're not," he said. "At least not yet."

He gauged her pensively, deciding how far to go.

"Look, I won't keep you against your will. But let me explain a few things first." He saw her eyes drop to the gun in his lap, forgotten in the fury of her assault. Slaton tucked it carefully under the seat, a show of goodwill. As he straightened, the sound of an engine announced a car approaching from behind. His eyes went to the mirror, his hands to the steering wheel and gearshift. A few moments later the car whisked by at speed. It disappeared around the curve ahead. He looked at her again. She seemed less tense.

"You could have bolted out and screamed for help from that car. You didn't."

"I'm glad you put that gun away," she said with some consolation. "But you still haven't told me who those men were. You knew them. You called one by name . . . Itzaak."

"That's very good — that you can remember details under stress. Most people can't. Who did they say they were when you let them into your room?"

"They told me they were investigators with a branch of the British government. Maritime Investigations or something. They called themselves Bennett and Harding."

"And they had IDs, although you didn't look at them closely."

She looked embarrassed. "They seemed professional enough."

"One was Itzaak Simon. The other I don't know by name, but I've seen him before. Both are assigned to the Israeli Embassy in London. Itzaak is the designated Assistant Attaché for Cultural Affairs. They're both full-time Mossad Officers, Israeli intelligence."

Christine laughed. "Spies? Israeli spies? What in the world would they want with me?"

"They'd want to find out how much you know about two things. *Polaris Venture* and me." Slaton saw by her expression he'd scored a hit. "That's what they asked you about, right?"

She nodded, "So you sank that ship and they're after you? You're with one of the Arab countries?"

He grinned. "No. I'm an Israeli too. And I didn't sink the ship. I think they did."

Christine sighed. "This isn't getting any easier." Her eyes narrowed as she studied him in the faint light of an overcast-shrouded midday sun. "You don't look Israeli. You're fair skinned."

"We come in all colors, shapes, and sizes. I have a lot of Scandinavian blood, but I was born in Israel."

"And you? You're a spy too? Why would Israeli spies be sinking ships, and killing one another in quiet English villages?"

"A very good question. I didn't know myself until yesterday. Then I got a letter from a friend of mine who had uncovered some information, and things began to make sense. I think there's a group of traitors within the Mossad. They're sabotaging operations, even targeting our own country and people."

She sounded suspicious. "You mean they're working with your enemies?"

"It looks that way, but I don't know much about them yet. It's an organization that's been around for a long time. Lately they've been less active, but more desperate."

"You say your friend told you all this in a letter?"

"He made a pretty convincing case."

"And does he know who these people are?"

"Some of them. Some he hadn't identified yet. In time he would have found them."

"*Would* have?"

"Yosy was Mossad. He worked at headquarters, outside Tel Aviv. Last week he came here to tell me all this in person. I was gone on *Polaris Venture*, so he left a letter where he knew I'd find it. He was killed before he could get back home, hit by a bus in Knightsbridge. It was ruled an accident."

Christine listened intently. Slaton went on for twenty minutes, telling her everything that had been in Yosy's report. He explained who Leon Uriste had been, and that he, too, had recently met a suspicious end. Slaton described a traitorous organization within the Mossad, a group who were bombing synagogues and shooting soldiers. He had no idea how many people were involved, but it seemed to include someone near the top.

Christine tried to make heads or tails of the information. And perhaps more importantly, of the psyche of this man who was talking to her. The weight of what he told her was numbing on a moral scale, but always logical and consistent. She also noted his physical appearance. It kept changing in subtle ways, as if he were a portrait whose artist was never quite satisfied, always insisting on one more stroke of the brush. The blisters on his face had largely healed and his beard, light in color, was getting denser. If it hadn't been for the eyes, she might not have recognized him at the motel. The intense blue-gray eyes that were always moving, scanning, processing all surroundings.

The few facts she could recall supported what he was telling her, and she suspected at least some of it had to be true. He finally finished with the sinking of *Polaris Venture*. Christine decided she knew the rest, and it left her with one particularly bothersome question.

"I still don't understand what these men wanted with me."

"They probably got word that you had rescued someone from a ship named *Polaris Venture*. They would want to know who you'd found. And they'd be curious as to what you knew about the ship."

His attention shot forward as a truck came around the bend. She saw it as well.

"This could be your ride," he offered. "You can go to the police and tell them everything. They won't be able to protect you, though. Those two men were going to kill you. You and I are threats to their organization. Probably the only ones, now that Uriste and Yosy are dead. They'll come after you, and a bobby standing guard at the door of a hotel room won't stop them. That's the best protection you're likely to get from the police. *If* they believe your story. Stay with me and I'll do what I can to look after you. I know how they think, how they work. It's your best chance."

Christine saw the slow-moving truck closing in. *Best chance?* She didn't know what to do, but there were only moments to decide. She opened the door and swung a leg out of the car. He made no attempt to stop her. There was time for one last question.

"Why is this all so important?" she asked. "What could I know about you or the ship that's worth killing people over?"

"You might know where *Polaris Venture* went down," he said. "Or you might know that she was carrying two tactical nuclear weapons."

❖   ❖   ❖

Hanit lay moored just outside the harbor of Marseille. She was a Sa'ar V class corvette and, at over a thousand tons, a regular and formidable presence in the regional waters off Israel and Lebanon. Here, however, in one of the busiest ports of the Mediterranean, she was nothing special. Huge freighters, tankers, and warships plied a constant stream among the swarm of smaller tenders and pilot boats. The Port Authority had not been pleased to have a foreign-flagged warship show up unannounced, and so *Hanit*'s captain gave little argument at having been banished to anchor in the outer mooring field. They wouldn't be here long, he reasoned, and they *were* under orders to be as unobtrusive as possible.

The captain stood with his executive officer on the wing platform, to the port side of the bridge. The two men eyed a small tender as it approached. It carried a crew of two seamen and a French port official, who would no doubt be grumpy and have a plethora of forms for them to complete. It also carried Paul Mordechai and two large crates.

Neither of the officers had ever met Mordechai, but they'd gotten the scuttlebutt. As the small boat pulled alongside, there was no mistaking their guest. He wore a bright print shirt adorned with flags of various nautical meanings. There were hurricane and gale warnings, along with a prominent SOS on the back. Mordechai spotted the two officers, came to attention, and offered a ridiculously snappy salute.

The exec rolled his eyes.

"All right," the captain said, "the orders are clear. We get rid of this Port Authority quack as fast as we can, haul aboard Mordechai and the crates, then get out of here."

"Aye," the exec nodded. He started to go below to supervise the detail.

"Oh, and Dani . . ."

The exec paused.

"Mind the crates."

Chapter Eight

"Ian!"

The bellowing summons had come from the adjacent room, the Scotland Yard office of Inspector Nathan Chatham. Ian Dark answered the call, entering Chatham's office to find his boss parked at his desk with a confounded look on his face. The object of his consternation was in hand, a small beeper that had activated.

"This!" Chatham roared, holding the offending device over his head. "What on earth does all this mean?"

Dark calmly took the device. The message line read:

SEE ACSO ASAP W/DSR CNX LV 12/1-12/8 REP CONF

"I suppose it all means something?" Chatham fussed.

Dark read the electronic shorthand, "The Assistant Commissioner Specialist Operations wishes to see you as soon as possible. You are to bring the daily situation report. He's also seen it necessary to cancel your holiday, which was to start tomorrow. You're to confirm receipt of the message by pressing this button."

Chatham waved his hand to indicate that Dark should go ahead and do it. He did. Dark had been working with Chatham for six months now, and he noticed more and more things happening that way.

Chatham got up from his chair, not bothering to straighten the papers that lay strewn in front of him on the desk. He was a tall, gaunt man, his face long and narrow, with a ski slope of a nose presiding over a broad, bushy mustache. Brown hair had given way to gray at the sides, all of it decidedly unkempt. His sage appearance was a constant counterpoint to Dark, whose own slight build, fair skin, and rosy cheeks gave no end of trouble when ordering a pint, even though he'd been of age for ten years.

"Assistant Commissioner, you say?" Chatham mumbled.

"Yes, the new man. Would you like me to come along?"

"No, no. I shouldn't think so. Probably just another silly staff meeting, that sort of thing." Chatham gave a crooked grin. "You stay here and fight the battle, eh?"

When he'd first started working with Chatham, Ian Dark had to keep from snickering at his boss. The endless military analogies, the technological ineptness. He kept picturing his boss in turn-of-the-century India wearing a pith helmet and shorts. It was an image, Dark later learned, that might well have come to be had Chatham been born a hundred years earlier. His grandfather had been a major in the Northumberland Fusiliers, serving in the Somme during the Great War. His father had battled Rommel in North Africa with the 1st Royal Dragoons. Only a ruptured eardrum had kept Nathan Chatham from continuing the family military tradition. It forced him to redirect his talents.

"They would not allow me to shoot the enemy," he'd explained to Dark one evening over a Guinness, "so I thought I should spend my time outthinking him." He had done exactly that.

Chatham had been at the Yard for over twenty years, and his reputation was second to none. Not only had he outthought the criminal enemy, but he often managed to better his superiors as well, a tactic that had more than once gotten him into hot water. It had also brought offers of promotion beyond his current rank of Inspector, offers that Chatham had repeatedly refused. He swore he could never be content "engaging the foe with pen and paper from a soft bottom chair." But if Nathan Chatham was troublesome to his overseers, he was even more notorious to those he investigated, at least ones who turned out to be guilty. A relentless pursuer and meticulous investigator. That was all Chatham ever cared to be, and something, by virtue of results, those above him would never be able to change. Like it or not.

Chatham went to the coatrack and wrestled an ill-fitting jacket onto his long arms. He left the room, then reappeared moments later.

"The new Assistant Commissioner," queried the man who had outstayed the previous six, "what was his name?"

"Shearer, sir."

Chatham nodded, then disappeared down the hall. Ian Dark chuckled. There was no job in the building he'd rather have.

Ten minutes later and two floors up, Nathan Chatham gave a cursory pat to his rumpled hair before being ushered into the office of the Assistant Commissioner Specialist Operations. The office was full of dark, weighty furniture that conveyed an aura of importance. Chatham was at least pleased to see that the new man had not redecorated the suite. The last one had made that his first order of business. He also lasted less than a year before moving on to a cushy private sector job. Chatham had berated the Commissioner himself over that appointment. "An abysmal choice. Nothing to the man. No substance!" he'd admonished. The Commissioner admitted it had all been about branch politics, and he promised to work against that kind of thing in the future.

Now Chatham was greeted by a well-groomed, genial man, probably in his early fifties. The new lord and master of Special Branch rose from his desk.

"Inspector Chatham, good to meet you. Graham Shearer." The tone was crisp, but friendly. Chatham shook hands, cocked his head slightly, then finally made the connection. The name hadn't rung a bell because he'd never known it. The face and voice were another story.

"We've already met."

The Assistant Commissioner looked surprised. "Have we?"

"Manchester. You were on the force. Inspector, I think. I was there to give evidence in the trial of a drug smuggler who had killed a rival here in London. Threw him out a tenth floor window as I recall. Nasty business that."

"Manchester, was it? That would be . . . thirteen years ago?"

"Fourteen. You were addressing the defendant's solicitor as I was waiting to give my deposition. You said, 'Your scoundrel is guilty and I have the evidence to prove it and if you don't like it you can bugger off!'"

The Assistant Commissioner's face stretched in thought and then the smooth veneer cracked as he broke out laughing. "Your memory is painfully precise, Inspector. I have calmed a bit since then." The Assistant Commissioner waved his arm toward a plush leather chair and retreated back behind his desk. "Please have a seat."

Chatham did so, encouraged that the Commissioner had taken his advice to fill the number two spot with a true policeman. As he parked his lanky frame in the chair, his eyes locked onto a box of chocolates on the Assistant Commissioner's desk. He was obvious enough and Shearer held it out.

"Please, Inspector. My wife gave them to me as an anniversary gift. I suppose I should find it encouraging that after twenty-two years she doesn't mind my being a couple of stone heavier."

The explanation was lost on Chatham who was engrossed in the most important decision he'd had on the day. He momentarily considered whether it would be improper to take two, but decided against it for the time being. Chatham plucked out a coconut crème and wasted no time.

"I've got a meeting at the top of the hour, so I'll get right to it," Shearer said. "We've had a bit of trouble down in Penzance. This morning two chaps from the Israeli Embassy were involved in some kind of row with a third man. One of the Israelis ended up dead and the other is in the hospital. The assailant disappeared, along with a woman he managed to drag off at gunpoint. She's another story altogether. The Israeli involvement has got Home Office in an uproar. They've asked me to assign someone to get to the bottom of it all."

Chatham's eyes closed and a near orgasmic expression set across his face. "Exquisite," he declared. "You say these two were from the embassy. Were they Mossad?"

"Ah, yes, one we're quite sure about, the other probably."

"What do we know about the attacker?"

"Nothing really, although forensics hasn't had a go at it yet. The motel manager got a look at him, but he was rather far off."

Chatham made a mental note of the brand name on the box of chocolates. The coconut crème had been quite nice.

"As I said, the woman is a story all her own. She was at this motel by courtesy of the local authorities. Yesterday she sailed into Penzance in a small boat that looked like it had just made its way through a typhoon. Seems she was on her way to the States when she found a man floating about in the middle of the ocean. She claims to have rescued the chap who, in turn, commandeered her boat and forced her to sail to England. When they arrived, near Land's End, he disabled the boat and left her stranded while he went ashore in a rowboat. Something like that."

Chatham looked up idly at the ceiling, "That would mean this woman has now been abducted twice in a matter of days. How unfortunate. Did the police take a description of this man she claimed to have rescued?"

"Yes, but I haven't seen it yet. Do you suppose the same chap has taken her again? Right after letting her go?"

"I don't think he took her the first time. It seems he took her boat and she went along for the ride. But to answer your question, I see three possibilities. First, that the same man did come back. Second, that someone else came looking for her because she'd rescued this man. Or third, that her story is not truthful, and she herself is involved in some sort of mischief."

Shearer pondered. "Or perhaps a combination of those things."

Chatham smiled at his new boss.

The Assistant Commissioner looked pointedly at his watch and stood up. "Well, the facts are a bit thin right now. I think it's gone beyond the sort of thing the local boys in Penzance are accustomed to handling."

"This woman, do you happen to know her nationality?"

"I believe she's American."

"Ah," Chatham said.

"I'll have to press on now, Inspector. As I said, Home Office is all revved over this one. Call me daily and let me know how things are progressing. Chief Bickerstaff is the man to talk to in Penzance. Glad I had the chance to meet you — again."

"I'll get right out to Penzance this evening." Chatham shook hands in parting and walked to the door, happy that the new Assistant Commissioner Specialist Operations was not nearly as big a twit as the last.

"Oh, and Inspector . . ."

Chatham turned to see Shearer holding out the remainder of the box of chocolates.

"Perhaps you should have these. Never been one for sweets myself. Just don't ever tell Mrs. Shearer."

Chatham made no effort to conceal his pleasure. He walked over slowly and took the box as though it held the Crown Jewels. "You have my word as a gentleman," he said reverently.

As soon as he was in the hallway, Chatham opened the box and selected another. Mint crème. Yes, he thought, this Assistant Commissioner would do nicely.

The morning air was laden in fog and a steady drizzle. Christine peered through the rain-splattered window of the Peugeot, barely able to see David at a newsstand across the street. They had spent the previous afternoon and evening driving to London, by way of a long, circuitous route. Stopping an hour short of the outskirts, Slaton had pulled off and found a quiet spot to park among a stand of trees. There, they'd gotten a few hours sleep. Christine had dozed fitfully, at least relieved that he no longer insisted on keeping an arm draped over her. At first light they were back under way, fighting the morning rush hour traffic into Kensington.

Christine yawned as she watched him jog back to the car, dodging traffic, with a pair of newspapers under one arm. When he clambered into the driver's seat, cold droplets of rain sprayed around inside the car. He tossed one of the papers into her lap.

"See what you can find," he said.

"Find?"

He leafed quickly through the *Times*, oblivious to the question. Seconds later he spotted what he was after on page six.

"Here it is." He showed her the headline: MURDER IN PEN- ZANCE. Slaton read silently while Christine opened up the *Evening Standard* and found it on page nine. A minute later, they swapped.

"They both say basically the same thing," Christine said. "You're wanted for murdering a man, putting another in the hospital, and possibly kidnapping me."

"They haven't gotten hold of a picture of you yet. That's good."

"You think they'll put *my* picture in the paper?"

"By this time tomorrow you'll either be a beautiful, rich heiress who's been kidnapped, or a devilish accomplice to murder."

"Accomplice? What are you talking about?"

"I mean the media, along with the police, are going to consider the possibility that you might be on my side in this. They know we were together on *Windsom*, so if someone sees us now, and you're not screaming and trying to run away . . . well, it could give the wrong impression. That's the kind of thing the press loves to get a grip on and spin as they see fit."

Christine was dumbstruck. "On your side? I just want my life back. But according to you, there are people out there who want to kill me."

"I know it sounds paranoid, but you saw it for yourself yesterday. Either way, this story will move up a few pages tomorrow. Especially once the papers track down some photographs and get a look at you."

She glared at him, but he was still engrossed in the article. Christine reckoned that was probably as direct a compliment as this man ever paid a woman. Her doubts returned, and she wondered again if she'd made the right choice. Had the two men at the motel meant her harm? Or was this man beside her the threat? She tried to convince herself that if she just went to the police and told them everything, things would work out. Certainly they could protect her.

Slaton tapped an index finger on the newspaper. "There's no reference here to the fact that Itzaak and his friend worked at the embassy. The police must know that by now, but they're keeping it quiet. It's either a diplomatic favor, or my government requested it."

She fell silent and he looked up, seeming to sense her indecision.

"Still not sure about me, huh?"

"No," she said, "not completely."

"Can't say that I blame you."

The interior of the car grew quiet, the only sounds coming from outside — people and machines, sloshing through rain on their daily routines.

"I'm a little confused myself," he said, finally breaking the silence. He pointed out the window. Cars and trucks streamed by incessantly and scores of people scurried in all directions on the sidewalks. "You can still go if you want," he offered. "We're in London. It's a big place. Lots of people, police everywhere. I wouldn't have brought you here if I wanted to hold you prisoner. I've got work to do, and this is where it starts."

"Where does it end?"

He looked away and didn't answer, which gave Christine no comfort. Did he not want to tell her? Or did he not know?

"I feel like I should believe you," she said. "I think you're right. Those two men were going to kill me. But what you did to them — that scares me too." An image came to Christine. The man she knew as Harding, his face frozen in death. As a doctor she had seen bodies before, but there had been something else yesterday. Something in the man's last, terminal expression. Surprise. Or maybe fear.

"Yesterday when you were questioning that man, you said you would find them. You said 'Tell them the *keeden* will find them.' Something like that. What does it mean?"

He gazed at the gloom outside. His hesitation told Christine she'd hit on something, and if an answer came it would be the truth.

"*Kidon,*" he finally said, still looking away. "It's a part of Mossad. There are only a few of us, and we have a very special mission."

Christine steeled herself. "And what is that?"

"Kidon is Hebrew for bayonet. We're assassins."

Prime Minister Jacobs arrived at his office following a tedious working breakfast with the Foreign Minister. Anton Bloch was waiting, his bulky frame planted squarely in the center of the room. Jacobs didn't like the brooding look on his face.

"Now what?"

"*Polaris Venture* again."

Jacobs stiffened. "Good news or bad?"

"We've found Slaton. He was picked out of the ocean by a private boat."

"That's wonderful! He made it—"

Bloch waved a hand. "Yesterday, in England, he killed one of our London men and put another in the hospital."

"What? He's killed one of our own people?"

"I didn't believe it at first either, but the man in the hospital is sure. It was Slaton."

Jacobs sat down gingerly, his mind spinning through the possibilities.

"Let me tell you all of it," Bloch started. "We got a tip from a source in Scotland Yard. It seems a small sailboat pulled into Penzance, that's a port in southwestern England, and the skipper claimed to have rescued someone from a ship that had gone down. The name given was *Polaris Venture*."

"So Slaton was on this sailboat?"

"Not when it pulled into port. The American was alone."

"What did this fellow say happened to Slaton?"

"*She* said he got off hours earlier and rowed ashore in a dinghy . The situation was pretty murky, so I ordered London to send a team to find out what was going on. They were supposed to be discreet, but for some reason they approached this woman and ran into Slaton. He killed one of the men, put the other in the hospital, and ran off with the American woman in tow. I don't know much more. We haven't been able to talk to Itzaak yet. He's the one that survived. The local police are keeping a close eye on him, and I'm sure Scotland Yard is involved now."

Jacobs sank even lower in his chair. "Why would Slaton try to eliminate two of his own? And why take this woman with him?"

"I don't know about the woman, but I *can* tell you without a doubt that he wasn't trying to kill Itzaak."

"How could you know that?"

Bloch dropped a thick file onto the Prime Minister's desk. Absent were the usual title and security classifications. Jacobs opened it and winced at the one word emblazoned in red on the inside cover — KIDON. Beneath that was the standard Mossad black and white, official glossy of David Slaton. Jacobs knew men like this existed, and he knew it was the kind of thing that could be poison to a politician. Yet it bothered him on an even more basic level.

"If this man had wanted Itzaak dead, we wouldn't have a team headed to the hospital right now."

Jacobs rubbed his temples. "Do you think he sabotaged *Polaris Venture?*"

"The American woman, a Dr. Christine Palmer, spoke to the police yesterday. Said she found Slaton nearly dead, floating around in the middle of the ocean. If that's true, he either wasn't the saboteur, or he mucked up his escape in a big way. Knowing Slaton, I doubt that."

"You say, 'If that's true.' Do you think this woman might be lying? Could she be involved?"

Bloch shrugged his beefy shoulders. "It's something we'll have to look into. None of it makes much sense right now, but I'd sure like to talk to Slaton."

Jacobs shook his head. He'd have to call yet another Cabinet meeting. What a shouting match that would be. He looked again at the file on his desk.

"How well do you know this man, Anton? Do you still trust him?"

"I know him as well as anyone. I recruited him. His father was an officer in the Haganah. He helped design the guerrilla tactics that made us such a thorn to the British and Arabs. In the War of Independence, Ramon Slaton was the leader of the underwater demolition team that sank the *Emir Farouk*. Nine men destroyed the flagship of the Egyptian Navy."

"Ramon Slaton . . ." Jacobs pondered, "I've heard that name but I don't associate it with the War of Independence."

"After winning the military battle we were faced with a very different set of problems. We had to start up a nation. Infrastructure, schools, health care. You couldn't even mail a letter. It all took money and the new government had none. What it did have was a high level of support from expatriate Jewish communities. That and a world whose conscience was still haunted by the Holocaust. Ramon Slaton became an unofficial emissary, working the public and private coffers of Europe to get everything from missiles to plowshares."

"Ramon Slaton — Cyprus!" Jacobs said with a burst of recognition.

"Yes, that was where it ended. He and his wife were gunned down on a street corner. A bodyguard killed the attacker, an Egyptian." Bloch pointed to the folder on Jacobs' desk. "The boy was nine years old at the time."

"Where was he when it happened?"

"At school in Geneva. He was the only child, and with no other immediate family he was taken in by some friends of his parents. They lived on Kibbutz Gissonar. Later, when we screened him for recruitment, these years were given special attention. For the most part he channeled his grief constructively. He continued as a superior student and was strong athletically. But he also acquired an interest in the military. His adoptive father was a company commander in the Reserves, and he gave the boy a basic introduction to the tools of war. He spent two years at this new home, finally getting stability back into his life. Then it happened. He was home on Kibbutz Gissonar on the eve of the Yom Kippur War."

Jacobs envisioned it. "Directly in the path of two Syrian armored divisions."

"As a country, we were completely unprepared. The few armored units we had in the area were forced to pull back until reinforcements arrived. The people of the kibbutz used every car, truck, and bicycle to evacuate the women and children. When the Syrian tanks arrived, two dozen men and three World War II vintage rifles were all that stood between the Syrian army and the main pumping station of our National Water System. Some of the men hid. The ones who tried to fight were mostly mowed down by machine gun fire from the leading tanks and armored personnel carriers."

"And the boy?"

"It was chaos, but he used his head. He acted alone, with nothing more than one of the old rifles and his knowledge of the area. He moved along the perimeter of the village looking for an opportunity. It came in the form of an APC with an overheated engine. The thing ground to a stop, spewing smoke. The rear door opened and soldiers began to stagger out, coughing and rubbing their eyes. The Syrians didn't seem worried about being out in the open, probably thanks to the lack of resistance they'd seen so far. They milled around and began arguing. The boy saw his chance. He held his fire until he was sure the APC was empty. Then he let loose on the five soldiers, taking four before his gun jammed. The last one ran to the village for cover. The boy removed the bayonet from his rifle and killed the man by hand."

Jacobs shook his head, "I've heard other stories," he said, "but a child . . ."

Bloch nodded.

"Did the boy tell you this?"

"Eventually he filled in the blanks, but during his initial Mossad screening interviews he refused to talk about it. Most of it came to light by way of a witness, this idiot Captain who was in the Signals Intelligence Division. When the Syrians crossed the border, this fellow had to take a jeep and collect code books from a series of command bunkers that were about to be overrun. He was racing just minutes ahead of the Arab tanks when he lost control of his jeep passing through Kibbutz Gissonar. Went into a ditch and the jeep turned over on him. Broke his leg badly. The fool managed to take cover, and from there he had a bird's-eye view of the whole thing."

"I see," Jacobs said, lowering his head in thought. "And is this what brought Slaton to the attention of Mossad?"

"In part. It also had to do with the fact that his father was a very influential man, one who died in service to the state."

"What happened to the boy after the war?"

"He went back to school, eventually entering Tel Aviv University. He studied Biology and Western Languages. He had an exceptional gift for languages. Textbook speech is fine for the university or ordering dinner in a restaurant, but our section prefers those who have been immersed in a native country — regional accents and usages, slang. You can only get that kind of proficiency by living in a place, and the boy had spent time at several schools in Europe. He tested out at the highest level in three languages. We usually hope for one."

"How old was he when you recruited him?"

"We began actively screening when he was nineteen, in university. Two years later we approached him with the offer of a "government position." It usually takes six months of interviews, background checks, and psychological evaluations before the recruits get an idea of the kind of work they're being sized up for. We watch closely for a reaction."

"And what is the usual reaction when a person realizes they're being chosen to work in the world's most elite intelligence agency?"

"Mild surprise, perhaps. We hope for as little reaction as possible. These people are used to being the best and brightest in their class. But to say they've been chosen is premature. Most don't pass the screening, and of those, less than half complete the entire training process."

"Ramon Slaton's son made it through."

"He was at the top of his group, both academically and physically. We also discovered that his success against the Syrians was no fluke. As a boy, he apparently did a lot of hunting. Rabbits, quail, that kind of thing. By the time he got to us, his marksmanship was uncanny. He outshot every instructor at the range on his first day. Slaton was clearly something special, so in view of his performance and his family history, we elected to train him as a kidon."

"And what does that education consist of?"

"There's no set curriculum. Contrary to popular belief, there aren't legions of them roaming the world. We only train a handful, and they're rarely deployed."

Deployed, Jacobs thought. Like an artillery piece.

"We trained to his strengths. He was sent to the IDF Sniper Course. As a former officer, you know what that school is like."

"Yes, I know. Marksmanship is the least of it. They teach weapons, tactics, and stalking. All with consideration for the sniper's most demanding trait — patience."

Bloch nodded. "His scores on the tactical range were off the scale. Altogether, Slaton spent three years being shaped into what he is today."

"And the rest is in here?" Jacobs queried, looking at the file. The Director's reply didn't come right away and Jacobs sensed a red flag. "Anton? You know what's at stake here. I want to know everything. Is there something that's not in here?"

Bloch sighed, clearly not liking where he had to go. "There is one thing. It involved a girl. As far as we know, the only serious relationship he's ever had. The two had known each other from the kibbutz, and they married during his second year at university. We researched her background and found her history unremarkable. They had been married a year when she gave birth to a baby girl. It's all in the file."

Jacobs dug through the folder to the appropriate section and his eye was caught by a photograph of a strikingly beautiful raven-haired girl. The photo had been taken at a café, probably candidly since she seemed unaware. Her face was alight with an infectious, somewhat mischievous smile. She was sitting at a table that held two coffee cups, and a single red rose lying atop an envelope. The photograph was not wide enough in angle to show the companion with whom she was sharing her humor, but Jacobs had no doubt.

"Two months before completing his final term at the university, right when we were considering him as a recruit, there was a tragedy. Slaton's wife and daughter, who was not quite two years old at the time . . . they were both killed."

"What happened?"

Bloch told him and the Prime Minister shook his head. "What a miserable, terrible waste," he said, leafing idly through the file. Looking up, he sensed discomfort in the usually unflappable Anton Bloch. "What is it? What else?" the Prime Minister demanded.

"There's one thing that's not in the file." Bloch took a deep breath, then finished the story.

The Prime Minister considered the implications. "It could mean nothing. Or it could explain everything." Jacobs interlaced his fingers and brought them under his chin as the weight of the day began to settle. There were so many tangents. "You said this is not in the file. I can understand why, but how many people know about it?"

Bloch shrugged, "Very few, and . . . well, it's been many years."

"Yet it's possible he knows."

"Slaton? Yes, but a lot of things are possible."

A light blinked obviously on Jacobs' phone. The Prime Minister wished he could put all the world's events on hold so easily. He jabbed a thumb toward the file. "You seem to know a great deal about this man, Anton."

"I've seen him work," Bloch said matter-of-factly. "He's our best."

Jacobs considered that, wondering if it was a good thing or bad. He sensed Bloch was finished. "All right, have London find out what the hell's going on. Send in more people if you need to. Cabinet meeting at noon." The Director of Mossad walked to the door and, as he did so, Jacobs noted for the first time that he moved with a slightly uneven gait.

"Anton . . ."

Bloch turned.

"Where were you during the Yom Kippur War?"

The stone face of Anton Bloch cracked into a rare grin. "I was an id-iot Captain in the Signals Intelligence Division."

Jacobs couldn't hold back a snort of laughter, but as Bloch disap-peared the Prime Minister of Israel sobered, focusing on the dossier that lay before him. He turned back to the front cover, to the photograph of David Slaton. He then began to read.

Poring through the record, Jacobs recalled from his infantry days the IDF sniper course, known informally by its contorted alias — Finishing School. The training regimen was brutal, but only later did the real test come. No one was a true graduate until they had made their first kill. To look through a gunsight at an unsuspecting human and have the coldness to pull the trigger. This was the true commencement of Finishing School. The more Jacobs read, the more he realized that David Slaton was indeed among the best. A pure killer, vacant any trace of hesitation or remorse. My God, he thought, can we really create such a person?

Chapter Nine

Inspector Chatham arrived at the Penzance station at eight that morning. His first sight on entering the building was the burly Chief of Penzance Police ushering a young woman with a tape recorder out of an office and toward the door. The man's tone was brusque, Chatham thought, fully commensurate with his appearance.

"That's all I can say now, miss," Bickerstaff barked.

The woman offered a few well-practiced words of protest and indignation, only to have them cut off when the door shut in her face.

Bickerstaff sighed and leaned his bulk against the door, as if expecting the irksome woman to try shoving her way back in. He addressed the sergeant at the main desk, "No more of those, Patrick, or I'll 'ave those stripes."

The sergeant behind the desk waved his hand dismissively.

The police chief finally noticed Chatham. "Well, hello. You must be the Inspector from Scotland Yard I've been hearin' about."

"Does it show that badly?"

"You're the only one come to see me this morning that didn't have a camera in one hand and a notepad in the other."

Chatham took the Chief's outstretched hand and, not unexpectedly, endured a bonecrushing grip. "Inspector Nathan Chatham, Special Branch. Good to meet you. I arrived late last night."

"You could have called me right off, Inspector. I'd have filled you in."

"That's quite all right. I suspect that finding this fellow may take some time. Rest can be our ally. We'll march on steady and with a clear mind, while the enemy grows tired from maneuver. Let him make the mistakes, eh?"

Bickerstaff seemed to chew on that, then jabbed a blunt thumb to the door where he'd just evicted the young reporter. "I've already made one mistake today by letting her in. Pesky lot, they are."

"The media? I suppose, but they have their uses."

Bickerstaff smiled and gestured for Chatham to join him in his office. The place was a mess. Papers and files were strewn across all furniture that was not regularly attended, and the lone bookshelf was bursting with odd, unmatched volumes stuffed in at all angles. Chatham was encouraged. This was a place where work was done.

Bickerstaff sifted through the pile on his desk, found the paper he was after, and handed it to Chatham. "Here's the preliminary report, Inspector. Let me tell you what I know so far."

Chatham browsed the report while Bickerstaff talked. He decided that, in spite of his brutish texture, the chief was a reasonably proficient investigator. He also didn't seem concerned about turf — some local police got bothered when Special Branch came waltzing onto their stage. It took Bickerstaff five minutes to hit the highlights, and, in the end, he was apologetic for letting things go as long as they had. "I really thought there was nothing to this at first, but now I see I should have called for help right away."

Chatham nodded and put down the written report. "Perhaps, but let's not worry about that. Far too much to be done." He steepled his hands under his chin. "This man, the attacker, no one got a good look at him?"

"The Israeli chap who survived. He's in the hospital. Took a nasty bump on the head, he did. Claims he can't remember a thing." Bickerstaff scrunched his considerable brow. "Do you think it's a diversionarial tactic, Inspector?"

Chatham tried not to cringe at the chief's recreational grammar. "It is our job to distinguish evidence from coincidence."

Bickerstaff nodded and a look of stern concentration fell across his mug. Chatham had the impression he was mentally recording the phrase for future use.

Bickerstaff continued, "The motel manager saw our suspect, but he was awfully far away. We know the bloke's a bit on the tall side, thin, light-colored hair, and a scruffy beard. That's all he could tell us, basically the same description Dr. Palmer gave me the day before."

"*Doctor* Palmer?"

"Right, the woman who's disappeared. She's a physician, American. Just finished her schooling. I made some calls to the States to verify that part. Everything she told me about herself checked, which was why by yesterday morning I was starting to believe her story after all. Certainly nothing to suggest she'd be tied up with Israeli spies and all."

"Spies, you say?"

"Well," Bickerstaff retreated, "they were Israelis I know, and I heard they worked at the embassy. I just assumed . . ."

Chatham stood and began walking slowly back and forth. "Forensics. What have we got so far?"

"The man from the lab in Exeter has been here. He's found a few partial fingerprints that might be from our man. They came off the BMW. The door handle, the steering wheel, and shifter."

Chatham was not encouraged. He had a feeling that whoever this man was, his prints might not be on record. At least not anyplace Chatham had access.

"All right," he said, "let's set the order of battle. We have a young lady in our lab who's very good at this sort of thing. I'll bring her over to have a look. We'll try to match those prints from the car to any on the sailboat, then eliminate those that are Doctor Palmer's. By doing so, we can erase any doubt that the same man is responsible for both abductions. Since you've already started verifying this woman's story, I'd like you to press on with it. Find out if she's spent much time abroad. Go back, let's say five years. What countries has she been to? How long? That sort of thing. I'll have Ian Dark help you with it. He's my assistant back in London. Good man."

Bickerstaff began scribbling notes on a yellow pad.

"We'll have to go over this house he broke into after coming ashore. And we'll need a precise description of the motorcycle he's taken. If we can find it, we'll know where he's been, and perhaps get an idea of where he's headed."

"You don't think he's still around here?"

"Not likely," Chatham replied distractedly, his thoughts already having moved on. "The Israeli in the hospital, is he well enough for a few questions?"

"I don't see why not. He took a few knocks in all the argy-bargy, but they tell me he'll be fine."

"Good. That's where I'm headed then."

"Do you think he can tell us who this fellow is?"

"Can he? Almost certainly. I just hope that he *will.*"

"All right, Inspector. I'll have Edwards here run you over to the hospital."

Bickerstaff summoned Edwards and issued the assignment. As Chatham was about to leave, the chief added awkwardly, "I'll do whatever I can to help. I feel badly about this, Inspector. The woman, Dr. Palmer, she seemed a nice lady, she did."

"We'll just have to find her then, won't we? Carry on, Chief."

Two hours later, Chatham left the hospital no better off than when he'd gone in. Itzaak Simon, the Israeli who'd survived yesterday's scrum, was recovering nicely. He was alert, lucid, and not about to say anything of use. Chatham wished he'd arrived sooner, before the man's pain medication had worn off.

The supervising nurse confirmed that Itzaak Simon had taken no visitors other than the police. He had, however, spent a good amount of time on the telephone earlier in the morning, and Chatham was sure he knew who was on the other end. The questioning process had gone badly. After conceding a few basic, obvious facts, Simon claimed to not remember anything else, a convenient excuse given the bump on the crown of his head. Chatham had pressed, asking why the Assistant Attaché for Cultural Affairs had been so far away from his desk at the embassy, in the company of another embassy employee who was carrying a gun. From that point, things were openly hostile, and when the Israeli eventually used his trump card of diplomatic immunity, Chatham stopped wasting his time. He was sure Itzaak Simon knew the identity of the killer, but he recognized a dead end when he saw it.

Exiting the hospital, Chatham stopped at the first telephone kiosk he could find and dialed his office. Ian Dark answered on the first ring.

"Hello, Ian."

"There you are, Inspector. I tried to ring your cell phone about an hour ago, but I couldn't get through. Have you lost another one?"

Chatham hated the infernal thing. It always seemed to interrupt at the worst possible time. Right now it was crammed into the glove box of his seldom used car, along with that blasted beeper that was always blinking and vibrating — like having some huge, angry bug in your pocket. He ignored Dark's question. "I'm getting nowhere here. Our witness is maintaining a very professional silence. I'm also quite sure that the man we're looking for is no longer anywhere near this place. Tell me, what have you found?"

"Well, Bickerstaff was right on one count. There were no ships lost in the Atlantic last week. Nothing at all. Of course it might have been a small vessel, something that might go unreported."

"Or . . ." Chatham prodded. There was a slight pause.

"Or a sinking that someone didn't *want* reported. Smuggler, maybe, that sort of thing?"

"Right. Go on."

"Oh, yes. There was one stroke of luck. I was cross-checking the things you mentioned through our data files and I got one hit. It seems another Israeli national was killed in London about a week ago. After some digging and a few calls to the Foreign Office, I'm quite sure this person was also a Mossad officer."

"Hmm. A hazardous occupation. What were the circumstances?"

"It was an accident, apparently. The poor sod walked straight in front of a bus. The local division investigated but didn't find anything suspicious."

"You say this man was Mossad?"

"According to our Foreign Office, he was assigned to the London station a few years back. Then he went back to Israel and they lost track of him. The police investigation clearly took him to be another tourist here on holiday."

"I see. Better have a look at it."

"Do you think this same fellow might have been responsible?" Dark queried.

"No telling. Better protect the flank, though. Get me a copy of that accident report."

"Right."

"I haven't seen Mrs. Smythe from Forensics yet. When is she due here?"

"She checked in from Bickerstaff's office about an hour ago. Ought to be catching up with you any time now, sir."

"Good, good. She and I will have a quick look around the crime scene here. I'll leave her to tally things up while I take the 11:30 train back to London. Set up a conference with Shearer. Someone at the Israeli Embassy must know what this is all about. If I can go there with some official weight, it might save us all a lot of work."

Slaton strolled out of the gift shop, got in the car, and handed Christine a small box.

"Merry Christmas."

She opened it up to find a hideous Casio watch. It was pink and green with an ugly, thick plastic band. The price tag in the box said twenty pounds. She had a feeling he'd paid less.

"Gee, thanks. It's the nicest thing anyone's given me this holiday season. Of course, it is still the first week of December."

He put the little car in gear. "Sorry. Can't spend a lot on Christmas presents this year. Besides, you really shouldn't expect much. I'm not even a Christian."

Christine tried it on for size and, unfortunately, it fit. They had spent an hour earlier in the morning buying things — or rather he had. Clothes mostly, and a few toiletries. It seemed logical at first, since neither of them had more than what was on their backs, but Christine thought his selections had been curious. If her bodyguard, as she'd come to think of him, had any sense of fashion, he kept it well hidden. Cheap jeans, expensive shirts, some brightly colored, others subdued. He made her try on a few things, while others he bought when they were obviously too big. It finally clicked when he'd picked out the reversible windbreakers and a couple of cheap hats. He was putting together disguises — all different shades, shapes and sizes — so that they might better conceal themselves. Her first urge had been to laugh, but awful memories of the previous day spoiled any humor Christine could dredge from the situation. He had rounded out the ensembles by purchasing sunglasses and some cheap, off-the-rack, clear reading glasses — cheaters, he called them.

"It's twelve-twenty and thirty seconds," Slaton said, glancing at a somewhat more handsome, but equally inexpensive watch on his own wrist. "I've already adjusted yours. It should stay synchronized to within a few seconds. That'll be close enough."

Christine studied her watch with a guarded expression as he went on.

"I've got an errand to run."

An errand, she thought. To most people that meant going to the corner for a loaf of bread.

"You're going to drop me two blocks from here. Can you drive a manual shift?"

Christine looked at the unfamiliar right-hand drive arrangement. "I'll manage," she said confidently.

"Drive around the area. Get familiar with the streets and the car." Slaton referred to a street map that was folded carefully to show the relevant section of town. "At one fifteen do a circle around Belgrave Square — here," he pointed. "Enter the square from Chapel Street and circle once. Work your way to the inside lane. If you don't see me, head back the way you came, toward Buckingham Palace and the Park. Keep driving and come back every fifteen minutes. If I haven't shown up by two-thirty, leave and come back once at nine tonight."

"And if you're still not there?"

"Drive away and ditch the car. Take the tube to another part of town and pay cash for a hotel room. In the morning go to Scotland Yard. Talk to Inspector McKnight. I worked with him once and he seemed like a competent fellow. Tell him everything."

Christine looked at him, realizing what he was saying. His eyes were still empty. No fear, no trepidation, just alertness. Scanning, always scanning the traffic ahead and behind. Every car, every face on the sidewalk scrutinized for an instant. Slaton pulled the car into a parking spot and left it running.

When he reached for the door handle, Christine grabbed his arm. "But you said the police wouldn't be able to protect me."

"It's your best chance if we get split up," he said smoothly. "Remember, you'd have to convince them everything I've told you is true."

Christine sighed, "That might be tough, since I'm not even convinced myself." Then she added, "So please show up."

"I'll do my best."

He got out and mixed in with the crowds on the sidewalk. In no time, he disappeared.

Hiram Varkal sat impatiently at a booth in his favorite Chinese restaurant in Knightsbridge. It was dimly lit, like Chinese restaurants all over the world, but that didn't bother him. What bothered him was the crowds. The place was incredibly busy today and his order was taking forever. To a lesser extent, he was also troubled that the booths at Lo Fan's seemed to be getting smaller. Either that, or . . . he looked down at his stomach. Varkal was a huge man in every proportion. When younger, he'd actually been trim and athletic, but the curse of time brought a slowing metabolism that, augmented by an unabashed love of culinary excess, had taken him to his present state. Varkal sported a rolling girth that was unending, unfit, and, around Mossad's London station, unmistakable. Still, for all his mass, Varkal harbored no regrets. Good food, good drink, good cigars — there was the stuff of a good life and he embraced every calorie.

Varkal pushed the table away slightly as he spotted Wu Chin coming his way. He was delighted to see an extra large helping of sweet and sour pork. The waiter gave a slight bow as he slid the heavy plate in front of his regular.

"So sorry for waiting, Mr. Varkal. Cook very busy today."

Varkal took a hand and idly combed a few strands of hair from one side of his head, over the bald spot, to the other. He couldn't be upset after seeing the huge portion Wu had brought, no doubt to make up for the delay. The waiter rushed off and Varkal tucked in his napkin, calculating how much time remained for the pleasure of savoring his meal before the afternoon staff meeting.

He had just shoveled the first big helping of pork between his jowls when someone slid into the booth's opposing seat. Looking up, his eyes became huge circles. Varkal choked and coughed spasmodically, spewing the food back onto his plate.

"*Jesus!*" he sputtered.

"Hardly."

David Slaton pushed a glass of water toward the huge man.

Varkal took a messy drink from the glass. "What the hell are you doing here?" he asked in a harsh whisper.

"Get your hands on the table."

It took Varkal a moment to decipher the implications of that directive, then a look of worry glazed over his face as he realized that Slaton's hands were out of sight underneath the table. Varkal plopped his fat fingers across the hardwood as if he were expecting a manicure.

Slaton was confident the man would be unarmed. Varkal had never been a field agent. He was a politician, a bureaucrat who had worked his way up. But having seen him in action, Slaton knew to be careful. What-

ever the man lacked in tactical experience and polish was more than
compensated for by a shrewd nature and an outstanding intellect. Varkal
had excelled in a cutthroat organization, and he was near the pinnacle —
he headed up Mossad's London station, a vital post that wasn't handed
out lightly. Slaton would have to work hard to keep the man off balance.

"What do you want?" Varkal asked.

"I want to submit my resignation."

"What?"

"I quit. I resign my position, effective immediately."

Varkal's eyes narrowed. "Your position? I don't even know what your
position is. You don't work for me."

"Not really, I guess. But you could pass it on for me. I'm sure you
know the right people."

Varkal frowned.

"I also need to find out a few things. I thought you might be able to
help."

"Such as?"

"Such as who killed Yosy Meier."

Varkal's face wrinkled in confusion. "What do you mean? Yosy
killed? It was an accident."

"Said who? The London police?"

"Yes. And we did a quiet investigation ourselves. Accidents do happen, David, even to Mossad officers. Particularly here in England. Until
the Brits learn to drive on the right side of the road like the rest of the
world, there'll be no end to mowing down the tourists—"

"Don't give me that!" Slaton spat. "You knew Yosy. If there was an investigation, it didn't go very deep."

"All right," Varkal admitted, "I thought it was strange. But there really wasn't any evidence of foul play. We pressed hard on a couple of in-
formants, but none of the Arab groups here seemed to be involved."

Varkal was recovering. Slaton caught him glancing to the entrance.
He was wondering where his security was. The chief of an important
Mossad station didn't wander around town without someone to look after
him. It was time to tighten the screws.

"They're gone."

"Who?"

"The guy standing out front. Rosenthal, I think is his name. And some new thug in a car across the street. You know, this is a very good restaurant, but you shouldn't be so predictable. Same time, same day every week. It makes for bad security."

"What did you do to them?" Varkal asked guardedly.

Slaton had already decided not to overplay the answer to that question. He pulled a small radio out of his pocket and shoved it across the table. It was the size of a cigarette pack, with an earpiece and microphone, the standard issue for Mossad security work. Slaton had retrieved it from his apartment, but he wouldn't need it again. "Somebody reported a gun in the ambassador's wing. Your boys ran off to help. The place ought to be locked down tight by now, but it'll take fifteen minutes to figure out there's no intruder."

Varkal nodded. A thin sheen of perspiration had begun to mat the strands of hair on his scalp. It was decision time for Slaton. His instincts told him to go with Plan A.

"All right, listen," he said. "I think there's a group within the Mossad that's making trouble, and I have a feeling you're not part of it."

"What do you mean making trouble?"

"Killing Yosy, for starters. Sending a ship and fifteen crewmen to the bottom of the ocean. There's a lot happening, but I haven't got it all figured out yet. I only know that it comes from inside our organization. Deep inside."

"What? You're saying our enemies have infiltrated the service?"

"I don't know. If that were the case, I'd expect it to be one or two people. And they'd just stay quiet, get as high as they could within the organization to pass information. From what I've seen there's a lot going on, a lot of people involved."

"Like who?"

Slaton made a quick scan of the restaurant. "Why did Itzaak Simon and his buddy go out to Penzance?"

"We got a message from Tel Aviv. It instructed us to keep an eye out for anything that had to do with a ship named *Polaris Venture*. We found out from a source in Scotland Yard that a woman had sailed into Penzance in a boat that was beat to hell. Said she had picked up a man in the middle of the ocean, who then turned around and commandeered her boat. Supposedly he was a survivor from a ship that had sunk, and the name she gave was *Polaris Venture*. We sent that much back to Tel Aviv and they replied right away, told us to monitor the situation closely."

"How?" Slaton said impatiently.

"What do you mean *how*?"

"Were you supposed to contact her? Question her?"

"No, the order was very specific. Just watch from a distance. No contact."

"All right. I'm sure you've talked to Itzaak by now. How did he describe what happened in Penzance?"

Slaton saw suspicion in Varkal's face. The uncertainty and fear were wearing off.

"He said that he and his partner, Freidlund, had set up surveillance. They spotted some guy trying to get into this woman's room and decided to approach him. Itzaak recognized you and asked what was going on. That's when you went off and attacked the two of them. They weren't ready for it and you got the better of them."

"Simple enough. Now let me give you my version." Slaton allotted one minute to explain what had happened. It wouldn't be long before security at the embassy figured out his ruse. When he finished, Varkal was skeptical.

"You're telling me Itzaak and his partner were going to bury this woman? Why would they do that?"

"I don't know exactly, but I've got a feeling it has to do with *Polaris Venture*. That ship had a very unusual cargo, the kind of stuff people *get* killed over. Tell me, how did Itzaak's team get assigned this specific detail? Did you send them out?"

Varkal looked skyward, as if rewinding his mental gears. "When I got the message, I went straight to the duty swine. He told me Itzaak and Freidlund were already on the way."

"Isn't that kind of strange?"

"At the time I didn't like it, but I wasn't worried. It was Priority Two. When I got to my desk that morning, it had been there for at least an hour. Somebody saw the message and acted on it."

"Or maybe Itzaak and his buddy knew it was coming."

Slaton watched it sink in, then saw something else register.

"Itzaak . . ." Varkal said thoughtfully.

"What about him?"

"I told you we looked into Yosy's accident. Well, Itzaak was in charge of the investigation."

"Who gave him that job?"

"He volunteered for it. Said he was a friend of Yosy's and wanted to do it for personal reasons. I didn't see anything wrong with that — figured he'd be motivated to do a good, thorough job."

Slaton watched Varkal closely and could see the facts sinking in. The man was no longer concerned about his immediate, personal well-being. Slaton had been able to plant the seeds of a more insidious, familiar danger, and the station chief was reacting predictably. If it was all true, if there really was a threat from within, then there was also a golden opportunity. Varkal would want to break it open in such a way as to reflect maximum credit upon himself.

"You see the pattern. And the more you look, the more you'll find."

"That's what you want from me? You want me to investigate this?"

"I want you to pass what I've told you on to Anton Bloch. Tell him that's why I'm running around England killing his people. Tell him I haven't turned against Mossad. It's turned on itself."

"But if what you're saying is true, how can you know who to trust?"

"You mean how can *we* know."

Varkal frowned, then his eyes went to the window at the front of the restaurant.

Slaton checked his watch. "They're back a little soon."

"Yes," Varkal said quietly.

"Well, it's that time. In the next ten seconds you have to decide whether I'm full of crap or not."

Varkal's hands began to fidget on the table. He made no move to signal anyone. Slaton couldn't see the front entrance directly, but he'd been keeping an eye on the mirror behind the bar. If anyone came within twenty feet of their table, he'd know it. Slaton heard the door open, and at the same time, Varkal made his decision. He smiled. Trying to look casual, Varkal waved away whoever it was.

"It's Streissan. He heads my detail," Varkal said under his breath. "I tried to wave him off, but he's coming over anyway. Probably wants to tell me about the false alarm. If he gets one look at you . . ."

Slaton wasn't listening. He was about to lose the advantage of surprise. He spotted Streissan in the mirror, twenty feet over his shoulder and closing fast. Worse yet, the man had realized someone was at the table with Varkal.

Slaton's hand went into his jacket and gripped the Berretta. In one motion, he swung out of his seat and leveled the weapon at Streissan's head. To his credit, the Mossad officer froze, realizing it was his only chance.

A customer at the bar saw the commotion and yelled drunkenly, "'ere now!" Only when one of the barmaids screamed did the whole room go quiet. All attention in the establishment went to the man with the gun.

Slaton wondered whose side Streissan was on. Was he a traitor? Or just a guy on security detail doing his job? He'd like to ask some questions, but there was no time. He had to get out now. As he backed toward the rear exit, two figures appeared on the sidewalk outside. Slaton had a clear view through the big plate glass windows at the front. The men were moving quickly. Too quickly. He didn't know either, but in an instant they recognized Slaton and their weapons were drawn. His options were gone.

Slaton shifted aim and fired, the room's silence disintegrating into a crackling hail of gunshots and crashing glass. He let go two quick rounds at each of the moving figures outside, then leapt for cover behind the end of the bar. Halfway there he felt a stinging pain in his forearm.

A few of the restaurant's patrons tried to run for the front door as bullets whizzed by. Most fell to the floor and turned over tables, seeking any protection they could find.

Slaton popped up from behind the bar and loosed a rapid succession of shots at someone jumping in through the shattered window. He saw another man down, writhing on the sidewalk outside. He quickly ducked back down as return fire scattered around the bar. He distinguished two guns now, one to his left, and one to the right. The one on the right had to be Streissan, with a standard issue Glock. Four rounds fired. The one on the left was different, maybe a Mauser. Five shots. His left arm blazed in pain.

Suddenly the Mauser started spraying shots wildly around the room. When the count reached nine, Slaton moved slightly right, stood full, and spotted Streissan, poorly protected behind a booth divider. He fired twice before Streissan could shift his aim and the big man sprawled back with a shout, then stopped moving. Slaton shifted his aim to where Mauser would be changing clips, but saw nothing. Whoever it was had to be holed up behind a large, particularly solid table, waiting for help. That would be the smart thing to do. There would be ten more Israelis here within two minutes — with bigger weapons. The local police would be right behind. It was time to go.

Slaton moved to the rear of the bar, took one good look to clear the area, then fired a shot in Mauser's general direction. One second later, another. One second, a third shot, and the cover pattern was set. He dashed low to the rear exit, and was almost there when Mauser let go a single shot. Slaton looked back to take aim with the next round. He was still running low when a big drunk who'd been hiding near the rear door made a lunge for the same exit. The two met shoulder to shoulder and both went down. Slaton fell awkwardly on his injured arm and the pain seared in. But he had to keep moving. Scrambling, he made it to the passageway and out of Mauser's line of sight. He took one last look back at the wreckage that had moments ago been a popular restaurant. The sight was vivid. Screaming people, broken glass, overturned chairs — and the massive body of Hiram Varkal splayed out on the floor, his face bloody, and his eyes wide and still in death.

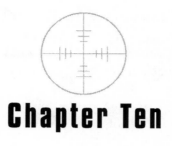

Chapter Ten

Christine began her third spin around Belgrave Square. She checked her ugly watch. One forty-four and ten seconds. The first pass, half an hour ago, had been two minutes late. After that, she'd gotten a better take on the traffic and the second pass had been right on. She wondered, for what seemed like the hundredth time today, what in the world she was doing. Driving a rented Peugeot in timed circles around a quaint London landmark, searching for her . . . Christine didn't even know what to call him. Her protector? Her killer? Her spy?

Whoever he was, he appeared out of nowhere halfway around the square. No waving or shouting to draw attention. He just stood in an obvious spot on the sidewalk, knowing she would spot him. Christine pulled over and he slid into the passenger seat.

"Turn left," he ordered. "Work over to Kensington Street."

And hello to you too, she thought. Christine edged the car back into heavy traffic while he immediately began scanning again for some unseen enemy. She noticed a small scrape on his hand.

"So, kill anybody while you were out?" She'd meant to lighten the mood, but it came out sounding crass. He gave her a hard look.

"Sorry." Christine heard the asynchronous wail of sirens in the distance, and she felt a shudder of unease. "Where are we going now?"

"We're going to get out of London for a day or two. Let's head back west, on the M3. And if you see a pharmacy along the way, stop."

Christine took another look at him. He was wearing a tweed jacket she'd never seen before. A small thing, she thought. He goes off wearing one jacket, comes back in another. There must be a harmless explanation. Then she noticed a dark stain on the sleeve. She pulled the car over.

"What are you doing?" he asked.

Christine replied by reaching over and gently coaxing the fabric up to his elbow, revealing a fresh wound.

"My God! What happened?"

"I took a round, but it's okay. I think it passed right through." He pulled his arm away.

"Well, your expert medical opinion aside, I should have a look at it."

"Keep driving. The bleeding has stopped, it's just sore. We'll be fine if we can put some distance between us and . . ."

Christine's stomach turned over.

"Go!" he insisted.

She pulled back onto the street. "All right. I'll keep going," she spat. "And maybe we can take a bullet out of that gun for you to bite down on. That's how you macho types deal with pain, right?" Christine's anger surged. "But while I drive, you tell me what happened back there. You go off without telling me where you're going or what you're doing, and then come back with a *gunshot*. If I'm being dragged into this, I want to know what's going on! Tell me or I'm leaving!"

He didn't say anything right away, and Christine glanced over at him. He was staring at her, concern evident through the scraggly beard that masked his face. Finally, he spoke. "You're correct, doctor. I was wrong not to include you. Maybe I thought the less you knew, the safer you'd be. But we're clearly past that now."

Christine eyed the bloodstain on his jacket and wondered what the other guy must look like.

"I went to see Hiram Varkal. He heads up the Mossad station here in London. I was guessing he had no part in this organization I've told you about, and I wanted to find out what he knew. If Varkal seemed safe, I was going to tell him everything so he could send it right to the top, to the Director himself."

"The last two Israelis you met up with didn't fare too well. Wasn't this guy a little nervous about meeting you?"

"He would have been if he'd known about it."

Christine listened intently as he explained how he'd cornered Varkal in the restaurant. He then went over their conversation and offered a brief version of the battle that ensued. She drove on in grim silence, acknowledging events she would never have thought possible two weeks ago. When Slaton was done, she realized things had gotten deeper yet.

"So you think you killed at least one of the three?"

"Yes," he replied evenly. "Maybe two. I had no choice. They'd drawn their guns."

The body count rises again, she thought. "What about this guy, Varkal? If he believed you, he'll pass on what you told him, right? And maybe he can convince the police you were acting in self-defense."

"No."

The reply was too simple, too quick. Then Christine understood. "You mean you killed *him?*"

Slaton shook his head, "I hit two of the security guys. But one of them took out Varkal."

"What?" She looked at him with disbelief, "Why would his own bodyguards shoot him?"

"Simple. Because he'd been talking to me."

Christine nearly ran a red light. She jammed on the brakes and the little car skidded just short of a crosswalk. Pedestrians moved cautiously in front of them, and an old man jabbed his cane at Christine with a disapproving stare. She held a deathgrip on the steering wheel. What else? she wondered. What more could happen?

She said, "Tomorrow this will be in every paper in England, won't it? Your picture and mine right next to it with a big question mark underneath."

"If my picture makes the paper, that's a very bad sign."

"I probably shouldn't ask, but why?"

"Because there aren't many photos of me," he said evenly, "and the ones that do exist are held by a particular agency of the Israeli government. The one that trained me to be what I am."

Christine considered that. "You mean the only official photos—"

"I mean the only pictures. No family albums, no vacation pictures, no Polaroids with my schoolmates. None of that. The ones that existed before I became a kidon were destroyed. That's how it works."

The light turned green and Christine drove on slowly, giving thought to what he'd just said. It all seemed so cold and cynical, even cruel in a way. It was yet another part of an existence she could never have imagined.

Slaton went on, "Granted, I've been a busy fellow for the last eight-

een years. It's possible our enemies might have snapped one or two can-
did photos. But if a mug shot shows up on the BBC evening news, it's
there courtesy of my government. It would mean the Mossad thinks I've
turned. They'd be throwing me to the wolves and they'll go after me
themselves. Hard. Governments don't like their disaffected assassins running around. Far too messy for — there!" he spat out, his head whipping
to one side.

Her heart spiked. "What?"

He pointed back to a sidestreet they'd just passed. "There was a pharmacy down that street. Turn around."

Christine breathed a sigh of relief and wheeled the car around. She
looked at his wounded arm. He seemed completely unbothered by it. She
remembered all the other scars she'd seen across his battered body. How
could anyone live such a life? And now she was being pulled into it. Again
she tried to imagine some way out.

Christine said, "If we went to the police and told them everything
right away, wouldn't that give you enough insurance?"

"Everything on my side is speculation. They can tie me to one dead
man, maybe more. They'll think I'm a lunatic, and before they figure out
otherwise — well, like I said, there are a lot of people who would be very
concerned if I were sitting in a jail cell answering questions."

She tried a new tack. "What about the newspapers? Go tell them
everything. Once it's made public, no one could come after you."

"Do you really think anyone would print something like this? Who
would believe it?"

Christine found a parking space directly in front of the pharmacy.
Who would believe it? she thought. Why do I believe it? The question
pounded in her mind. She had always thought herself to be an intelligent,
reasonable woman. A person of science and logic. But she did believe
him. He had kidnapped her. Twice. She had seen him kill a man, yet for
some damned reason she sensed that everything he told her was true.

She felt him watching her. It made her uncomfortable and she
forced herself to a new line of thought. Christine leaned toward him.

"Hold still," she said in her best professional voice. She pulled the
jacket carefully from his wounded arm, then unbuttoned his shirt cuff
and eased it back to get a better look at the wound. It would be impossible
to tell without an X-ray whether any part of the bullet remained in his

body, but she could clearly make out an entry wound on the anterior fore-arm, and an exit wound in back.

"We need to clean and dress this. Then we should get an X-ray to check for any damage we can't see."

"Hospitals are out for now, so let's just clean it and be done."

Christine frowned. She was mentally logging what she'd need from the pharmacy when she suddenly noticed their closeness. She felt his breath on her neck and her gaze shifted. With their faces only inches apart, the two locked eyes. He looked at her openly, for the first time with-out calculation, without the cold alertness that had permeated his every action. And then there was more. His expression seemed to hold familiar-ity, as if he was looking at someone else, someone he knew far more inti-mately. In the silence, Christine felt awkward. She pulled away.

"All right," she said, collecting herself. "I'll go get what we need to repair you. Something to cleanse the wound, gauze, tape. Maybe an over-the-counter pain medication. Anything else?"

"Yeah, get me a razor and some shaving cream."

"Okay."

As she grabbed the door handle, he reached out gently and held her by the wrist.

"Christine . . . I'm sorry about that. You reminded me of someone."

She nodded thoughtfully, then smiled. It was the first time he'd ever called her by her first name. "Well, I can honestly say that you don't re-mind me of anyone I've ever known."

He produced a thin smile of his own, but then, in a moment, it dis-appeared. He returned to his duty of evaluating all activity on the streets and sidewalks. The kidon was back as quickly as he'd gone.

"I don't like it," Chatham declared. Back in his Scotland Yard office after the midday train ride from Penzance, he held a copy of the police acci-dent report on the death of one Yosef Meier.

"I must say, sir, I really didn't see anything suspicious in it myself," Ian Dark offered.

"No, nothing suspicious. Nothing at all! This wasn't an investiga-tion. It was someone filling an administrative square." Chatham jabbed a finger at the bottom of one page, "See, only one eyewitness interviewed. One!" Chatham tossed it aside.

"It's been less than a week. Perhaps we should look into it ourselves."

Chatham shook his head. "I wish we could, but we can't deploy our forces too thinly. Right now it's only us and Mrs. Smythe. Which reminds me, has she reported in yet?"

"She had Chief Bickerstaff call in. Seems this entire affair has raised quite a row in Penzance. No less than a dozen locals have gone in to see Bickerstaff this morning, all of them claiming to have witnessed some part of what went on yesterday. One woman actually identified the BMW, but she saw it leaving the motel. Nothing we didn't already know. As for the transfer car, a number of people are certain they spotted it."

"And?"

"Could be anything from a black Lamborghini to a Tripley Bread van."

Chatham sighed. "What about Smythe?"

"She's still trying to identify the car our man switched to, using those tire imprints you pointed out. Bickerstaff was curious as to what drew you to those particular tracks. He says there were tire marks all over the place, a lot of them closer to the abandoned BMW."

Chatham shrugged, "A bit of logic, but mostly guesswork. All we have at the moment, I'm afraid. Smythe can probably identify the type of tire, but even then, they're all so common nowadays. If we find the right car we'll be able to match irregularities and prove where it's been."

"But first we have to find it," Dark said, realizing they weren't much beyond square one.

The telephone rang and Chatham wagged his long index finger in the air as he walked to pick it up. "This is what we need, I think." He picked up the handset, "Chatham here."

The conversation was a very one-sided affair. Chatham's eyes narrowed and his jaw tightened as he listened. At the end, he dispensed a few pleasantries and set the phone gingerly back on its cradle, silently ordering his thoughts.

"What's happened?" Dark asked.

The question broke Chatham's trance. "It was the Assistant Commissioner, about the meeting we were supposed to have this afternoon with the Israelis. A few hours ago he arranged it with a fellow named Hiram Varkal."

"Varkal? Who's he?"

"It's an ill-kept secret that he's Mossad's Chief of Station here in

London. Or, at least he *was*. Just after noon he was killed in a shootout. It happened at a restaurant in Knightsbridge, a few blocks from the embassy. One other Israeli was killed and a third wounded."

"Good Lord! They're dropping faster than we can count."

"Yes, and that's not all. It seems today's killer matches the description of our man quite nicely."

"The media will go wild."

"I think those were the Assistant Commissioner's very words. This business has become the Yard's top priority. The Commissioner himself has seen fit to name me as being in command of what is now a highly public investigation. I've authority to use any assets necessary to apprehend this fellow."

The phone rang again, and Chatham motioned for Dark to pick it up. He did, and after exchanging a few words he held the phone to his chest.

"It's Security down in the lobby. They say there's a throng of reporters outside looking for you. It seems the word is out that you've been put in charge of a big investigation and they want a statement. Apparently they're quite agitated."

Chatham checked the time. "Of course they are. The deadline is fast approaching to get something onto the evening news. Tell them we'll have a briefing in fifteen minutes."

Dark relayed the message.

Chatham went to the rack and retrieved his great coat. "Our manpower problem has gone, Ian. Let's call in the reserves. Get through to Inspector Grant, Homicide Division. He and his best five men will reopen the investigation of Yosef Meier's death. Call Shearer back and tell him to find out who's running Mossad affairs at the embassy now. I must see that person, tonight if possible. Get a half dozen people out to Penzance to help Smythe with anything she needs. Have forensics send . . ." Chatham snapped his fingers in the air, trying to remember the name, "Moore, yes, that's it. Sharp lad. Have him meet me right away at the Lo Fan Restaurant in Knightsbridge. That's where I'll be if you need me." Chatham strode to the door.

"But sir! You just scheduled a press briefing in fifteen minutes."

"Right," Chatham called over his shoulder. "And I'm sure you'll do a cracking good job."

❖　　❖　　❖

They arrived in Southampton at 4:30, Slaton at the wheel as they made their way through City Centre. Ten minutes earlier he had pointed out a hotel called The Excelsior, but the car didn't stop. They traveled two blocks away from the hotel, toward the waterfront, a blatantly mercantile trap anointed the Town Quay. From there, he circled back to The Excelsior, and eventually repeated the exercise from three different directions.

"Do we have to be that careful?" Christine asked as he finally pulled into a parking spot a block from the hotel.

"Just doing a little reconnaissance. It's quicker than walking." He shut off the engine, but left the keys in the ignition. "I'm going to see about a room. I'd like you to stay here. I'll explain when I get back."

She eyed him, "You'd better."

Slaton checked in as Henrik Edmunson, the name taken from his Danish passport and the associated credit card. He requested, in poor English, a room facing the front street, explaining that he and his wife had stayed in a similar room at The Excelsior years ago while on their honeymoon. The clerk seemed troubled by the request, explaining that availability was minimal, but he eventually found an acceptable room at a ruinous price. Slaton made a show of flinching at the cost, but took the room anyway, a dutiful husband determined to show his wife that there was still some romance left in the old boy. Once registered, he went to the room, spent fifteen minutes inside, then headed back to the car.

Christine realized she was acquiring a number of disturbing new habits. She found herself watching men and women, even children on the sidewalks, trying to decide who might be paying her too much attention. She resisted an urge to move to the driver's seat, not wanting to succumb to paranoia. She spotted David instantly as he rounded the corner. He climbed into the driver's seat.

"All right," he said, "there are two reasons for our being here. First, we need to let the world quietly pass us by for a day or two. We'll read newspapers and watch the BBC to see just how much trouble we're in."

Christine moaned, never having been in trouble before on a national, newsworthy scale.

"Second, I can't get to the bottom of all this without freedom of movement. I've got to be able to travel. The documents I'm using now were issued by Mossad. In theory, there were no records kept, so they shouldn't be traceable to me."

"But you think that's not the case?"

"I think we need to find out. The people after me know I'm running. They know I need documentation and they'll try to uncover it. Until now, the only thing I've used this identity for is the car. Knowing about it would help them, but only so far. It's a moving target. Now I've used the credit card to check into a hotel."

"So they might be able to find us here."

"They won't find us because we won't be at The Excelsior." He pulled out a wad of twenty-pounds notes and peeled off a dozen. "Here. There's another hotel right across the street from The Excelsior. It's called Humphrey Hall. Go there and get a room. It has to face The Excelsior and be on the second or third floor."

"I can't use my own name, can I?"

"No, just pick one you'll remember, a friend's name. Something you'll recognize if a clerk calls as you're passing by. You won't have ID, but if they do ask, be reluctant, tell them you'll have to go back to your car and get it. If they persist, tell them you're going to get it, come straight back here and we'll leave."

Christine sighed. She felt like a student taking Espionage 101.

He continued, "Honestly, I don't think ID will be a problem. I suspect it's the kind of place that won't ask much as long as you're paying cash up front. It's just best to think these things out ahead of time."

"Of course."

"Once you get the room, go straight to it. Open the window halfway and draw the curtains half closed. That way I'll know what room you're in. I won't come up right away, I've got some things to do. It should take a couple of hours."

Christine grew anxious, remembering the last time he went off on his own.

"Don't worry. I've just got to do something with this car."

"And what's the secret knock for me to let you in?" she queried, trying to lighten the mood.

His reply was humorless, "I'll just knock and tell you it's me. The people we're worried about wouldn't bother knocking at all."

David had been right about getting the room at Humphrey Hall. Once the clerk had cash in hand, he produced a key and a simple registration card on which Christine hastily scribbled the pseudonym Carla Fluck.

Carla had been one of her best high school friends, a girl who married badly soon after graduation, some thought simply to escape so many years of adolescent suffering under the weight of her unfortunate maiden name.

The stairs to the second floor creaked as Christine made her way up. It was the kind of place that would be granted "character" or "old-world charm" by the more generous tourist guides. The room turned out to be old and damp, like the rest of the building, but reasonably clean. It was a suite, one main room facing the street, and a separate bedroom and bath to one side. She arranged the window and drapes in the main room to the proper configuration, then looked down to the street. Christine knew David was out there somewhere. She couldn't see him, but he was there, perhaps watching right now. It was oddly comforting.

She decided to take a shower, knowing he'd be gone for a while. She closed the bathroom door and was about to lock it when she remembered what had happened on *Windsom* — the look on his face when he had burst in and seen her naked. He had stared for just a moment, a shocked, confused look on his face until he finally turned away. He'd expected to find her up to no good, brandishing some newfound weapon or a radio. Instead, he had miscalculated, his surprise compounded by Christine's indecent state and his own obvious lack of trust. Christine thought about that. Things had certainly changed. Through all the madness she was sure of one thing about David Slaton — he trusted her now. He had left her alone in the car. Right now she could be sitting in this very room with a police contingent, awaiting the arrival of a thoroughly dangerous man. But he trusted her. And so much of what he had told her seemed to make sense.

Earlier, she'd found herself staring at the phone, seriously considering a call to her mother, who had to be worried sick by now. David had specifically warned her against it, reasoning that any angst her mother was going through now was nothing compared to the mourning of a dead child, which might be the case if any traced calls gave away their location.

Humphrey Hall compensated for its lack of ambiance by having an abundant supply of hot water. Christine soaked in the shower for a full twenty minutes, allowing the warm, high-pressure stream to work deep into her muscles. She let her mind wander home, contemplating what she might be doing in a week or a month; sooner or later the nightmare would end and she could get back to her life. A rotation to all-night shifts in the ER would seem mundane now. Christine followed with even better thoughts. Home with her mother cooking Christmas dinner; having coffee, bagels, and aimless, giggling banter with her sisters at Le Café Blanc.

When Christine left the shower, clouds of steam permeated the suite and meandered out the half-open window in the next room. On the bed, she opened her small rollerbag, the one David had bought for her at a secondhand store. They hadn't purchased any clothes specifically to sleep in, so she put on a loose-fitting pair of cotton sweatpants and a T-shirt, also from the secondhand store. It was gloriously comfortable. Christine didn't take anything else out of the suitcase and she repacked the dirty clothes she'd been wearing earlier. *Never leave anything behind without reason. Always be ready to go on a moment's notice.* Reluctantly, she was learning.

She went to the living room and relaxed on a couch, wondering what other diversions might work. The phone still beckoned, but she'd promised not to try. The morning's local newspaper sat on a table by the door, but that wouldn't do. It would undoubtedly contain an article she had no interest in seeing at the moment. The same went for the television. Christine envisioned two grainy photos behind a news anchor, one of her and one of David. *"Be on the lookout for these two outlaws . . ."* Just like Bonnie and Clyde. Had it gone that far yet? She didn't want to know.

Christine felt a chill as brisk evening air began to settle in through the window. She wondered if it would be all right to close it. Surely David had seen the signal by now. With a sigh, she decided to leave it open. She retrieved a blanket from the bedroom, settled back on the couch and tried to drift toward the good thoughts.

The knock roused her from a deep sleep. It took a few moments for Christine to orient herself. She glanced at her watch and saw it was nearly ten o'clock in the evening. Another gentle knock.

She got up and made her way to the door, keeping the blanket wrapped around her shoulders to ward off the cold that had descended on the room. Her eyes were narrow slits as they adjusted to the light and her hair lay severely askew, having dried while she slept. She opened the door without asking who it might be.

When he saw her, he grinned.

"What's so funny?" she said.

"Nothing. It's just that you look . . ." Slaton paused and the grin suddenly disappeared.

"What? Is something wrong?"

He seemed uncomfortable. "No. No, never mind." He eased by her into the room. "It's cold in here."

Christine wondered what that was all about. Since he was obviously trying to change the subject, she decided not to pursue it.

"I know. I wasn't sure if I should close the window."

Slaton moved around the room, turning out all the lights. When he was done, only one shaft of light remained, emanating from the adjoining bedroom. Next he went to the window and closed it, leaving the drapes halfway open.

"Sorry, it's my fault," he said. "You're not used to this kind of thing. I should have told you to close this up after an hour. You did the safe thing, though. That's good."

"You'll make a spy out of me yet," she mused.

Slaton looked out the window and beckoned Christine over with his hand. He pointed across to The Excelsior. "See the room directly across? The one with the light on?"

"On the third floor?"

"Right. It's a suite like this one. A living area and one bedroom, only the bedroom has a window as well, off to the right, see?"

"Sure." The lights were off in the bedroom, but Christine could see the vague outline of a big bed and a few pieces of furniture. "Compared to Humphrey Hall it looks a bit more . . . I think the English would say, posh? Next time let's do this the other way around."

"Next time."

"So now what? You think if these people can trace you to The Excelsior that they'll come looking for us?"

"If they can trace the documents, then yes, I'm sure of it."

"That could take days, couldn't it?"

"Possibly. But like I said, we have to stay out of sight anyway. This way we use the time productively."

"So you're just going to sit there and watch?"

"I know it sounds boring, but that's what people like me spend a lot of time doing. Why don't you get some more sleep. Sorry I had to wake you."

His eyes were alternating now between the room at The Excelsior and the street below. Christine looked at his profile in the dim light. His beard was thickening, each day's growth further eclipsing his facial features. Only the eyes were clearly visible, and they were obscure in their own way, seldom giving insight to the soul beneath. Christine went back to the couch and got comfortable.

"You've got to rest sometime, too," she said. "Wake me in a couple of hours and I'll take a shift."

"All right," he replied.

She knew he wouldn't.

There was no noise this time, but rather a hand on her shoulder, a gentle squeeze. The room was completely dark, but Christine's night vision was well adapted. She saw him move to the window. He said nothing, but curled his index finger to draw her over. She got up against her body's weary protest, and went to stand next to him.

His attention was fixed on the room at The Excelsior. Christine studied it closely but saw nothing new. It was vacant and still, the lights burning steady in the main room. Suddenly she was afraid. Bile began to churn in her stomach. Then it happened.

Two men burst in the door. They were wearing ski masks and had weapons leveled, sweeping across the room in search of a target. Within seconds they ran to the unlit bedroom. Christine jerked involuntarily as a faint strobe of light lit the bedroom for an instant, followed by a half dozen more. She knew it was from the guns, but there was no sound. Even from this far away there should have been some kind of sound. The guns must have been silenced.

A light came on in the bedroom as one of the men went to the bed and threw back the covers, revealing two long sets of pillows. Something like snow seemed to be floating eerily over the bed, and Christine realized it was a cloud of feathers, remnants of the bedding that had just been annihilated. The two men saw they'd been taken. They looked around the room frantically, then glanced out the window toward the street. Christine knew there was no chance she and Slaton could be seen in their dark nook, but she froze instinctively. The gunmen exchanged a few hasty words, then left the room as quickly as they'd entered, turning out the lights and closing the door neatly behind.

Christine could do nothing but stare at the darkened windows across the street. Whatever doubts had remained were now gone. She had just witnessed her own execution.

The world seemed to spin and then a strange vibrating sensation caused her to look down. Her hands, shaking uncontrollably, were enveloped in his. She took a few deep breaths to calm herself.

Slaton brought a thumb and forefinger up, gently lifting her chin until she met his gaze.

"We have to go now," he whispered.

Christine nodded. Her reply was even and controlled. "Yes. We do."

Chapter Eleven

It was nearly midnight as a lone Chevy Suburban crept across the Libyan Desert south of Tripoli. To go any faster was out of the question. The "road," as it was referred to locally, was in miserable shape. Recent heavy rains had added deep ruts to the already rocky trail surface. It was more of a path, really, an old trader's route that meandered through the desert in such a way as to avoid the highest hills and the deepest *wadis*. With no moon to help, the desert was particularly dark, and the big truck's headlights bounced along through the surrounding blackness, illuminating only the most obvious trouble spots.

The driver kept to his pace. In the rear, Colonel Muhammed Al-Quatan frowned impatiently. The fact that they were three hours late could easily be blamed on the flight that had been so annoyingly behind schedule in delivering their guest. None of the truck's occupants knew their good fortune — it was the closest Libyan Air Flight 113 from Paris had been to being on time all week.

The driver brought the big vehicle to a crunching halt. Since leaving Tripoli there had been constant banter between the two Arab men in front, and now with a fork looming in the road ahead, they began to argue over navigation, each pointing adamantly in a different direction. Colonel Al-Quatan interjected in rapid-fire Arabic, his authoritative tone doing more to settle the dispute than his words. The driver gloated obviously and the pounding journey resumed.

Al-Quatan settled back into his seat, idly wondering where they found some of these imbeciles. Many of the newest ones were almost children, a fact that would unbalance any sense of right or honor in a more conventional commander. But this was not a conventional war, and no commander could ignore the arsenal they provided. That odd, almost divine self-discipline that let them walk into a crowded café with five kilos of high explosives strapped to their chests. Al-Quatan knew he had such men and women in his camp. Unfortunately, for every one of *them* he had ten idiots like the ones up front, a fact that constantly sidetracked him from more important matters. He glowered silently, just waiting for one of them to make another mistake. If they made fools of themselves again, he would take the butt of his pistol and make a very sorry example out of somebody.

Al-Quatan took another discreet look at the truck's fourth occupant, who sat beside him, the one he'd been sent to retrieve. Since leaving Tripoli, the man had been quiet. His round, dark eyes were now cast aimlessly out the window, looking for — *what?* A way out? It was too late for that. A friend? Not for a thousand miles, if there were any left. Perhaps just a rock to crawl under. At least he'd had the balls to come, Al-Quatan thought. Or perhaps he was just scared out of his mind. The man's physical appearance was not in keeping with his post. He was a sergeant in the Israeli Defense Forces, yet looked nothing like a soldier. Probably five-foot-five, he carried forty extra pounds in all the wrong places. His eyes and hair were dark, yet his skin pale and taut — a man who spent little time outside an air-conditioned office cubicle. Al-Quatan thought he looked soft, like a large spoiled child who'd been ruined by too many trips to the sweetshop, not a square-jawed warrior from Aman, Israel's vaunted military intelligence arm. Shrewd and cunning, then? Clearly not, based on the hole he'd dug for himself.

No, Al-Quatan had been blessed by Allah with a knack for sizing up people, and this one was a weakling. Clay ready for firm hands to mold. Perhaps the Zionists weren't ten feet tall after all. At any rate, he had at least been respectful, which was more than Al-Quatan usually got from foreigners. In particular, he disliked the Europeans. The French, the Germans, the Brits — they were all so maddeningly arrogant. But the dog sitting across from him had its tail between its legs, and Al-Quatan couldn't wait to see him squirm under Moustafa Khalif's merciless heel.

The Colonel took out a pack of Marlboros, tapped the box until one protruded, then held it out to the Israeli. It was a gesture of kindness akin to what a condemned man might get from the commander of his firing squad.

The man's eyes focused on the offer. "No, thank you," he muttered in rapid English.

Al-Quatan shrugged, took one for himself, lit up, and took a long draw. He wore a very satisfied expression. "We are nearly there," Al-Quatan announced. "Moustafa Khalif wishes to see you right away."

Sergeant Pytor Roth nodded and straightened up in his seat. He looked out across the Libyan desert, still unable to detect any lights on the horizon. There hadn't been any for over two hours. The drive from Tripoli had been longer than expected, but then the roads were in abysmal shape. From the airport he knew they'd gone south toward Marzuq on what was one of the few high-quality roads in the country. Eventually they'd turned onto a semi-improved dirt road and made reasonably good time. The last hour, though, had found them traveling on a surface that was far better suited to camels than large sport utility vehicles. It was another glaring disconnect in a country that seemed to be trying to catch up with the rest of civilization in one giant leap. Roth mused at the progress represented by the big black Chevy Suburban. The Americans might be infidels, but exceptions were apparently made for reliable transportation. Twenty years ago it would have been a rattle-trap Russian Zhil limousine. And twenty before that, strictly dromedary.

The flight from Paris had been equally strange. Absent were the Italian suits and gold-trimmed briefcases. Those few legitimate businessmen who ventured here generally preferred the big European carriers. The passengers on Libya's state airline had been young students, weary vacationers, and a significant contingent of swarthy characters who seemed to eye one another continuously. Each was no doubt engaged in his or her own brand of illicit behavior, and the specter of professional overlap had weighed heavily throughout coach; the black market, smuggling, and terrorism were a way of life in these parts.

Roth looked at his watch and wondered how much deeper into this godforsaken sandbox they'd have to go. He'd seen Libya in satellite photos, yet Roth never imagined he'd get to see it up close. He wondered idly what corner of the country they were in now, but the thought passed quickly. Knowing wouldn't do him any good. The possibility of escape was nil. He was deep inside the Libyan Desert, in the hands of his sworn

enemies. And he was about to make them an incredible offer. If they accepted, Roth would be driven back to the airport with the promise of becoming a wealthy man. If they refused, he wouldn't see the light of the
next morning.

His hand squeezed the armrest on the door and he wondered for the
thousandth time how he'd gotten himself into this mess. He felt like a
pawn in a chess game, only he was neither black nor white — simply a
lone, errant piece trying to exist between two battling armies. Still, there
was a chance. Roth could survive, maybe even profit if it all worked out.
All he had to do was talk. He'd always been good at that, and he already
knew what to say. If they believed his offer was legitimate, and of course it
was, the only question would be price.

Al-Quatan shifted forward in his seat and peered through the front
windshield. The Colonel then leaned back and used his thumbs to tuck
in some loose shirt around his waistline. They were getting close.

Nothing about the journey had really surprised Roth so far, nor had
anything about Colonel Al-Quatan. He was a short, compact man, with
the olive skin tone so common among the Bir al-Sab Bedouins of the
Negev region. He sported a thick black mustache, and a bristle of close-
cropped hair served as base for his maroon beret. The shoes were gleaming, the fatigues pressed and heavily starched. To complete the package, a
leather holster was wrapped around his ample midsection, one hip displaying a large caliber ivory-handled revolver, the other a satellite phone.
Roth knew the colonel's commission was self-appointed, never having
been issued by any particular country or army. But he was, without doubt,
the organization's military commander, and he had no hesitation in
flaunting the title of rank, as had been the case earlier when introducing
himself at the airport.

The truck rounded a hill and a small city of tents appeared. The area
was well lit, the tents grouped tightly together. Roth saw laundry hanging
from lines between tent poles. A large pile of trash had accumulated off to
one side of the complex. They had obviously been here for weeks, if not
months. It was a place where they felt safe. Roth wished he had some kind
of mental navigation device. The coordinates of this place might be worth
a lot to the right people.

The Suburban neared the perimeter of the compound and its headlights illuminated two men sitting next to the road on an overturned fifty-
five gallon drum. One stood up lazily and Roth was surprised to see, of all

things, an Israeli-made Uzi strapped loosely across his chest. The other man didn't even get up, his Russian weapon leaning on a rock, its butt in the sand. These would be the guards. The one who was standing smiled and waved at the familiar truck, which passed without stopping.

Al-Quatan gave a directive to the driver in Arabic. Roth correctly interpreted the command and a surge of adrenaline jolted through his body. They were going directly to Khalif's tent. Roth was not fluent in Arabic, especially given the numerous dialects, but he had a basic knowledge of the language, a fact he would certainly keep to himself for the next day or so.

Al-Quatan looked away for a moment and Roth quickly wiped a mist of perspiration from his upper lip. It was going to happen fast now, the balance of his life to be determined in the next twenty minutes. He had to keep his wits.

The Suburban stopped sharply in front of a large, centrally located tent.

"Stay here," Al-Quatan ordered Roth. The colonel got out of the car, disappeared into the billowing tent for less than a minute, then returned.

"Moustafa Khalif will see you now. Abu will take your bag."

Roth followed Al-Quatan to the tent. At the entrance were two armed men, these more serious and professional than the ones on the perimeter. It only made sense that Khalif would have his best men nearby. They gave their Israeli guest a rough pat down and a hard stare, then ushered Roth inside as Al-Quatan followed.

In the tent, Roth found a random, asynchronous atmosphere. Plywood floors were partially covered by ornate carpets. A scattered assortment of chairs, couches, and tables were strewn about the place, none seeming to match. A Louis Quinze desk was shoved into one corner, and on top was a ten-gallon jerry can with the word PETROL stenciled in big block letters. A large crystal chandelier hung from the center of the tent's frame, half its light bulbs burned out.

The two security men took up post at the entrance, out of earshot, but with a clear line of sight toward the Israeli. Roth was sure their aim was excellent. Al-Quatan moved off to one side and stood silently. Only then did Roth notice the other person in the room. He rose from a plush sultan's chair, a tall man with huge olive eyes, a salt-and-pepper beard, and weathered features. Roth recognized him instantly. The man's arms outstretched in greeting and, dressed in the traditional Arab *jellabah*, his robe flowed outward, giving the appearance of a huge bird airing its wings.

"Mr. Roth, I am Moustafa Khalif. I am pleased that you have come."

Roth nodded politely, noticing Khalif made no effort to amplify his greeting with any of the traditional physical add-ons — no Arabic embrace or Western handshake. He looked much like the photos Roth had seen so often in the newspapers back home, perhaps older, a bit grayer.

"I hope your journey was not a difficult one," Khalif said. His English was measured and deliberate, almost without accent.

"Not difficult, just long," Roth said.

"Good. I know we are not conveniently located, but you can understand our reasons." Khalif waved a wing toward an open chair. "Please have a seat."

Roth chose a sturdy dinner chair as a man in an ill-fitting white servant's jacket presented a tray of tea. So far, so good.

"Traveling. There is something I am no longer able to do. When I was a child, my parents took me to Italy and Austria. The Sistine Chapel, Vienna, the Alps. I remember it like it was yesterday."

Khalif gave a wistful sigh and Roth tried to imagine the terrorist as a child. He couldn't.

"Here, I am a prisoner, surrounded by a desert and a people that are not my own. Still, we are safe, and for the moment that is important. From this place we can pursue our freedom, and someday, if it should be the will of Allah, we will return home. Perhaps then I can travel once again."

Roth wondered if Khalif really believed it. He sipped his tea with a level gaze, not sure where this was headed.

"Where are you from, Roth? What part of Palestine?"

The bait was obvious and Roth decided the Arab was testing him. "Haifa," he said. "And it hasn't been called Palestine for a long, long time."

Khalif's eyes narrowed, a hawk gliding above its prey, deciding when to strike. Roth tried to hold steady under the piercing stare. The isolation of his tactical situation suddenly seemed overwhelming. He was alone, unarmed, and surrounded by the enemy. He took another sip of tea, trying to gather his wits. Meandering wouldn't be to his advantage, so he moved right to the point.

"Did you view the loading process in South Africa?"

Khalif paused before answering, obviously deciding if this was where he wanted the conversation to proceed. He relented. "Of course. We sent one of our best agents. He photographed the loading and we have studied the evidence."

Roth knew, in fact, that Khalif had rushed his nephew, Fareed, down to South Africa. Hopelessly inept, but completely trustworthy, Fareed had been the only one to meet both requirements — the proper documents to travel on short notice, and a rudimentary knowledge of photography. Roth was also aware that Khalif's technical range for photo surveillance and imagery interpretation was nothing beyond Fuji film and a magnifying glass.

Khalif continued, "The cargo was in canisters. How do we know what you say about them is true?"

"You saw my partner there. And the kidon. What else would Israel be taking out of South Africa with that kind of secrecy?"

"I would not venture a guess," Khalif said dryly.

Roth reached under the lapel of his jacket. He sensed a brush of motion from the two security men by the door. He gave the guards a plaintive look as he slowly pulled out an envelope and handed it to Khalif.

Khalif found four photographs in the envelope. He laid them out on a table and gestured for Al-Quatan to join in. The two men studied the photos carefully for a few moments. Roth watched their expressions intently.

"How can we be sure?" Al-Quatan said in a harsh whisper.

"My associate inspected them before they were canistered," Roth explained. "He also took these pictures for my government. It wasn't easy to get copies."

Khalif looked at the photos again, then asked, "Where are they now?"

"At the bottom of the Atlantic Ocean."

The two Arabs looked at one another in amazement.

"Imbecile!" Al-Quatan exploded. "You said you would—"

Khalif cut him off with a sharp wave.

"You must be patient," Roth said.

"How?" Khalif wondered. "How will it be done?"

Roth told them how the weapons would be retrieved, his eyes dart-

ing back and forth between his customers. The explanation seemed to settle Al-Quatan and eventually drew a smile across Khalif's thin lips. Roth
could tell he liked the plan.

"And you also have the technical data?"

"Of course. That was part of our agreement. But there is one thing,"
Roth added, his voice cracking just slightly. "It has become more expensive than I thought. I'll need more money."

Khalif raised an eyebrow, but it was Al-Quatan who spoke angrily.
"We have already agreed on a fair price! You are in no position to negotiate!"

Roth looked at Khalif, pointedly ignoring the underling. "The cost
of executing our plan is greater than I expected. And afterwards, it will be
very difficult, very costly for my friend and I to disappear. You know how
my country can be about tracking down its enemies."

Khalif turned away. Clasping his hands behind his back, he moved
slowly across the room. Roth felt his heart pulse. Sweat began to bead
again.

When Khalif turned back, the wrath in his eyes and the hiss of his
voice were venomous as he leveled a finger at Roth. "You are not an enemy to your country! An enemy fights with honor. You are a traitor! And
you and your friend would betray me as quickly as you have betrayed your
own people. I will pay the agreed upon amount. Half soon, then half
when we have received the shipment and verified it to be authentic. What
happens to you afterwards, I do not care. But trust in this — if either of
you attempt to deceive us in any way, we will come for you. And we will
give evidence to your own country that you have betrayed them."

Al-Quatan laughed, "For once Palestine and the Zionist pigs would
be united in a cause. That of finding and destroying two wretched little
weasels."

Khalif was apparently finished with his outburst and Roth stayed
calm. A gradual smirk came across the Arab's face and he clapped his
hands twice.

From behind, Roth heard a familiar, sultry woman's voice, "*Mmm,
Pytor. It's been so long.*"

Roth turned to see Avetta. She looked better than ever, her silken
black hair framing classic features and flawless skin. The layers of her robe
could not hide the full, ripe young body that swayed beneath. Sweeping

by Roth, she looked just as she had the first day he'd seen her, almost a year ago, only now the expression was different. The chin a bit higher, the black oval eyes no longer innocent but knowing, and her full lips showed the hint of a smile. She moved beside Khalif, victorious.

"I believe you know one another," Khalif prodded.

Roth frowned, briefly wondering what her real name might be. He was also curious as to why Khalif had seen the need for her presence. "You don't have to prove your point," he said.

"I think I do," Khalif countered. "I think it is important that you know exactly where you stand." Khalif produced his own small stack of photographs and handed them to Avetta. She walked over to Roth and held up a few for the Israeli to see. Grainy and undeniable, they'd been taken in a cheap hotel in Beirut, showing the two of them engaged in various acts of indiscretion. Roth looked right past the photographs as Avetta waved them tauntingly in front of him.

"I've seen them before."

"Some of them," Khalif said. "There are others. But this thing you do for us now, there is little evidence of it. Understand, traitor, we can give these to your government at any time, along with samples of the documents you passed on to us. You were very cooperative when your paramour asked for these things."

"I was cooperative with a prostitute who was blackmailing me."

Avetta dropped the photographs and slapped Roth hard across the face. The room was silent for a moment before Colonel Al-Quatan started to laugh. Avetta gave him a hard look that was mirrored by Khalif, and Al-Quatan's humor evaporated.

"A prostitute acts for money," Khalif spat, "but not my Seema. She had a far more honorable purpose, and she succeeded magnificently."

"Your who?" Roth queried.

"Seema is my eldest daughter. Doesn't it make the pictures even more meaningful? You, a sergeant in Aman, a married father of four, taken by the daughter of your country's most bitter enemy."

Roth was caught off guard, amazed that Khalif could use his own daughter in such a way. He'd never understand the things these people did in the name of religion. Holy War was enough of an oxymoron, but this was new territory.

"I understand my position," Roth admitted. "As of today, my career in the Israeli army is over. I'm a deserter." And an ex-husband, he thought, even though the marriage had been cold for years. "A successful outcome is more important to me than you. It's my only chance."

"Good. Then we understand each other."

Seema was dismissed and Roth felt the worst was over when Khalif and Al-Quatan pursued the details of the financial transfer. Finally, they discussed how the delivery would take place. Roth's idea bred hesitation at first, but Al-Quatan liked it, so Khalif consented. "It's the safest way," Roth said of the transfer. Then he tried to sound casual in reciting the precise words he'd been forced to practice a hundred times.

"Keep in mind, these are highly complex devices, not to mention valuable. I trust you've made plans as to how you'll handle them once they're yours?"

Al-Quatan answered. "We have made all the arrangements. Security and technical help will be the best."

Roth nodded and Khalif raised his voice to summon the two guards. "Escort Sergeant Roth to his quarters. He will return to Tripoli in the morning."

As he left, Khalif reminded him, "Nine days, Mr. Roth. Nine days."

The makeshift control room was set up in the officers' mess aboard *Hanit*. The room had been chosen for logistical reasons — adequate electrical supply, good ventilation, and right next door was the ship's hardened Weapons and Maneuver Control Center. The ship's officers were not consulted, most finding out at the evening meal that their lone retreat had been commandeered by the annoyingly chipper little man who had boarded two days earlier in Marseille. Paul Mordechai had transformed the dark, formally decorated dining area into an entropic scattering of equipment and wires.

The ship's captain looked over Mordechai's shoulder as he sat glued to a video monitor. The sprightly engineer had been in the same seat for over three hours, yet showed no lack of patience or enthusiasm. He wore a headset with a boom microphone and his face was illuminated by the machine's flickering glow.

The ROV was a "fly out" model. Sent to the bottom on an umbilical, it then separated and took guidance signals out to two hundred meters. A 50-watt quartz halogen light was boresighted to track the digital camera, and images were transmitted to the docking rig, then relayed top-side by way of the umbilical.

To the uninitiated, the pictures might have seemed relentlessly monotonous. The flat mud on the ocean floor had almost no contour, like the moon without craters. The highlights for the last hour had included a crumpled beer can that looked like it might have been there since World War II, and a pair of undulating worms who poked their heads out of the muck, miniature cobras swaying to the song of some unseen charmer.

"Shouldn't we have found something by now?" the captain asked.

"Needle in a haystack, Captain."

"But we're still getting two good signals from those beacons. Strong signals."

Mordechai manipulated a joystick and the view on the monitor began a shift to the right. "Just makes the haystack smaller, needles don't get any bigger."

The captain frowned.

"Our biggest problem is stability." Mordechai pointed to the display. "Your ship is drifting. Not much, but enough to screw up our search matrix. We can only use the engines to adjust forward and aft. I could make a better system. Put a differential GPS on the drone, something to compare its exact position and drift relative to the ship. Then we'd install some side thrusters with digital control on *Hanit* and write up software to automate the corrections. The way it is now, with everything done manually and only one axis of movement, by the time we correct one way, the drone is drifting to the other. Ends up with divergent oscillations. Same thing can happen in aircraft flight control software."

"How comforting," the captain deadpanned, obviously lost.

Mordechai smiled and keyed his microphone, "Ten forward."

In the adjoining control room a lieutenant engaged the screws to push a thousand tons of warship gently ahead, then reversed them momentarily to stop.

"Still seems to me we should have found something by now. *Polaris Venture* was 150 feet along the waterline. Even if she broke up, there ought to be some pretty big pieces down there."

Mordechai had no reply, primarily because he was more and more bedeviled by the same question. They had locked onto both beacons, getting good signals every thirty minutes. By his own calculations, considering antennae errors and thermal deviations, there was a ninety percent chance that *Polaris Venture* was within a two-square-kilometer area on the ocean floor below. They had covered that entire search box once already and found nothing. The other ten percent was weighing greatly on Mordechai when he finally saw something.

"There!" he shouted.

A grainy, squarish image appeared on the monitor.

Mordechai yelled into his microphone, "Mark one!" He worked the joystick furiously, repeatedly pressing a button that took magnified pictures of the image almost two miles below. Rocking nervously in his chair, he now understood why *Polaris Venture* had been so hard to find. "Where's the other one? Where's the other?" he mumbled.

"I don't know what that is you've found," the captain said, "but it's not part of a ship. At least not any part I recognize."

Mordechai held his drone directly over the small box, then tilted upward so the camera and beam of light spread out level across the bottom. He then slowly rotated to the left. The small cone of illumination arced across a barren submarine landscape, a tiny lighthouse in one of the world's darkest corners. After ninety degrees of rotation he stopped and zoomed in.

"There," Mordechai said.

Another object, a twin to the first, came into view.

"Mark two, bearing three-three-zero, ten meters from mark one. Captain, have the radio operator stand by for a secure uplink. We've got a very important message to send."

"That's it? I thought we were looking for a ship."

"We are," said a dispirited Mordechai. "But we won't find it here."

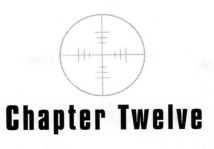

Chapter Twelve

Christine guided the small Ford through Dorset countryside as they made their way back to the region where the odyssey had begun, the rural Celtic counties of the southwest coast. They had abandoned the rented Peugeot in Southampton, leaving it a few blocks from The Excelsior in a crowded lot. How David had acquired this car was a mystery to Christine. It seemed mechanically sound, but was frightful to look at. Probably twenty years old, it seemed held together by an amalgam of rust and putty. The back window was plastered over with stickers, supporting the likes of the Green Party and a musical group called Throbbing Gristle. The odometer had simply stopped working at 217,768 and both rear fenders displayed damage from what looked like two separate incidents, although Slaton had assured Christine that all required lights and vital moving parts were functional. She guessed that he'd stolen the car, hoping no one would miss it, or perhaps figuring the owner was likely a budding criminal or an anarchist, the type of person who would avoid any intentional contact with the police.

David was asleep in the passenger seat. Christine had offered to drive, knowing there was no way she'd be able to get any rest. The image of two masked men and the flashes of their weapons kept flooding her thoughts. Once again her protector seemed to be a step ahead of these madmen, but how long could it last? She heard David rustle, as he'd done time and again over the last two hours. He wasn't sleeping well, but Christine suspected it had nothing to do with what had gone on at The Excelsior. His eyes opened groggily.

"Where are we?" he asked, with a glance at his watch.

"Almost to Dorchester."

He straightened up and stretched. "You made good time."

"Feel any better after the rest?"

"Sure."

Christine thought he still looked tired. In the days she'd been with him he'd never slept more than a few hours at a time. That wasn't good. She'd worked enough twenty-four hour shifts in her residency to know that recurring lack of sleep could seriously cloud a person's judgment.

"So where did you find this beauty?" she asked with a glance up at the ripped headliner. "Is it hot?"

He laughed, "You mean stolen? No, I bought her fair and square. Nine hundred pounds sterling."

"The seller won. Who was he?"

"A young kid. Heroin addict, I think. Wanted to sell the car fast, probably for a quick fix. Once I offered cash, he signed it right over. I made a copy of the papers, then sent off the registration, but I neglected to sign at the bottom. Some clerk will see the mistake in a couple of days and send it back to an address that doesn't exist. It will all take time, and for a few days we'll have a beat-up car that's been legitimately signed over to us."

"Whose name is it in?"

"Yours."

"Mine?" she exclaimed.

"Well, Carla Fluck's."

Christine smiled, and then from somewhere deep within a laugh emerged, followed by another and another. It was contagious and he succumbed until both were laughing uncontrollably. It felt good, and Christine realized that even through all their troubles, all the death and deception, there could still be laughter. There could still be life.

She sized him up.

"What?" he asked, clearly wondering what was on her mind.

"Oh, I've just never seen you laugh like that. I suppose I thought a person like you would always be . . . serious or something."

"A person like me?" he said, his voice harsh. "A killer, you mean. That kind of person."

"No, I didn't mean—"

"Oh, yes, we're serious. One has to be when all you do is go around killing people all day. But we do all the rest. We laugh, cry, feel pain, a whole spectrum of emotions."

Christine fixed her gaze on the road ahead, not sure what to say. The ensuing silence was stifling.

"I'm sorry," he finally said. "I don't know where that came from."

"You don't have to explain. I know how much pressure I feel like *I've* been under. I never stopped to think that you might—"

"Get ready to turn off!" he interrupted.

"What?" She noticed he was concentrating on the side mirror. Christine looked back and saw a pair of headlights in the distance behind them. A chill spiked down her back and her grip on the wheel tightened.

"Is someone following us?"

"Probably not." The little Ford went around a curve and the headlights behind disappeared temporarily. "Turn! Turn there!" he said, pointing to a small gravel side road.

Christine braked quickly and swerved onto the road.

"Take it in another fifty feet, up next to those bushes. Kill the lights and put it in park." Christine did as he instructed. "Make sure your foot's off the brake pedal or else the brake lights will stay on."

Christine moved her foot as far away as she could and they both sat in silence. A long ten seconds later the car whipped by behind them, showing no signs of slowing.

"Okay, turn us around and be ready to go."

Christine extracted the car from the side road, did a three point turn, and backed into their hiding spot. They sat silently for nearly ten minutes, the little Ford's feeble engine idling.

"All right," he finally said, "we're safe. Let's press on."

Christine let out a deep breath. "You haven't told me where we're going."

"We're going to put some distance between ourselves and The Excelsior. We still need to get lost for a day or two, and I think I know just the place.

Prime Minister Jacobs' morning staff meeting ended at 10:00. He had tried to show interest in the daily crises briefed by his various Cabinet members and their underlings. More Katyusha rockets flinging in from the Lebanese border, a severe influenza outbreak in the primary schools, and the Americans again. This time their Senate had tied up an international aid bill, threatening the start of the new Hadera desalination project. In spite of his efforts, Jacobs' distraction was evident to all. When the meeting finally dragged to a close, the staffers were asked to leave, while Cabinet Ministers remained. General Gabriel and Ehud Zak looked worried. Sonya Franks and Ariel Steiner eyed one another contemptuously.

Jacobs got things going. "What's the latest, Anton?"

The creases in Bloch's brow seemed to have attained a permanent etch. "We found the ELTs. But not *Polaris Venture*."

"What does that mean?" Steiner pounced.

"The ELTs were exactly where we expected to find them. Only they weren't in the wrecked hull of a ship. They were simply lying next to each other on the ocean floor."

It was a result no one had predicted, and silence prevailed as the group digested the information.

General Gabriel said, "So the ship might have been hijacked, and whoever did it threw these things into the ocean to throw us off?"

"Maybe," Bloch said. "All we can say for sure is that somebody's trying to confuse us. The question is, *why?*"

Jacobs forced hope into his voice, "*Polaris Venture* is a big ship, Anton. Surely if she's still sailing around somebody will spot her soon."

"Yes, I've already sent out a message to watch for her. And our satellite people are going to give all the Arab ports a good look over the next few days."

"A few days might be too late," Steiner suggested.

Franks said, "I have to agree. Isn't there something else we can do?"

Jacobs was stung by the rebuke from one of his closest allies. He sensed the political sands shifting.

"There's more," Bloch said. "I sent a flash message yesterday, about our London Chief of Station being killed in a gun battle."

"I know Anton, I saw it. It's an awful thing. We'll do what we can to solve that when the time comes, but for now we have to concentrate on *Polaris Venture*."

"This *is* about *Polaris Venture*. This morning I talked to London. It seems our people got a good look at the assailant."

"You don't mean —" General Gabriel started.

"I'm afraid so. It was David Slaton."

Jacobs felt like he'd been punched in the stomach. "God Almighty," he said.

"What's going on, Anton?" Zak demanded. "One of your people sabotages our most delicate operation in years, then runs off and starts killing his co-workers?"

Bloch said, "We don't know that he was responsible for hijacking or sinking *Polaris Venture*. And we don't know why he's been on a tear through England."

Zak showed a rare glimpse of impatience, "You can't justify what he's done now, Anton. This man is a menace."

Franks said, "I agree. He's turned against us, for whatever reason. We don't know what happened to that ship, but we know he was involved somehow. And there seems to be no doubt he's responsible for decimating our London station."

The room fell quiet. Political allies exchanged knowing glances, adversaries glared at one another. All waited for Jacobs to speak.

The Prime Minister stared at the table in front of him. Bloch had explained the tragedy in Netanya. Had Slaton gone off the deep end? Jacobs decided it didn't matter. Not now.

"Anton," he said, "is there anything you can tell me in Slaton's defense?"

Bloch's pause was brief. "No."

An ocean of grim faces descended on Jacobs.

"Then you know what has to be done."

"I'll issue the order," Bloch said.

By noon, Nathan Chatham's patience was running thin. He had spent the entire night in his office, and though he'd directed two cots to be set up in a side room, so far his own was unused. The room was abuzz with people scurrying in and out, most of them leaving a paper or two on Chatham's desk. He quickly scanned each and directed it to one of two places — a growing manila folder on his desk, or the trash can on the floor next to it.

A man who Chatham didn't even recognize came in carrying a heavy binder, at least 200 pages long. He handed it to the inspector with a kind of ceremonial reverence.

"What the devil is this?" Chatham demanded.

The owlish man peered through round eyeglasses and explained succinctly, "It's your personal copy of the Commissioner's new policy manual. It explains everything we all need to know. New information security procedures, parental leave, and a greatly expanded statement on sexual harassment that—"

"Balderdash!" Chatham bellowed. He got up, threw the brick of a manual straight into the trash can, then stomped on it for good measure. The clerk from the upper floor looked stunned.

"Out with you!" Chatham said, his voice booming. "Out!"

The bewildered clerk bid a hasty retreat and shot a look of warning to the next victim, who was now standing in the doorway. Ian Dark held back his snicker until the poor man was out of earshot.

"Sexual harassment indeed," Chatham fussed. "More worried about being kind and gentle to one another than catching killers. That's what's wrong with this place nowadays."

Dark's tone was conciliatory, "You might have been a bit hard on him, sir. He's a new lad on the upper floor."

Chatham's terseness eased and he began to fidget, putting his hands in his back pockets. "Yes," he muttered, "perhaps. Well, we'll make it right then, won't we?"

"I'll go up later and ask for a new manual, maybe have a word with the fellow."

"Yes," Chatham fudged, "that's the ticket. So, what have you found?"

Dark held up a file and a videotape. "First of all, I just got off the phone with ballistics. From what they've seen so far, there were at least four shooters — three Israeli security men and the assailant. The Israelis surrendered their weapons for evidence. The attacker dropped one of his weapons on the way out."

"One of them, you say? Good Lord, how many did he have?"

"The one he dropped was a Mauser, one round fired. Rough tests show it's probably the one that killed Varkal. The rest of his work was with a 9mm, maybe a Berretta. We'll have it all worked out soon. Are the Israelis cooperating?"

Chatham had spent a good part of his morning at the embassy. "Things are rather chaotic there, as you might expect. The media have made the connection between yesterday's events and those in Penzance. There's a phalanx of reporters standing watch outside the embassy. Unfortunately, the woman I eventually spoke with wasn't giving anything up. In fact, she was downright evasive."

"I imagine that's how it will be until Tel Aviv decides otherwise."

Chatham strolled to a tray of sandwiches that had been put on his desk sometime last night. Blindly grabbing a sample, he took a bite and his mouth puckered. "Ugh! Bloody awful!"

"I'll send for something fresh."

Chatham found a carafe of water and reconstituted his fouled palate. "And so," he said, "the question then becomes, why? Is this fellow a threat to the Israelis? Has he done them harm? Does he know something important, perhaps embarrassing? Find the answer to that, then we're on the way to his identity, and eventually his location." Chatham paced the room, wringing his hands behind his back. "What about this American woman? Any sign of her yet?"

"No," Dark responded, "she hasn't been seen since he hauled her off two days ago. I shouldn't give odds on her still being alive. Whoever this fellow is, he manages to leave a steady trail of bodies in his wake."

"What have you found out about her?"

"Nothing extraordinary. She's a doctor, well liked. No radical friends or fringe politics. Everything we've found points to a nice young woman caught up in bad circumstances. Maybe he took her from the motel as a hostage."

"Kidnapped her? The same person in the wrong place, again?" Chatham stopped pacing, closed his eyes and pinched the bridge of his long nose.

"Bad luck, perhaps?" Dark offered weakly.

Chatham shrugged, "We'll come back to it. What's that?" he asked, gesturing to the videotape Dark held.

"Ah, a stroke of luck, or at least I thought it was. Remember yesterday, you told me to look into Yosef Meier's death? Well, I found a jewelry shop about 100 feet away from the accident scene that had a security camera set up. It doesn't show the actual point of the incident, but it gives a view out the front of the shop, toward the street. You can see the people on the sidewalk clearly. I went over it earlier, covered the ten minutes before and after the event."

"And?"

"Nothing, I'm afraid."

"Let's have a look then." Chatham eyed the seldom used TV and VCR that sat on a cart in the corner of his office. He dug around on his desk and found a remote control for the TV under some papers in the OUT box. He managed to turn the device on, but then quickly transformed the picture into a mesmerizing array of blue and green lines. Realizing this wasn't right, he kept jabbing buttons, next commanding the set to auto-program ninety-nine channels of static.

"It's the devil's own work, it is," Chatham grumbled. He handed the control over to his subordinate. "You wrestle the beastly thing."

Ian Dark fixed the picture, then ejected a movie that had been left in the tape player. Chatham frowned when he saw it was a Swedish porn film. Someone had been using the equipment while they were out. Dark tucked it discreetly among a stack of Metropolitan Police training videos.

"The accident occurred at quarter past eleven in the morning," Dark said, "but I'll cue it to start ten minutes before. I did impound all the tapes for that day. The owner of the store keeps seven days of tapes on file. Apparently in the jewelry business it's easy to overlook one or two small things that might be missing, something the smart thief knows. This fellow inventories once a week and keeps enough tapes on record to cover it."

"Hmm, yes," Chatham mumbled, concentrating on the video.

The image was black and white, but good quality, and the time and date in one corner made it easy to get to the right spot. People on the street were clearly visible, though not for long. Only those few who stopped to gawk in the store's windows were captured for more than a few seconds. The tape ran to the time of the accident, which Dark noted, then continued. Roughly ninety seconds after the accident would have occurred, Chatham waved his hand.

"Stop! There—"

Dark paused the tape. On the screen were an elderly woman with a shopping bag, who held a vague resemblance to the Queen Mum, and a couple of teenagers wandering aimlessly.

"Inspector, the lads look harmless, and the little old woman—"

"No, not the people," Chatham snapped impatiently. He waved his hand in circles. "Go back, back a few seconds."

Dark obliged, rewinding frame by frame until Chatham stopped him.

"There it is!" Chatham got up and tapped on the glass screen. "This car!"

Dark studied the vehicle. "I can't see the driver with that camera angle. The top half of the car is cut off. But one thing's for sure, it's a BMW.

Do you think it could be the same one we found in Penzance? There's a lot of those running around London, you know."

"Not like this one," Chatham said. "Look at the license plate."

Dark squinted, "I can't read the numbers, the angle is impossible. But it looks vaguely familiar. There's something different in the border."

"It's a diplomatic plate," Chatham said with certainty, "and I'd wager that if it's not the same car, it's at least drawn from the same motor pool."

Dark strained to make sense of it, "You think the Israelis killed this Meier chap? Maybe the car was from another embassy. The Syrians, or someone like that."

"Hmm," Chatham murmured, lost in a multitude of his own thoughts. "What we have to do is send this down to our technical people. Perhaps they can make something out of that license plate. In any event, I'm more inclined to believe that Yosef Meier's death was nothing near an accident."

"I suspect you're right," Dark agreed. "There's a lot of killing going on here, and possibly more to come. It's frustrating that the Israelis must know something about it, but aren't letting on."

"*Something?*" He crossed to the window and stood with his hands on his hips. "They know all of it!" he growled. Chatham strode to the door and yanked his coat off the rack. "I'm going to have a word with Shearer."

They arrived in the late afternoon. As a seasonal matter, the beach access road had been blocked off. Slaton got out and dragged a wooden barricade far enough aside for Christine to maneuver their ragged little car through the gap, then shoved it back into place. He didn't bother to smooth over the tire ruts in the muddy gravel — there were already others, so they were clearly not the first to circumvent the barrier. But on this day, with a chilly breeze and low, heavy clouds that seemed to promise rain, they would likely be alone. A small car park just inside the entrance lay vacant, and likely had been for days. Even during peak season, the beaches along this stretch of the Devon coast were not among the most popular. They were remote, rocky, and the water was nearly a mile from parking at its closest point.

They drove slowly on a road that seemed to have no end, meandering deeper and deeper into a maze of sandy hills that were covered with outcroppings of coarse, tough vegetation. After ten minutes, Slaton announced his intention to find a place to park that would conceal the small car. There were plenty of hiding spots. Unfortunately, the same loose sand that created a warren of twenty-foot dunes also served to make the valleys impassable to lightweight, two-wheel-drive sedans.

It took twenty more minutes of weaving before Slaton found a spot he deemed useful. A turnabout was situated between two dunes, and farther back a thick, straw-like stand of grass gave some firmness to the ground. Slaton got out and studied the area. Content, he guided Christine to pull the Ford back behind a large hill and into a stretch of brambles. This time Slaton yanked off a few long strands of grass and used them to sweep clear the car's tracks. He went back to the main road and stood with his arms crossed, evaluating how well they were concealed.

"That should work," he decided. "We'll sleep in the car tonight. By morning, I'll have the next steps worked out."

Christine looked at the surrounding dunes. They seemed desolate and barren, yet comforting. No people or cars to watch and worry about. Only sand, thicket, wind, and wide-open space. It was the safest she'd felt for a long time.

"Have you been here before?" she asked.

"Once or twice. During the summer it's busy. But this time of year it might be a week before anyone wanders by."

A gust of wind swept in and Christine felt a chill. She reached into the car, fished out a cable-knit sweater and put it on. Slaton began rummaging through two bags of provisions Christine had purchased earlier at a small village grocery.

"Hungry?" he asked.

"I suppose. How far away is the ocean?"

Slaton's head was still buried in the back of the car. "Oh, maybe a mile."

"Why don't we take our dinner there. A walk would feel good after sitting for so long."

Slaton lifted his head out of the car and looked at her, then shifted his gaze up to the solid gray sky that hovered threateningly overhead. He shrugged. "Okay. If you want." He took a bag of groceries, then went to the driver's seat and grabbed his jacket and the Beretta.

Christine tensed at the sight of the weapon. She watched as he started to wrap his jacket around the gun, no doubt to keep out any rain or sand. She remembered the first time she'd seen it — pointed at her in a Penzance hotel room, by a man who was now dead.

Though David didn't seem to be watching her, he suddenly stopped what he was doing. He studied the gun obviously for a moment, then said, "Ach, no need to lug this thing along." He put it back under the driver's seat and locked the door, then opened the trunk and pulled out a stack of three heavy blankets, requisitioned from Humphrey Hall. "But we might need these." Slaton closed the trunk and set off for the shoreline at a casual pace. When she didn't fall in right behind, he turned.

She stood staring at him, an inescapably warm smile on her face. "What?"

"Nothing," she said, the smile still etched in place.

They followed a winding path between the dunes. The soft sand made progress slow, but neither was in a hurry.

"So what are your plans after you finish your residency?"

The question caught her by surprise. It was the kind of thing she used to give a lot of thought to. "I'd like to be a family practitioner, probably in a small town. A lot of my classmates are set on specializing — surgery, radiology, anesthesiology. They'll say the pay is better or the hours more reasonable. When they finish school they'll go to work in some big hospital, an assembly-line operation where they never even get to know their patients. That's not being a doctor. Not in my book. And not in Upper's."

"Who?"

Christine laughed, "Dr. Upton N. Downey, my resident adviser and hero. He's a Texas Type A. Constant slow motion. He'll lope through the halls in his Tony Lama snakeskins and drawl non-stop to a half dozen fledgling residents. Winks at the kids, winks at the nurses, never misses a thought. Upper is a really smart man who's proved to me that good medicine is part science, part art. The science for a good FP is knowing a little about all the specialties. And the art is in getting to know your patients and their families, getting them to trust you."

"You'd be good at that. The trusting part."

Christine smiled.

"So what was your favorite rotation? Isn't that what they call them?"

"Yes. OB-GYN. I delivered a baby a few months ago. It was the most incredible thing I've ever done. Have you ever seen a child born?"

He hesitated on the question, one that should have required no thought. "Once," he said.

For the thousandth time Christine wondered what was going on in his head. They shuffled ahead silently and she hoped he would explain, that he'd lift the veil for once and show a part of himself. When nothing came, she decided not to push.

"This reminds me of a beach back home," she said. "I used to go there when I was a girl. The dunes seem endless. Then, just when you think you'll never reach the water, it appears out of nowhere."

"Was this in Florida?"

"Yeah. Where I grew up."

He nodded, "It's good to have a place you can call home. Someday you'll probably be taking your daughter to that same beach."

She laughed, "I never thought about it, but I suppose you're right. As long as someone doesn't stack it with condominiums first."

They crested a rise and suddenly the Atlantic was before them. The waters were dark, almost black in color, punctuated by white streaks of foam. Waves broke up and down the beach, producing a never-ending series of hollow thuds, weary travelers slamming down to announce their arrival, then churning and clawing the last few feet up to shore. They stood in silence, mesmerized by nature's perpetual show.

"Every beach sounds a little different," Christine said.

"Yes," he agreed. "Lots of variables. Sandbars, the steepness of the upslope just offshore. Then the bottom might be any combination of sand, rock, coral, or loose pebbles."

"Now that's one thing I've never tried to deduce scientifically."

"But you are a scientist, Dr. Palmer."

"Maybe, but some things are better left a mystery."

He dropped their belongings to the sand and set out toward the waterline. Christine followed suit.

"It was part of some training I took many years ago, waterborne assault. The water might be an ocean, a lake, a swamp, or a ditch full of sewage. Whatever it was, you had to know the line where water met earth like the back of your hand. A moonless night or zero visibility in the water was no excuse. Use the compass and watch, feel your way if necessary." His voice grew detached as he went on, "The water was your way in, your way to get close, the sanctuary you owned. But sooner or later the time would come to get out. And you'd better be in the right place. Not too far from your partner or too close to the guard shack where . . ." his voice trailed off. "Sorry, here you are trying to show some heartfelt appreciation of nature, and I give you a short course on covert amphibious assault techniques. You're right. Some things are better left a mystery."

She gave no reply.

"I guess I've learned a lot of peculiar things over the years."

Christine remembered, "When I found you in the ocean there were shoe laces tied around the bottom of your pants legs. Was that one?"

"Yeah. It's a cold-water survival trick, on the same concept as a wet suit. If you can't keep cold water out, at least contain a narrow warm layer next to your skin. It buys a little time. I don't remember where I picked that one up. Probably on a beach at three in the morning with some big guy behind me screaming it would save my life someday." He stopped and shifted his gaze to sea. "Maybe it did."

"Then I'm glad you learned it." Christine watched for a reaction, but like always, there was none. He simply stood staring at the frigid ocean.

They sat down together facing the water. Neither spoke as the bitterly cold ocean rose and fell to meet the shore. An occasional cry from a seagull punctuated the surf's rhythmic chaos. Evening was fast approaching and the overcast skies accelerated the loss of light. Christine looked to their right up the coastline. It was straight and featureless as far as she could see. In the other direction the beach made a gradual curve out to sea, then turned back in, disappearing from view four or five miles away. There, at the point, she could barely discern a pair of faint, yellow lights. The only other sign of civilization was an old fishing dory overturned on the beach behind them. It was parked above the high water line, probably for the season. The isolation seemed almost complete.

"It feels good to be out here, away from everything," she said. "It's as though I'm back on *Windsom*."

"But you're not alone here."

"I don't need to be alone to feel relaxed," she paused and then added, "do you?" Christine suddenly realized the question might seem barbed. "I'm sorry," she fumbled, "I didn't mean to imply anything."

He looked at her squarely, his eyes holding more feeling than she ever thought he might possess. But Christine couldn't tell what that feeling was. His reply caught her completely offguard.

"I saw a child born once. My daughter. I was there in the delivery room, and you're absolutely right — there were doctors, nurses, lots of blood. But all I can remember is the moment my tiny daughter came into the world. It has to be the most magnificent, awe-inspiring event on earth."

Christine was stunned. She had weighed this complex man in so many ways, from so many angles, yet it had never crossed her mind that he might have a family.

"You have a daughter!" she exclaimed. "That's wonderful!"

He turned back to the ocean and shook his head. "She's dead."

The weight of the earth came crashing down. Christine felt helpless as she grasped for something to say, something beyond the standard, pointless, "I'm so sorry." Nothing came to mind.

He pulled out his wallet, delicately removed a photograph and handed it to her. The picture was of a small girl, probably two years old. She was laughing as a woman pushed her on a swing. The young woman had beautiful, dark features, and a vivacious sparkle in her eyes, a characteristic unmistakably reiterated in the little girl.

"She's beautiful," Christine said, trying to recover. "This is her mother?"

"My wife. She's dead as well."

"My God! What happened?"

"Katya, my wife, and little Elise were riding a bus home from the library and . . ." he struggled to find words and Christine noticed his hand digging into the beach, a fistful of sand squeezed remorselessly.

"Was there an accident?"

"No. It was no accident. It was three men with AK-47s and grenades. They got on the bus and wiped out twenty-two people, three of them children." His hand kept clenching, faster and harder. His voice rose, "My daughter survived for a few hours. But I couldn't get there in time to be with her. Do you know what a fragmentation grenade does to a two-year-old body, doctor? Do you?"

Slaton closed his eyes and Christine put her hand over his. She held it until the grasping stopped, then kept holding. Neither said a word.

Gradually, the light faded, and an occasional drop of rain gave promise of more to come. Neither seemed to care as they sat watching the open sea, both mesmerized by their own private thoughts.

It was Slaton who finally broke the silence. "You know, I thought about becoming a doctor myself. A long time ago, back when I was at university. There must be a tremendous sense of satisfaction, working to save lives."

"You make it sound like we're all saints. I know a lot of people who went to medical school just because they wanted to make good money, or satisfy their egos."

"Maybe. But even those types can justify what they do. It's a noble calling."

Christine handed back the photograph and he slid it carefully into his wallet. She shivered as a gust of wind swept by.

"It's getting cold." he said.

"A little."

"Let's get a fire started, then we can eat."

They both went foraging at the high tide line and easily scavenged enough driftwood and dry grass for a small fire. Slaton set up camp next to the old wooden dory, using it as a windbreak. The boat, about fifteen feet in length, had probably not been used since the summer. Only a few flakes of red bottom paint remained on its weather-beaten hull. Behind the boat was a rusty old fifty-five gallon drum. Slaton gave it a kick and the hollow rapport confirmed that it was empty. He started building a fire right next to the boat.

"The weather's about to take a turn for the worse," she said, pointing out at the water. The dark clouds that had hung over the sea now seemed to reach down and touch it. A heavy, moisture-laden blanket was enveloping the horizon to the east and north.

"I think you're right."

"I'd hate to head back to the car," Christine lamented. "I like it here. The rest of the world seems so far away."

"It does, doesn't it?"

A light drizzle started to fall. The fire caught and began to burn steadily, notwithstanding the occasional hiss of a raindrop. Slaton threw on a few more sticks and looked at the boat.

"I've got an idea."

He went to the boat and lifted one side slightly to test its weight.

"What is it?"

He rolled the empty metal drum right up to the boat. "I'll lift this side up, you roll the drum underneath."

"All right."

Slaton put both hands under the gunnel of the dory and heaved up with all his strength, raising it just far enough for Christine to maneuver the drum underneath. With the drum in place, he lowered the side of the boat to rest on it, creating a makeshift lean-to. He gave the arrangement a few shoves to ensure it was solid, then spread out a blanket under their newly formed shelter. Moving the rest of their belongings in, they found enough room to be able to sit up.

The wind calmed as the drizzle thickened to a steady, light rain. The fire was situated just outside their new shelter, its smoke drifting up and away, but the radiant warmth filling their refuge. Dinner was a loaf of French bread, tart cheese, and bottled water. They took the meager meal in silence, both enjoying the simple fare and, accordingly, the simple sound of raindrops tapping the thick wooden hull overhead. Afterwards, they watched as the fire's flames danced and reflected obscurely off the rusted metal drum.

Christine spoke in a quiet voice, not wanting to interrupt the rain's soothing echoes. "How long can we stay here, David?"

Their eyes met, and Christine noticed how completely he was looking at her. There was no caution, no glancing over her shoulder. The alertness that had always encompassed him was now completely gone.

"We can stay as long as we like."

No other words were spoken. On their knees, they faced one another. She leaned forward and kissed him gently. She felt him tremble as she ran her hands up his arms to his shoulders. She slowly unbuttoned the front of his shirt, and with each unclasping he took a breath. When she finally removed his shirt and put her hands on his bare chest, he drew in a short, sharp gasp. It was as though he was being touched for the first time. Christine ran her hands along his naked back, feeling the hardness and the scars. Then she leaned back, unbuttoned her own shirt and pressed her naked chest to his. His hands began to respond, enveloping and stroking. Her own breathing quickened and they laid down.

The kidon's hands trembled no more as he reveled in a glory he could scarcely remember.

Chapter Thirteen

The rising sun stirred them both from a deep sleep, its warming rays reflecting into their quiet retreat. Their bodies lay entwined in a blanket beneath the old fishing dory, still and close. Neither wanted to disturb the sanctuary they'd discovered, and so both maintained a deliberate silence. Words could only lead back to reality.

Christine was watching a seagull glide silently by when she felt him tense. He cocked his head, then sat up abruptly.

"David, what is it?"

Slaton scrambled over to the fire, which had long ago died out, and began shoveling sand over the spent ashes. Then Christine heard it too — the unmistakable sound of a helicopter approaching. With the fire well covered, he pulled her back as far as they could go under the boat. The noise from the aircraft got louder and louder, drowning out the sounds of the sea that had held them for so many hours.

"Do you think it's the police?"

"More likely the military. I doubt they routinely patrol the coastline here, so it's probably just a crew making a sightseeing run up the beach. But they could have some kind of infrared sensor. That's why I doused what was left of the fire."

"It burned out hours ago."

"There might still be enough heat in the embers to contrast with the cool sand."

The sound reached a crescendo, then changed in pitch as the helicopter passed overhead. They peeked out to watch the big bird. Christine saw it maneuver inland, then reverse course back to the coastline, a big sweeping S turn. The sound began to fade, and soon the craft disappeared into a curtain of haze.

"He didn't seem very interested."

"No . . ." Slaton replied.

They dressed and came out from under the shelter. Christine stretched her limbs while Slaton stood alertly, a hand shielding his eyes from the glare of the low eastern sun. His attention was still fixed on the sky, as if he expected the big machine to come swooping back at any moment.

"We've got to go," he announced.

Christine said nothing. Of course they had to go, she thought. They had no food, the water was almost gone, and their accommodations were comical. Yet after last night, not running like a hunted animal, but feeling secure, relaxed, even loved. She wished they could stay here forever.

"They may have seen our car."

"Would the engine still be warm?" she asked.

"No. But the car is metal. At dusk it cools faster and at dawn it warms more quickly than the sand and vegetation. It would stand out like a star in the night sky on an infrared scope."

"So you think they saw it?"

"Actually, I doubt it. But there's no way to be sure. If they did spot it, the fact that it's parked back in the scrub would only make it more suspicious. We can't take the chance. If we get caught out here in the open there aren't many ways out."

"All right," she said. "Where do we go?"

"Back up the road, to Sidbury."

"I almost hate to ask, but what are we going to do there?"

"Well, I don't know about you, but I'm hungry."

When the food came, Christine found she'd worked up a surprising hunger. She polished off her eggs and toast faster than Slaton, who wasn't dallying, and now she was shoveling through a bowl of fruit.

"I see you've found your appetite," he said.

"Being hunted like this," she mumbled through a mouthful of cantaloupe, "it seems to crank up my metabolism a notch. Maybe when we're all done and nobody is shooting at us anymore, I can write a diet book and get rich."

Slaton grinned and flipped open a newspaper he'd purchased. He held up page four next to his face and Christine gagged when she saw it, a rough pencil sketch of him beneath the headline — *KILLER STILL LOOSE!*

"Good Lord, put that thing down!" she whispered harshly. Christine glanced uneasily around the half-full cafe.

"Nobody's looking," he said. "And besides, it's really not a very good likeness."

Christine had to admit the resemblance was poor, but it was still unnerving. "I suppose I should be happy my high school graduation picture isn't right there next to you."

"It will be."

She frowned and was about to register her displeasure when the waitress scurried over to fill her coffee cup for the third time. The waitress moved on and Christine took a long, steamy sip. She was beginning to feel the zing. "You know, we can't just run forever. We've got to do something. I say we go to the police, tell them everything." She reached over, grabbed the newspaper and began scanning. "Here . . . 'Inspector Nathan Chatham, one of Scotland Yard's most experienced investigators, has been put in charge of the search for a suspect who's wanted for —'"

"Christine," he interrupted in a patient tone, "you're right. We do have to take the initiative." Slaton reached down to the floor and grabbed a large plastic bag he'd brought in from the car. "We have to figure out what's going on, and I think it might start with this."

Christine had wondered what was in the bag, but hadn't asked, knowing he'd get around to it. Slaton pulled out a large, flat book titled *Hammond's World Atlas*. He shoved aside their plates and opened it on the table. The page he selected covered the northwest coast of Africa and the adjacent Atlantic Ocean, the area where she'd first found him.

"Where did you get that?"

"I stole it from the public library in Southampton. I went there while you were checking into Humphrey Hall."

"I guess we can add that to the list of crimes they'll be after you for. Let's see now, we have murder, assault, kidnapping, auto theft, forgery, vandalizing my boat . . . and now pilfering from the local library. Have I missed anything?"

"Plenty," he said distractedly as he ran a finger over the map. "I've been giving this a lot of thought and things are starting to make sense, but I need more."

Slaton pointed to a line he'd penciled onto the map. It started at the bottom, in the southern Atlantic, and curled up along Africa's western coast. "This is the course *Polaris Venture* was supposed to have taken. At least that's how I remember it. Now, show me where you found me. Be as precise as you can."

Christine studied the map and found the Madeira Islands, the best reference she could remember. Then she took a table knife and laid it over the mileage scale. She measured off 280 miles, marked it with her thumb, then moved her rule to the islands along the proper bearing.

"Here," she said, putting the point of the knife on the spot. "If I had parallels or a protractor I could do better, but I'd say this point is good to within ten miles."

Slaton pondered her estimate, cupping his chin. "I was in the water for a day and a half. Which way do the currents run?"

"The Canary current comes in from the northwest, maybe a knot or two. The wind might have affected you. It was out of the northeast, I think, but pretty light. I'd say you drifted south, but it's hard to say how much. Thirty miles, maybe forty. I still can't believe you survived so long in that cold."

"So *Polaris Venture* went down about here." Slaton shook his head, "No, that's still off the course we were supposed to have taken. A good thirty or forty miles west."

"How were you navigating?"

"It was all hooked up on the autopilot, which gets its position from GPS."

"Did the South Africans load the waypoints for your route?"

Slaton slouched in his seat and his head flew back, "Oh, no!"

"What?"

"He did that, too."

"Who did what?"

"Viktor Wysinski. There were two of us in South Africa to set this up, but I was the only one to actually go along for the ride. Wysinski gave the course data to the ship's captain. And he was there when it got programmed."

"He's Mossad?"

"Yep. I had a lot of time to think while I was floating around out there. I suspected Viktor, but I couldn't believe he'd turned. He was hardcore, used to be a commando in the Israeli Army. A real patriot, or so I thought. But I can't see it any other way now. He had access to make it all happen. Wysinski installed the explosives on the ship, and he must have set them to go off at a specific time and place."

"Explosives?"

Slaton explained, "We were ordered to install scuttling charges on the ship. That way if there was a hijacking we couldn't repel, at least we could sink her. I'm certain that's how *Polaris Venture* went down. I was out on deck, and I remember hearing the charges go off. Unfortunately, most of the crew were down below, asleep."

"None of them got clear? Not even the ones who were above, on duty?"

He shook his head, "I never saw anyone else. In the dark, all I could find was that cooler."

"So Wysinski is one of the people who are making our lives so awful."

"Has to be. And he is now on my list."

Christine didn't know what that meant, except that it was probably bad news for this Wysinski fellow.

As Slaton concentrated on the map, Christine tried to sort through all the blips on her very cluttered mental radar. "So this guy changed the ship's course and sent her down using the explosives. But I don't see why. I mean if he, or the people he works with, are trying to get those nuclear weapons you told me about — well, what have they accomplished?"

Slaton banged a palm on the table in frustration, "That's what doesn't make sense! If you sink her in ten thousand feet of water, the weapons are gone. The whole affair might embarrass our government, but that's not worth the risk, not worth killing sixteen people." Slaton stared at the atlas, looking like a frustrated chess player with fewer ideas than pieces.

Christine fixated on the small dent her knife's tip had made on the page. "Wait a minute!" She took the atlas and flipped to the index.

"What is it?"

"David, this isn't a nautical chart, it's an atlas. The page we were looking at leaves out one very important part of the picture." Christine turned to the rear of the book and found the page she wanted.

"Look at the same spot here!"

Slaton did, and his troubled expression washed away. This page covered the entire Atlantic Ocean, but also showed a relief of the ocean floor.

It presented the vertical development beneath the surface, all the trenches and ridges that lay unseen in the dark depths. There, right where they had calculated *Polaris Venture*'s demise, was the answer.

"The Ampere seamount! That's it! Sink her on the seamount, then you can recover the weapons."

"It wouldn't be easy," Christine said. "It's a hundred and thirty feet. I've done some diving and that's pretty deep."

"No, it's well within reach. If you breathe a special mixture, you wouldn't even have to decompress."

The waitress came by and Slaton waved off a refill on their coffee. She left the check and went on her way. Christine stirred in her seat.

"There's more," Slaton warned.

"What?"

"The codes, the ones that activate these weapons. The South Africans gave them to us for safe keeping. They were hand-carried back to Israel after we loaded *Polaris Venture*. Guess who."

"Wysinski again?"

"Touché. Whoever's running this will have both the weapons and the codes to use them."

Christine closed her eyes and wondered aloud, "Can it get any worse?"

"Probably."

"Do you think someone would actually use these things?"

"There are only two reasons to steal a nuclear weapon. To use it, or sell it to someone else who will."

It was sturdy logic, but Christine was amazed he could remain composed at such a thought. "David, we can't just keep running. Sooner or later someone will catch up. If it's not these lunatics, then it'll be the British police. We know what these people have done. Now we have to tell the authorities."

Slaton sat back and took a deep breath. "I don't know," he said, shaking his head. "I'm not sure who to trust with something like this. Wysinski and his bunch have infiltrated Mossad. But I have no idea how high up it goes."

"We could tell Scotland Yard. But it does sound so far-fetched."

"We have no proof of anything. No *Polaris Venture*, no weapons. My government wouldn't admit to any part of it. They'd just tell the Brits that I'm the assassin who's been running around killing people. Even if we convinced someone this is all happening, the first thing they'd do is go out to the seamount and look for the ship. That could take days or weeks, and it's already been . . . what, ten days since *Polaris Venture* went down? Given how carefully this operation was planned, I'll bet the salvage has already taken place."

"We have to do something, David."

He wore a look of grim determination. "Yes. And I think it's time we went on the offensive."

Emma Schroeder used her ample hip to wedge a bag of groceries against the door jamb as she flipped through a massive key ring, trying to find the one that would let her into her flat. She finally found the right one, and at the same time the phone inside began to ring. Fumbling, she opened the door and trundled over. Emma balanced the groceries on the back of the couch with one hand, and picked up on the fifth ring.

"Hello," she said breathlessly.

"Hello, beautiful."

She stood straight and lost her grip on the bag, which fell to the couch, a half dozen oranges spilling out and thudding to the floor. There was no mistaking the voice or the greeting.

"Where the hell are you, David?"

"I'll bet that's the million dollar question around the office, isn't it?"

"Don't be cute, dammit." Recovering, Emma saw the door was still wide open. "Hold on a minute." She went over and closed it, then picked back up. "Do you know what's going on?"

"No, Emma. You're the source. I called to find out."

"They're saying you killed Varkal . . . and Freidlund and Streissan. Itzaak Simon's still in the hospital." Emma waited for a response, but only got silence. "David, tell me you didn't do these things."

"I didn't kill Varkal," he said flatly.

"And the rest?"

"The rest I did, but only in self-defense. I had no choice, Emma. There is a group of traitors inside. I don't know how many, but they're on the verge of something really terrible."

"I saw an ops order today that was really terrible. Basically, it instructed the entire station to drop everything and look for you. They want to bring you in, David, one way . . . or the other. I've seen a lot of orders, but I've never seen one like that."

"I have," Slaton replied. "But they're pretty unusual. And this one's a mistake."

"You mean it's a bogus message?"

"No, darling, it's a legitimate message. But the reasons behind it are all skewed. I don't have time to explain now, but I can tell you that the people behind it are the same ones who killed Yosy."

Emma was dumbstruck. "Killed Yosy? You mean as in *murdered* him? It was an accident, David."

"Trust me. I know about things like that. It wasn't an accident." He paused, as if letting it sink in. "Emma, I need your help. I know I'm putting you in a bad spot, but I'm asking you to trust me and not—"

"What do you need?"

"Emma, understand, I could get you in trouble here."

"I expect trouble from you, you scoundrel. Now what do you need?"

"We have to be quick," Slaton said.

Emma realized what he was suggesting — that her phone might be recorded, or even live-monitored. "Go on."

"See if you can find out where a guy named Viktor Wysinski is. You've probably never heard the name, he's a headquarters puke. But I really need to find him. I'll call you back tomorrow at—"

"Eastbourne."

"What?"

"He's in Eastbourne, at the Harbor Hotel."

"Dear, you've always been a model of efficiency, but how on earth could you know that?"

"Alpha roster. One went across the acting Chief of Station's desk yesterday and I got a peek at it. I guess he wanted to find out exactly who we had in country, probably so they could all go out and look for you."

"Wonderful."

Emma explained, "This guy Wysinski was the only one listed as being in the U.K., but not checked in here at the embassy. I remember things like that."

"You always amaze me."

"That's why you love me so, you and . . ." Emma felt tears well up in her eyes. "Do you really think somebody did that to Yosef?"

"I'm afraid so, Emma. Listen, I'm sorry to mix you up in this. I'd better go now."

"All right. Be careful."

"You do the same."

"And call me if you need anything else. You know how good I am."

"You're the best, beautiful. The best."

It had been frustrating to wait all day for Emma to get home from the office, but Slaton had seen no other way. Calling her at the embassy would have been far too risky. Since then, things had gone well. He and Christine made good time from Devon, pulling into Eastbourne shortly after midnight. With little chance of spotting Wysinski at that hour, they found a secluded spot to park and struggled for some shut-eye. The previous night at the beach already seemed like a lifetime ago.

Slaton was always cautious, but his instincts told him to be particularly aware now. An hour before sunrise, he sent Christine off with instructions. She'd run a few errands when the shops opened, then, much as they'd done at Belgrave Square in London, she would drive the car periodically by a designated rendezvous point.

It began perfectly. Slaton spotted Wysinski soon after setting up watch, headed toward Dunn's Harbor Hotel from the direction of the harbor. He granted the stocky ex-commando a wide berth. Slaton would rather lose sight and pick him up later than be spotted. Wysinski turned into the lobby of the hotel and disappeared into an elevator. He seemed both casual and alone, characteristics that Slaton found troubling.

Slaton set up camp at a café down the street, well clear of the hotel entrance, but near enough to monitor the traffic going in and out. It was two hours before he picked up Wysinski again, this time leaving the hotel and heading back to the waterfront. Having already settled his check, Slaton waited for Wysinski to pass, then took up pursuit.

The sun had made intermittent appearances over the course of the morning, but dark skies to the north made for an easy forecast. Wysinski marched at a brisk pace into the ocean breeze, his thick legs churning near double-time. Minutes later he reached the waterfront and trundled down one of the five long piers that jutted into the harbor.

Slaton turned aside, wandering the path that arced along the harbor's perimeter, all the time keeping an eye on his quarry. Wysinski stopped at a slip halfway down the pier, boarded a big motor yacht, and disappeared into its cabin. Since he wasn't carrying any baggage, Slaton doubted the man was going anywhere. Wysinski had also ignored the use of tradecraft on his walk to the harbor — no double-backs, quick turns, or slowdowns. Just a casual stroll that Slaton disliked.

The harbor was quiet. It was the wrong time of year to begin with, and the impending dismal weather acted as a final blow to curtail the waterfront's more casual pursuits. The small rental sailboats were chained together. The trinket vendor's carts were all shoved aside in a line and locked down. A few boat owners scrubbed and fiddled with their prize possessions, and a handful of the scrappier merchants were open for business, probably more out of habit than anything else.

Slaton scouted for a position that would give an unobstructed view of Wysinski's boat. He selected an empty bench, adjacent to a kiosk whose optimistic owner hoped to sell T-shirts with pictures of waterbirds on them. Slaton unfurled the newspaper he'd been carrying all morning and settled in. Patience was demanding, but more so now as Slaton remembered the last time he'd seen Wysinski, on Pier Three in Cape Town. He had given Slaton a "see-you-later" nod as *Polaris Venture* pulled away from the dock — with full knowledge that the ship and her crew were doomed by the explosives he had so meticulously planted. Very simply, the man had tried to kill him. And Slaton knew Wysinski was associated with whoever had killed Yosy. He felt anger and hatred, just as he had for so many years, only now the source was different. Yet as strong as these feelings might be, Slaton knew how to push them aside. The kidon remained calm, for there was much to be done.

He looked across the harbor, registering all pertinent details. The roads that led to and from the waterfront, the maze of buildings and structures that sheltered people and channeled traffic. He checked lines of sight and noted those vantage points that would have a clear view of Wysinski's boat. Slaton studied the few people who were out, recording where they were and what they were doing. One man had a dismantled rudder up on a dock, applying a coat of red bottom paint. Another was installing some kind of antenna on a cruiser. A bored waiter at an empty café stood folding napkins, probably hoping for a break in the weather that might draw out a healthy crowd for lunch. Then he saw a young girl, probably no more than seventeen or eighteen. She was smiling as she tended the row of flower boxes that fronted the café. There was an open, genuine look of content about her, and Slaton imagined that, by innocence of youth, she was enamored with what her work would bring. In time, the boxes would explode with color, contributing to spats ended, weddings enhanced, or — best of all — the simple, romantic beauty of a lone magnificent flower, a gift from one lover to another. Seventeen, the kidon thought. Seventeen years old.

Suddenly there was movement on the boat and Slaton saw the ex-soldier astern, sorting through a pile of equipment. Wysinski was still in no hurry. The kidon cocked his head and looked back to where the young girl had been tending her flower boxes. For some reason he wanted to see her again, in all her faithful purpose and innocence. She was gone.

His approach was completely silent. The pier was wide, and along each side lay a solid row of boats and wooden finger slips that blocked the view almost continuously. If any passerby had happened to look in just the right gaps, they would have seen the vague, dark silhouette of a small inflatable Zodiac beneath the pier. It moved so slowly that anyone who might watch it for a moment or two would see nothing other than the motion one would expect from such a craft if it were moored on a loose painter, drifting randomly back and forth. Indeed, it moved in two directions — six inches slowly shoreward, then a foot toward the end of the pier. Six inches in, another foot out. In the dim light there was no way anyone could make out the man who was crouched inside, his head just clearing under the dock's stringer planks as he inched his way out.

Slaton worked his fingers into the gaps between the wooden two-by-sixes, careful to never let the tips protrude above the top surface. At one point, someone, probably a dockhand, walked directly overhead and stopped. Slaton, motionless, saw the soles of a pair of deck shoes through the cracks, and heard the man grunt as he tossed a sailbag onto the deck of a nearby boat. It landed with a thud, then the shoes retreated back up the pier toward shore. Slaton pressed on, finally stopping twenty feet short of Wysinski's boat. He pulled out the Beretta and released the safety.

For a full five minutes he listened, mentally logging the sounds, the patterns of movement, and selecting a point of entry. The boat was stern to the pier and had a large, flat swimming platform behind the transom. It was clearly the quickest and easiest way aboard, assuming he could get there unseen. The name on the stern was artfully scripted, *Lorraine II*, home port Casablanca.

Slaton wondered if this was the boat that had been used to retrieve the weapons. It was not a salvage ship by any means, but could have done the work. There were two small davits astern, of the type normally used to hoist and carry a small skiff. But there was no skiff, and a few strong men would have had no trouble swinging a pair of five-hundred pounders aboard.

Slaton heard Wysinski go below and he edged closer. The last ten feet would be the toughest. Wysinski would have a narrow line of sight, over the transom and under the dock. Slaton saw the coast was clear and moved fast to the platform. He stepped across silently while pushing the Zodiac back into the shadows, then stayed low until he heard Wysinski back on deck. When Slaton stood, the gun was sighted and ready.

Wysinski had his back to Slaton, but he sensed a presence and turned. Slaton saw something in the man's expression. But it wasn't surprise. There should have been surprise. And maybe a trace of fear, even in an old soldier. Alarms went off in Slaton's head. Something was very wrong. He quickly glanced up and down the pier but saw nothing out of the ordinary.

"Get below!" Slaton ordered, wanting to get out of the open. "Hands behind your back!"

A sneering Wysinski complied, moving slowly to the boat's cabin. Slaton followed, every sense on alert for the slightest deviation. Wysinski was a few steps in front as they reached the big main cabin, and as Slaton passed through the companionway, he assessed the interior. Aside from Wysinski's steady movement, there was nothing. Then he spotted the two descending stairwells, one to his left and one to the right, passageways that led back and down, probably to a stateroom below the aft deck. If he followed Wysinski forward—

A barely audible creak. Slaton heard the sound just as Wysinski's eyes gave it away. He twisted right, saw movement and fired without waiting to focus on the target. There was a groan as the man fell back, tumbling down the staircase.

Slaton spun left and saw a glint arcing toward him from the opposite stairwell. He lifted an arm to parry the blow, but felt the knife slice across his chest and wrist. In close, Slaton dropped his gun and grabbed the arm that held the knife. With all his strength he turned, letting the weight of his body do the work. The attacker lost his balance and stumbled against Slaton. At that moment a shot rang out from Wysinski's direction and Slaton felt the man he was struggling against go limp. He dove down the stairs to his left as another shot rang out, this one shattering a nearby porthole and spraying glass everywhere.

Slaton crashed painfully to the bottom of the stairs, banging his head against a rail. He saw the first man he'd taken, lying crumpled on the floor with a crimson pool spread across his chest. The man's gun lay on the floor and Slaton grabbed it as he rolled behind the central bulkhead for cover. He got his first look at the stateroom under the aft deck. It was stunning.

Not ten feet away, chained to a wooden cradle, was a ten kiloton nuclear weapon. Resting snugly in Eastbourne's harbor. He could easily see how they'd done it. There was a large hatch overhead, near the port davit, and Slaton noticed that the furniture and trimmings in the state room had been torn apart to make room for the weapon. He heard movement above. Wysinski wasn't giving up.

Slaton checked how many rounds remained in the gun's clip and was glad to find it full. He then looked down and evaluated his wound. The cut on his chest wasn't deep, but his arm was stinging in pain. The sounds above stopped. Wysinski was waiting for him to make the next move. Slaton wondered how long it would take for the police to react, then mused that, at the rate he was going, he could soon write an authoritative treatise on the subject.

He looked again at the hatch above the cradled weapon, then noticed that the port stairway had a privacy curtain at the bottom. It wouldn't stop bullets, but it would conceal his activities. Slaton reached across the stairwell and yanked the curtain closed, his action drawing fire through the flimsy fabric. Three rounds, one of them clinking to rest in something metallic. He looked at the bomb to see a nice round hole in the nose cone. Slaton was grateful it wasn't a conventional, high-explosive type, or he and Wysinski might both be at the bottom of the harbor. Curling his wrist into the starboard stairwell, he fired four shots blindly. He then ran to the hatch, unlatched it, and threw it open. The big fiberglass door swung up slowly on pneumatic lifts and stopped in a vertical position. Slaton moved quickly.

Victor Wysinski stood watching the two stairwells. He didn't see the hatch rise until it was nearly straight up. It hinged forward, blocking his view of the opening. Wysinski fired three shots that easily penetrated the thin fiberglass. There was a moan, and a gun slid out onto the deck. Then a muffled thud. Wysinski moved out on deck, keeping his firearm trained on the hatch. Slaton was nowhere to be seen, but there was blood around the opening. Wysinski rushed to the hatch and pointed his gun downward, certain he'd scored a hit. He saw nothing.

Slaton cued on Wysinski's hesitation. It only took a moment for the ex-commando to realize his mistake and turn, but it was too late. Slaton rushed him from behind, crashing a shoulder into Wysinski's side. He held his arm upright and they slammed headlong into the transom, Wysinski's gun going over the side and into the harbor. The two struggled and fell entwined, crashing heavily to the deck. Wysinski recovered first and saw the gun Slaton had lost lying a few feet away. He scrambled over and grabbed it. Slaton struggled to his feet, looking stunned and grimacing in pain.

"You're slipping, kidon," Wysinski said with a smirk.

Slaton looked down the barrel of the weapon and slumped to one knee.

Wysinski glanced toward shore. "You let an old paratrooper get the better of you."

"Those other two aren't so smug," Slaton said, gasping for breath.

"Joacham and Sergeant Heim? They were good men. You've been costing us a lot of good men lately, but not anymore."

"The police will be here any minute. Your revenue from this fiasco is about to be cut in half," Slaton said with a nod toward the hatch.

Wysinski laughed. "You haven't figured it out yet, have you?"

"What?"

"Do you really think we're going to all this trouble for a few million in cash? It's too bad you won't be alive in a couple of days to see. It's beautiful, the way everything will work."

"How what will work?"

"If only you could have been on our side, kidon. Unfortunately, the person in charge has some history with you. Or maybe I should say, you with him. That's why you're here. In ten minutes the police will find the killer they've been looking for — dead. And with an alarming surprise below decks."

"Where's the other weapon?"

"In the hands of Pytor Roth, a mercenary and an imbecile who will unwittingly shape the future of our country. It all fits perfectly."

Sirens and screeching tires announced the arrival of a large police contingent. Slaton stood straight, his eyes locked to Wysinski. "You say the person in charge has a past with me? Who?"

Slaton took a deliberate step forward. Wysinski straightened his arm and pulled the trigger. The gun clicked harmlessly. Slaton didn't even blink, his movement steady and strong. Wysinski tried to shoot again with the same result. His smugness disintegrated as he realized he'd been duped.

Slaton closed in. "*Who?*" he screamed.

Wysinski backed up, his eyes sweeping, searching frantically for something to use against the kidon. Wysinski spat out, "He was one of the shooters on the bus in Netanya."

Slaton stopped dead in his tracks. "What?"

"And the man who ordered Yosef killed. He's the reason you are here today."

"Netanya? That was the Palestinians, Anand's group."

"Rubbish! We never identified anyone, did we, kidon? We only rounded up the usual suspects. You of all people must know — no one was ever held responsible."

"You? You and your sick friends? Working with the Arabs?"

"No. Don't you see? It's exactly the opposite."

Slaton's head spun. Wysinski was only trying to save himself. Nothing more. "No, not Netanya," he said hoarsely. "No Israeli could do that. What would it accomplish?"

"Yes, what have we accomplished?"

Slaton took a step away, and slowly, agonizingly, he tried to comprehend the incomprehensible. A world he always controlled seemed to be spinning now, and he was at the vortex.

"And wait until you see what we accomplish this time. The policies of compromise for our country will be over. We will be strong once again and he will lead us there. He *is* leading us there."

The words swirled in Slaton's mind and one thought, one image overrode everything else. He was waiting outside the room, the nurse standing squarely in his way. *Let me in! I have to get in! Do something — anything!*"

The burly soldier charged Slaton, knocking him off balance, then ran. Slaton stumbled backwards as Wysinski clambered up to the dock.

"Who did it? Who?" Slaton stammered. He saw Wysinski racing away and realized the answers would soon be gone. All at once, the fog lifted. Slaton riveted on the man who knew, the one who could slay his nightmare once and for all.

Slaton bolted, immune to his pain, immune to feeling anything. He lunged across to the dock and caught Wysinski in ten strides, twisting an arm behind his back. Wysinski leaned ahead, clearly expecting Slaton to try and stop him. Instead, Slaton propelled him forward and the heavier man completely lost his balance. With all the force he could muster, Slaton slammed the stocky soldier head first into a concrete dock piling. Wysinski's body crumpled to the dock and lay motionless.

Slaton dropped next to him and put his hands around a throat that would never again carry a breath. "*Who?*" he screamed. "*Who did it?*"

"Don't move!" a voice commanded from somewhere up the pier.

Slaton was oblivious as he strangled the limp corpse.

Another shout, "You!"

This time he looked up. Three policemen were twenty feet away, approaching very, very slowly. Slaton looked down to see the lifeless eyes of Viktor Wysinski. It was the first time he had ever killed a man without planning, without premeditation. He had simply killed due to rage. The kidon had lost control. But now he had to regain it, because there was still someone else out there. Someone even more dangerous. And more deserving. Slaton stood slowly.

The policemen were an experienced contingent and they stopped five paces away, seeing no surrender in their suspect's posture. What they saw in his eyes was closer to madness.

"Here now," the one in front said, "let's do this the easy way."

It happened without warning. Their man dove to his right and disappeared with a splash into the inky water of the harbor.

"Bloody hell!" one of the bobbies said as they all ran to where the man had been. Two searched the water in vain while a third checked Wysinski, which didn't take long. "He's done," the policeman said with certainty.

Another policeman came running up the dock and more were in the distance. All converged on the pier. They searched the adjacent boats, not finding any trace of their quarry. Then, at the very end of the pier, an out-board motor churned to life. The two who were closest ran out and spotted a small inflatable boat, thirty yards off and speeding toward the harbor entrance. The driver was hiding under some kind of blanket or tarpaulin.

"He's makin' for open sea!" one of them yelled. The constable in charge barked orders to the nearest man. "Get to the harbormaster and commandeer a boat. Something fast!" He pulled out his radio and put in an emergency request for a helicopter from the Royal Navy in Portsmouth. They watched the Zodiac as it headed out through the channel. At one point it crashed into a seawall, before bouncing crazily back to open water.

"He's stark mad," one of the bobbies said.

Another nodded. "Did you see the look in his eyes? And the way he killed that poor sod?"

"I don't know about you, but it doesn't bother me one bit that someone else will have to wrap him up now."

Half an hour later, a Royal Navy helicopter, a Westland Sea King, intercepted the Zodiac. The little craft was two miles offshore, still at full throttle and making large, lazy circles on the choppy seas. The Westland's crew moved in for a closer look and immediately noted three things. First was a tarp that was flapping along loosely behind the craft, slapping in and out of its wake. Second was a rope, tied from beam to beam, and in the middle secured to the little outboard's steering arm. Of course the third, and most relevant observation was that there was no one in the boat.

Chapter Fourteen

The police in Eastbourne searched the Bertram and had no trouble discovering two more bodies in the suite below deck. Word was quickly sent to Scotland Yard that the man they were after, seen by three officers, was likely responsible. They also made note of a large, polished steel, cylindrical object on a stand near one of the bodies. The officer in command, understandably on edge as a result of the carnage around him, elected to assume the worst and ordered the entire dock evacuated. He called in the bomb disposal unit from London's Metropolitan Police.

The technicians from London arrived an hour later. The man in charge had considerable experience defusing all sorts of small, home-made explosive contraptions; credit that to the IRA. He took one look at the sleek, well-machined device on board the yacht and quickly decided he might let someone else have a crack. Whatever it was, it looked military, and the Army lads up at Wimbish would do better with it. In the meantime, he suggested that the evacuation perimeter be expanded. The few operating businesses on the waterfront were ordered closed, and a handful of year-round residents were rousted from their homes. By one o'clock that afternoon, only those with official purpose were allowed within a block of the harbor.

The 58th Field Squadron had existed, under various banners, for over a century. As one of the few Royal Engineers units to specialize in explosive ordnance disposal, the 58th managed a brisk business in places like Northern Ireland, Bosnia, and Kosovo. More recently, its charter had been expanded to conduct "search operations in confined and environmentally harmful situations," a euphemism for tangling with the occasional weapon of mass destruction.

Based in Wimbish, the soldiers of the 58th took nearly two hours to arrive. By then, crowds had begun to gather outside the cleared area, concentrated at those points that held a good view of the harbor. Reporters prowled the access points, peppering anyone in any sort of uniform with questions about what was going on. Aside from acknowledging that three bodies had been removed from the scene, little was said.

The 58th brought their best men and equipment, and got right to work. A robot might normally have performed the initial work, however their preferred unit was designed for streets, buildings, and warehouses. Its tracked wheels where wholly incompatible with stairs and, anyway, the contraption was far too big for clambering around such tight spaces. That being the case, the scene reverted to one not much different from what it had been back in World War I — one volunteer, in the best protective gear available, would go below deck on *Lorraine II* and deal with the weapon. Yet while the concept was reminiscent of another era, the technology was not. A small camera on the soldier's headgear transmitted real-time pictures to a mobile command center outside, where the officer in charge watched every move.

It was obvious they were dealing with some sort of military device, but unlike any they'd ever seen or been briefed on. It was similar in shape to an air-dropped munition — a five-hundred pounder, perhaps — and they all saw what looked like fin attach points at the rear. But the lack of any external fuse or guidance package seemed peculiar. The point man identified what seemed to be a serial number at the base of the cylinder, and technicians outside fed these numbers, along with a physical description of the weapon, into a laptop computer. The computer cross-checked through its substantial database of weaponry, but found nothing to match.

The officer in charge was vexed. He recalled his specialist, not wanting to risk anything more until he knew what they were dealing with. It was one of his subordinates who suggested they use their new machines from the States, Ranger and Alex. Both were made by a small, highly specialized American company. Ranger's function was to detect the slightest signature of certain radioactive isotopes, while Alex was used to identify a wide range of metals with potential nuclear uses. The machines had been unpacked only weeks earlier, but long enough for the curious engineers of the 58th to decipher their operation. Both were quickly brought

forward to bear analysis on the enigma that lay below *Lorraine II*'s stern
deck.

The results were immediate, conclusive, and stirred a convulsion of
anxiety in the control room. The soldiers there, among the steadiest in the
British armed forces, fought to maintain their professional equilibrium.

There were two immediate options. Evacuate the entire city, or tow
the Bertram out to sea. Since the first option would necessitate revealing
the need for the evacuation, a technique sure to incite panic, the second
was selected. Arrangements were made to commandeer a small tug while
the whole matter was sent up the chain of command. Far, far up.

It took twelve minutes to reach Nathan Chatham. He was already grim,
having received word earlier of the triple homicide in Eastbourne. The assailant, seen by police, was almost certainly their man. That on his mind,
he was called unexpectedly up to Shearer's office, where the Assistant
Commissioner filled him in on the latest bad news.

"We don't know where it's come from," Shearer said, "but our technical people are working on it. This is a military device, not something
slapped together in the IRA's basement. Perhaps stolen from Russia.
We've been worrying about that kind of thing for years."

"Or Israeli," a somber Nathan Chatham said, thinking out loud.

"What was that?"

"I said Israeli. It's either their weapon, or perhaps one that's been gotten hold of by their enemies. That's all that makes sense."

Shearer tried to follow. "What makes you so sure?"

"We've been able to identify one of the bodies from that boat. He's
Israeli."

"Mossad again," Shearer offered.

"We don't know much about him, but I can't imagine otherwise."

"And the fellow who got away?"

"It's him," Chatham fumed, wringing his hands together. His frustration was boiling over into anger. "Eastbourne?" he rumbled. "What in the
devil would he be doing down there?"

"Yes," Shearer agreed, "I thought that odd. As far as we can tell, this
thing is not armed, and with Eastbourne not a politically significant target, I think we can assume it was headed elsewhere."

"But it doesn't make sense to leave something like that sitting at a
dock. How long did you say the boat has been there?"

Shearer reviewed the message on his desk. "Two days. And there's no evidence they were about to move."

"Two days," Chatham huffed. "You might make port for fuel, but then you'd be on your way, wouldn't you?" He thrust his hands deep into his pockets and began pacing, his head bent low.

"I'm told the fuel tanks were nearly empty. And they hadn't made any request to put into the fueling dock."

"Wasn't there any kind of inspection? Customs?"

Shearer shrugged, "Seems they slipped through somehow."

Chatham scowled. "There's a reason for everything here. I'm just not seeing it yet."

"Needless to say, this has gone straight up. The Prime Minister has scheduled a meeting in an hour. I'd like you to be there. It's at Number 10," Shearer added, referring to the address on Downing Street.

Chatham looked at his watch. "Good," he said forcefully, "I've got a few things I'd like to discuss with the Prime Minister."

"Oh, and there is one other thing," Shearer added far too casually.

"What?"

"This weapon, it seems, is resting on some type of wooden cradle. There also happens to be a second cradle next to it."

Chatham cringed, "And the second cradle is . . ."

"Quite empty."

The first press release came at 4:10 P.M., London time. Thin on details, it insisted that the situation was under control. The yacht and its cargo were now almost a hundred miles out to sea, and firmly surrounded by a flotilla of Royal Navy warships that essentially blockaded the area.

By nightfall, no less than four thousand people had surrounded the harbor in Eastbourne, all wanting to see where the doomsday boat had been docked that morning. A far greater number had taken flight, leaving the city by car, train, and even bicycle, oblivious to the fact that the weapon was far out to sea.

Over the course of the evening there were no fewer than seven briefings by various government agencies. A weather expert from the Met Office gave assurances that, even if the weapon should go off in its present position, the upper level winds would drive any harmful effects southward, out to open sea. The man stood in front of a large map which displayed (those with true knowledge might say exaggerated) the distance of the threat offshore. The Prime Minister himself even made a plea for calm, just in time for the evening news broadcast. All repeated two main themes — the situation was well in hand, and those responsible would be held to account. None mentioned the possibility of a second weapon.

Slaton drove fast, pressing well over the speed limit in the rattletrap little Ford. Christine was unnerved. He was taking chances like never before. Even worse was his demeanor. Something had changed back in East-bourne. Earlier this morning he'd been calm and chatty, almost casual. Then he'd gone to look for Wysinski. When she picked him up at the designated spot three hours ago, he was a different person, restrained and alert, clearly on edge. And this time she had collected him soaking wet, with a few new contusions and a gash on one arm. From the rendezvous, they'd driven north, keeping to back roads, and he'd hardly said a word.

"Are you going to tell me what happened?" Her request met silence. "Where are we going?"

Slaton's eyes were riveted to the winding road ahead, probably a good thing given the speed at which they were traveling. She leaned forward to be sure she was in his field of view and stared at him.

"Circumstances have changed," he said abruptly.

"How?"

"I don't think you're in danger any longer."

"The way you're driving, I am!"

He ignored her critique. "I'm convinced the reason they went after you was because you might have blown their whole operation. You knew where you picked me up, and so you might have known where to look for *Polaris Venture*."

"That makes sense, I guess, but now you're saying I'm no longer in danger. What's different? *Polaris Venture* hasn't gone anywhere."

"No. But her cargo has."

"The weapons?"

Slaton nodded.

"How do you know that?"

"Because I saw one of them this morning. It was on a big cruiser, in the harbor at Eastbourne."

Christine jerked back in her seat. "You're telling me there's a nuclear weapon sitting on a boat back there? In the middle of a good sized city? Could . . . could it . . ."

"Detonate? Wouldn't make sense to me," he said doubtfully. "Eastbourne's not much of a target. But I really have no idea what it's doing there."

"What about the other one?"

"Your guess is as good as mine. They might only have salvaged one. But the point is that one of the weapons is there. The salvage has taken place, so you're off the hook."

Christine supposed he was trying to offer relief, but instead she felt bleak and hollow. The cat and mouse game they'd been playing was now much more encompassing, no longer simply the two of them scurrying from a few madmen. The lives of thousands could be at stake.

"So why are we in such a hurry?" she asked.

"Because along with the weapon there were three men on that boat. At least two are dead, and the police got a good look at me."

Christine didn't even flinch. A mild numbness set in and she wondered if she could be getting used to such things. Perhaps this was how he always stayed so calm — a series of psychological jolts that gradually, indelibly wore you down until there was nothing left. How much must David have seen in so many years of undeclared warfare? How much could he take? How much could anyone take?

She watched him concentrating on the road ahead and behind, summing up all the sights, sounds, and smells; categorizing everything as friend, foe, or neutral. Last night he had been a warm, caring man. Now he was altogether different. She saw a volatile fury seething within him that she didn't understand. Even more, for the first time since she'd pulled him from the ocean, she was frightened. Not for her own well being, but for his. Something was terribly wrong.

"David, are you all right?"

The softness of her voice captured his attention. At last, the man she had known last night reappeared. He eased off the accelerator and put a hand to her cheek. "We're going to get you safe now."

"How?"

Slaton told her. When he finished, she thought about the plan. It made sense and she could hardly argue against it.

"What about you? What are you going to do?" she asked.

The car accelerated and Slaton was again lost to the task at hand. He never answered, and Christine was left wishing she had never asked.

❖   ❖   ❖

Anton Bloch shifted uncomfortably in his seat outside Prime Minister Jacobs' office. He'd been there for nearly an hour, waiting patiently while shouts reverberated behind the two thick wooden doors. He looked at Moira who was, as always, implacable. She sat typing on her computer, as if unaware that the future of their country was being decided in the next room. Bloch had tried to catch her eye once or twice, but her professionalism was unyielding, and she kept tied to her task.

The news about one of the weapons turning up in England had hit three hours ago. The Brits tried to make the communiqué as diplomatic as possible, but the magnitude of the event transcended what little conciliatory language the Foreign Office could include. Great Britain strongly suspected Israeli involvement in the matter of a nuclear weapon turning up on their doorstep, and they demanded an explanation. The fact that the weapon had been dragged out to sea, and was no immediate danger to anyone, save the sailors who watched over it, carried little comfort. A multimedia feeding frenzy had begun. The world wanted answers.

In Tel Aviv, the news hit particularly hard among those who knew the details of the "*Polaris Venture* fiasco." For those in power the story ran wild, a fire driven by hurricane winds and jumping the feeble breaks that were security clearances and chains of command. Now the true elite, the Knesset leaders and coalition makers, all knew the facts, and they realized it was only a matter of time before the whole thing would land with a crunch at Israel's diplomatic feet. A political bloodletting of the highest order was under way in Jacobs' office, and Anton Bloch sat quietly, impotently on the sidelines, knowing he was as much to blame as anyone.

Bloch tried to imagine what was happening in England. Slaton and Wysinski had gone to South Africa together to load the weapons, then they had split up. Now both of them, and one of the weapons, turn up in a quiet English harbor. Viktor Wysinski and two other Mossad men, dead. David Slaton the killer. Again. And God only knew where the other nuke was. It all made Bloch reel.

Finally, Jacobs' office grew quiet. The heavy mahogany doors flew open and a stream of the most powerful men and women in Israel filed out. Some looked at Bloch contemptuously as they exited, while others ignored him, more rushed and purposeful. The last few out simply looked defeated. Jacobs did not emerge.

Bloch got up and started into the office. He momentarily wondered if Moira would announce his entrance, but she stayed locked to her work. Passing her desk, Bloch got a good look and saw that her eyes were glistening. Moira knew what was happening, but she was doing her best to keep up a front. It was her way of dealing with it.

Jacobs was alone in the room, seated at his desk but facing away, toward the window behind. Bloch could only see the back of his head.

"Well?" he said, announcing his presence. "How did it go?"

Jacobs didn't say anything for a moment, then slowly eased his chair around. He looked thoughtful and subdued. When he finally spoke, he did so slowly, as if making a conscious effort to shift gears from the free-for-all that had just ended. "Badly, Anton. Badly."

Jacobs stood. He looked weary and his shoulders sagged. "We've sent word to the British ambassador here, admitting we lost the weapon that turned up in Eastbourne. We also admitted that there's a second one loose. I suspect we'll look for it together, quietly for now. But if we don't find it soon, Anton, I'm afraid word's going to get out."

"We'll find it," Bloch said, more with hope than conviction.

"I'll be making a speech tonight. I have to acknowledge Israel's part in this whole affair. It will also contain my statement of resignation."

"Resignation? You're kidding!"

Jacobs shrugged. "There's really no other way."

"There has to be! Say it was a Mossad screw up. I'll take the blame."

The Prime Minister came around the desk and put a hand on Bloch's shoulder. "I appreciate your loyalty Anton, but we can't get out of this so easily. A lot of people know that I approved the mission right from the start, and some of those people don't like me or my party."

"Fight them!"

"I did. I fought for all I was worth, but it was no use. It all comes down to support, numbers. There were too many against me."

"Politics," Bloch spat.

"Politics, my friend. That's what got me here, and that's how it ends." Jacobs struck a fist into his open palm. "Damn! If I only could have held it together. There were so many things in the works, things I cared about."

"Who will take over?" Bloch asked.

Jacobs laughed. "You should have seen them. The posturing, the threats, the blatant dealmaking. I'd say Steiner, or maybe Feldman. Whoever can scheme up the right coalition. For now, Zak will run things until a special election can be arranged."

"Zak? He was briefed on everything right from the start. Isn't he as dirty as the rest of us?"

"Of course, but somebody has to run the country for a couple of months, Anton. Zak's a Knesset member, and since he's always been in my shadow, he hasn't stepped on many toes yet. To tell the truth, I think the others see him as the least ambitious of the bunch. He agreed to not be part of the next government. And we'll erase his name from any records that might have put him at the meetings."

"Whose idea was that?" Bloch asked.

"It was mine. We have to insulate him."

"What about Greenwich on Monday? Will this threaten the Accord?"

"A few of the Arab countries will raise a predictable fuss, but we'll confess our sins carefully. At worst we'll look careless, but there's no new strategic ground. We've been nuclear capable for decades. No, the Accord will go forward. I'm sure of it."

"That's your peace agreement! You spent an entire year battling for it. You have every right to be the one who signs it and finishes the deal."

"No," Jacobs said, "this has to be done right away. Once I've taken responsibility for this mess, there's nowhere for me to go but out. I can't linger for a few days for something like that. My resignation will take effect at midnight. Zak will go to Greenwich and sign the Accord."

Bloch had never been more frustrated in his life. Again and again he tried to figure it out. How had the weapons been taken? How did one end up in England? And above all else, *why?* He'd give anything to talk to David Slaton for sixty seconds.

"And Anton," Jacobs added awkwardly, "I'm afraid you'll be going down with me."

Bloch nodded. "I expected as much. You'll have my letter in the morning."

Jacobs went to a small cabinet where a bottle of brandy was waiting, a prepositioned salve. He held out a glass, inviting Bloch to join him.

An agitated Bloch shook his head. "No. Maybe tomorrow, but not now."

Jacobs poured a stout bracer, snapped his head back and downed it in one motion.

Bloch headed for the door.

"Where are you going?"

"There's still one weapon out there, and I want to find it. I hate being made the fool!"

It was the kind of evening Nathan Chatham enjoyed, cool and clear. Living a mile and a half from the Yard, he generally eschewed the clunky old conglomeration of iron that passed for his automobile. He always felt that a crisp walk helped to clear his thoughts, thoughts so regularly muddled amid the daily scramble of people and information. Today had been particularly hectic, and he'd gotten no sleep the night before. Exhausted, Chatham had explained to Ian Dark that he'd be going home for dinner, a nap and, most critically, a few hours of quiet in which to think things through. He'd be back at the office by midnight.

Chatham walked at his typical brisk pace so as to take advantage of the cardiovascular benefits. No need then for a time-consuming exercise program. It also had the advantage of getting him home a few minutes sooner.

He reached the brownstone row where he'd made his home for the last twenty-one years. His particular dwelling was over two hundred years old, built for a sea captain, or so the property agent had told him. It was solid and well-maintained, two stories squeezed narrowly into a row of similar homes that ran the length of the street. Lately the address had become fashionable and, one by one, widows and pensioners were giving way to the *nouveau riche*, young advertising and financial princes who parked Italian cars in the street and spruced their housefronts in the most god-awful colors. Chatham didn't mind much. They were loud at times, but the walls between the homes were a full one meter thick and he had no trouble getting his sleep. (Neighborhood legend had it that even Hitler's V-2s had gotten no satisfaction here, one having bounced off the backside of a house to make a large crater in a resident's backyard. Old timers swore the defiant owner had filled the gaping hole with water and used it for many years thereafter as a duck pond, though Chatham had never seen evidence of it.) His only complaint was on Sundays, the day he liked to work in his garden. Occasionally the parties at nearby properties got out of hand, disturbing Chatham's cherished day of peace and reconstitution. It was during these instances that the Chief Inspector from Scotland Yard had no hesitation in putting his rank and position to good use.

He spent a few minutes chatting up Mrs. Nesbit, who was sweeping her porch two doors down. A great hater of the "bloody tele," she was probably the only person on the block who hadn't seen the evening news, and thus had no idea what Chatham had been up against all day. He found it a pleasant diversion to hear the neighborhood gossip — Number 20 at the end of the street had been sold to a speculator, and Mr. Wooley's gall bladder operation had ended favorably.

Chatham bid goodnight to Mrs. Nesbit and went to his door. He fumbled through his keyring, found the correct one and went inside, right away noticing the familiar, cool dampness that came from leaving the furnace off all day. When he closed the door, it struck him that the room seemed darker than usual, no illumination from the streetlights filtering in from the front window. Chatham tried to remember if he had closed the drapes for some reason. Then something else seemed off, though he wasn't sure just what. A moment later his instincts were proven correct. A light came on. When his eyes adjusted, he saw two people sitting comfortably in the matching armchairs of his living room, a man and a woman he'd never met. He recognized them instantly.

"Good evening, Inspector," Slaton said.

Chatham paused to regard his intruders. The man looked casual and relaxed, a manner at odds with the handgun lying obtrusively in his lap. The woman, rigid and nervous, was the far less worrisome of the two.

"Is it?" Chatham replied. He casually removed his topcoat, noticing the man's hand tense almost imperceptibly over the gun. "At ease, sir. I don't carry a weapon. And I might add, it is illegal to do so in this country." He calmly walked to the thermostat and turned on the furnace. "It will take a few minutes to warm. Can I offer you some tea?"

Slaton grinned. "No, thank you."

"Well that settles it then, you're not an Englishman. At least I had that much right. Are you Israeli?"

"I am."

Chatham was pleased. "Good, good. I was headed in the right direction, then. Let's see . . . Mossad?"

Slaton nodded, still allowing Chatham to lead, "I was. But I'm not sure if it still applies."

Chatham beamed and turned his attention to Christine, "And you, dear. I must say I have been vexed about how you fit into this."

"So have I, Inspector."

"We'll get to all that," Slaton said.

"Good," said Chatham, "although with that weapon so clearly in view I suppose you've not come here to surrender."

"No," Slaton replied.

"I have," Christine chimed in.

Chatham considered that. "I must say miss, from what I know, you're not the one who's committed the crimes here. It's your associate who's left a trail of bodies across this country. In all honesty, I wouldn't have been surprised if we had eventually found you in a shallow grave in the moors."

"You're wrong about that," she retorted. "David is the only reason I'm still here. Yes, he's killed and hurt people, but it was only in self-defense. We're being chased, Inspector. And it all has to do with those two nuclear weapons."

Chatham raised an eyebrow. His voice softened. "I see."

Slaton said, "Inspector, have a seat. I'd like to tell you a story."

Chapter Fifteen

Chatham listened as Slaton covered everything. How *Polaris Venture* had gone down, how Christine had rescued him and unwittingly gotten involved. The Israeli explained Penzance; that he had gone back guessing Itzaak Simon and his friend, or someone like them, would show up. Then he made a convincing case that he'd felt obligated to take Christine with him, to protect her from the danger he'd put her in. Chatham didn't interrupt once, but mentally filed away questions for later. Once the facts were laid out, the Israeli got to why they were here.

"When these people discovered that Christine had rescued me, she instantly became a problem. I don't think they'd been able to salvage the weapons yet, and she knew roughly where *Polaris Venture* was. That's why they went after her. I convinced Christine to not go to the police right away because they wouldn't protect her."

"We do that sort of thing quite well," Chatham disagreed.

"I didn't say you wouldn't be *able* to protect her. I said you wouldn't. Last week there was nothing concrete to support what I've just told you. I doubt anyone would have believed her."

"And now?"

Slaton nodded toward Christine, "This morning we figured it out. I think we know exactly where *Polaris Venture* is."

Christine, taking her cue, produced the atlas and opened it to the appropriate page. She moved next to Chatham and pointed out the seamount. "By our calculations, she went down here, in roughly 130 feet of water."

"Easily salvageable," Slaton added. "You wouldn't even need any fancy equipment."

Chatham eyed the book critically and tried to remember the description of the weapon found in Eastbourne. "How heavy are these devices?"

"A little over 400 pounds. Getting into *Polaris Venture* and dragging them clear would have been the hard part. Then you just attach a couple of inflatable salvage buoys. At the surface you could easily lift them out with a small winch. With good conditions, and if *Polaris Venture* settled favorably, it wouldn't take more than half a day. It looks like that salvage has already taken place." Slaton gestured to Christine, "And if that's the case, Christine is no longer a threat to these people."

"What about you?" Chatham queried.

"I'm very much a threat to them."

Chatham frowned. "So who are these Mossad villains you keep referring to? Pro-Arab Israelis? Are they being bought off? How could there be so many of them? And here in England, no less?"

Slaton hesitated, "That part I don't understand. We've had our share of spies and turncoats like any country, but I could never have imagined something on this scale."

Chatham wondered if Slaton was truly as mystified as he appeared. "Sounds rather fantastic, if you ask me."

"Any more fantastic than if I'd told you yesterday that you'd find a nuclear weapon on a pleasure boat in Eastbourne?"

Chatham tried to change tack. "So you're going to leave Dr. Palmer in my custody?"

Christine shifted restlessly, "I don't like the word custody. David—"

Slaton cut her off by raising his hand with a violent slashing motion. A moment later there was a knock on the door. A sharp, rapid-fire knock. Nathan Chatham knew precisely who it was.

From behind the heavy wood door a sing-song voice called out, *"Yoo-hoo, Inspector. I've got something for you."*

"It's Mrs. Nesbit," Chatham said at a whisper. "She makes tarts every Tuesday. Always brings one over."

Slaton shook his head and put a finger to his lips. Another knock, then silence. Slaton waited a full minute before speaking again.

"Will she come back?"

"Probably not," Chatham said. "She'll just keep it until tomorrow."

Chatham watched as Slaton weighed that response, deconstructing it to uncover any deception, deciding if Mrs. Nesbit might cause complications. Apparently satisfied, the Mossad man went on.

"Inspector, I know you'll evaluate everything we're telling you. I know you'll dig and cross-check, but the facts you find will reinforce that we're on the level. Christine is guilty of nothing more than being in the wrong place at the wrong time. She will cooperate fully," he shot her a pointed look, "and answer any questions you have. Before I leave, though, I want your assurances on a few things."

Chatham took a stab at the first. "You wish for her to have immunity from prosecution."

The two fugitives exchanged a glance. "Yes," Slaton said.

"I can't guarantee anything, but if your story holds true I can't imagine she'd be guilty of much more than aiding and abetting you, sir. As long as she cooperates, I'll do everything in my power to see that no charges are brought forward."

"Fair enough," Slaton said.

"What else?"

"There's another weapon out there somewhere. I want your military to start monitoring the area we've identified. Right away, in case the salvage hasn't been completed."

"Those forces are not under my command, of course, but I can probably convince the right people that this bears looking into. Anything else?"

"Yes. I want your word that you'll give Christine protection, just in case I've gotten it all wrong. Tight protection. Not just a hotel room or a cell in some minimum security area."

"I'll see to it. You have my word."

"Good. That's it then." Slaton went over to the modest dining area and grabbed a wooden chair from the table.

Chatham tried to guess what he was up to, figuring it out when he saw the Israeli pull out a big roll of duct tape. "Is that really—"

"Necessary? Well, let's see. If I asked you to sit still after I leave and not call in my whereabouts for two hours, would you?"

"No."

"Then it's necessary."

Slaton shoved the chair back against a banister at the bottom of the narrow staircase. He gestured for Chatham take the seat, and he did so re-luctantly.

The thought of trying to overpower the Israeli entered Chatham's mind. But it exited just as quickly. He had watched the man closely. For the most part he'd been pleasant and businesslike. But to the trained eye there was more. The way he moved, so efficient, with no wasted motion. The way his eyes registered every movement. And when Mrs. Nesbit had come to the door. He knew she was there before anyone, even before she'd knocked. No, Chatham thought, there was a fine line between brav-ery and foolishness, and he knew of at least a half dozen men in the last week who had made the wrong choice with this one.

Slaton secured him to the chair with duct tape. Then, for good measure, he connected the chair to the heavy wooden banister.

"I'm not going to worry that you might shout. I don't think your neighbors could hear you through these walls anyway, but if you do try, I've instructed Christine to tune your stereo to the most annoying heavy-metal radio station available and then set the volume on maximum."

"That," Chatham deadpanned, "could lead to criminal charges for her after all."

Christine watched tensely as Slaton secured the Scotland Yard man. She realized that in minutes they'd be parting ways for the second time in a week. The last time, he'd been rowing himself ashore, and Christine had hoped to never see him again. This time it was very different. The thought stuck stubbornly in her mind.

When he was done, he handed her a pair of scissors. "Two hours, no less."

She nodded. "I need to talk to you, David."

He looked up, scouted the room, and pointed to the kitchen. They retreated beyond Chatham's watchful eyes.

"What is it?" he asked in a hushed tone.

"You don't know?"

He looked at her directly, something he had seemed to avoid since they'd left Eastbourne. Christine felt a glimmer of hope.

"Look," he said, "I know what you're thinking. But things can't hap-pen that way."

"What way?"

"The way they were yesterday, and . . ."

"And that night?" she said. "Why not? What was so wrong with it?" She could see him withdraw, his gaze fading to obscurity. Christine wanted to rescue him once and for all. "David, they can protect you as well as they can me. I like Inspector Chatham. I think he believes us. Stay. Get out of this life you're so immersed in. It rules everything you do. You can't eat, sleep, walk, or talk without worrying about who's chasing you or who you should be chasing. You're not even capable of love if—"

"No!" he said loudly. "I—" he lowered his tone to a harsh whisper, "I had a wife and child once, and they were ripped from my life!"

"Oh!" Christine spat back, "So you're just going to spend the rest of your life destroying others to make up for it! That makes sense. You don't even know who was responsible for what happened back then."

"I can find out now!"

Christine watched him turn away and storm to the back door. There, peering out the window, he performed reconnaissance on a well-tended garden and the wall that surrounded it. That was how they'd gotten in, and that was how he'd leave.

"David, two nights ago I thought I finally knew you. I thought I saw the person you really are. But now these demons are back. Whatever it is, walk away! Stay here with me and we can both stop running!"

"You don't understand."

"No, you're right. I don't!" she yelled, not caring if Chatham heard. "I don't understand what you're doing, where you're going, or what you're thinking. For a short time I thought I did, but I was obviously wrong."

They squared off and glared at one another, both unyielding. Slaton finally broke the stalemate. He brushed by her and went for a last check of their captive. Apparently satisfied Chatham wasn't going anywhere, he walked right past her again and started out the back door.

She watched him, speechless, not believing he could leave it at that. But at the threshold he stopped. He spoke without looking at her, "All that I've brought on — I hope none of it has hurt you."

"Only one thing," she said quietly.

He didn't move for a moment, as he stood staring out the half-open door. Then he was gone.

Christine folded her arms tightly and tried to hold her composure. She took a few deep breaths before returning to the adjoining room, where an inspector from Scotland Yard sat calmly taped to his dining room chair.

Chatham eyed her.

"Is it really true that you found him in the ocean? You've never seen him before that?"

Arms still folded, her hands clutched at her sleeves. "Yes. Why do you ask?"

"Well, the way the two of you interact. I'd suspect you might have known one another longer."

She turned away briefly, not wanting him to gauge her reaction. When she turned back, Chatham made a show of inspecting the bindings that held him to the chair.

"I don't suppose I could talk you into cutting me out of this predicament?"

She shook her head.

"No. No, I really didn't think so."

She sat gingerly on the stairs beside him.

"You look tired. Been a tough week, has it?"

She nodded.

"I can help him."

Christine studied the inspector, "How?"

"I don't know yet, honestly. But I've a great deal of manpower at my disposal."

"He's just a terrorist to you. Perhaps the most dangerous one ever, if you believe what's in the press."

"The press," Chatham scoffed. "I believe only what I can verify. You and that fellow say you're the victims here. Surprisingly, I have an urge to believe you. However, I must support that urge with evidence." Chatham softened his tone, "I will find him. Hopefully before anything more happens. But in order to do that, I must know who he is, what he's going to do next."

"Who he is?" Christine hunched forward, bringing her knees to her chest. "I don't think he even knows that. What could I tell you?"

"Anything. Everything. Tell me he's six-foot-one, a hundred eighty pounds, with a round scar on the back of his left hand, and two small moles on the back of his neck at the collar. Tell me he's got a scruffy beard with some recent scarring underneath, probably a result of the exposure at sea. His English is good, but the accent is continental. He seems well-educated, perhaps proficient in other languages. He also favors his left arm as though it's been injured recently."

"You're very observant, Inspector."

"I've been at this a long time. I repeat, I *will* find him."

"You might, but he's also very good at what he does, Inspector Chatham."

"Right, and since we have some time here, that would be a good place to start. What *does* he do?"

Christine thought about that. As far as she knew there was only one true answer, but she couldn't bring herself to say it. *He kills people, Inspector. He shoots them and kicks them in the face so hard that their necks break.* She had to tell this policeman everything without condemning David. There had always been circumstances to support what he'd done, and she knew there was another side to him, another person within. One night she had seen that person, held him, even loved him. But there were two David Slatons, and the one that had just walked out onto the streets of London was the one she would probably never know or understand. Perhaps it was because of the ghosts, the demons that always tore into his dreams. In any event, Christine knew she had to do everything possible to help him. She would not let him fight the world alone. He'd been doing that for far too long.

"His name," she began, "is David Slaton . . ."

Christine released Chatham after exactly two hours of captivity in his own living room. He made a lengthy phone call and, before the end of it, a large sedan pulled up directly in front of the house. When Chatham finally finished his call, he and Christine got into the car.

The inspector said nothing to the two men in front, but within minutes the driver had whisked them to a back gate at Scotland Yard. Through security checkpoints and a labyrinth of passages, the car deposited Christine and Chatham at an entrance, which posted no signs to guide the unfamiliar. There was simply a door, more security, and an unmarked elevator. They got on the elevator and, to Christine's surprise, went down, mocking the huge multi-story structure that towered above them.

All the while, they kept in tow the two quiet, solidly built men who had been in the car. Christine found herself watching the bodyguards, studying them. Alert and expressionless, they never once seemed to look at her or Chatham. They were simply fixtures — silent, watchful and ever-present — and she realized that they reminded her of David. At any rate, Christine decided Chatham was keeping his word. The security men made her feel safe, notwithstanding the fact that she was now tucked away in the headquarters of one of the world's preeminent police organizations.

Christine was ushered into a small, utilitarian room and told to wait. She tried to get comfortable, figuring it could be a long night.

By coincidence, the press releases were issued almost simultaneously. From Scotland Yard came word that a suspect had been identified in connection with the nuclear weapon in Eastbourne, indeed the same man who had been sought concerning shootings in Penzance and a West End restaurant. The American woman who had purportedly been abducted by that same man was now in police custody, and being questioned about her involvement. An excellent drawing of the man, courtesy of Nathan Chatham's memory and the Yard's best computer-aided sketch man, was issued with a request for the widest possible dissemination.

From Tel Aviv came a communiqué admitting that the weapon found in England was of South African origin, and had been hijacked while under transport to Israel for safekeeping. Three cleverly worded paragraphs managed to avoid placing any blame on the state of Israel. It also dodged, just as the British had, any mention of a second weapon. Both governments wanted to sidestep whatever panic that announcement might incur.

In a brief speech half an hour later, Israeli Prime Minister Benjamin Jacobs announced his resignation, citing tragic security lapses that had taken place under his watch. The failures had irretrievably undermined the support of his governing coalition. Ehud Zak was named as acting Prime Minister, until elections were held in two month's time. Zak vowed to cooperate completely with the United Kingdom and all other nations to bring those "guilty persons or organizations" to justice.

CNN could barely keep up.

Chatham had allowed her to phone her mother. The call was brief, and the Inspector himself had listened to every word. In roughly a minute, Christine assured her mother that she was safe, and would be home soon. That conversation should have provided final relief for Christine, a confirmation that, for the first time in weeks, her own personal safety was not at question. Instead, she still felt uneasy and the reason was clear. David remained very much in danger. He was being hunted down by the world's top police forces, not to mention a shadowy band of killers.

Nearing midnight, Christine was comfortably seated in the ante-room to Chatham's office. At the hallway entrance she saw two big, famil-iar shoulders, one on each side of the door frame. Across the room, Chatham was barking instructions to a harried staff.

"Heathrow in particular, but don't forget Gatwick, Stansted, and City. He's got a head start, but not a big one. Containment! That's the thing. Take those men off the tube and put them on National Rail, all the big stations. And the car. He'll have to ditch that ridiculously conspicuous car. Check all the rental agencies, particularly the smaller ones. We must know about anyone trying to deal in cash . . ."

On and on Chatham went, and after a final verbal boot to their col-lective bottoms, a half dozen men and women scurried out of the office and dispersed down the halls. The inspector appeared and beckoned Christine into his office.

"Dr. Palmer, if you please."

Christine went into Chatham's office. It seemed a dark, haphazard place. The appointments were tasteful, though dated, and papers and files lay strewn about the place, with a big pile stacked loosely on the floor in one corner. The furniture looked comfortable but had to be fifty years old, judging by the worn fabric and scratched wood surfaces. Christine saw scant evidence of the twentieth century, let alone the twenty-first. There was a telephone at his desk, and a television and VCR sat on a wheeled cart. The digital clock on the VCR was insistently flashing 12:00 and, given that the stroke of midnight was approaching, would soon be correct for the second time today. The rest of the room's furnishings had likely been in place for generations.

Chatham got straight to the point. "Tell me again how he purchased the car, the last one you were driving."

"He said he bought it from a young kid," Christine said.

"Do you know how he found it? An advertisement of some sort?"

Christine's patience was spent. "Inspector Chatham, I've gone over this. I've answered all your questions. I want to help you as much as possi-ble, but so far, everything I've heard leads me to the conclusion that you're putting all your efforts into finding David. If you believed what we've told you, you'd be searching for the people who really hijacked *Polaris Venture*. They're the ones who have a nuclear weapon."

"Dr. Palmer, I understand your frustration, but your friend Mr. Slaton remains a very dangerous man. He's proved it time and again."

"David is not the danger here!" she said angrily. "You're after someone who's on your side while the real murderers are out there, maybe plotting to kill thousands of people." Christine glared at the Scotland Yard man, ready to jump on any reply.

Chatham's stony face broke and his lips curled into a grin. At that, Christine's posture relaxed as well. Chatham walked over to the door and closed it quietly.

"I'm not accustomed to being second guessed in my own office," he mused. "But then I wish more of my staff would force a good point when they have it. Most nod their heads without thinking."

He took a seat next to her on a worn leather couch. Chatham spoke in a hushed tone, not that anyone would hear them beyond the solid oak door. "Let me start by saying that I believe you. I think David Slaton is not our biggest problem. In fact, he might well be out there trying to find that weapon, just as we are."

"Then why not let him go and look for the real criminals?"

Chatham sighed with exasperation. "Quite simply, because I have no idea who they are."

"Well they're Israeli . . . traitors or something. That's what David thinks and it makes sense."

"Does it? Dr. Palmer, I know most of the people he's gotten mixed up with were Mossad. We figured that much out days ago. But my government has asked Israel for an explanation of all this weapons business — at the highest levels, I might add. Do you know what we were told?"

"What?"

"That your Mr. Slaton is responsible for everything."

"You don't believe that," Christine implored.

"No, I don't. Which leads me to one of two possibilities. Either the government of Israel is lying about it, or they don't know what's going on any more than we do. Given the amount of heat they're taking over this whole affair, I'd say the latter is the case. They're as stumped as we are. And with the Greenwich Accord next week, I think they'll do anything to finish this embarrassment as quickly as possible."

"What do you mean by *anything*?" she asked guardedly.

Chatham leaned closer and tilted his head to one side, his long face awash in seriousness. "I'm looking for David Slaton because he's the best lead I have. But I must add that I think he'd be safer in our hands than roaming across the world with a bull's-eye on his back."

Christine cringed, though Chatham was only reaffirming what she already suspected. She took a deep breath, held it, then let out a long sigh. "I can't wait to get back to medicine. It's so much easier."

"And I don't want to risk losing my Tuesday tarts this summer."

"What?"

"If I don't tend to my roses soon, Mrs. Nesbit will have nothing for her centerpiece come Easter Sunday. She's very unforgiving about these sorts of things."

Christine smiled and Chatham put a hand on her shoulder.

"Help me find him," he pleaded. "The sooner we do that, the sooner we can all get back to our boring old lives."

Chapter Sixteen

Slaton sat quietly in a dark corner of a subdued pub shortly after midnight. The mood in the place had been more raucous an hour ago, but England's rugby team had lost a close one, to France no less. As soon as the match had ended, someone changed the channel on the television, and the bartender got busy pouring a round of consolation.

Slaton had chosen the pub simply to be lost in a crowd while he took a meal. He hadn't eaten since breakfast and wasn't sure when another opportunity might arise. He wore a cap with a wide brim that largely concealed his face, and aside from two requisite visits from the waitress, he'd been largely ignored. The plate in front of him was empty now, the pint of beer half gone. He'd ordered the beer only because he otherwise would have been the only person in the place without one. Along the same lines, he felt obliged to drink it, taking no pleasure in the taste, nor the knowledge that his senses would be ever so slightly degraded. He took another swallow but stopped before finding the mug's bottom, lest the barmaid have ideas about swinging by with a replacement.

Slaton found himself awash in thought. He was convinced that Christine was safe now, in part because he felt Chatham was competent and would keep his word. But Slaton was also increasingly sure that his reasoning was correct. Christine had become a target only because she might have compromised *Polaris Venture*'s location. Now that didn't matter because the weapons had been salvaged. He still didn't understand the rest, though. Wysinski's words ricocheted through his mind again and again. The second weapon would *shape the future of our country*. What could that mean? And who was behind it all? There had been truth in Wysinski's taunting. *The shooter in Netanya . . . the man who killed Yosef . . . he will lead us there . . . he is leading us there.*

But who? Had someone high in the Mossad sold out, or been black-mailed? Yet there were too many involved. Too many ex-soldiers who had bled for their country, too many well-screened Mossad officers. It didn't add up.

"Here, turn that up mate," someone barked.

Slaton watched the bartender raise the volume on the TV as a BBC late night newscast came on. Everyone knew what the top story would be. The crowd eased their grousing enough to listen. The bartender looked surprised. "Haven't seen it like this since that Falklands business," he grumbled, casting an eye at the screen himself.

Distant aerial footage showed the harbor in Eastbourne, while the anchorwoman danced around the news that there was no news. She reit-erated the few known facts before the video gave way to Slaton's own im-age. Actually there were two. Police sketches, far better than what had been in circulation. One showed him as he was, with a thickening beard, the other an estimate of what he'd look like without it. Inspector Chatham wasn't wasting any time. Slaton imagined that a dozen sets of eyes at the bar should be going back and forth between the television and his table, but, in fact, no one even glanced his way. He heard a few mumblings about "bloody terrorists" this, and "IRA" that. Slaton suspected they might even get a picture soon, courtesy of his government. And his life would get that much harder.

Eventually the newscast moved on to a related story, that of the suc-cession of government in Israel, a country that was, for the moment, on everyone's shit list. The newly installed Israeli Prime Minister was speak-ing to a frantic gathering of the media. A man of medium height, Zak's heavyset frame was masked behind a podium, and his nearly bald head shone under bright camera lights. Slaton had never met the man. Like most other Israelis, he'd only regarded Zak as a background fixture, stand-ing behind Benjamin Jacobs' right shoulder, smiling and nodding at all the appropriate times. Slaton knew the man was an ex-IDF officer himself — the public would never support a candidate who hadn't done his service. Zak's demeanor now began to reflect that past. There was a no-nonsense, almost imperious expression, and he seemed cool and at ease fielding the verbal grenades being hurled his way.

"Did Israel steal this weapon from the South Africans?" some imbecile asked.

"No!" Zak retorted.

"Will Israel ask for the device, now that it's been dismantled?"

"We are presently consulting with the British government as to what would be the safest, most responsible disposition of the weapon."

"Some suggest that the weapon was hijacked by an Arab country," a female reporter said. "Do you think it might have been intended for use against Israel?"

"I cannot speculate. As you know, we are cooperating with the British authorities and Interpol to apprehend an Israeli citizen who we think is involved. We don't know if he acted alone or in concert with others. But there is no evidence to suggest involvement by any of our Arab neighbors."

The same female voice, "Will the Greenwich Accord still go forward Monday?"

Here, Zak took his time. "Peace has been a long time coming. After years, we have finally agreed with our adversaries to co-exist, to stop the insanity of violence that has plagued us for so long. The Greenwich Accord has been negotiated and ratified by our government. As long as our Arab neighbors continue along this same path of peace, I see no reason for us to not do the same. I will be in Greenwich next Monday to sign the Accord."

Slaton felt a chill shoot down his spine. Something Zak had said. Something. He watched without listening. Zak's thick forehead was gleaming, his blunt finger raised to make a point. *As long as our Arab neighbors continue along this path*—

Slaton sat transfixed. It didn't happen instantly, but was instead a slow, simmering path to recognition. He relived the past weeks and put everything in a new light, trying in vain to disprove the sick idea that was making more and more sense with every moment. Each old piece fell perfectly into the new mold, all along so obvious, yet so insane. He'd had it all wrong. For twenty years. *The man who had Yosef killed . . . the shooter in Netanya . . . he will lead us there . . . he is leading us there!*

Slaton finally understood. For twenty years he had been fighting the wrong enemy, exorcising the wrong demons. There were so many implications. The second weapon would be used, but how and where? Slaton couldn't think about it. All he could do now was stare at the television until Zak's picture finally disappeared. The newscaster began talking again, and over her shoulder was a photograph of the National Observatory at Greenwich. Through all the emotions, the hatred and confusion, one thing became clear. Crystal clear. Slaton battled to regain control as the waitress strolled up and took his empty plate.

"Anything else, luv?"

"No, nuttin'," he managed.

The waitress left a check on the table. When she returned five minutes later, the man in the corner booth was gone and his mug finally empty. She found enough money on the table to cover the tab, and an extra pound for her own troubles. The usual.

"We've found the car, Inspector," Ian Dark said, rushing into the Scotland Yard cafeteria.

Chatham immediately put down the knife and fork he'd been using to saw through a particularly tough steak, then ran a napkin across his mouth and bushy mustache. "Where?"

"The Barcomb Insurance building. It's . . ." Dark hesitated as Chatham closed his eyes dejectedly.

"Straight across the street from this building," Chatham finished. "How long ago?"

"Twenty minutes. One of our special teams found it. They were going through the big parking garages, just as you instructed."

Chatham shoved aside the daily special with few regrets. "Tube, rail, car," he murmured rhetorically, "how will you move now my friend?"

"Shall I concentrate our forces?" Dark suggested.

Chatham frowned, "I'm worried this might be a diversion, but yes, there's really nothing else to do. Keep up surveillance of the major transportation centers, but get everyone else over here. Start with a two-mile radius, then work outward. Talk to every cab and bus driver who's been through for the past . . ." he glanced at the wall clock, "four hours. Question the ticket agents at all the nearby tube stations. And car hire agencies, check them all. Also, see if there were any security cameras in that parking garage."

Chatham set off briskly toward the elevator. "The Israelis promised us a photograph. See if it's come in yet. That drawing is good, but nothing like a current photo."

As they waited for the elevator, Dark pulled out his cell phone and

began punching buttons. By the time the elevator call light had extinguished, Chatham had his answer.

"The picture came in ten minutes ago. They're reproducing as we
speak, and it should be out to the field within an hour."

"Capital," Chatham said distractedly. He looked at the little device
in Dark's hand, grudgingly accepting its utility. "Perhaps I should learn to
use one of those after all."

Dark smiled at the small victory. "Really nothing to them, Inspector," he said, holding it up. "Anyone can learn how."

Chatham eyed it with suspicion as he reached out and punched a
button on the elevator. The moment was ruined by the elevator's fire
alarm bell. Scotland Yard's top detective glared furiously at the illuminated red button on the control panel, the one he had just pushed.

"Blast!"

Slaton stood at a bus stop where no bus was due to arrive for over an hour.
Earlier, a kindly old passerby had brought the matter to his attention, but
Slaton simply thanked the man, explaining that he didn't mind having to
wait on such a lovely morning. The old man had looked up at a solid overcast, shrugged, and gone on his way.

In fact, Slaton had seen two buses come and go. The reason for
his loitering had nothing to do with them. Adjacent to the bus stop,
behind a chain link fence, lay his true objective — the loading dock for
the New Covent Garden Market, the biggest and busiest produce market
in London. Slaton had spent the morning watching the operation. Big
lorries brought in huge loads from the ships in port. There were bananas
from Panama, oranges from Spain, and Haitian sugar. Intermixed with
the big trucks were smaller versions that came from across England,
and a few from the continent. These brought their own cargo, moderate
in quantity and even more limited in range — beets, potatoes, broad
beans, and onions — the narrow range of tubers, leeks, and vegetables
that comprised the bulk of agricultural production in Northern
Europe.

Slaton had already culled his search to these smaller trucks, which
were mostly from family farms, engaged in bringing the fall harvest to
market. Conveniently, the sidewalls and doors of these vehicles were often stenciled with the names and locations of the farms they serviced.

He'd been watching for nearly three hours when his patience was finally rewarded. An ideal prospect rumbled into the yard, a boxy red contraption that advertised Smitherton Farms and Dairy, Thrapston, Northamptonshire. It was the first to meet all his requirements. Not just an open air crate, this truck's bed was completely enclosed with a roof and rear cargo door. The driver was alone, a wiry, older man. And no doubt a Smitherton, judging by the care he exercised in unloading the forty or so boxes of turnips that made up his load. Most important was the address in Thrapston. It wasn't the exact place he was looking for, but Slaton doubted he'd get much closer.

The old farmer set his last box onto the loading dock and stood waiting for a foreman to come round. That was the important part, the paperwork which would eventually route a deposit into the likely modest coffers of Smitherton Farms and Dairy. As Slaton watched, the dock foreman shouted something to the old man and spun a finger in the air. The old man raised his hand in acknowledgment, walked over to his truck and got in.

Slaton worried for a moment that his first choice was about to drive off. He saw the old diesel chug to life and maneuver away from the loading dock. Then he understood. The old man parked his rig toward the back of the lot and another truck, much bigger, took the now vacant slot at the busy loading pier.

The driver walked back to the platform to patiently wait his due. Slaton grabbed his backpack and began to move.

Anton Bloch was cleaning out his desk. He'd been informed of his ouster only hours ago, yet Zak wanted him out immediately. Bloch's ties to the "*Polaris Venture* debacle," as it was now internally known, were inescapable, and his downfall a fait accompli. Still, he was surprised at how quickly the end had come. In two hours, the new Director of Mossad would be quietly sworn in.

Bloch fished through the drawers of his desk. There were few personal effects to deal with, a result of his efforts to compartmentalize his life. The office was for work, and private mementos could only distract. One wall was accented with a few obligatory family photos, poor ones his wife hadn't minded parting with. Bloch had brought them in at the suggestion of one of his staff, a woman who'd dryly noted that the only preexisting decoration, a large framed *Code of Ethics*, did little to soften the room's tone. (The *Code* was a vestige of the previous Director, who had thought it marvelously funny given that Mossad's chartered mission was to lie, cheat, and steal.)

Then there was the sword mounted by the door, a relic from Bloch's days at the military academy. It was inscribed with one of those cryptic Latin phrases, the meaning of which he'd forgotten over the years. Bloch had nailed the thing up on the wall of his office because that was about all you could do with something like that.

All in all, there wasn't much to give insight into the person who sat behind the Director's desk, and scant evidence that he held a life beyond this building. At the outset, Bloch had made a reciprocal promise to himself that he wouldn't take his work home. On that count, he'd failed abysmally. It was easy enough to not take the papers and files home. Since most of it was classified at the highest levels, it would have constituted a severe security breach to do so. However, the unconscionable nature of his position could never be left behind. Bloch's work was a never-ending sequence of troubling events. Sometimes he even arranged them. He couldn't remember the last night he'd gone to sleep with fading thoughts of a good dinner, his granddaughter's laugh, or loving his wife. Maybe it would be different now.

Bloch pulled files out of his desk and stacked them to be returned for safekeeping in Documents Section. Had his departure been under more favorable circumstances, he might have browsed through and reminisced over the missions they represented. But on this day, he had neither the time nor the inclination. He was elbow deep in the bottom drawer when the secure line rang with its distinct high-pitched tone. He picked up and was rewarded with the voice of a trusted friend.

"We figured out where the *Lorraine II* came from, boss."

"Casablanca. She was chartered for a fishing trip two weeks ago. The Moroccan captain and first mate have both disappeared, but it doesn't take a genius to figure out where they ended up."

The caller sounded crestfallen. "How'd you know that?"

"The British told us this morning. They're taking this pretty seriously. Have you got anything else?"

"Uh, no. Sorry."

"All right," said an exasperated Bloch. "Stay in Morocco and keep looking. And if you call me again, I want you to use a different number." Bloch gave his home phone number, lacking any better ideas, and hung up. He sat tapping his fingers on the desk. With only a few more hours as

Director, if he was going to use his authority, he'd have to do it now. There were two immediate problems — David Slaton and a ten-kiloton weapon, both of which had disappeared into thin air. To get answers, a multitude of options came to mind, but they all carried a common theme. Bloch picked up the phone and dialed. A female voice answered.

"Flight dispatch."

"Anton Bloch," he said authoritatively, "I want a plane ready in thirty minutes."

"Number traveling and destination, sir?"

"One passenger. London."

The search had gone on for six hours when Chatham called the first meeting. Four supervisors, one from each twenty-man team, assembled at the Yard with Chatham presiding. There was a painful lack of new information. The first three teams had reported six possible sightings of their quarry, all thin in detail and none that got Chatham's hopes up. Lieutenant Barnstable was the last chance, however his solemn expression matched those who'd gone before. Just as he began, Ian Dark walked in and quietly handed Chatham a copy of the evening *Times*.

Barnstable stood before the large city map that dominated one wall and went over his troops' findings. Chatham let his eyes wander across the newspaper. The headlines were still bold. *NUKE DISARMED! SUSPECT IDENTIFIED!* The picture of David Slaton was on the front page, in a bottom quarter. Rough and grainy in the print reproduction, it had lost a good deal of clarity. If the paper had known another weapon was unaccounted for, Chatham suspected the photo would have covered the entire front page. He scanned idly while Barnstable droned in to an approach and landing.

"Altogether, we've identified only one possible match," he said. "A bus driver claimed to have seen a fellow at a bus stop who looked something like our man."

Chatham browsed to page four.

"I interviewed him personally," Barnstable said, in an ode to his own efficiency, "but he didn't seem very sure. Apparently he didn't get a good look at the bloke either time."

"Either time?" Dark asked.

"Well, yes," Barnstable explained. "It seems the same fellow was at this stop on two consecutive passes."

Dark queried, "You're saying this bus got around to a stop twice, and the same man was there both times? A man who bore some resemblance to our suspect?"

"Right."

"Did he get on the bus?"

"No," Barnstable said.

Chatham surprised everyone by jumping in. "How much time had elapsed between those two stops?"

Barnstable fished a notepad from his jacket and began searching. Finding the times, he did the math, "One hour and forty minutes, sir."

Chatham's attention was now complete. "Ian, get a city schedule. I want to see if there were any other buses he might have been waiting for." He turned back to Barnstable, "Lieutenant, did this driver have anything else to say?"

Barnstable shuffled through his notes. "No. No, he just said the fellow was standing around. He didn't seem to be paying much attention to the buses."

"A man standing at a bus stop, but not waiting for a bus," Chatham commented.

"Well, yes. I suppose," Barnstable mumbled. He had the look of a man waiting for the boot to drop.

"Have you been to this stop, Lieutenant?"

"Not recently, but I'm familiar with it."

"What else is nearby?"

"It's right next to the New Covent Garden Market. Overlooks the backside, the loading docks."

Chatham grinned knowingly at his crew. They looked back blankly, not seeing it yet. "We are assuming he's trying to leave the city. Put yourselves in his shoes. He knows we'll be watching all the usual means of transportation."

Dark was the first to speak. "The lorries. They're in and out of the market all day."

"Empty when they leave," Barnstable added.

"Right," Chatham said encouragingly. "Barnstable, find that bus driver and get the exact times he saw this man. Let's see if any other buses went by the same stop. If so, we must talk to those drivers."

"Yes, sir," Barnstable said. "And I'll make sure the fellow I talked to didn't pass by that stop later in the day. If he did, and our man *wasn't* there . . ."

"That's the idea," Chatham said. Next, he pointed to Jones on the left, "Go straight to the market. They must keep some kind of log, a record of deliveries. Find out what trucks passed through at the time and where they were headed." Then it was Cole's turn. "Once we identify the trucks, we'll have to track down the owners and drivers. We must find out exactly where they've been. Get over to Motor Division and be ready."

The investigative team leaders had an air of urgency as they went off to their respective assignments. Chatham sat back at his desk and looked again at the *Times*, still open to page four.

"If we only knew what he was up to," Dark pondered aloud.

Chatham nodded contemplatively, "When I spoke to him, I could tell there was a plan. One very clear objective. If we can guess what it is, we'll know where to look."

"Any ideas at all?"

Chatham raised an eyebrow and turned the newspaper around to face Dark. It was folded so that one article displayed prominently.

> SECURITY TIGHTENED FOR GREENWICH ACCORD
> *Reuters, London*
> *Security measures have been strengthened for the upcoming Greenwich Accord. The treaty signing ceremony will be under increased scrutiny in light of the recent discovery of a nuclear weapon on a motor yacht in Eastbourne. According to a Scotland Yard spokesperson, "We see no relationship between the events in Eastbourne and the peace talks, but it serves to reinforce that terrorist elements take no holiday. Security arrangements for the Greenwich Accord will be intensified as we anticipate the signing of a treaty which will help bring an end to just this kind of threat."*

The article went on to describe some of the more obvious precautions being taken. Dark's youthful face was heavy with worry. "Do you think that second weapon will turn up in Greenwich?"

Chatham leaned on a table and drummed his fingers. "I have no idea, Ian. But something tells me our man Slaton is headed there."

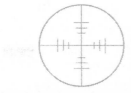

Chapter Seventeen

Cold sandwiches and lukewarm tea. Supper was easily ignored as Chatham and Dark poured over information that was now coming in from all quadrants. Foremost at the moment was a status report. The American's Nuclear Emergency Search Team, or NEST, was enroute, and scheduled to arrive early the next morning. Chatham was surprised to see how inadequately prepared his own country was to undertake such a search. Scotland Yard and the military had held a few joint maneuvers, but these had more to do with disposing of a known weapon, as had been the case in Eastbourne. The process of searching for a nuclear device hidden in a large city, or for that matter a country, was a far more daunting task. Success depended on an immensely complex network of sensors and computers, which had to be driven and flown across targeted search areas.

"The Americans are bringing their best gadgets," Dark said.

"Well," Chatham grumbled, "I suppose they do have a knack for this sort of thing."

"I'm told these sensors have a limited range, though. They're not much use if you don't know where to begin."

"Which is precisely why we must locate Slaton. I'm still convinced he's our best lead."

"We've had a few more sketchy sightings, but none sound promising." Dark held up a clipboard with a half dozen loose fax pages, "We've accounted for seven delivery trucks that were at the market this morning. They belong to one of the big co-operatives in Birmingham and their

routes were all tracked by computer. We talked to each driver, and forensics has tracked down all but two of the trucks. So far, nothing suspicious."

Chatham wasn't surprised. "No, no. This fellow spent hours at that
bus stop looking for something in particular. He had to get out of London,
but there was a destination in mind. I think he waited for a truck that was
going where *he* wanted to go."

"Of course!" Dark said. "He stood at the bus stop and shopped for
one that was bound for the right place. Now if we only knew where that
was."

"Give me the log."

Dark handed over the clipboard and Chatham leafed through the
pages.

"Sixty deliveries in our time frame."

He mulled the list, then took a pencil and circled an even half dozen
entries. Scooping thumbtacks from the top drawer of his desk, he went to
the road map of England, which had been hastily stuck to the wall right
next to the room's only artwork, a cheap oil rendition of the Battle of
Trafalgar. Chatham ran a finger over the map to find the towns he'd selected, then jabbed a red tack into each. All were conspicuously in the
same general area. East Anglia and the East Midlands.

"Let's track these down first. Talk to every driver. Find out the routes
they took after leaving London, especially where they stopped to purchase
fuel, eat, or use the toilet. We'll have a look at the trucks as well."

"Just in case he's gone and left evidence behind?"

"Yes, it's worth a try, although I doubt he'd make that kind of mistake. Our best hope is that someone might have seen him." Chatham
looked at the map again. "We're not far behind, but we've got to spot him
again soon. Otherwise, we're sure to lose track."

The Smitherton Farms and Dairy truck hit a big rut and Slaton was nearly
thrown to the floor of the cargo compartment. He'd been trying to brace
himself but there wasn't much to grab. Aside from two empty wooden
crates, the back of the truck was barren. It was also dark. They'd been going non-stop for four hours since leaving the London market, and the sun
had set along the way. There were only two spots where light could enter
the compartment to begin with. One was a fist-sized hole in the ceiling
that had been taped over — Slaton had removed the tape — and the
other a horizontal slit between two of the front end panels. During the af-

ternoon, the gaps had allowed just enough light to see the corrugated sidewalls of his temporary quarters. But now he sat in almost complete darkness, wishing Mr. Smitherton could have afforded a new set of shocks and springs to keep the old contraption from bottoming out with a crunch on every pothole. Slaton tried to be thankful they weren't carrying a full load.

Periodically, he looked through the thin opening in front. He could see past the rear window and into the driver's cab. Ever present was the back of the old man's head, his attention locked forward as the truck bounced onward, steady and true.

Slaton wished he could make out road signs to confirm they were headed in the right direction, but the angles of view and lack of light made it impossible. That being the case, he was forced to dead reckon. For this, he looked past the old man to the instruments on the dashboard. The speed had averaged forty miles an hour for the first one and three-quarters hours. Seventy miles, but then distance was the easy part. Direction was far more problematic. Initially, he'd used the sun as a reference, its reflections clear as it set to the left. They'd been headed northbound, probably on the A1.

Then the first turn had come. Fortunately, the night skies had cleared and Slaton could see up through the hole in the ceiling. He was able to identify the Little Dipper and Orion, situated to suggest a more easterly track. Not very precise, but the best he could manage under the circumstances. And significant, because he knew that Thrapston would have been a westerly turn off the A1. They were headed elsewhere.

Slaton conjured up a mental image of the East Midlands and tried to deduce where they might be headed. No clear answer came to mind. He was still mulling the possibilities when the truck suddenly braked and turned onto a road that was in noticeably worse condition. Smitherton slowed to a crawl, smashing heavily over a series of potholes, water splashing into the wheelwells with each dip. When they finally came to a stop, the old man honked the horn once before shutting off the engine.

Slaton reached in his backpack for the bottle of rum he'd bought earlier. It was half empty now, after he'd discreetly spilled much of it into a dumpster. With the bottle in hand, he waited, squinting into the driver's cab. The old man was waving to someone through the front window, and as he slid out of the cab, Slaton heard the voices of children.

"Grandfather! Grandfather!" they squealed gleefully.

"Hello, lads," the old man said.

A high-pitched voice pleaded, "Can we play in the truck? Can we? I want to be the chicken!"

Another howled exception, "You were the chicken last time! You're the pig now!"

"No, I *won't* be the pig!"

"Easy now," the old man broke in. "Tell me, has your mum saved me some supper?"

Slaton then heard a different voice, this one an adult female in the distance. He couldn't make out the words, but the tone was universal.

"Oh, mum," the children whined in unison.

"Come on then," the old man said, "let's have our supper. Then I'll have a word with her." He added in a stage whisper, "And remember at the end to tell her how delicious the pudding is."

Slaton heard their footsteps fade off and then a door banged shut. The cargo compartment was almost completely dark now, virtually no light creeping in through the two openings. He felt for his bag and stuffed the rum back inside. Had the old man gone to open the rear door, Slaton would have splashed the liquor around and sprawled to the floor, simulating a drunk who'd sought some shelter and passed out. He'd done it before, convincingly, but it wouldn't be necessary this time.

He went blindly to the back of the compartment and his hands searched until they found the thin strand of rope, which went under the door to disable the latch on the outside. He untied the knot that held the arrangement in place, then raised the door a few inches to get a look outside. The only structure he could make out was a barn fifty feet away. A fence bordered an open field in the distance. As far as he could tell, there were no people. And better yet, no dogs.

He opened the door high enough to slide out, then quietly rolled it back closed, noting that it did so without the trace of a squeak. The equipment might be dated, but old Smitherton cared for it well. Slaton considered spending the night in the barn, but decided against it. If he were discovered, the connection to Smitherton's truck and the London market would be all too easy. He reckoned there were probably a lot of other barns around, maybe even something more comfortable. The question of how far off course he'd gotten would have to wait. Tonight he needed a place to rest. His body required it, and he suspected the opportunity might not come again for some time. Slaton ran low to the barn, planning to use it for cover as he distanced himself from the house. Ten yards away, the barn door creaked and swung open.

Slaton froze, caught helplessly in the open. A dim shaft of light cast from the entrance, and a little girl, probably no more than six or seven, backed out through the door. She held a bucket with both hands and was clearly struggling with its weight. She closed the door, turned and then stopped, her eyes wide as she saw the unfamiliar man standing straight in her path.

Slaton smiled quickly and assumed an Irish brogue, "And hello there. You must be Charlotte."

The little girl was clearly put off by the stranger's presence, but she didn't seem afraid. "No, I'm Jane."

Slaton raised a brow. He pulled out his wallet, opened it sideways and squinted, as if struggling to read a very small book. "Jane . . . Jane . . . no." He flipped through the cards in the wallet, then held one up. "Oh, Mary above! I've got the wrong week."

"Wrong week for what?" she asked cautiously.

Slaton smiled again and looked over his shoulder at the farmhouse. He could hear the faint sound of voices inside. He bent down on one knee. "To deliver the surprise."

Jane put down her bucket. "Surprise?" She eyed his backpack hopefully.

He spoke in a whisper. "It's in me truck, up at the top of the drive. I just come down here to make sure I knew where it was going before I tackled that road."

"What is it?" she asked, curiosity overriding caution.

Slaton wagged a finger for her to come closer. The girl left her bucket and closed the gap, still stopping a few feet away.

"Well now, I don't think I should really be telling ye that."

Her eyes lit. It was clearly the answer she wanted. "Is it for me?"

"Ahh, Miss Jane, I canno' speak of it. But listen," he said, holding up his now closed wallet, "I'm not supposed to deliver this until next week. If my boss finds out I've messed up another delivery, I think he'll sack me."

The girl wore a look of forced concern.

"I'll be back this same time next week to deliver it. But I need you to help me out of this jam," he said seriously. "Don't tell anyone I've been here. Not your parents or your friends. Nobody. That should keep me out of trouble, *and* it'll keep my delivery schedule on time next week."

"It's a Christmas present, isn't it?"

He winked and the little girl squealed. Slaton put a finger to his lips, but it was too late. The front door of the house creaked open.

"Janie?" a voice called out.

"Yes, mum?" The girl looked to the house. Jane could be seen from the porch, but Slaton was behind the truck, still out of sight.

"Janie, who are you talking to?"

"Oh, no one, mum." Jane lied with that complete lack of conviction reserved for children. She went back for the bucket. Struggling to lift it, she sloshed some of the fresh milk onto her dress.

"Do be careful!"

"Yes, mum." The girl shuffled her feet under the load and made her way to the house. As she passed Slaton, who was still in the shadow of her grandfather's truck, she looked directly at him. Slaton put an index finger to his lips again, which only made her giggle.

"Jane?"

Slaton heard footsteps, hollow across the wooden porch, then crunching over the gravel and dirt driveway. He eased into a shadow and saw Jane approach her mother, the girl's head-low posture a model of contrition. The woman stood with her hands on her hips. After watching her daughter pass, she walked down the drive to where the girl had been standing. With a quick look around, she shook her head.

"That girl will be the end of me," she muttered, turning back to the house.

When the door closed, Slaton ran at full speed up the drive to the main road. It had been a small mistake, but years in the field had convinced him — it was the small mistakes that killed you. There was a good chance the girl wouldn't say anything, or if she did, that it wouldn't be believed. Still, her mother might have heard something, and Slaton had to assume the worst. After five minutes, he slowed to a sustainable pace and checked the time. It was quarter past seven in the evening.

In fact, it took less than an hour. Angela Smitherton-Cole's suspicion had been aroused. And Jane was a rotten secret-keeper. Right after dinner the girl confessed that a delivery man had come to bring the big Christmas present, but that he was early and he wasn't supposed to deliver it until next week and he might get sacked if she told anyone and, by the way, he was very nice.

Jane was the fourth child, so her mother and grandfather were both well versed in children's storytelling, experts at distinguishing fact from fantasy. Jane's account had details and a touch of guilt that left no doubt in their mind. She *had* been talking to a man outside.

When Jane was done with her confession, she was dismissed to her room to get ready for bed. Angela and her father exchanged a serious look and went outside. He retrieved a tire iron from the cab of his truck, then walked back to the cargo door. There were large footprints in the fresh mud all around the rear bumper. He gripped the iron and threw open the door, only to find the compartment empty. He did notice a small piece of rope tied to the latch that had never been there before. Old man Smitherton looked at the tracks on the ground again. He could see where the person had moved around to the far side of the truck, and then, judging by the gap between steps, run back up the drive toward Brightly Road.

"I don't like it," he said to his daughter. "Might have brought him here all the way from London."

Angela held her arms across her chest as if she were cold. "He's gone now, at least. Whoever it was."

She waited for her father to confirm this thought. Instead, he said, "Let's call Rodney."

Rodney was Angela's younger brother, and a brand new constable on the local police force. Rodney thought the issue serious enough to take it up with his sergeant, who nearly dismissed the matter before remembering the new message from Scotland Yard. Something about trucks that had recently been to the London produce markets. By 8:45 it got to Nathan Chatham.

Slaton decided he'd keep moving until three in the morning, then look for a place to hole up. If he couldn't find satisfactory shelter, he'd stay in the woods. It wouldn't be comfortable, but as long as he kept them searching a wide enough area, it would be safe. He wondered if he was being overly cautious, if perhaps little Jane had kept quiet after all. Or maybe her mother wasn't the suspicious type. Then a car would come into view, or a plane would fly overhead and the thought would be vanquished.

He considered hopping into another truck or stealing a car, but the area was thinly populated. There would be few such opportunities to choose from, and, more to the point, few for Chatham to check out. Slaton was glad he'd met Chief Inspector Nathan Chatham. He wondered what the man was up to. Was he still mired down questioning Christine, hoping she held some key to it all? At least she was safe now, Slaton thought. Maybe the great inspector was pacing furiously in his office, empty-handed and trying to predict the unpredictable. Or were men swarming around a little farm nearby, taking photographs, searching a produce truck for some shred of a hair, and slinging pointed questions at a bewildered little girl? Perhaps not.

Slaton had, however, settled on one point. Of all the people looking for him now, there was one man at Scotland Yard who was the biggest threat. He had the resources, home field advantage, and something else — that calm self-assuredness that emanated from people who regularly got what they were after. Chatham would be tenacious, and there was only one way for Slaton to get the man off his tail. He had to give Chatham that second weapon, along with those responsible for taking it. And to do that, he had to get clear.

To begin, Slaton could only assume that the encounter at the farm had exposed his position. If Chatham started a search, he'd get a map and place a big marker on the farm. From there, he'd blockade all roads and rails leading away from the area, the distance of the inspection points being proportional to the amount of time since Slaton had last been seen. Then another circle would be drawn, this one corresponding to that same amount of time, but smaller because it assumed travel on foot. The allowance would be generous, probably six or seven miles per hour. Within that circle, the search would proceed methodically, as many men around the perimeter as possible, an effort to contain, and dogs in the center to track and flush. That's how it would happen, and so Slaton's tactics were set. Stay clear of the major roads and lines of communication. Move on foot, but move fast.

There was advantage in knowing what the inspector had to do. Adding to it, Chatham could never guess where Slaton was headed. The only question was how best to get there. He took another look at the touring map he'd found in the addict's car, and the name of the village jumped out at him. Uppingham. It lay fifteen miles farther to the northwest. This was his immediate objective. Slaton had been there before, on more casual business, and he knew the area. The more he thought about it, the more Slaton liked the plan. It would provide a number of critical tools for the work ahead. And it would screw one particular inspector straight into the ceiling.

❖   ❖   ❖

Chatham was ecstatic when the news came in about Jane Smitherton-Cole's encounter with a stranger. In minutes he'd been able to confirm that her grandfather had indeed been to the New Covent Garden Market that morning, and almost certainly carried someone from there to his daughter's farm. And while Chatham wouldn't typically put much emphasis on the testimony offered by a six year old, Jane's description had matched Slaton squarely. The command center at Scotland Yard was put into action.

The local police began a search of the immediate area around the farm near St. Ives. Chatham ordered a blockade of the roads leading away from the district, and a checkpoint was set up along each end of the rail line that traversed three miles to the south. The police from four surrounding counties were dispatched, with another two hundred to arrive within the hour. Two military posts had deployed nearly their entire detachments, three hundred at last count. The troops would provide a wide-ranging assortment of tools to aid the search, everything from all-terrain vehicles to dog teams. Then there were other things Chatham had never heard of, let alone understood, including four Westland helicopters, equipped with low-light TVs, searchlights and infrared something-or-others. The helicopters would cycle through a search pattern that centered around old man Smitherton's truck.

Within the hour, west Cambridgeshire would be overrun by an authoritarian cast of thousands, all in the interest of finding one man. Never in his twenty-eight years at the Yard had Chatham seen such an array of forces brought to bear. He only hoped that soon he'd have something to show for it.

In the first hour, Slaton estimated he made nine miles, but only by staying on a secondary road that was light on traffic. It helped considerably that he was only carrying the backpack, now looped over his shoulders, and lighter after getting rid of the bottle of rum. Slaton ran at a steady clip along the shoulder. By staying on the road, he knew his chances of being spotted were greater. For the time being, though, speed was all-important. Also, the cloud cover had thickened, allowing no moonlight through. This would make moving to the fields and forests painfully slow, not to mention the increased chances of turning an ankle or tearing up his clothing.

Every five or ten minutes, a passing car would force Slaton to scurry aside and conceal himself in the overgrown hedgerows, those that seemed to so conveniently border all English roads. He estimated eight miles in the second hour, then the clouds began to break and he decided to move to the fields. There, on choppy, uneven ground, his pace slowed considerably. He circumnavigated a few flocks of sheep so as to not make any disturbance, and kept well clear of the few buildings he could make out. Most were barns and sheds that looked like they hadn't been used in years, but Slaton couldn't allow a repeat of his earlier mistake.

Cresting a hill shortly after ten o'clock, he spotted a small village in the distance. Nestled low in a valley, its lights cast a subtle yellow hue into the misty air above. Slaton moved perpendicularly to the city, and a few minutes later came to a road. Staying behind the ancient, ivy-covered stone fence that ran alongside, he followed along until he came to a road sign. It declared the place two kilometers ahead to be Oundle.

He found a grassy spot and sat down, leaning back against the wall. Slaton stretched out his legs and felt immediate relief in the tired muscles. The sweat on his exposed face and neck began to feel cool in the night air, no surprise with a temperature near the freezing point. He noted that his shoes and the bottom of his pants were covered in mud and grass. One shirtsleeve was sodden from a slip he'd suffered crossing through a gully.

He took a long draw from the water bottle in his pack, then pulled out the map and a small penlight. Slaton wished he had the luxury of a topographical map, something that showed terrain contours, but at least the one he had was of sufficient scale to identify the smaller roads and towns. He instinctively held the map in a concave manner, shielding the source of light — the reflected illumination only found his eyes and the wall behind. Slaton quickly located Oundle, then estimated where he'd gotten off Smitherton's truck. He was disappointed, but not too surprised, to find that he'd only made twenty-one miles, two less than he'd hoped. Still, the going had been rough. Recent wet weather had made the fields exceptionally soggy, and footing for the last hour had been a real problem. He'd have to go back to moving along the roads.

Taking another drink, he folded the map to display the area he'd be covering in the next hour. It was then that he heard the engine of a truck approaching. He killed the light. His senses went to full alert, discerning that there were actually two heavy diesels. They sounded identical. And at this time of night—

He shoved everything into his pack and quickly glanced left and right. The wall, about four feet high, extended as far as he could see toward town, but ended twenty feet to his right. Since the trucks were coming from town, it would give plenty of cover as they passed. With the belching engines directly behind him, Slaton could feel the ground vibrate. Then came the unmistakable squeal of brakes.

The big rigs paused and then, judging by the grinding of gears, maneuvered back and forth a few times. Finally, the engines stopped and their cavernous rumble was replaced by an even more troubling sound.

A young man's voice called, "This how you want it, Sergeant?"

"Right, that should do the trick. Leave the headlights on."

"You sure this is the right spot?"

"The major said two kliks this side of Oundle. Now keep those weapons handy lads. No leaving them about."

"For show, right?"

"That's it."

Slaton hadn't stumbled onto a roadblock. The roadblock had stumbled onto him. For the second time tonight his luck seemed cursed. He sidled against the wall to the only cover, a spot where the vegetation had gotten out of control. He tried desperately to move behind the dense foliage without causing any movement of the vines that grew up and over the top of the wall.

Slaton listened as five, possibly six, soldiers settled in. They bantered about the things soldiers typically bantered about and exchanged theories on the terrorist they'd been assigned to hunt. None of their ideas were of interest to the Israeli who sat silently concealed not ten paces away. Slaton continued to dig in and pull cover around himself. Across the wall, the group's mood ascended, becoming more loose and lighthearted. Then the first car came.

The sergeant barked terse instructions and Slaton heard a safety click off on at least one weapon. The car stopped and its driver, a woman, was asked, "Have you seen this man?" Slaton reckoned the picture was a pretty good likeness by now. The bewildered driver replied she had not, and consented to a brief search of her car. Minutes later she was cleared to go on, everyone seeming happier at that point.

Slaton wondered how effective his concealment was. Through gaps in the foliage he had a good view of the end of the wall — he doubted any-one would find reason to vault straight over — but it was hard to tell if any part of his hunkered down body was visible. Thankfully he'd had the fore-sight to choose dark clothing. And he no longer cursed the mud that had splattered over his extremities on that foray through the ditch. Slaton del-icately moved branches here and there to fill in thin spots, and slowly raked dead leaves around his legs. He was still fine-tuning his camouflage when he saw movement. Slaton froze.

One of the soldiers, a squat, fireplug type, appeared from around the end of the wall. He had an automatic weapon hung loosely across his chest and was coming straight at Slaton. With the man only steps away, Slaton prepared to take him, knowing it would be impossible to do qui-etly. The kidon was an instant away from lunging into a melee when the man stopped. He undid his fly and began to urinate. Midway through, someone shouted a question and the sergeant turned slightly to answer. On doing so, his stream splattered squarely on Slaton's left foot. Once fin-ished, the man zipped up, turned, and trundled back through the muck and around the wall. Slaton took a deep breath, wondering if his luck wasn't quite so bad after all.

An hour after taking up post, the soldiers had searched three cars and a truck with nothing to show for it. They were getting bored. The prospect of staying up all night to harass a few civilians was causing mild dissen-sion, and the sergeant allowed two men to sack out in the cabs of the trucks. The others would get their turn. Soon after, a deck of cards ap-peared and a half-hearted poker game broke out.

Slaton planned his egress carefully. He could move only one way, left and low behind the wall. Fifty yards in that direction the road and wall curved out of sight. There were no obstacles, nor any cover, save for the wall itself. His only concerns would be complete silence, and to not cause any movement that might be seen from the other side. Slaton waited for the next vehicle. It would provide a distraction, and also be the least likely time for anyone else to serve a call of nature.

The car that finally came was perfect. The driver was middle-aged, his passenger a much younger woman. They were both loud, argumenta-tive, and quite drunk.

Amid the shouting, Slaton got up carefully and inched free from his hiding place, the muscles in his legs aching the instant he did so. Moving silently behind the wall, he made a good hundred yards before venturing a look back. The driver was standing by the hood of his car, hurling insults and jabbing a finger in someone's chest, oblivious to the fact that he was grossly outnumbered by heavily armed soldiers. His companion got out of the car, ostensibly to help. She teetered momentarily on stilt-like high heels, then fell flat on her face. Slaton was almost tempted to stay and watch the show.

He drank the last of his water, then put the empty bottle back in his pack. It was getting late. The roads would be nearly deserted in another hour. A hundred yards farther down there was no line of sight to the road-block. With the coast clear, Slaton vaulted the thick stone fence that had served him so well and started out at a trot along the shoulder. Blood came back quickly to his legs and the stiffness that had set in during the delay began to subside. For all the inconvenience, Slaton knew he was safe for the next few hours, outside Chatham's perimeter of search. He noted the time on his watch and gradually picked up speed.

Chapter Eighteen

A distracted Nathan Chatham ambled down the corridor from his office deep in thought. The operation had outgrown his own wing, and been moved to the far end of the building, where an intricate and unfamiliar tangle of conference rooms buzzed with activity. Chatham turned and weaved through a half dozen interconnecting offices, only to find himself back in the hallway where he'd started. He scowled and tried again. On the second attempt he found a wilting Ian Dark splayed out on a couch, staring blankly at another of the endless stream of messages that had been pouring in for the last two hours.

Chatham caught his associate in mid-yawn. "Dark!"

His number two sat up straight.

"What have you got?" Chatham asked, maneuvering his big frame onto a folding chair that looked far too delicate for the task. Dark handed the latest over to his boss.

"Nothing much. This one says the American NEST team has begun a search of central London."

Chatham harrumphed, "Discreetly, one would hope."

"Oh, yes. The vehicles are unmarked, and if anyone asks they'll only say they're a survey team. No need to incite a panic."

The inspector looked down his nose at the message through half-cut reading glasses. He cast it aside with a flick of his wrist.

"But why central London?" Dark asked. "Do they know something we don't?"

"No. We haven't any idea where to start, so London was suggested."

"By who?"

"Shearer, who was under the gun from above. It seems all the Members of Parliament who know about this second weapon are in London themselves, as are many of their families."

"Good Lord! You mean they can't see beyond their own personal well-being?"

"Achh!" Chatham spat, throwing his hands in the air. "It doesn't matter, man. We don't have any better ideas about where to send these Americans. At least this way it makes the pompous ninnies think we're doing something for them."

"Do you think they can find the weapon, assuming it's even there?"

"No. We were briefed at Number 10. This equipment is very limited. Give them a stadium or a small neighborhood to look in and they'll find it. But a city the size of London? Not a sausage."

A slightly built man knocked on the open door. He had a plethora of identification badges hanging around his neck, and Chatham thought he resembled a small bird with delightful plumage around the breast. Then he remembered. The name escaped him, but this was the very competent fellow who headed up Grounds Security at the Yard.

"Inspector, we've got a visitor who'd like a word with you."

"David Slaton, perhaps?" Dark offered wryly.

"No," the security man replied humorlessly. "He says his name is Anton Bloch. He seemed to think that would mean something to you."

Chatham imploded in disbelief. "You've got to be joking!"

The man shrugged, "He's sitting on a bench in the main lobby, between a pimp and a solicitor. Shall I send him down?"

Chatham looked at Dark, whose expression held equal parts excitement and puzzlement. There was only one answer. "Immediately!"

The two Scotland Yard men exchanged pleasantries with the stocky, serious Israeli. Ian Dark, lacking an invitation to stay, made a discreet exit, closing the door on his way out. Chatham offered Bloch a chair and the two men sat facing one another awkwardly. Chatham decided a touch of hospitality might be the right thing.

"Can I send for some coffee or tea?" he offered, not sure which they took in Israel.

"No, thank you," Bloch said, "I just finished an eight-hour flight and I was swilling caffeine the whole time. Frankly, I'd like to get straight to business."

Chatham made no argument as Bloch cast a suspicious eye around the room. "Is this place secure?"

The question took Chatham by surprise. "Secure? This is Scotland Yard, man." Chatham saw that his guest seemed less than convinced, so he tried to remember what Dark had told him about that sort of thing. "Yes, they . . . ah, what was the word now . . ."

"Sweep?"

"Right, that's it. They sweep the place with some sort of electronic contraption. Every day, I'm told. I suppose one can never be too careful."

Chatham saw doubt creep in to Bloch's face, but it seemed to disappear when he asked, "Does anyone in your government know you're here?"

"No," Bloch admitted, "aside from the two pilots who flew me in. And I should tell you," he added sheepishly, "I entered your country this morning with a . . . a less than accurate passport. Sorry."

Chatham dismissed it with a wave of his hand. "What's brought you here? In particular, why Scotland Yard and not the Foreign Office, or something along those lines?"

"I'll have to explain further, Inspector. You see, I'm no longer the Director of Mossad. I was forced to resign earlier today."

"Going down with your Prime Minister's ship, eh?"

"So to speak," Bloch grumbled. "My resignation is not public record. We keep these things to ourselves for a number of reasons, but I don't mind if you want to pass it on to your MI-6."

Chatham nodded in appreciation of the gesture.

"Inspector, I'm here to help you find that second weapon."

"I see. And where exactly did it come from?"

"As we explained yesterday to your ambassador in Tel Aviv, the weapons were South African. Beyond that . . ." Bloch hedged. "Inspector, I don't represent my government any longer. I'd rather not get into how this all came about, or why."

Chatham relented. "I can see you've gone and put yourself in an awkward position, so I'll take whatever information you can offer."

"And I would like to keep my visit here private."

"Obviously. That's why you showed up at the reception desk downstairs and announced yourself by name and not title. No one in the building would recognize you, and few would be able to associate your name. Direct, yet unobtrusive," Chatham said approvingly.

"Thank you for understanding. Have you had any luck yet?"

"Finding the weapon? No. But I've spoken with your man Slaton."

Bloch was clearly surprised, "You found him?"

"Well, I must admit, it was *he* who found me. When I went home last night he was waiting for me, with the American woman."

"The doctor, the one who pulled him out of the ocean?"

"Yes, Dr. Christine Palmer. Slaton asked me to take her into protective custody."

"And you did?"

"Of course." Chatham nodded toward the door. "She's right down the hall." He watched the Israeli's reaction carefully.

"What's she like?"

"Attractive," Chatham found himself saying. "Slaton insists she's quite innocent with respect to all that's been going on."

"Maybe I could have a word with her later," Bloch suggested.

Chatham's reply was off-hand, "Perhaps."

"What about Slaton?"

"We're still looking for him. We've tracked him to a small farm outside St. Ives, in Cambridgeshire."

"You won't catch him."

"Time will tell," Chatham countered. Spooks were always so full of themselves. "He put forward a rather incredible version of our recent events."

"You must know more about the whole thing than I do then."

"Perhaps. But I think there were a few parts he left out."

"I'd like to hear everything," Bloch suggested. "Maybe I can fill in the gaps."

Chatham eyed his guest, calculating the possibilities. Had the Israelis sent Bloch to find out what the Yard knew? Would Bloch offer truth, or a carefully guiding script? There simply wasn't time to dwell on all the ramifications. Had he been of a more self-promoting nature, Chatham might have succumbed to the professional risks of divulging sensitive information to a foreign national. Instead, he possessed a singular mindset.

That of finding his quarry in minimum time. Being two strides behind Slaton, and probably farther behind that second weapon, Chatham decided he'd press ahead, listen carefully, and decide later whether he trusted what Bloch could add to the puzzle.

It took twenty minutes to cover it all, with Bloch asking questions and filling in the occasional blank. Afterward, Chatham had questions of his own.

"You say you found these electronic beacons that were installed on *Polaris Venture?*"

"Yes, in eleven thousand feet of water. But not the ship."

Chatham put this together with what Slaton had told him. He was struck by the inescapable beauty of the plan. "So there you are. A lovely bit of deception. Someone put these beacons in deep water, assuming you'd then consider the weapons lost and out of reach. Safe, in a sense."

"Right. But we finally did something right by pressing ahead with the search. Other than that, we don't know much. Except that Slaton has turned up here in England and is decimating our U.K. contingent."

"But if Slaton is going around killing your people, then isn't it reasonable to assume that he's one of those responsible for stealing the weapons?"

Bloch spoke grimly, "Officially, my government has no doubts. Slaton is the guilty party. But if you're asking me, I can't believe it. I know him, Inspector. He's the last person I'd ever expect to turn or sell out."

The phone suddenly rang and Chatham filed that answer away for further consideration. It was the Commissioner himself on the line, and Chatham promptly directed his superior to standby. He put his hand over the mouthpiece and addressed Bloch, "Sorry, this might take a few minutes. I doubt the Commissioner would find it amusing that the head of another country's spy service was loitering in my office."

"Ex-head."

"Right. How long will you be here in London?"

Bloch shrugged, "My calendar is suddenly very empty. I'll stay as long as I can help. That is, if I'm not deported. I am here illegally, you know."

Chatham winked. "I'll take care of that. And Dark will set you up with a place to stay."

"Thanks." Bloch added introspectively, "You know, Inspector, I wish I could talk to David. I think he'd trust me enough to tell me what he knows." He let that float for a moment, then as an apparent afterthought added, "Oh, and do you think I could have that word with Dr. Palmer?"

Chatham had already decided on the matter. He made a show of looking at the clock on the wall, which read ten minutes after eleven. "First thing in the morning."

Slaton arrived at the compound shortly before sunrise. He was disappointed in his timing, having arrived too late to make a move in the pre-dawn hours, the preferred schedule for attacking an unsuspecting adversary. With that chance gone, Slaton granted himself a break. He'd essentially run a marathon last night, after little rest in the last three days. He could feel the tendrils of fatigue setting in fast, sapping his strength and, more ominously, clouding his thoughts. Certain that he was outside Chatham's immediate search area, he allowed himself a tenuous combat nap in a thick, quiet stand of trees overlooking the post.

It lasted nearly two hours. Just before eight, a storm of noise, dust and diesel exhaust violated the still morning air. Three truckloads of troops lumbered to the front gate, where a single guard sat slouched on a chair inside the small gatehouse. Slaton watched as the guard stepped from the shack to exchange shouted obscenities with his departing mates. When the trucks disappeared, the man quickly moved back to the warmth of his shelter.

The Royal Engineers 119th Field Squadron, a mile outside the village of Uppingham, was not a high security facility. The soldiers here were an engineers regiment, a contingent whose time was spent in the practice of building temporary encampments, bridges, roads, and runways. Of course, they remained soldiers first, which was why the bulk of the force had been rousted from their normal duties and, Slaton was quite certain, sent thirty miles southeast to beat bushes for Scotland Yard.

He watched from the treeline, a hundred meters away, as a slight young man walked from the barracks to the headquarters building. Minutes later, a young woman performed the reciprocal act. Shift change at the command post. Somewhere a small gas engine, probably a generator, droned continuously. The sentry looked bored, and was probably miffed that he'd been left behind on post while his mates had gone off to track down the world's most wanted terrorist. David Slaton, the object of that search, waited twenty more minutes before he was satisfied. All was quiet.

He reckoned there might be a dozen troops remaining, mostly for

command and control, and maybe a guard or two for the next shift. He
started to move, making a wide half circle to the rear of the facility. There
were thirteen buildings of various sizes strewn across the compound. A
few were obviously barracks. Then there was a headquarters building, a
mess hall, and a couple of others he discounted for various reasons. He
decided his objective lay in one of those five buildings whose purpose
seemed indeterminate. Slaton moved in closer.

Yesterday there might have been a roving sentry, perhaps with a dog,
to patrol the fence surrounding the post. But clearly not on this morning.
The fence itself was a simple twelve-foot high chain-link variety, with
bands of razor wire across the top for show. Slaton had raided a barn a few
miles back and requisitioned a set of bolt cutters. As long as there were no
motion or vibration sensors on the perimeter, which he strongly doubted,
getting in would be easy.

The ground outside the fence had been stripped of all vegetation,
leaving a fifty-yard clear zone all around. At the rear of the post, a second
road, this one gravel, came in from the surrounding forest and led to a
back gate. This gate was heavily chained and looked as if it hadn't been
used in years. Just inside the rear entrance were the remains of the motor
pool — a small armored troop carrier, a drab olive Land Rover, two dump
trucks, and three bulldozers. There were large voids in the parking area,
empty spots where the troop trucks and command vehicles had no doubt
been last night.

Under other circumstances he might have watched for a few more
hours, but he knew he had to move. Chatham would be widening his efforts soon, and the head start Slaton had earned would quickly evaporate.

He clawed up some dirt and rubbed it over his face and hands, an exercise of redundancy since he was already filthy from head to toe with the
mud from three English counties. Hygiene aside, it made for excellent
camouflage. The backpack he'd been toting contained his worldly possessions. One spare change of clothing, British identification documents,
cash, map, penlight, an empty water bottle, and the bolt cutters. He
didn't want to take the bag since it might prove cumbersome. On the
other hand, he couldn't leave it here. If anything went awry, he might not
have time to retrieve it. Slaton settled on a middle ground. He took the
identification papers, along with his remaining British pounds, and
stuffed them into a filthy pocket. The papers were probably compromised, as the Danish documents had proven to be at The Excelsior. They

were, however, all he had left, and might buy a few minutes in an emergency. Slaton extracted the bolt cutters, then zipped up the backpack and slid it under a prominent bush beside the gravel road.

The cutting tool in hand, Slaton made one last survey of his target. With no one in sight, his gaze settled on the motor pool, and a particularly wicked idea came to mind. He moved off low and fast toward the fence.

Chapter Nineteen

Chatham was asleep on one of the back room cots when Ian Dark gently rattled his shoulder.

"Inspector," Dark said.

Chatham's eyes opened and he gathered his bearings.

"Something you should hear, sir."

Chatham looked at his watch and saw it was nearly noon. "What is it?"

Dark motioned for him to follow. Chatham made an effort to smooth the wrinkles from his clothes and ran his bony fingers once through the matted tangle of hair atop his head.

A man in uniform was waiting in his office. Dark introduced Chatham to Colonel Edward Binder, the Defense Ministry Liaison to Scotland Yard. Colonel Binder repeated what he'd told Dark five minutes earlier, and any cobwebs remaining from Chatham's slumber were swept away.

"Are you telling me our suspect has broken into a military facility and taken weapons?" Chatham stood rigid.

A contrite Binder replied, "We don't know who it was, Inspector. No one got a look at this person."

Chatham fumed, having no doubt whatsoever. "What exactly did he take?"

"We're not completely sure yet, but an inventory is under way. We do know he's taken two L96A1s."

"Two what?"

"L96A1s. They're rifles. He's also taken a handgun, some ammunition, a vest and . . . there was one other thing."

"A main battle tank, perhaps?" Chatham ripped.

"Actually it was a Land Rover, the military version."

Chatham exploded, "One of the most wanted men of all time has walked onto a post and taken guns, ammunition, and a truck? Without anyone even seeing him?"

Dark came to Binder's defense, "Inspector, Colonel Binder is only the messenger."

Binder went ramrod straight as he returned fire. "Security was lacking because nearly the entire post was thirty miles off, hiking around the countryside looking for this man! If anyone's to blame, they'll be right here in this room!"

Chatham stood to full height and the men glared at one another. Dark moved physically between them, but the intervention proved unnecessary. Chatham turned away, realizing he did have to share the blame.

"All right, all right," he said, banging a fist into his palm, "we've no time for this. At least we know where he was this morning. What have you done to find this truck?"

Binder stood down and said, "The local constabulary are on alert."

"How did they know it was stolen," Dark asked, "and not just taken in a mix-up among the troops?"

"The theft was obvious," Binder said. "The motor pool is at the rear of the facility and the gate there was locked tight. He got out by cutting a rather large hole in the perimeter fence and then driving through it."

Chatham flinched, but held fast. He strode to the map on the wall and removed the pin that was stuck on Smitherton's daughter's house. After a brief search, he jabbed it on Uppingham.

Dark said to Binder, "Can you say when the truck was last seen in the motor pool?"

"No, but I'll look into it."

"You see," Dark explained, "if we know the earliest possible time he might have taken it, then we know how far away he might have driven."

Chatham shook his head vigorously. "No, no Ian. That's not it at all. You're not putting yourself in his place. He's taken a vehicle that's going to be easy to spot. And he left a gaping hole in the fence, so he really didn't try to hide the crime. He won't keep it for more than an hour, I'd say.

He'll make a mad dash." Chatham looked at the map and the answer was clear. "Leicester! That's where he's headed. Trains, buses, taxis, even an airport we're not watching. And he's had all morning." Chatham slapped his open hand over the map. "Blast! He could be anywhere by now!"

Dark echoed Chatham's frustration. "So where do we start?"

Chatham set his jaw. "Maybe it's not as bad as all that." He tapped a finger on Leicester. "First we find the missing Rover. If he's ditched it near a transportation hub, it might get us back on track. We take the picture and show it around. Remember, he's got some oversized luggage now that must stand out."

Colonel Binder frowned. "Inspector, the L96A1 is a very special type of weapon. Do you know what it's used for?"

Chatham confessed he had no idea.

"Special operations equipment. It's a sniper's rifle."

Dark cringed, while his superior remained impassive.

"And why two of them?" Binder added.

"Yes," Chatham mused, "why indeed?"

The British Army Land Rover was spotted within the hour by Constable Hullsbury of the Leicester Constabulary. Hullsbury had been driving home in his personal car when he saw a Rover with the unmistakable drab green color scheme. A quick call-in on his cell phone confirmed that this was indeed the one everyone was after. An excited dispatcher at headquarters instructed him to keep the vehicle in sight at all costs, but added a warning to not get too close. The policeman didn't bother to reply that he'd been to the briefing on this fellow — he wasn't going anywhere near without a small army of back-ups.

Hullsbury followed from a distance, glad to be tucked discreetly into his small compact. The Rover moved erratically, speeding one minute, then slowing to a crawl. Eventually the driver turned into a large construction site, ten or twelve acres of freshly turned dirt and mud. A pair of graders and a huge payloader sat dormant, their crews nowhere to be seen, probably gone for lunch.

Constable Hullsbury watched in amazement as the most wanted criminal in Europe spun a wild circle in the loose soil. He called in an update on the suspect's position while the Rover sped back and forth, mud flying thirty feet into the air. Within minutes, backup units began to arrive, discreetly taking station all around the construction site.

Ten minutes later, the Rover was caked in so much mud that Hullsbury could no longer tell what color it was. It also appeared to be stuck,
axle deep in a muck that even its nimble four-wheel-drive power train
couldn't overcome. The truck sat motionless, mired to the midsection,
with its wheels spinning occasionally to no effect.

Then, on some unseen cue, it happened. More sirens than Hullsbury had ever heard in his life, a veritable symphony of justice coming
from all directions. A half dozen police cars sped by and three more appeared from the opposite side of the construction site, along with an armored car and two smaller camouflaged Army vehicles. He threw his
little Ford into gear and followed, feeling more comfortable now with the
numbers. They all careened wildly through the wet dirt and came skid-
ding to a stop, Hullsbury a bit too late as his car clipped the fender of a
black and white. Settling roughly a hundred feet away, the authorities
formed an uneven circle around the stranded Rover, which sat motionless, spewing steam from under its hood.

At least three dozen policemen and soldiers, Hullsbury included,
scrambled out of their vehicles and took protection behind doors and
quarterpanels. Some of the policemen had pistols, while the Army blokes
were sporting automatic rifles and at least one grenade launcher. Hullsbury had instinctive doubts about this circular strategy. If bullets started to
fly he'd take good cover, happy that the bloke with the grenade launcher
was right next to him and not opposite.

In the rushed conglomeration of firepower there was no clear leader,
and so no one bothered to insist that the suspect should, *Come out with
your hands up!* The omission proved immaterial, as the present show of
force rendered any such suggestions superfluous.

Hullsbury took a good look at the Rover and noticed for the first time
that there were two people inside — or at least two sets of eyes, white and
wide in amazement. The driver's door opened, then the passenger's, and
two suspects emerged. The driver was skinny with orange hair and a large
silver barbell pierced through one eyebrow. He was no more than nineteen years old. The other had blue hair, a large tattoo on one arm, and was
even younger and skinnier than the first.

The younger boy was trembling, while the older one had enough
sense to at least put his hands in the air. He smiled nervously and called
across the divide, "We was just havin' a bit of fun, we was."

❖   ❖   ❖

The car was a Porsche. Flashy, but the only other options had been a Maserati and a Bentley. Obey the appropriate traffic laws, Slaton reasoned, and everything would be fine. Best of all, there were no suspicious rental clerks, salespersons, or stolen vehicle reports. The car was completely untraceable, and part of the reason he'd chosen the Engineers Squadron near Uppingham.

The arrangement was similar to the one at the lodge. The Porsche was owned by another sayan, this one a middle-aged commodities broker, fabulously either good or lucky, who had retired early to the downs of east Leicestershire. The man's parents, however, were not blessed with like fortune. Orthodox Jews of modest means, they were settled tenuously in the tumult that was Gaza. No doubt guilty about his copious wealth, the financier had proven an easy recruit for Yosy. His home and vehicles were always available to the cause, a minimal sacrifice since the sayan was often abroad, as had been the case this morning. Slaton needed only to disable the garage alarm (the code being 1–9–4–8, the year of statehood for Israel), then simply select a set of keys off the rack. On the empty hook went the Star of David medallion, which hung on a nearby nail. There would be no questions. At least, not for a very long time.

Slaton had selected a circuitous route back to London. First he would travel southwest, through Coventry and Swindon, before turning direct. He made his one stop after sixty miles, in the Cotswolds. It was a remote section of the district, and aside from a few villages, sparsely populated. The terrain held a gentle contour of easy hills, where pastures blended into random outcroppings of hardwood forest.

Slaton followed a meandering series of gravel side roads, scouting back and forth until he found what he wanted. Exiting a stand of trees, he came upon a relatively flat area, a long, open meadow of grass that sloped softly downward for a few hundred yards, ending in another group of beeches and oaks. He parked the car at the far end, where a clear brook rambled quietly over a timeless bed of stones and pebbles.

Slaton got out of the car and stripped naked. With a towel he'd pilfered from the sayan's garage, he walked to the stream and stepped in. The water ran over his feet like ice as he waded toward the center, scouting out the deepest spot. Drawing a quick breath, he dropped into the frigid water. The stinging cold seized his body like a glacial vice, giving strong encouragement to expedite the task. He scrubbed hard and vigorously to loosen a thick accumulation of dirt, grime, and sweat.

Finished, he went back to the car and toweled off, the sun aiding by way of a brief appearance. Slaton donned his last set of fresh clothes — a pair of Levis that nearly fit, and a long-sleeve, cotton button-down shirt that felt remarkably warm. Next he opened the trunk, which was at the front of the little sports car. The rifles had fit, but barely. He took one and inspected it for the first time, checking the breech, barrel, and testing its action. It was well-oiled and clean, credit that to the meticulous Royal Engineers. Slaton checked the other, then plucked out a sturdy piece of cardboard and some duct tape he'd also taken from the sayan's garage, along with a box of ammunition. Back at the garage he had trimmed the cardboard to an egg shape, roughly ten inches in height and eight in width, and drawn a black reference circle, the size of a one-pound coin, in the center.

He hauled his collection to the line of trees at the end of the meadow and found a medium-sized beech, whose trunk was in full sun. He taped the cardboard securely to the tree at shoulder height, then walked up the slight rise, counting paces to estimate distance. At one hundred meters, he stopped and loaded the weapon. Slaton had never used the British version of the rifle, but it had a good reputation. The telescopic sight was another story. He was intimately familiar with the tight, reliable Schmidt & Bender 6x.

Slaton surveyed the ground. He needed support for the shot, but the biggest thing here was a shin-high rock. He eased down and tried to get comfortable among the loose stones and grass. Settling his left wrist on the rock, he trained the familiar gunsight on his target and studied the picture it presented. He shifted the reticle to other points, getting used to the weight and balance of the gun, then settled back on the cardboard oval. The kidon lightly touched his finger to the trigger. The trick was not to squeeze. That involved motion. Gradual pressure . . . track . . . gradual pressure . . . and when the weapon actually fired it would almost be a surprise. Almost.

The shot rang loud through the heavy morning air, scattering a pair of pheasant from the underbrush. The birds were probably stocked game from the hunting club he'd seen a mile back to the south. Slaton had chosen the area for just that reason. Not only was it isolated, but the few people who did live or spend time here were used to hearing the occasional report of a shot.

He shouldered the rifle and walked through tall, dew-covered grass to the target. The bullet had struck high and right, about four inches at two o'clock. Good, but not good enough. Slaton walked back to his perch, made a minor adjustment to the sight, and issued another round. His second shot was inside two inches. He took the other rifle and repeated the process. The second troubled him, striking high three shots in a row.

He then walked all the way to the end of the meadow, again measuring paces to estimate line-of-sight distance to the target. Unfortunately, it was necessary to calibrate the rifles for a wide variance of ranges. Eight rounds later he was getting consistent with both weapons. He could still improve, but Slaton decided not to risk any more attempts for fear of drawing attention to his work. In any case, the primary was well set.

Slaton collected his gear and made one last trip to the beech at the far end of the clearing. There, he ripped the obliterated target down from a pock-marked tree trunk and tossed the remnants into the stream.

Christine's quarters at Scotland Yard were rudimentary. The bed was comfortable enough, but the rest of the tiny room was set up as an office, no doubt its customary function.

It had not been a restful night. A large man with crew cut red hair loomed outside her door. He had seen to it that she'd been left alone, but Christine still heard the constant commotion outside. A copier whirring across the hall, footsteps passing. Occasionally someone would stomp by on a dead run and she'd wonder. Why the urgency? Had something happened to David? Chatham had originally mentioned a hotel with heavy security, which certainly would have provided fewer distractions, but Christine asked to stay at the Yard, telling the Inspector she might be able to help bring David in safely. In reality, of course, she was just desperate for information. And she suspected Chatham knew it.

It was nearly noon when a hand rapped softly on her door. The knock was followed by a muffled voice, one she recognized as that of Chatham's assistant, Ian Dark.

"Dr. Palmer?"

Christine went to the door. "Yes, what is it?" she said eagerly, surprised to find Dark backed by a beefy, dour-looking fellow who seemed to be trying to smile.

"Good morning, Dr. Palmer. I've brought someone who'd like a word with you. This is Anton Bloch, until a few days ago he was—"

"David's boss," she interrupted.

Bloch said, "Well, one of them. He's told you about me?"

Christine remembered vividly. Anton Bloch was the person David had wanted to talk to, the one he would trust. "Yes, he spoke of you." She wondered if she should invite them in to the sparse little cubicle she called home. Dark answered the question for her.

"There's a meeting room down the hall."

Dark led the way, turning into the plushest room Christine had seen at the Yard. There were leather chairs on royal blue carpet and a table that might have been solid oak, an entire suite that had somehow evaded the pragmatic misers who'd furnished the rest of the building.

Dark left them alone and closed the door, although Christine noticed that Big Red, the guard, had tagged along and was lurking just outside. She took a seat and Bloch did the same, the leather squeaking as he settled his big frame. He looked around at the walls and ceiling, frowning openly.

"What's wrong?" she asked.

"I'm paranoid by nature. I feel like someone's watching us," he grumbled.

Christine looked suspiciously at the light fixtures and picture frames.

"Ah, well. No matter," Bloch said. "So, I understand you've had quite an adventure over the last two weeks."

Christine sighed, "Yes. Not the kind of stuff I'm used to."

"Me either, to tell you the truth. In fact, I think David has even found some new ground."

"I think so."

"David probably told you I run Mossad."

Christine nodded.

"That was true up until yesterday. Unfortunately, I've been booted out, along with much of the Israeli government."

"I'm sorry," she offered, not really sure if that was the right thing to say in such circumstances.

He waved his hand dismissively, "Bah! A good job to be rid of."

Christine found the answer less than convincing.

He looked at her, his eyes narrow with curiosity. "How well have you gotten to know David?"

She almost laughed at the loaded question. For the head of one of the world's top spy organizations, this guy didn't have much guile. "Well enough," she said with a shrug. "He saved my life. More than once."

"And you his."

"I was in the right place at the right time. Anyone would have done what I did. I only wish I could help him now."

"So do I," Bloch concurred. "But to do that, I'll need your help. Can you tell me the story?"

Christine sighed. She'd been over the whole thing so many times. But this was the man David had wanted to talk to all along, the one who really might be able to help, so she went through it once more. The Israeli listened carefully. When she finished, he had a few of the usual questions, and Christine tried to offer accurate answers. That done, he grew more circumspect.

"You know, David was lucky to have been found out there in such a big ocean. And luckier still that it was someone like yourself."

She had the feeling he meant it. "Have you known David long?"

"Since he began with Mossad. I recruited him, so I suppose you could say I got him into this mess."

"Did you ever know his wife and daughter?"

Bloch shifted in his chair as the witness turned the table. "I was never introduced, but I know a little about them. Did he tell you what happened?"

"He told me they were murdered, by an Arab group. And I know he still has nightmares about it." Bloch listened closely, but showed no surprise until the next question. "Who was responsible for their death, Mr. Bloch. Do you know?"

"Specific names? No, we never found out who attacked that bus. I don't think we'll ever know. And now, it's so long ago . . ."

"He knows," she said quietly.

"What?"

Christine stared off into space, verbalizing what she'd known since his last words to her yesterday. "David knows. After all these years, he's figured it out. And that's where he's going. To find that person."

"What makes you think that?"

"It happened yesterday in Eastbourne. He found something out from a man named Wysinski, one of the men he . . ." Christine couldn't bring herself to say it. She took a deep breath and closed her eyes. *David, you'll never get what you're looking for. Not that way.*

"Wysinski knew who attacked that bus twenty years ago? Who?"

Christine regrouped. "David didn't say. But he knows, I'm sure of it."

Bloch studied his hands for some time before asking, "Did David say anything at all regarding this nuclear weapon, the one that's still out there?"

"No, but I think it's tied to the rest. Find who killed his family, and you'll find that weapon."

They both sat silently, lost in their respective thoughts. It was Anton Bloch who brought things to an awkward close. "Dr. Palmer, I'd like to talk some more, but I have a lot to do."

"I understand. Will you tell me if you hear anything about David?"

"I will," he promised.

"You know, David trusts you. So I will too."

"Good."

Bloch left the room and asked the guard where he could find Ian Dark. As he wound his way through Scotland Yard's byzantine corridors, he thought back to the tragedy. Twenty years ago the Mossad and Shin Bet, Israel's internal security service, had done a quick rundown of a murderous attack in Netanya, basically relying on the police report. It was rare to find the actual culprits in such an attack. The killers would hit, then disperse, disappearing into homes, markets, and mosques within seconds. Israel had taken to a policy of retribution versus legal justice. No need to find out who pulled the trigger. Just keep a list of the combatants and commanders. For every Israeli killed, take out two of the enemy. It was a campaign of numbers. A simple, logarithmic, escalation in-kind. The policy was shaped by continuous, small-scale violence, and limited resources. But it gave little solace to victims' families on either side. And now, perhaps, it was coming back to haunt them.

For years Slaton had tried to find out who was responsible for the massacre in Netanya, while the Mossad had shown little interest. A fearful Anton Bloch began to think it should have been precisely the other way around.

Slaton worked his way south to Swindon, then rode the M-4 back to the bustling anonymity of London. He crossed to the East End, arriving at the onset of dusk. Here, the tired warren of streets were void of the tourists who flocked to the more trendy boroughs. The people he saw were locals — born here, lived here, died here. And not many drove Porsches. Slaton knew he couldn't do as he had this morning. Then, he'd known the Land Rover would be missed immediately, and he figured that leaving the keys in the ignition might buy an extra hour or so. The Porsche would not have been reported missing, but if it turned up wrecked from a joyride or vandalized, Chatham might make the right connections and know where to start looking.

Slaton scouted for twenty minutes until he found what he was looking for — a bank with a public parking garage that looked like a fortress. He decided to circle the place once to make sure. On the backside, the neighborhood trended downward, a row of dilapidated brownstones. They were weather-beaten and crumbling at the edges, but clearly occupied.

Slaton slowed for a group of schoolboys playing soccer in the street ahead. They stopped their game and parted enough to let him pass. If he'd been driving a Ford the boys probably would have glared down the intruder who'd interrupted their match. Instead, they looked on Slaton, or actually the car, with a certain reverence. The sleek machine was innately the kind of thing that young men aspired to, especially when in the company of other young men. Slaton waved as he passed and wondered how old they were. Eight or ten? Maybe eleven? He really had no idea. Slaton watched as the game resumed in his rearview mirror, then turned at the next corner. The bank would have to do.

The Benton Hill Inn was a seedy establishment, even by East End standards. A well-constructed young woman sauntered across the enlarged hallway that passed for a lobby. She wore a loose-fitting top that shifted a great deal as she moved, offering intermittent and ever-changing views of her considerable cleavage. Her pants took another course altogether, tight to the point of being a second skin, notwithstanding their lime green hue. She stopped at the front desk, which was really nothing more than a well-worn counter separating the entrance from the owner's "suite." She slammed her hand down on a bell and its ring pierced the early morning silence. A clock on the wall confirmed that it was nearly five in the morning. Hearing no response from the room behind the counter, the woman banged on the bell a few more times. "Roy!" she shouted in a husky voice.

A bleary-eyed man finally emerged from the doorway behind the desk. He wore a rumpled T-shirt and old brown boxers. "All right! All right, Beatrice! Keep your knickers on!"

Beatrice grinned through an earthen hardpan that blurred the distinction between cosmetics and masonry.

He squinted at the clock. "Working late are ye?"

"I've got a bloke taking good care of me, I 'ave."

The proprietor looked past her to see the figure of a man hunched over by the staircase. He was wearing a run-down overcoat and a brimmed cap. He was also swaying as though he were on a ship in a storm, his hands locked to the banister in a determined effort to stay upright.

The man behind the counter chuckled. "He's been taking care of *you*, you say?"

She produced a wad of crumpled bills and handed over the usual fee. There were two fivers left over and she managed to wedge them into the back pocket of her pants.

"I want him out by noon," he whispered loudly.

"I'll leave a note, luv, but it might be a touch later."

The man behind the counter shrugged, handed over a key, and disappeared into the back room.

Beatrice went to the foot of the stairs and put an arm around her newfound friend. "All right, third floor." The man muttered something unintelligible and they started up.

Five minutes and a couple of shin bruises later, she let them into Number 36. The room was dark and musty, and looked like it hadn't been swept in years. Beatrice was at least happy to see the bed had been made. She gave her ward a playful nuzzle and guided him to the bed.

"It ain't the Ritz, now, but it ought to serve our purposes, eh ducks?"

The man was clearly feeling it. She helped him take off the old greatcoat and threw it over a chair as he flopped onto the bed face first. "Now you just lie there a minute or so, luv, whilst I freshen."

Beatrice made her way to the bathroom. There, she took her time, primping her bleached hair and rubbing over a few smudges in the spackle. After ten minutes, Beatrice opened the door a crack and peeked out. Happily, she saw the bloke right where she'd left him, on his belly, with one leg hanging off the bed. And snoring mightily. She tiptoed over to make sure. His face was scrunched sideways on the mattress and a string of drool leaked from the corner of his mouth. Beatrice smiled, pleased that he'd gone down over easy. She reached smoothly into his rear pocket and slid out the wallet, the same one he'd been drawing twenties out of all night at the Burr and Thistle. She counted two hundred and ten quid.

"Let's see," she thought out loud, "that was going to be fifty. Or did I say seventy?" She gave herself the benefit of the doubt, and then some. In the end, she left forty-five quid, and resisted a temptation to snag the credit card. If she took everything, he might get mad and come looking for her. This way he'd just kick himself for spending what was probably a week's wages, and that would be that.

Before she left, Beatrice couldn't resist a look through the small tote bag he'd been lugging around. She opened it and found some duct tape, a magazine, a pair of eyeglasses, shaving gear, and a jumble of toiletries. Nothing of any interest. She took a last look at the poor sod passed out on the bed. He was rather dirty and had a rough beard. Still, from what she could see of his features, he probably wouldn't have cleaned up half bad.

She bent down close enough to smell his whiskey breath and whispered, "Next time, eh luv?" Beatrice left, closing the door with a deft, practiced softness.

Slaton didn't move for a full five minutes. He heard her footsteps descend the creaky stairs, and soon after, the sound of a door closing and her high heels clacking on the sidewalk outside. Then there was nothing, save for the usual sounds of late night — the occasional passing car, a dog barking in the distance.

When he got up he did so quickly, which was a mistake. Slaton wasn't used to the liquor. He had staggered into the bar sober, and discreetly spilled most of the first drink on his clothes, rubbing it over his chin and face to create the right air about himself. Once Beatrice had latched onto him, however, there was no choice but to take a few the proper way. Now he would have to fight the haze, at least for a short time. Only when the room was safe could he allow a much earned rest.

He latched the deadbolt on the door, realizing the old rotted frame probably wouldn't hold against a stout kick. His wallet was on a table next to the bed and he noted what she'd done. Beatrice was no beginner. Walking down the street earlier, he'd felt her patting down the pockets of his coat as she coaxed him along in a straight line. He knew she wouldn't be able to resist a check of the duffel as well, so while Beatrice had been engaged with the proprietor in the lobby, he'd removed a few things from the duffel — the handgun he'd stolen from the Royal Engineers (a Heckler & Koch 9mm), a bottle of hair dye purchased earlier at a pharmacy, and most of his remaining cash. These he had stuffed into a hip pocket of his overcoat. He kept her on the opposite side as they ascended the stairs, and after taking off the coat in the room, she'd made no effort to go through it again. He was glad, because otherwise he would have been forced to make use of the duct tape. And he'd have lost a lot of valuable time.

Slaton took the money and hair dye from his overcoat, and put them back in the duffel. He then removed his shoes, shirt, and pants. The clothes he laid neatly across the back of the chair by the bed, trousers on top. The duffel went to the seat of the chair. He took the shoes to the bathroom and washed off the remnants of mud from yesterday's excursion, then set them on the floor to dry next to his shirt and pants. Next, he pulled a small night table toward the bed, positioning it to a point midway along the rail. The H&K went on the table to be precisely at arms length, barrel left and away, safety off. He put his hands on his hips and did a quick inventory. If he had to go, he could be dressed with the money in one hand and the weapon in the other in no more than twenty seconds.

Finally, Slaton laid down, which seemed like an effort in itself. His body still, he felt fatigue fall over him like a heavy blanket. He had done well. In the forty-eight hours since leaving London he'd gotten safe, and, along the way, acquired tools that would be vital to his plan. The rifles were still safely locked in the trunk of the Porsche. He'd collect them tomorrow. The only glitch in the last two days had been the little girl, Jane, who had seen him get out of Smitherton's truck. She had forced him to move faster than he would have otherwise.

Presently, the only person who could place him in this room was Beatrice, and Slaton doubted she was having any second thoughts about the poor drunk she'd just rolled for a hundred and sixty-five quid. He had to assume that a photo would soon be released, or was perhaps already circulating. If Beatrice should see it, there was a chance she'd recognize him. But the police wouldn't be focusing on neighborhoods like this, and Slaton doubted Beatrice read many newspapers. Right now she was probably headed home herself. Professionals of all sorts needed sleep to function.

As Slaton lay still, the soreness in his muscles became more pronounced, his body's protest to last night's pounding run. It would improve with rest. The last time he'd gotten any true sleep was on the beach. It seemed so long ago. An image of Christine came to mind, the two of them back on the beach, talking about something unimportant. She was laughing, a deep, easy laugh, from the soul of a contented person. He hoped he'd done nothing to change that.

Slaton pushed the thoughts away. Now was the time for sleep. There would be few opportunities in the days ahead. He tried to mentally go over the next day's timetable, but the schedule began to blur. Slaton finally succumbed and drifted off, his right hand inches from the H & K.

Chapter Twenty

He'd taken the first available flight. Then the first cab. The taxi now stood still, anchored in traffic two miles from the hospital. So close, but he might as well have been where he started, halfway around the world. He pounded his fist on the door in frustration. Cars and trucks everywhere, a mass of mechanization choking on its own fumes, and brake lights as far as the eye could see.

He dug into his pocket, pulled out a wad of money and threw it into the front seat. The door of the rickety old cab was jammed shut and it took a solid kick to swing it open. It never entered his mind to set a pace. He just ran. Sprinting along the sidewalk, in and out between idling cars and buses. People stared at him. Hadn't they ever seen a man running for his life before? The first half mile was easy, then his body began to protest. His breaths came with every stride, legs pounding ahead, churning across the concrete and asphalt. *Faster. Faster.* Halfway there, his body told him to slow. Lungs aching, he could feel the sweat beading on his face. None of it mattered. There was only one thing. *Faster!* Then he saw it in the distance and seeing it gave a rush of adrenaline. For the last hundred yards his feet barely seemed to touch the ground. He burst through the building's entrance and slid to a stop on the slick floor, gasping for every breath. People in white stood staring at him.

He shouted with all the air he could expel, "Where? Where is she?"

"On the top floor," one of them replied, a finger extended upwards.

He ran to the elevator and slammed the call button. When it didn't open immediately, he looked for the stairway. It had to be quicker. He would make it quicker. He took the stairs three at a time, and big numbers on the doors at each floor kept track of his progress. *Three . . . four . . . five.* His lungs heaved inward, swallowing every wisp of air. Progress was slower now, wobbly as his body demanded he break the pace. He ignored it. So close. *Eight.* The muscles in his legs quivered spasmodically, not wanting to take him any higher. *Nine.* How many more could there be? His head and heart were pounding, harder with each step. *Ten . . . eleven. Faster!* And then the stairs ended at a final door. He burst through and fell sprawling to the hard floor. The room seemed incredibly bright and he squinted, trying desperately to see down the long corridor ahead. He leaned against a wall and managed to claw his way upright. Just a few more steps.

More people in white. They looked at him knowingly and pointed to the end of a brilliant tunnel ahead. He got up a head of steam and stumbled forward with all that was left in him. At the end of the corridor was a single doorway. It was open, and a diminutive old woman stood at the threshold. She faced him, her hands clasped in front of her.

"Let me by! I have to see her!"

She shook her head and he stopped. "I'm sorry," she said, her voice practiced in soothing, in caring. "You're too late. It happened only moments ago."

"No!" he shouted. "No!" He moved forward and tried to squeeze by the old woman but she wouldn't budge. He noticed for the first time that the room behind her was darker than the rest of the place. He couldn't see anything inside. "I've come so far," he pleaded. "I have to see her!" He tried to push the frail woman aside, but again she wouldn't move. He wedged himself against her with all his strength and tried to break through her blockade, but somehow he was thrown back into the hall. The diminutive woman simply stood there, the nurse's hat on her head cocked compassionately to one side. "I'm so sorry," she said.

He was overcome by pain. It sliced into every fiber of his flesh, and he fell to his knees and looked skyward.

David Slaton screamed, and then woke.

He got out of bed quickly, forcing away the familiar demons. As usual, the sleep had eased his physical fatigue, but nothing more. It was noon.

Slaton went to the bathroom, turned on the faucet at the sink, and splashed cold water onto his face. He was particularly thirsty and, not seeing any drinking glasses, he twisted his head down into the basin to drink from the tap. Standing straight, he stretched, noting a few new sore spots from his trials of the last few days. He took the bandages off the wounds on his arm — one from a gunshot, one from a knife. They were still painful, but seemed to be healing. Next, Slaton turned on the shower, letting it run a full ten minutes before succumbing to the fact that there was little, if any, hot water at the Benton Hill Inn. For the second time in as many days he braced himself for a frigid immersion. The icy shards hit like a shot of electricity, and the last numb tendrils of sleep disappeared. This time having a bar of soap as an associate, he scrubbed to remove the dirt and scents that had escaped yesterday's dip into a tributary of the Avon River. Once finished, he was at least grateful to find a clean, dry towel. It was time to get to work.

Slaton stood in front of the mirror over the washbasin, made a mental picture of what he saw, then went to his backpack and brought it to the bathroom. The first thing he tackled was the two-week-old beard, which no longer served any purpose. Chatham had seen him this way, and if the inspector circulated composites there would certainly be versions that included facial hair. He shaved it all off, leaving conservative sideburns. Next came the hair dye. It was a simple process, ending with a dark brown hue. Anything more severe might have turned an unnatural appearance, but as it was, the hair held a legitimate color, many shades removed from its beginning. He kept a portion of dye in reserve, calculating that one touch-up might eventually be required.

The color change complete, he went to work using a pair of scissors and a hand mirror, cutting away the bulk of his hair to roughly an inch in length all around. Next, he used a set of electric clippers, giving an even shorter, uniform cut. He then took a copy of *Men's Fitness* magazine from his pack, turned to a page near the end and propped it against the wall at the back of the washbasin. He studied the picture in the advertisement carefully, wanting to match it as closely as possible. With a good quality razor he began shaving the hair just above his forehead. He worked from the center, then outward slightly and back, all the time referring to the picture. At times he had to use the hand mirror along with the wall mirror to track his progress.

The process slowed as he neared the end, but after a careful thirty minutes it was done. Slaton stepped back to get a good look, using the mirror to see different angles, and comparing the appearance to that of the man in the magazine. It was good, but there was more to be done.

He'd anticipated a conspicuous difference in skin tone, the top of his head having seen less sun than the forehead. Fortunately, the exposure from his days floating in the Atlantic had caused his face to blister and peel. Now healed, this new skin was relatively light in complexion, a state not undone by the sunless British winter. With another recent purchase, a small jar of make-up, he judiciously touched up the tan lines, masking and blending until there were no remnants of the natural demarcation. Satisfied, Slaton pulled a pair of thick-framed reading glasses from his bag and applied them to his face. Finally, he compared the image in the mirror to the one he'd seen when he started.

Slaton was pleasantly surprised at the magnitude of the change. He now had a severely receding hairline and was quite bald on top. Short, dark hair on the sides further distinguished this new image, and the glasses served to interrupt his facial features. He wondered for a moment if even Christine would recognize him, but then Slaton quashed the thought. Of course she would. And it didn't matter anyway.

His new appearance would take some upkeep. He'd have to shave the top each morning, keep the make-up properly toned, and perhaps refresh the tint once during the weekend to be on the safe side. But overall, Slaton was assured. Confident that his new image would grant the freedom he required.

The kidon strolled casually through Greenwich Park. The business suit was an expensive make, but rather ill-fitting, since he'd purchased it at a second-hand store. The proprietor had offered to make alterations, however the process would have taken three days. Slaton had graciously declined before paying the man in cash.

The day was uncharacteristically sunny, the temperature nearing fifty degrees. Still, he carried an overcoat folded across one arm — a frequent visitor from abroad whose past experience had given broad confidence in England's meteorological inconsistencies. In his other hand was a thin leather attaché, which contained today's *Financial Times* and a sampling of tourist brochures regarding the local area.

The tremendous expanse of Greenwich Park had been authored by Le Notre, Louis XIV's celebrated landscape architect. On commission from Charles II, Le Notre transformed a featureless riverside tract into a vast Royal playground. Acre upon acre of green grass lay divided and bordered by wide, tree-lined walking paths. Over the years the Park had matured and been gradually encircled by the stoically urban City of Green-wich. Its character, however, remained intact, and as monarchs gave way, the Park reverted to a more public domain, granting the masses a chance to stroll like kings.

Centuries old beech, oak and chestnut trees loomed over Slaton as he meandered the trails. There were more people out than usual this day. Throngs of tourists made their way to the Royal Naval Observatory at the top of the hill, and a smattering of locals strolled and exercised their dogs in the grassy clearings. In the center of a western knoll, workmen were busy constructing the stage, which three days from now would be the center of world attention. Today it was Slaton's focal point.

He'd probably walked fifteen miles since arriving in the early after-noon. Starting from Greenwich Station, Slaton had circled the huge park, committing the surrounding roads and buildings to memory. He knew the location of every tube, bus, and ferry stop within a two mile ra-dius, and Slaton had already purchased an unrestricted day pass for each system. If he needed to leave in a hurry, he didn't want to be scrambling for change or banging his fist on a broken vending machine.

He had spent the last hour in the park itself, watching from a dis-tance, considering different angles and elevations. The stage was a simple enough structure. Large wooden planks formed the base, about four feet above ground level. Behind the stage was a tall plywood backdrop, and the entire framework would no doubt soon be festooned with all the trap-pings and regalia always required of such sideshows — flags, curtains, rib-bons, and probably a big banner depicting two hands clasped in friendship, perhaps an olive branch above. It was all very predictable, which made Slaton's job that much easier.

There was no heavy security yet, perhaps a few more bobbies than usual. Slaton surmised that Inspector Chatham had not yet deduced his intentions. That could change at any time and, in any event, things would get much tighter in the days to come. Slaton had been on the other end before, arranging security for just this sort of event. He knew how hard it was. With three days to go, preparations were being made, details as-signed. Each day would bring more severe measures and eventually there would be spotters with binoculars and sharpshooters on the rooftops, hel-icopters circling at a discreet distance, and roving plainclothes types checking IDs randomly in the crowd. Sunday would be very different, in-deed. But by then it would be too late.

Slaton walked up the pathway that led nearest the stage for his first and only close pass. Most of what he needed to know he could ascertain from afar, yet he wanted one good look. The carpenters were nearing completion of the wooden structure, and next would be electricians to rig for light and sound. The asphalt path took him within twenty feet of the stage. A few people had stopped along the path to watch the project unfold. Slaton kept moving — his disguise was good, but not infallible — and he expressed the same idle curiosity that a hundred passers-by had shown in the last hour.

At a glance, he gauged the height of the stage at standing level and its dimensions. The width was roughly seventy feet, the depth half that. To each side, in back, were stairs that led down and behind the structure. This was where the participants would amass, concealed by a temporary arrangement of tents, blinds, and men with dark glasses. They would arrive on a schedule drawn in proportion to their importance, lesser dignitaries forced to mill about for up to an hour, the most vital appearing only minutes in advance. Then, in a carefully choreographed scene, all would make their way to the stage, again segregated. Peons to the left, leaders to the right. Or perhaps the other way around. The poor security chiefs had to grasp straws of unpredictability wherever they could find them. Slaton passed the stage and looked back once over his shoulder, knowing he would not get this close again. He saw nothing to alter his plan.

He continued out of the park and walked north along Crooms Hill Road, the street that bordered its western edge. He turned a few times to gauge his distance from the stage, and also to check the trees. A single row of huge beeches, their branches void of foliage for the winter, stood encircling the park, arboreal guardians whose presence delineated the preserve from its harsher urban surroundings. There were occasional breaks in the treeline to accommodate pathways and service roads. Slaton lingered at two of these gaps and reckoned the angles and distance to the stage. One was roughly fifty meters closer, but either would work.

Across Crooms Hill Road were rows of shops at street level, and above those the second and third floors seemed to be residential, some likely occupied by the shopowners, others rented out as apartments. Slaton had so far spotted two buildings with TO LET signs in the window. He immediately discarded the idea of attempting to rent, or even view either of them. It would be one of the first things Chatham checked, and any vacant rooms would be searched and monitored.

He continued walking down the street, counting his steps. A middle-aged woman swept the sidewalk in front of a pub. A slight young man parked a bicycle near an alleyway and disappeared into a side entrance. At five hundred yards he stopped. Anything more would be ludicrous. He looked back along the far side of Crooms Hill Road. It had to be done here. Somewhere.

Slaton crossed the street and covered the same ground in the opposite direction. The busiest place was a restaurant, the Block and Cleaver, which drew a steady stream of customers. Next to it was a souvenir store, then a small tobacco shop with a FOR SALE sign in the window. Slaton was three steps past it when he paused. He turned and looked at the small shop, then up above. Strolling back, he stopped at the FOR SALE sign and turned to see the stage in the distance. He had a partial line of sight, with one tree close-in on the right. Slaton judged it to be a hundred and ninety yards, perhaps a bit more.

He looked again at the advertisement in the window and read a brief description of the property, noting that it encompassed not only the shop, but two individual flats on the upper floors. He committed this information to memory, along with the asking price, and the name and number of the property agency, then again crossed the street. Slaton surveyed the front of the building, checking windows and the angle of the roof. He saw furniture on the second floor, however curtains were drawn on the window of the top flat and he couldn't tell what was inside.

He took a seat on a bench and pulled out the *Times*. For twenty minutes he alternated between the paper and the building. He watched the comings and goings at the tobacco shop, and decided the place was meager from an entrepreneurial standpoint. On further study of the facade, Slaton saw three windows on the upper levels, two on the second floor and one on the third. He also took note of a small, slatted vent at the apex of the roof. He thought of what might go wrong, and a dozen fatal scenarios came to mind. They were, however, the same disasters that would likely apply to any spot along this street next Monday morning.

Slaton got up and walked south to the first intersection. There, he turned away from the park and quickly found the alley that ran behind the Crooms Hill Road shops. He spotted the back of the smoke shop and studied it for a moment. Satisfied, he went back to the side street and walked west, away from the park. Two blocks later he found a pay telephone and rang up E. Merrill at Burnston and Hammel Associates. The E., as it turned out, stood for Elizabeth.

"With what might I help you, sir?" queried a stridently proper, if rather high-pitched voice.

"Yes," Slaton replied, inserting a pointedly continental hue to his speech, "I'd like to enquire about a property on Crooms Hill Road in Greenwich."

"Which would that be?" E. Merrill quizzed, as though she held agency on the entire block.

"It's a smoke shop, across from the park."

"Oh, yes. An excellent location and a good customer base. I think it does something on the order of two hundred thousand a year, gross."

"To tell you the truth, I probably wouldn't keep it the same. That is, I wouldn't be interested in the inventory. Do you think the owner might consider that kind of arrangement?"

"Well, the owner is retiring. But I'm sure something can be done," E. Merrill said accommodatingly. Slaton had a vision of the woman sitting in a cubicle halfway across town with a forged smile on her face.

"Tell me about the upstairs units. Are they sublet?"

"No. The owner lives in one, and of course he'd move out with the sale. The other unit was sublet, but it's vacant at the moment." Slaton gave no immediate reply and E. Merrill clearly felt the need to expand her answer. "The lease values for flats in that part of town are quite attractive."

"I'm sure," Slaton said, his tone strictly at odds.

"Perhaps I can arrange a viewing."

"Well," he hedged, "there is another property I'm very interested in . . . but all right. No harm in having a look."

"Are you available this afternoon, Mr. . . . ."

"Ahh, terribly sorry. Nils Linstrom is the name. Yes, shall we say four thirty?"

"That would be fine," Elizabeth Merrill replied.

Slaton spotted the woman who had to be E. Merrill outside the Greenwich Smoke Shop at precisely four twenty-five. She was in her fifties, he guessed, professionally dressed, and wearing a bit more make-up than she should have. He introduced himself as Nils Linstrom and the two exchanged pleasantries, then went inside to meet the owner. His name was

Shrivaras Dhalal, an Indian man who was undoubtedly nearing retirement age. Dhalal didn't say much and seemed stand-offish. Slaton suspected he'd been briefed by E. Merrill that this prospective buyer wasn't
interested in the store's inventory, and thus any offer would certainly reflect the point. Sensing the social loggerheads, E. Merrill gave Slaton a
quick tour of the shop and then led upstairs.

"These units are really quite nice. They've been updated in the last
few years. Were you planning on taking one yourself?"

"Oh, no. I live on the continent most of the year. This would serve
strictly as an investment."

"If it's an investment you want, this might well be the place. When
it first came on the market I took a good look at it myself."

"And when was that?" Slaton asked.

The property agent hesitated, having been cornered on a matter of
record. "Well, I suppose it's been about a year now." Then E. Merrill
added abruptly in a low tone, "Mr. Dhalal wasn't very motivated at first,
but I think he's getting serious."

They took a quick tour of Shrivaras Dhalal's flat. Slaton roamed
enough to get a good look out the window, then suggested they go to the
third floor. The upstairs flat was a mirror of the one below — a main living room overlooked Crooms Hill Road and the park, the kitchen fell in
the center, and a single bedroom and bath to the rear. The only difference
here was a vaulted ceiling.

Slaton wandered around, forcing himself to spend time in the
kitchen and bathroom before ending up by the front window. Someone
had opened the curtains for the showing. He looked out and saw a clear
line of sight to center stage, just to the left of the tree he'd been worried
about. Slaton backed into the room and looked at the ceiling. It angled up
in an inverted V, except at the very apex. There, near the front wall, was a
flat section five feet across and ten feet long. He realized that the vent he'd
seen from the street had to be there.

"What's up there?" he asked.

"Oh, back when these places were built, the local architects tended
to add in things like that. I suppose you could call it something of an attic. I'm sure it's very handy."

"Yes, I'm sure." Slaton saw that the attic ended halfway into the room
by way of a small triangular wall hung from the roof, and in the center of
that was an access door. Slaton strolled back to the front window and

looked out, his hand to his chin as if making calculations. Which in fact he was.

"You know it's really not all that bad. Would Mr. Dhalal permit me to see his books?"

"I imagine he would, but I didn't think you were interested in his line of sales."

"Business *is* business, you know. I'd like to go back a few years, of course."

"Oh!" E. Merrill grew visibly excited and lost some of her veneer. "Yes. Ah, let me go see."

She hurried out and Slaton heard her clatter down the stairs. He quickly went to the hallway and grabbed a short wooden ladder he'd spotted on the way up. Placing it under the attic door, he climbed up. The door to the compartment was perhaps two feet wide and slightly less in height. It took a sharp tug before it swung open, and Slaton turned his head as a cloud of dust belched out. Immediately inside the enclosure was a dusty old shoe box which he shoved to one side. With that out of the way, he could see all the way to the vent at the far end. There were rafters above on an angle to support the roof, and at the bottom were crossbeams every eighteen inches. There was also an array of dead bugs, dust, and not much in the way of light.

Slaton hadn't known this morning exactly what he was looking for, but now he suspected he might have found it. The plan grew quickly, details fell into place. He swung the door open and closed a few times. It was stiff, yet seemed sturdy enough. Of course, it would be a tight fit. Still . . .

Voices from below forced his thoughts to accelerate. He knew the end point, and from that critical reference he worked backward, devising a way to put everything in place. He got down off the ladder and hurried to the bedroom where he unlocked the rear window. He then went back and climbed to the attic door. Inside the attic, nails protruded from the ceiling. He hooked the sleeve of his jacket on one and pulled, ripping a small tear in the cuff. Next, he took off his wristwatch and placed it in his pocket. He waited.

Elizabeth Merrill and Shrivaras Dhalal were climbing the stairs, he with a half dozen ledgers under one arm. The property agent was running commission numbers in her head when she heard a loud thump and a shout from above. She quickened her pace, Dhalal right behind. Arriving at the top floor, she found their potential buyer sprawled on the floor next to the ladder.

"Damn!" he cursed, in obvious pain.

"Mr. Linstrom, what happened?" she cried.

"You are all right?" Dhalal chimed in as they both went to help.

Elizabeth Merrill watched Linstrom grimace as he struggled to a sitting position. He grabbed a shoulder and moved it in a rolling motion. "*Ah*, stupid of me! I was having a look up there," he said, pointing to the attic. "My jacket caught on something and I lost my balance."

"Should we call for help?" she asked guardedly.

"No, no," he insisted. "Just a knock." He started to stand and Dhalal put a hand under his elbow to help.

"You really should not do that," the merchant chided with a finger pointing upward. "Very dangerous."

Elizabeth Merrill knew he'd fret over liability issues. Linstrom held up an arm, displaying a tear in the cuff of his jacket. To everyone's relief, though, he seemed to recover quickly.

"I'm fine, really. No harm done. Let's go look at those books, eh?"

The trio went downstairs, Dhalal keeping a close eye on his accident-prone suitor. Safely on the first floor, Dhalal brewed tea and the three spent nearly an hour going over the books. Linstrom asked questions that went straight to the bottom line, and while his comments were sometimes critical, all in all he seemed content with the numbers. He eventually made his pitch while Dhalal was assisting a customer.

"I'm going to have a word with my banker this evening," he announced.

Elizabeth Merrill's lack of reaction was well practiced.

"Today is Friday," he continued. "I can probably have something for you on Monday. Can we meet . . . say around ten in the morning?"

"That would be fine. Where shall we meet?"

He paused. "We'd better make it here. Sometimes my banker has specific questions about a property, things he wants me to check on. Of course we'd be contracting for a proper inspection should we reach an agreement."

"Of course," she said. Then it dawned on her. "Monday. You know, things will be busy around here that morning. There's going to be a big ceremony in the park."

"Oh yes, all that commotion outside."

"Huge crowds," she said pointedly, suggesting heavy traffic for the shop. "You might come a bit early, but I don't see why there should be any difficulty in our meeting here."

"Good, because I've got a flight to Hamburg that afternoon. If we don't meet Monday, it might get pushed back a couple of weeks, until I'm in town again."

Elizabeth Merrill smiled. The two shook hands, exchanged best wishes for the weekend, and went their respective ways. Ecstatic that she might finally unload Dhalal's stagnant listing, the property agent bustled off to her car.

The kidon took up a more casual pace.

He loitered briefly at a crosswalk, then a newsstand. He absorbed every detail while meandering back to Greenwich Station. There was still much to be done, but one thing was now certain. Barring sudden death or severe injury, he was absolutely convinced that Elizabeth Merrill would be in the shop come nine forty-five Monday morning.

Chapter Twenty-One

Slaton got back to his room at six-thirty that evening. The Forest Arms Hotel in Loughton had been a compromise. More respectable than the Benton Hill Inn, but not above taking cash up front for a short stay. The lies had come fluently. Having lost his wallet, the fastener salesman from Antwerp had been forwarded enough cash to get him through the weekend. A bored desk clerk had surrendered a room key with distinct lack of interest. Slaton had been alert, watching the young woman for any shred of doubt, any momentary glint of recognition which would tell him he'd been spotted. There was nothing.

He bolted the door and dropped his most recent acquisitions on the rectangular coffee table — a box containing a four-foot long window blind, a set of eight adjustable metal brackets with woodscrews, a small battery-operated screwdriver, a standard screwdriver, a pair of pliers, and a sturdy pocketknife. The ensemble of hardware coalesced nicely for a man who was going to install a window cover.

From the closet, he pulled out a half dozen small blocks of wood he'd scavenged earlier from a construction site, and then one of the weapons. The rifle's steel barrel was cold, its solid weight familiar in Slaton's hands. He set it down across the arms of a chair, taking care not to disturb the sight he had calibrated the day before. He took a wood block, actually a small section of four-by-four, and held it against the butt of the rifle, tracing an outline with a pencil. He then sat down with the pocketknife and began to carve. It was a laborious process, even though the

wood was relatively soft. Power tools would have made the job much easier, but the noise would have been impossible to explain if any of his
neighbors were to lodge a complaint. After twenty minutes he evaluated
his progress. Deciding he'd gone too wide, he started over with a different
piece of wood.

The first block took forty minutes to complete. The second was
quicker, being a more simple design. Next he drilled guideholes, eight in
each block of wood. The electric screwdriver was quiet enough that it
wouldn't be heard outside the room.

Slaton then went to the long box containing a retractable window
blind. The box was held together with two plastic packing straps and a few
staples on each end. He removed the staples one at a time with the screwdriver and pliers, inflicting minimal damage on the cardboard carton. He
then carefully worked the plastic straps over the ends and opened the box.
Taking out the wood blind, he set the cardboard container aside. The
blind had a cord for actuating the contraption, and at the bottom was a
small pulley designed to anchor the cord to the side of a window frame.
He removed the pulley, then cut the cord into three segments, each
roughly four feet in length. Having purchased an expensive brand, the
cord was good quality.

He then gathered the bulk of the blind and the unused blocks of
wood. These, he shoved to the back of the upper shelf in the closet. The
shelf was probably seven feet up, and stepping back, he decided no maid
less than six-foot-six could have any chance of spotting it. Even if it should
be noticed, there was nothing particularly alarming involved.

He laid the box on the couch and began packing. The rifle went in
first. He used the carved wood blocks, the bubble plastic that had come
with the blind, and a few towels from the bathroom to cradle the weapon,
again taking care not to disturb the sight. Then he fit the hardware and
tools around the weapon and closed up the box, reworking the staples and
plastic straps neatly back into place.

As a final touch, he slid the paper receipt underneath one of the
straps, giving the complete impression of one freshly purchased window
covering. The appearance was right, the weight was right. Slaton only
hoped the more serious security precautions hadn't yet begun. Sunday afternoon or Monday morning was out of the question. There would be
overt and covert security at every turn, and he'd never get within a mile of
the stage with a package like this. But tonight the watch would be thin,

England's security forces still scattered across the country hunting a nuclear terrorist. At least he hoped that was the case.

Shortly after nine o'clock that evening, Switchboard Two at Scotland Yard took a call from a man wishing to speak to someone in Nathan Chatham's office. It was routed to an assistant, who was busy typing on her computer.

"You want to talk to who?" she asked.

"Christine Palmer," the man repeated.

"Whoever she is, she doesn't work in this section," the operator said, clearly hoping that would be that.

"No, no. She doesn't actually work there. Look, could you ask around darlin'?"

The assistant stopped typing and frowned. "Say," she said over her shoulder, "has anyone heard of a Christine Palmer?"

Most of the room shot her a blank look, but there was one reply. "Who wants to know?"

The woman recognized the voice of the boss's right-hand man and her attention ratcheted up a few notches. "Some doctor from the States."

Ian Dark took the handset.

"Hello. To whom am I speaking?"

"Howdy. This is Dr. Upton Downey. I run the residency program at the Maine Medical Center. I'm trying to locate Dr. Christine Palmer."

"How did you get this number?" Dark asked.

"Her mother gave it to me. Say, is this really Scotland Yard?"

"Yes, it is."

"Well, Christine's mom wouldn't tell me much, except that she's probably going to miss her next rotation. I can't imagine Chrissi bein' in trouble over all this stuff."

"No, I don't think there's anything to worry about."

"That's good. I can rework her turn in radiology, but after that things get a little sticky."

Dark hesitated, then said, "Perhaps you should speak to her directly, Dr. Downey. Hold on for a moment."

Christine was reading a newspaper when the rap came on her door. She smiled on seeing who it was. She couldn't help but like Chatham's calm, amiable counterpart who'd gone out of his way to make her feel less a prisoner and more a guest.

"Hello, Ian."

"Hello," Dark said, returning the smile. "Tell me something. Is there a doctor back in the States who acts as your supervisor or mentor, that sort of thing?"

"I have a resident advisor, yes."

"What's his name?"

"Upper Downey. Or Upton, if it's official."

Dark looked puzzled by the silly name. "Is he a Texan?"

"Even worse. An Aggie."

That clearly went past the Englishman. "Yes, he's a Texan," she said.

Dark wagged his finger for her to follow, "He's on the phone out here. Why don't you come talk to him."

Christine followed Dark down the hall, Big Red in trail as always. The thought of talking to Upper seemed strange. She'd been in his office for an interim evaluation only two months ago. The hospital, her career. It all seemed like a previous life. But Upper would be the one who'd smooth things over when she got back.

Ian Dark quietly admonished her to not say anything about the ongoing investigation, then handed over the phone and disappeared.

"Upper? Are you there?"

"Hello, darlin'."

Christine froze. The accent was right, but the voice was distinctly not. To her credit, she avoided blurting out "David!"

Slaton held quiet while she recovered.

"How are you?" Christine asked, managing to avoid the instinctive and far more delicate *where* question.

"I'm fine," he said quickly. "How are you? Are they keeping you safe?"

Christine hesitated, wondering if she should try to keep some kind of verbal ruse going.

He read her thoughts. "Don't worry. They're probably monitoring this conversation, so let's not bother talking in circles. I want you to pass some information on to Chatham."

Christine didn't want to pass information. She wanted to talk to David, she wanted to convince him to turn himself in so they could be together in the fortress that was Scotland Yard.

"David—"

"Darling," he cut her off, "we have less than a minute. I need your help."

Christine bit her lip. "You always know just what to say. All right, go ahead."

"I think I've figured this out, or part of it anyway. There is a group in Israel, very high up in the government, who are committing terrorist acts themselves that can be blamed on others. They've been doing it for years, and now they've stolen these weapons. They're going to use the second one this weekend, or possibly Monday morning."

"What?"

"Don't you see? They don't want the Greenwich Accord. If a nuke goes off at the right place and the right time, the deal would be dead."

"Lots of people could end up dead. Where would it happen?"

"That's the part I don't know. In the past they've attacked inside Israel, but they can't do that now. Not without destroying — well, you can imagine."

"Yes," she said breathlessly.

"But they'll use it in some way that creates a clear threat to Israel."

"Who are these people?"

"You've already met some of them."

Christine remembered Harding and Bennett and the black-clad figures at The Excelsior.

"There's someone named Pytor Roth. I think he may know where that second weapon is. And there's one person who runs it all." Slaton told her who.

"Dear God, David! If you're right—" she stopped, realizing what else it meant. "David, no! You can't mean he's the one responsible for—"

"Time's almost up."

Christine finally understood what he was going to do. Why he was still out there. She felt ill, but nothing she could say in the next few seconds would change his mind.

"Tell Chatham everything," he said.

"What about Anton Bloch?"

"Anton?"

"He was here. I met him yesterday."

This time she'd surprised him, but he answered right away. "Yes. Chatham and Bloch, but nobody else. They'll know what to do."

"All right David, I'll do it if it will help you."

"It will. I've got to go."

The call ended with a click that seemed deafening.

❖   ❖   ❖

Christine told Ian Dark she had to see Inspector Chatham right away, with the irregular caveat that Anton Bloch also be present. Dark seemed tentative, so she explained who they had both just spoken to. He was stunned.

Chatham was already in the building, and Dark managed to catch Bloch as he was checking out of his hotel. Twenty minutes later, Christine was rehashing the phone call with two men whose interest was nothing less than absolute. She told them about a hawkish group within the Israeli government that was terrorizing the country's own citizens.

"This is incredible," Chatham said. He deferred to Bloch, "Could this possibly be true?"

Bloch's dire expression was an answer in itself. "If you think about it, there's a terrible logic. It would connect a lot of things."

Christine said, "He thinks the second weapon you're searching for is in the hands of somebody named Pytor Roth."

Bloch and Chatham looked at one another hopefully, but Christine could see the name meant nothing to either.

"David thinks it's going to be set off in the next few days."

"To torpedo the Greenwich Accord," Bloch correctly deduced.

"Yes," she said.

"Set off where?" Chatham wondered. "Here in London?"

"David thinks it will be in a way that makes it look like Israel is being attacked or threatened."

Bloch said, "Of course. And another country, one of our enemies, will take the blame."

Chatham said to Bloch, "If it goes off in Greenwich and kills your Prime Minister — *that's* a threat to Israel's security, not to mention Great Britain's."

"It won't happen in Greenwich," Christine warned.

They both looked at her with a plaintive expression that asked, *What else can go wrong?*

"David believes he knows who's leading this group," she said.

Chatham raised an inquisitive eyebrow. "Who?" he asked guardedly.

"Ehud Zak."

Chatham scowled. "Oh, now that's rich. I can just see it." Putting his hands behind his back, Chatham took a few paces and drew a tone of mock seriousness, "I've come to 10 Downing today, Mr. Prime Minister, to inform you that the investigation had been badly unstuck, but we've finally figured things out. You see, this fellow we've been chasing over hill and country isn't the culprit after all. No, he called this morning and told us that it's been your counterpart all along, the Prime Minister of Israel. We've sent a large party over to the embassy to drag him in."

Nobody laughed. Bloch sat stoically, obviously working the angles, trying to validate such an incredible accusation.

Chatham gesticulated wildly toward the Israeli, "Surely you can't buy into this? I've met your man Slaton, and I agree there was a certain legitimacy about what he had to say, but this is extraordinary!"

Bloch didn't respond. Chatham turned to Christine and demanded, "What evidence does he have?"

"Think about it," Bloch interceded

"Think about what?"

"What's already happened. Two nuclear weapons hijacked. One turns up harmlessly in Eastbourne. And then what? The Israeli government has a swift and predictable shift. Zak becomes Prime Minister. They tell you Slaton is the guilty party, without offering anything to back it up. Remember, he wasn't supposed to survive the sinking of *Polaris Venture*. But since he did, he would have been a threat, the one person who might unravel everything."

Chatham said, "Sir, I'll grant that politics is not my strong suit, but how could this make sense? Zak is only temporarily in charge, until elections are held, isn't that the case?"

"That's how it works on paper. But go on to what Slaton is suggesting. Let's say that second weapon *does* go off Monday morning. Maybe it detonates fifty miles off the coast of Israel, on a ship. The government, Zak's government, says it was a botched attempt at finishing off the Israeli state once and for all. The country faces her greatest threat. The Greenwich Accord is dead and a nation rallies around its leader. That's what happens in times of crisis."

They all saw how it fit.

"This can't be happening," Christine said wishfully.

"Proof!" Chatham insisted. "There's no way to prove any of this. And without it we can't act!"

Bloch stared at the floor. "Proof? There might be some. I could do a quiet run-up on Zak and this Pytor Roth fellow, whoever he is. Over the years there has to be a trail, something incriminating. But it would take time, a couple of days at least."

"There's one other thing," Christine said.

The two men looked at her numbly. Christine addressed Bloch.

"You know David had a wife and daughter, and that they were killed in a terrorist attack many years ago. But it wasn't the Arabs. He believes it was this group, Zak in particular, who was responsible." There was no easy way to say the rest. "I'm afraid David is still out there because he intends to assassinate the Prime Minister of Israel."

Bloch and Big Red escorted Christine back to her quarters.

"I'm going straight to Tel Aviv," Bloch said. "Hopefully, I can dig up some hard evidence and explain everything to the right people."

"You don't have much time. I think David's shooting for Monday." Christine winced at what she'd said. Bloch didn't seem to notice.

As they approached her room, Bloch took her by the arm and stopped. Big Red's gaze sharpened, but the security man made no move to step in. He crossed his thick arms and stood a few paces away, giving them a degree of privacy.

Bloch spoke quietly, "There's one thing I'd like to tell you, in case David calls again. It's something only a few people know, and it really isn't important anymore. Except maybe to him."

Christine eyed him warily. The unflappable stone of a man she'd gotten to know over the last two days seemed to be, for the first time, unnerved.

"I've wanted to tell him myself, many times," Bloch said searchingly. "There were moments when it seemed like the right thing, but I never. . ."

She thought he looked pale. "What is it?"

"It has to do with his wife and daughter, how they died."

"I don't see how the details are important. There were some killers and David believes Zak was among them. They stopped a bus, got on with machine guns and grenades." She paused at the terrible thought. "And they didn't stop until everyone was dead."

"Yes. That much happened. And it might have been Zak. Except David's wife and daughter weren't on that bus."

Christine drew back and her voice went to a whisper, "What?"

"They were waiting for a different bus, over a mile away. A drunk driver bounced up on the curb and ran them down. It was an accident. The kind of tragic, senseless thing that happens every day, even in war zones."

Christine leaned back against the hallway wall. "But why? Why did you let him think . . . what he thinks."

Bloch sighed, "Someone knew David was being recruited. I don't know who, and it's not important. But when they found out about the accident, it dawned on them to make a connection. The police reports and autopsies were quietly altered. His wife and daughter were gone, so it was used."

"You mean — ?"

His voice filled with angst, "What better way to motivate a prospective assassin than to make him hate the enemy. To make him think they'd murdered his family."

Her body half-turned, crumpling against the wall. She felt like she was choking, drowning in a sea of deception and hatred. Then the anger began to well.

Bloch said, "I know, it sounds barbaric."

Christine exploded. "You're monsters, all of you!" she shouted. She lunged toward Bloch, but Big Red intervened and Christine felt herself being tugged away. "You tortured him all these years! Just to use him, to make him as hateful as the rest of you!"

Heads peered from doors along the corridor as people tried to see what the ruckus was about. Two more sturdy men, obviously cohorts of Big Red, materialized in seconds and positioned themselves between Bloch and the agitated American doctor.

She lowered her voice, but only slightly. "There's no way to justify something like that! I don't care if it was somebody else's doing. I don't care if there was a war going on. It was wrong! Wrong!"

Bloch could only nod, a defeated expression on his leathery face, "Yes. It was wrong."

Big Red gently pulled her away and the other two men guided Bloch in the opposite direction. "I think we should put an end to this visit," the security man said.

Bloch acquiesced, "Yes, I understand." He spoke over his shoulder as he was being ushered off. "If you talk to David again, you have to tell him. It's time that he knows."

Big Red's arm was draped around her, steering her down the hall. Christine shrugged away, still seething. A few days ago she never would have believed there were such warped, manipulative people in the world. Christine wished she could rescue David from all of them. *I'll tell him,* she agonized. *I'll tell him if I ever see him alive again.*

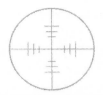

Chapter Twenty-Two

Slaton left the hotel at 9:20 that evening, having settled on the time after some deliberation. He would have to climb up the fire escape and let himself into Dhalal's upper flat, the type of task usually best left for the small hours of the morning. The problem was the box. Home improvement shoppers weren't typically out at 3:00 A.M. lugging packages around. This in mind, he'd settled on the late evening. It would be dark, but the streets still busy with people ending their day's business and beginning a night's leisure. He would blend in on the sidewalks, then disappear into the alley behind Dhalal's.

He took a cab, not wanting the exposure of the tube on a busy Friday evening. The driver tried to chat at first, but Slaton was minimally receptive and the fellow finally gave up. When they arrived at the prescribed address, two streets south of the tobacco shop, Slaton handed over his fare along with an average tip and bid the driver a courteous good evening.

From that point Slaton walked quickly, a man with things to do. There were plenty of people about, and he realized that by holding the box upright as he carried it, he could partially shield his face from oncomers. When he reached the mouth of the alley, he stopped. Slaton pulled the receipt from his box and pretended to study it. He might have been looking for an address that had been scribbled down, or double-checking the price he'd just paid. When the sidewalk was clear, he slipped deftly into the narrow passageway.

To his left were the businesses that lined Crooms Hill Road. Among them, fifty yards ahead, was Dhalal's smoke shop. To the right the configuration was similar — the backsides of small buildings, some with residences above. At this hour the businesses were all closed, except one at the very end which Slaton recalled was a restaurant. The alley was much darker than the street had been, only a few shafts of illumination straying from the flats above. To each side lay a shadowy assortment of trash cans, crates, and grungy boxes. Slaton heard a stereo playing soft jazz, and somewhere overhead two jagged voices, a man and a woman, were locked in a profane argument.

He reached the back of Dhalal's shop and gauged his task. The building opposite was unlit and quiet. Unfortunately, Dhalal's was not. A light shone brightly from the window of the owner's second-floor flat, and Slaton could hear a television blaring a variety show. The fire escape was also a problem. It looked in worse shape than Slaton remembered, rusty and crooked. Strangely, something else came to mind — another fire escape, the one that had been by the window at Humphrey Hall. Slaton had spent hours looking past it as he tried to concentrate on The Excelsior Hotel. As he tried to spot the enemy. As he tried not to watch her. She had fallen asleep on the couch, her long limbs stretched languidly under a blanket, her lovely profile silhouetted in a soft, indirect light. It was a captivating, distracting picture. Until the two men had come. Then he'd woken her and brought her back to the nightmare of reality.

A loud voice echoed at the end of the alley, interrupting Slaton's mental excursion. Backing into the shadows, he waited and listened for a full minute before deciding there was no threat. Slaton cursed under his breath. He studied the ladder, briefly wondered if there was any better way up. He felt exposed standing at the bottom of the fire escape.

With a good look to make sure no one had just entered the alley, he scrambled up the steps. The crusty metal framework creaked and groaned under his weight, flakes of rust sprinkling to the ground. He was making too much noise, but there was no turning back now. Sacrificing stealth for speed, he made it to the third floor in seconds. Fortunately, Dhalal had not discovered the open lock on the window. Moments later, Slaton was in with his package, closing the window behind. He fell to the floor and listened.

The television still blared from below. He heard voices outside, but soon realized it was only the argument flaring louder in the other building. He realized how incredibly stupid that had been. Why had he been in such a hurry? What if the window had been re-locked? Slaton lay still.

He closed his eyes tightly, but the vision would not be pressed away. She was there, sitting on the beach, an inquisitive look on her face as she tried so hard to understand —

The television suddenly went silent in Dhalal's flat. He heard rustling downstairs, then someone on the inside staircase. The soft, quick steps were receding, going down. Creaks as the front door of the shop opened, closed, and then a faint click as the lock tumbled into place. Shrivaras Dhalal was going out. Slaton remained motionless. What was happening? He'd lost focus and done a completely amateurish thing. It had to be the fatigue.

Slaton forced his mind to acquire order. He listened carefully for ten more minutes, then went to work. It might have been a simple task had it not been for the small confines of the attic. It was little more than a crawl-space, and he had to keep movement to a minimum as the business end of forty-year-old roofing nails scratched at him from above. It also didn't help that he had to perform the entire job by illumination of a small pen light, held in his mouth. After forty minutes, though, the preparations were complete. Complete to give him the one chance he needed.

Ehud Zak looked out the window of the BBJ, Boeing's 737 business jet derivative. The night sky was clear and the blinking lights that had been their escort of Israeli F-16s were no longer in sight. The aircraft had peeled off, he was told, back when they'd entered Italian airspace. Over the open Mediterranean you could never tell, but the Italians didn't shoot down transiting heads of state.

The pilot announced that they were over central France, and Zak looked down to see a network of lights across an otherwise black void. It reminded him of a starry sky, except the lights were clumped together in bigger groups, impossibly dense constellations connected by spindly off-shoots that must have been roads. He had never been to France, but he would go soon.

Zak settled into a huge leather chair and played with the buttons that made it move. The back tilted down, a leg rest moved up, and something bulged under his lower back. He chuckled. He'd been on the new state aircraft once before, having taken it to a funeral in India. It hadn't been quite important enough for Jacobs himself to attend, and the Foreign Minister had been in South America, so the duty had fallen on Zak to convey official condolences. On that trip he'd traveled up front. Nice enough, but nothing better than a typical airline's first-class section. The rest of his entourage was milling about there now, while he enjoyed the solitude of the Prime Minister's suite that had previously been off-limits. Zak looked around appreciatively. He was surrounded by the finest in furniture, fittings, and accessories. Dark wood, royal colors, crystal fixtures. And in back, in an adjoining room, was a sleeping compartment with a huge bed, an entertainment system and mirrors everywhere. Zak delighted in the prospects.

A knock at the mahogany door interrupted his thoughts. "Enter," he said loudly. He had meant the reply to be weighty and important, but it came off sounding imperious. No matter.

A steward marched in and directly replaced the warm coffee pot with a fresh, hot one. "Will there be anything else, sir?"

"No," he said, "not now." Zak suppressed a smile. That had been better. Dismissive, but keep the fellow on the hook.

The steward disappeared, and Zak again looked out the window. A huge area of lights was coming into view. It could only be Paris. Zak sat mesmerized and reflected on how far the merchant's son had come. He wished his father could see him now, the bastard. He had gone and died four years ago, but even then the old goat had seen him rise to become a Knesset member, far above what anyone could have expected from the son of a second-rate peddler. The old man might have had money, but his son had acquired power, now more than ever.

Strangely enough, Zak and his father had been born with the same gifts. They had used them, however, in very different ways. His father had been the definitive trader. Imports or exports, textiles or condoms, whatever sold. Talk fast and think faster, that was the key. As a boy, Zak had watched and learned. Learned it was all right to buy out a struggling partner for pennies on the dollar, or foreclose on a competitor's widow whose insurance had lapsed. It wasn't being heartless. It was simply business. Send a check to the local homeless shelter and the conscience always came around. The trader's son had shown great promise, and expectations were universal that he would carry on the family business, perhaps even exceeding the mercantile standards set by his elder.

Unfortunately, those dreams were dashed — as so often is the case for young men — by a woman. At nineteen Zak became infatuated with Iricha, a waitress at the Café DuBres. It was a romance both fast-paced and passionate, and after four weeks young Zak had gone to his family to declare enduring love for the woman. And to announce their intent to marry. His father gave no doubt that, in his eyes, the union was beneath consideration. Not only was Iricha a divorcée and ten years older than young Ehud, she was also Palestinian. Zak brought Iricha to meet his father, to prove what a wonderful wife and mother she might be, but the elder refused even to see her.

He had fumed at his father's bigotry, but the rift solidified. Soon his father decreed that if the marriage should come to pass, Zak Trading Ltd. would not. In fine adolescent form, the defiant son answered with the most rebellious act he could imagine. He joined the Israeli army.

This had two results, first being that his father made good on his threat to sell the business, retiring early and well on the proceeds. The second, and the one that took him completely by surprise, was a sudden coolness that developed in his relationship with Iricha. She eventually made a tear-laden confession that, although her love for him was boundless, life as the spouse of an enlisted man in the IDF was not the idyllic future she had envisioned. She then went about devising any number of schemes by which they could rescind his enlistment and return to the good graces of his family. Her favorite idea was to fake a pregnancy, which she imagined might lead to a hardship discharge for Ehud, and a softening of his father's stance. Then, a quick marriage-miscarriage strategy would put them back on the road to enduring happiness and prosperity.

It was here that Zak united the concepts of love and war. He had grown up watching his father, the master artisan of trade, deal his way to success. Getting a customer to pay more for less while believing it was *he* who had gotten the bargain — that was the elusive masterpiece. Yet it was Iricha, the buxom, raven-haired waitress from Haifa, who made him realize that slickness and manipulation were not limited to the world of commerce. He finally saw that his fervent Palestinian lover had been negotiating her own contract, one in which he, and the security of his family's wealth, were the commodities in question.

Then there was the matter of his enlistment. Zak's father was not without influential friends who probably could have orchestrated the loss of his enlistment papers. But the choices had been made, and his father would make him live with them. Stung by this realization, Zak did the only thing he could. He jettisoned his bride-to-be and stuck with the Army.

The string of events served to form Zak's life in many ways. He knew in the recesses of his mind that he could just as easily have been duped by an Israeli woman, or for that matter a Greek or a Latvian. But resentment grew within, and he started to despise and distrust that entire race of people who were generally considered "the enemy." This ember was fanned easily, as Zak lived and worked within the IDF. Like most military sub-societies, the culture was close-knit, conservative, and completely suspicious and intolerant of the enemy. That meant all things Arab, and particularly all things Palestinian.

Within the first year of his service, Zak received word that Iricha had gone on to marry a wealthy Lebanese banker, a man more than twenty years her senior, and the flame was stoked ever more brightly. First Zak had lost his family and fortune, then his soul, all to an amoral temptress. It created a vast emptiness within him. But the void filled quickly with hatred, with an urge to extract payback on the people, the way of life, whose product was Iricha and her carefree evil.

He was not a warrior in the conventional sense. He had never been one to strike out with fists, nor was he physically strong or athletic. Yet he looked for ways to use the weapons that had always served him. Wits and cunning, the ability to manipulate. Those were the instruments he'd use against the vile people who were both his national and personal enemy. Iricha had turned the tables on him, but Zak vowed to never let it happen again. And someday an opportunity for retribution would come.

Early on, he made every attempt to put these troubling thoughts aside in order to focus his considerable talents on a fledgling military career. It got off to a promising start when, as fate would have it, he was assigned to be the supply clerk of a large infantry unit, something akin to placing an arsonist in charge of a fireworks factory. He quickly learned the intricacies of the military bureaucracy and turned them, wherever possible, to his advantage. Within eighteen months, the 6th Infantry Regiment had caviar and the finest Scotch each Thursday afternoon, the commanding officer was riding around in a Mercedes staff car, and corporal Zak had found himself recommended for a commission.

Having never intended to make the military a career, he reconsidered, and decided life as an officer might not be bad, especially in view of his limited prospects outside the service. That in mind, he accepted the promotion, but only with his commander's personal assurance that he could switch specialties. A career in supply and logistics was tempting, but Zak had already seen its limitations. In choosing a new field, he fell back on one of his estranged father's favorite maxims — *scientia est potestas.* Knowledge is power. And so it was, Lieutenant Zak requested, and was granted, appointment to a new division. Aman. Military Intelligence.

For the merchant's son, it was an atmosphere in which to flourish. Lies and deception were the stock in trade, a veritable playground for Zak's shrewd mental games. It was also his chance for payback. He felt increasing satisfaction each time he embezzled money from a Hamas bank account, or bribed a shopkeeper in Gaza. Each success brought gratification, but also whet his desire for more. His stock rose quickly in this shadowy corner of the IDF, and his commanders gave him increasing freedom, opportunities for bigger and more meaningful operations. However, here Zak had gotten carried away. He lost sight of the fact that this obtuse branch of the military was still just that — a branch of the military.

Zak hatched a plan to place a bomb at the upcoming meeting of a pro-peace Palestinian group. The bomb wasn't supposed to go off. It would simply be a dud, one that could be readily identifiable as being of Hamas origin (easy enough, since the Israeli military was constantly defusing and confiscating just such weapons). The resulting in-fighting amongst the Arabs, Zak reasoned, would be a joy to watch.

His commander, a recalcitrant lieutenant colonel, didn't see it that way. He thought the whole idea absurd, if not downright dangerous, and ordered Zak to kill any further thoughts of it. Two weeks later, a bomb did indeed detonate at the meeting in southern Gaza, and an anonymous caller claimed credit for a rogue offshoot of Hamas.

Zak's commander launched a ballistic accusation up the chain of command. Things always fall heavier than they rise, and the lieutenant colonel was immediately reassigned and told to shut up. An ominously quiet investigation got underway. Zak, of course, insisted he had nothing to do with planting the bomb, which was true in the most literal sense. He passed a lie detector test with flying colors, an easy thing to do when you understand how they work, and in the end there was scant evidence. Certainly nothing to hang a court-martial on. Still, the military has its ways. The senior leadership was highly suspicious, and Captain Zak was quietly informed that he would never be anything more than Major Zak. He was reassigned to Signals Intelligence Division, or SIGINT, graveyard of careers lost.

Zak's remaining years in the service seemed professionally quiet. This, however, was not a consequence of his having been idle. In his eyes, the bombing in Gaza was a great success. The Palestinians quarreled and became suspicious of one another. Editorials in the Arab press pointed fingers everywhere. Everywhere except at Israel. If nothing else, Zak's time in the intelligence world taught him the value of the media, and of public opinion. Time and again, governments made decisions based not on facts, but rather on opinion polls, the mood of the people. This caused Zak to expand his original ideas, and give them one further, devastating twist. He quietly espoused his thoughts to those who had helped in the first attack, along with a few other carefully chosen friends, men who felt as adamantly about the cause as he.

The second operation took place six months after the first. A small car bomb at a pizza shop. An Israeli pizza shop. One Jew killed, two wounded. The headlines were loud, and the Israeli response clear. Helicopter gunships took ten times as many Arab lives. Zak found the success intoxicating, and his group grew larger. More attacks were arranged, but each with the greatest of care. He realized the inherent danger. If his group were ever discovered, the media's sway that now aided him would deal a massive counterpunch. Israelis attacking Israelis, blaming the Arabs. The world would cringe.

After a dozen attacks in the first three years, Zak began to feel the risks outweighed the benefits. He scaled back, making the strikes big newsgrabbers, but fewer in number, and only when the chance of detection was low. They were also planned to coincide with the occasional efforts at peace, torpedoes to any truce that might give land to the dirty squatters.

Zak muddled through four years in SIGINT before accepting early retirement, with the rank of major, as promised. It was a divorce, in a sense, one that caused both parties to breathe a sigh of relief. By then, his organization was well established. Still young, and with a clear goal in mind, he searched for even more effective ways to manipulate the will of his countrymen. He found it in politics.

The merchant's son was a natural. All he had to do was tell people what they wanted to hear. Tough words at the Veterans Society fundraiser, suggest peace at the university commencement speech. It took two years to land a seat on the Knesset. There, his career might have stalled among the lawyers, generals, and other merchants' sons, had it not been for one stroke of luck. Zak managed to tie himself to the coattails of a rising star by the name of Benjamin Jacobs. The timing was impeccable. Within ten years of leaving the service under a cloud, he had become the second most powerful man in Israel, at least on paper. From there, there had only been one place to go.

And here he was. The lights of Paris had faded, along with those of the French countryside. Now he saw nothing but blackness below, and he decided it must be the English Channel, that little strip of water that had so often saved the British from their enemies. Zak wished he had a Channel. One he could throw all the Palestinians into. A chime sounded and he saw the light flashing on his private intercom. He waited a few moments before picking it up casually.

"What is it?"

He recognized the pilot's voice.

"We're beginning our descent, Mr. Prime Minister. It might get bumpy and I wanted to make sure you were buckled in."

"How long until we land?" Zak demanded.

After a slight pause, the pilot replied, "Seventeen minutes, sir."

The pilot was a colonel in the Israeli Air Force, and had probably received his commission about the same time as one retired Major Ehud Zak. Timing *was* everything.

"Make it sixteen." He hung up and smiled.

By coincidence, ten miles to the south another Israeli executive transport, this one much smaller, was climbing as it began its six-hour journey back to Tel Aviv. Inside, Anton Bloch was also talking on a handset, he to a hotel in Casablanca. His expression was both grim and determined.

When Anton Bloch arrived in Tel Aviv there was no limo waiting. Instead, he'd called ahead and his wife was there to give him a ride, escorted by two bodyguards. For all the privileges Bloch would lose, the muscle would be around for many years. No one would particularly care if he were blown to bits, but ex-Directors of Mossad knew far too many dirty secrets to risk capture.

Bloch was exhausted after the all-night flight from London, and he sat with his wife in the back seat as they went straight to his office. Or what used to be his office. On the way there, the Blochs made a feeble attempt at conversation. They covered the weather, their leaking bathroom sink, and finally ventured to more tender ground, the status of their recalcitrant daughter who had been mucking up her first year at university. The last subject was a sour one, and they both knew he couldn't give the issue the attention it required. At least not now. Arriving at Mossad headquarters, Anton Bloch shot his wife a look that told her she'd have to handle it for the time being. As he was about to get out of the car, she grabbed his arm.

"Oh, wait. I have something for you." She dug into her purse and handed over a message, scripted in her own meticulous handwriting. "Some fellow named Samuels called you at the house. He said this was important."

He took the note, kissed his wife more than dutifully on the cheek, then hurried inside.

Bloch was recognized immediately by security at the entrance and ushered straight to his old office. His successor, Raymond Nurin, wanted a word with him. The choice didn't surprise Bloch. Nurin had never spent much time in operations, but he was competent, and a safe pick who would neither stir controversy, nor go in and turn the place upside down to put his personal stamp on things.

Once alone on the elevator, Bloch read the message his wife had taken.

> *Sunday, 6:00 A.M.*
> *Found second boat chartered from Rabat in Pytor Roth's name. 34' Hatteras. Name Broadbill, registered in Morocco. Went to sea two weeks ago, no sign of boat or crew since. Advise.*
>   *Samuels.*

Bloch crumpled up the note and vowed to call Nathan Chatham as soon as he could with the name *Broadbill*. He suspected there might have been a second boat, one to carry the second weapon. The first had been chartered in Casablanca, by Wysinski and his bunch. From there it had been a dead end — but now Rabat. Roth's name had been the key. Bloch suspected a little research might turn up more on the man. Find him, and maybe they could get to that second weapon in time.

The elevator opened and Bloch was shown to his old office. Not much had changed. There were some new, half-opened boxes of junk to take the place of his own lot, which was presently shoved against the far wall. The desk was already buried under a maelstrom of papers and files.

"Anton," Nurin said with false familiarity and a smile. Bloch had met the man a few times, but he'd always worked in other sections, socialized in different orbits.

"Where have you been?" Nurin asked guardedly, clearly uncomfortable in the company of his predecessor. The man almost seemed intimidated, and for the very first time Anton Bloch wondered how the rank and file of the Mossad had always seen him. Perhaps some gruff and surly tyrant? Bloch discarded the thought. He didn't much care.

"In England," Bloch grunted, "but you already know that."

Nurin looked embarrassed. "Well, yes. But what were you doing there?"

"Trying to figure out where that missing weapon is."

The new boss tried to exert some control. "Anton, jetting off to Europe is not the Director of Mossad's job. We have people who do that kind of thing. And you left your personal security detail behind."

"I'm not the Director anymore."

"There's a lot of people who were nervous about where you'd gone."

"Like who?"

Nurin huffed, clearly not liking the vector of the conversation. His tone eased, "Look Anton, we've got to figure this out. I'm sorry about all that's happened, but we have to work together."

The last thing Bloch wanted was a togetherness speech. "I went to England to find Slaton and look for any leads on where that second weapon might be."

"Did you have any luck?"

"No," Bloch said, not bothering to add, *And if I did have anything, I wouldn't share it with you right now.*

Nurin sighed, glancing at his watch. "I'm expecting a conference call from the Prime Minister any minute, but I've got to see you later today. There are some ongoing projects I'd like you to brief me on."

Bloch tried to look enthusiastic. Then a thought came to mind.

"Yes, I'll brief you on everything this afternoon. You know, it would help to have the files. That way we could go over them together."

Nurin looked at a day planner on his desk. "How about three o'-clock? I'll cancel the rest of my afternoon."

"Fine," Bloch said. "Do I still have authorization? Two days ago I was the Director, but if they've gone by the book, those pencil-necks downstairs might have pulled my access."

Nurin looked surprised, "Oh, of course. I'll make sure they give you whatever you need."

Bloch retained his business-like expression. The new Director had just made his research a lot easier.

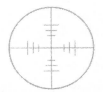

Chapter Twenty-Three

Inspector Chatham stood fast against the cold drizzle and brisk wind that whipped his face. It was a long face, longer than usual, and beads of precipitation peppered his mustache. He was standing on the ceremonial stage in Greenwich Park, and under his feet were two pieces of tape. They formed an **X**, this being the very spot where the signing table would be tomorrow morning. From this spot, the leading powers of the most embattled region on earth would commit to a lasting peace. That is, unless David Slaton got in the way. Or a nuclear weapon, or . . . what else? Chatham wondered fretfully. Perhaps a meteor from the heavens? It was his job to worry about things. All sorts of things. Yet, at the moment, he had an ill feeling he'd missed something.

A tireless Ian Dark came slogging across the wet sod and climbed up to the stage. Chatham's gaze remained fixed on the horizon as his assistant came alongside and stood silently, apparently allowing rank its privileges.

"You know," Chatham began, without taking his eyes off the park, "I've been at it a long time, this business of chasing after criminals. And I've had some success in hunting them down, putting them behind bars as necessary. Some were quite stupid, made the job easy. Others were actually rather clever. But they have all—" Chatham finally looked at his colleague, "*all* been done in by one thing. The predictability of human nature. It has always amazed me. They'll rob a bank, then a week later when the money's gone, they'll rob the same one again. We're very much creatures of habit, Ian. People go to work, eat lunch, exercise, and cheat

on their spouses with amazing punctuality. My sister has gone to the same
hair stylist at ten-thirty on Wednesday mornings for the past twelve years."

Chatham began to stroll the platform. "My first case was a hit-and-
run. Some poor chap got run down on a backstreet intersection at four in
the morning. No witnesses, no physical evidence to speak of. I went out
and stood on that corner from three to five in the morning for two weeks.
Finally, a woman drove up one night and paused at the intersection. I was
in uniform, and as soon as she looked over at me I knew. We both knew.
I'll never forget the look on her face. She confessed. She was a nurse,
worked the late shift every other Saturday. She'd gone home sleepy that
one night and missed the stop sign. Hit the fellow and panicked, kept going."

Chatham moved slowly, almost as if conserving energy.

"Creatures of habit?" Dark asked. "Predictable? Even Slaton?"

"Especially Slaton!" He stopped and waved a hand out across the
park. "Here. He'll be here tomorrow, somehow." Chatham strode back to
the X. "While Israel's Prime Minister is standing on this very spot!"

Dark looked around doubtfully. "Ten plainclothes men are already
here, and twice as many uniforms. Tomorrow will triple that count, not to
mention the head-of-state protection details of a half dozen countries.
They'll stop and question anyone having the faintest resemblance to Slaton's photo. The trash cans are gone, the sewer covers bolted closed. And
the only cars permitted within three blocks will be those carrying the participants. I can't see how, Inspector."

"Nor can I, Ian. But just because we don't see it — that doesn't
mean it's not there. An opening. Somewhere." Chatham looked out at the
Queen's House in the distance. "What about that, over there? Too far?"
he wondered aloud.

"Oh, yes. I've talked to some of the Army chaps who do this sort of
thing, the sharpshooters. They tell me four hundred yards is the outside,
and then it would require a good bit of luck to hit a target the size of a person. The Queen's House is nearly a thousand yards." Dark raised one arm
up at an angle. "You'd have to raise the gun up like this and loft the bullet
in the general direction of a target. Hitting anyone would be sheer luck."

Chatham eyed his assistant. "You *have* been busy."

Dark grinned. "Those Army lads are really top drawer. I spent some
time with them this morning. You see, I thought that of all the people I
know, they're the most like him. They make their livings much the same

way he does, knowing how to hide and shoot. They'd know how he might go about doing it. I'm going to meet two of them in an hour, right here. I'll have them look over the area firsthand and tell us what they think."

Chatham cocked his head and nodded approvingly. "Yes, I see." He went back to scanning the park. "Hadn't thought of that."

He rarely issued compliments, and when he did, they often seemed to come obtusely. But Chatham saw this one had hit home. Dark couldn't have looked giddier if the Queen Mum herself had just touched a sword to his shoulders.

"Of course," he added pensively, "that assumes he's going to use the rifle."

"What do you mean?"

"Well, it occurred to me that he might have stolen those rifles in order for us to think these exact thoughts. For example, if we were concentrating on looking for a concealed sniper with an outsized rifle, we might ignore the more obvious. A well-disguised face in the crowd, an impostor on one of the security details. Remember, he's stolen a handgun as well."

"Yes. I suppose."

"Still," Chatham reasoned, "we've got to cover everything. You meet with those Army lads and tell me what they say."

"Right, sir."

"Oh, and anything yet on that boat Bloch told us about, the *Broadbill?*"

"No. I think we've gone over every harbor and slip in the country. Nothing."

With a thumb and forefinger, Chatham slowly groomed his moustache, brushing away the accumulated droplets of rain. It might not be in England, he thought, but it was out there.

Most of the East End shops were closed on Sunday, so Slaton phoned the hotel concierge. Once he'd explained his needs, the sprightly young woman efficiently directed him to a shopping area a mile north of the hotel. She then offered to call a cab, but he politely declined the transportation. The streets were quiet on Sundays. He would walk.

The concierge was right about the shopping complex. Slaton quickly found what he needed. He made his first purchase in a clothing shop, then two in an electronics store. Avoiding crowded areas, he paid cash and kept his contact with the sales assistants to a minimum. On his way back to the hotel, he considered stopping at a restaurant for one last good meal. As tempting as it was, there was no point in taking chances. Not when he was so close.

He stopped at a small grocer he'd spotted a few blocks from the hotel, picked out a baguette, some sliced ham, and a container of orange juice. He took a spot in line to be rung up by a disinterested young woman who was chewing gum like a cow might chew a mouthful of grass. She mumbled an obligatory greeting of some sort, then summed up Slaton's purchase. He proffered a ten-pound note and she plopped a few coins in his hand in return, dropping the food in a plastic sack. She mumbled again, this time probably "Thank you," with little more than a glance at her customer. Slaton left the store pleased that his groundwork was complete.

The customer who had been standing behind Slaton, a well-dressed elderly man, shoved his tea and fudge in front of Prudence Bloom. She ran it through the scanner, distracted as she did so. After ringing the man up, she stood staring at the rack behind him, forgetting to give him his total.

The customer patiently leaned forward, trying to see the display on the cash register. "Four pounds, six?" he queried. "Is that right?"

The question broke her trance. "What? Oh, yeah. That's right."

He pulled a handful of change from his pocket.

"Did you see that bloke in front of you," she asked, "the one that just left?"

"Yes, I suppose. Why do you ask?"

"It was him," she said with certainty.

"Who?"

"Him!" Prudence pointed to a rack of newspapers behind her customer.

Every front page blazed with pictures of the terrorist fellow the police had been after. The man looked, then turned to Prudence, his skepticism evident.

"You saw him better than I did, but . . ." he ran a hand obviously over his own thin crown, "he had less up here than I do." He pointed to the photograph, "This fellow's got a full head. And he doesn't wear glasses."

Doubt settled in as Prudence studied the face in the newspapers. Obviously wanting to move things along, the man grabbed one and handed it to her. She studied it up close.

The customer had clearly had enough. He squirreled together the exact change, dropped it on the counter, and put the tea and fudge in a bag himself. He bid her, "Good day, miss," with mock politeness.

"Good day," she said, not looking up. Fortunately there were no other customers in line.

Prudence spotted a phone number at the bottom of the article, one to call in order to give information. She bit her bottom lip. Anybody could put on a pair of glasses, she reasoned. He was right about the bald spot, though. Nothing was mentioned about a reward. But still, if she could be the one to nab a killer like this! What a story to tell her boyfriend Angus and his mates. She picked up the phone next to the cash register and dialed.

"Crime Line," said a young man.

"Yes," she said excitedly, "I've seen the man you're looking for!"

"Which man is that, ma'am?"

"The killer, that terrorist bloke! He's in all the papers, he is!"

"Right. And your name is?"

"Prudence. Prudence Bloom. I run the till at Hartson's Grocery in Loughton. I just saw him, right here in front o' me!"

"Can you describe him?"

"Well, he looked just like the picture here in the paper."

"How tall?"

She thought hard. "Six-foot, I suppose. More or less. But it was him! I'm lookin' at the picture right now. Add the glasses, and take some hair off the top."

"Sorry?"

"He had glasses. And there was some hair gone on top, not like in the picture. But it was him all right."

Fortunately for Prudence Bloom, she couldn't see the expression on the man's face. The hotline operator took down information for five minutes. When he was done, he promised that someone would drop by to investigate.

"I hope it'll be soon," she said, looking suspiciously toward the street. "He could still be right outside."

The operator tossed Prudence Bloom's report into a stack of seven others he'd taken in the last hour. And there were nine men and women filtering calls behind him. "As soon as we can, ma'am."

❖   ❖   ❖

"As soon as we can" turned into two hours. The officer in charge of the hotline operation was handed the most promising prospects immediately. If he concurred that they were worth checking, an investigative unit was instantly dispatched to gather more information. Once the priority tips were handled, he waded through the other ninety-five percent. He read Prudence Bloom's information and yawned. The fact that the suspect was now balding didn't even register a chuckle. So far today, the suspect had been seen with a red Mohawk, two hundred extra pounds, and in one case had somehow transformed himself into a black woman.

The supervisor wasn't particularly excited by what he read, but the standing orders were to check out *everything*. He also had the advantage of manpower. Virtually every policeman in the city was working this weekend, like it or not. He put the report in a queue, and eventually a copy was faxed to the local division.

When Constable Vickers walked into Hartson's Grocery, Prudence Bloom was getting ready to go home. She was upset it had taken so long, but the cashier told her story all the same. She'd seen someone who matched the pictures in the paper, albeit with a few adjustments. Beyond that, the patrolman garnered only one other useful scrap — when the man had gone out, he'd turned right. As Vickers departed, a frustrated Prudence Bloom was explaining everything to her manager and asking for the next day off.

Vickers had nothing more to do, so he turned right as well. He spoke to a few of the merchants down the street and showed them a picture, but nobody remembered the man. He was ready to give up when he came upon the Forest Arms Hotel. He went in and made his pitch at the front desk, with no luck, then moved to the bell stand.

He held up the picture to the man on duty.

"Seen this fellow? Maybe missing some hair on top and with a set of thick brown-framed eyeglasses?"

The bellman thought. "Well, like that . . . I s'pose it looks a bit like the chap up in 37. He came in a couple of hours ago."

"Was he carrying anything?"

"Two shopping bags, I think."

Vickers smiled. He'd found his suspect. That would make his sergeant happy. It always made them look on the ball when they could call back to headquarters and tell them to strike one off the list. He took the lift to the third floor, found Number 37 and knocked loudly. There was no answer. He frowned and went back down to the front desk, wondering if they'd let him have a look without a warrant.

"Who's in Number 37?" he asked.

The desk clerk looked at her log. "That would be Mr. Forger, the Belgian. Is there a problem?" The clerk looked nervous. She had obviously made the connection as to who Vickers was asking about.

"When did he get here?"

"Two days ago. I checked him in. He paid cash in advance, through the weekend. I—"

A shrill, pulsating screech cut off all normal conversation.

"What's that?" Vickers yelled.

"The fire alarm!"

A hysterical maid came running down the stairs. "Fire!" she screamed. "Number 36! There's smoke coming from under the door!"

The clerk called the fire department.

"Bloody hell!" Vickers stammered. He drew out his two-way and called the station.

Benjamin Jacobs was at home. It felt strange after spending so many years on the move, traveling abroad, dashing from a speech here to a committee meeting there. His days and nights running the country had been spent mostly at the Prime Minister's Residence in Jerusalem, with occasional forays to Tel Aviv. And twice a year Jacobs would stray to the requisite oxymoron of a "working vacation," typically a resort with magnificent views, wide-ranging recreation opportunities, and no chance to enjoy any of it. On the few occasions when Jacobs had tried to sneak back to his own house, it was invariably surrounded by the media. They clicked and clamored, hoping for a sound bite or a picture — some snippet that could be turned into either a meaningful diplomatic signal or an awkward personal gaffe. The latter usually got better ratings. Jacobs swore he didn't miss any of it.

His resignation had been effective last Wednesday night. What surprised him was that by the next evening he'd fallen off the face of the earth, professionally speaking. Jacobs fully expected to spend a month or two debriefing, tying up the administrative and procedural loose ends of an executive administration that had lasted almost two years. Instead, his calls to Zak's office had gone unanswered, and even his old staff seemed

to be avoiding him. Lowens' phone extension suddenly changed. Moira
had been transferred to a different office, but nobody seemed to know
where. The Deputy Assistant to the Minister of Transportation had hung
up on him. Jacobs tried not to take it to heart. They were all in the career
survival mode. A simple case of out with the old and in with the new.

So it was, when Jacobs' green secure phone rang in its familiar,
piercing tone, he picked it up expecting someone from the Ministry of
Communications to be on the other end. No doubt to remind the sacked
PM that he had to return the phone so it could be used by someone who
was still important.

He lifted the handset and growled, "What is it?"

There was a pause before Anton Bloch's distinct voice rumbled, "Ah,
it's me, Mr. Prime . . . or . . ."

Jacobs had to laugh, "Benjamin will do, Anton. How are you?"

"Fine," Bloch said quickly, no real regard given to the question. "I've
been busy."

"At least one of us is. I feel like a leper."

Bloch didn't laugh, his usual humorless self. "I've got something I'd
like to talk to you about."

"Old business?" Jacobs guessed.

"Yes, in a way."

"Come over tomorrow afternoon. Our housekeeper, if we still have
one, makes a terrific seafood pasta dish."

"Actually, I was thinking of something sooner."

"My wife and I have plans to go out tonight, Anton. It's been some
time since we've been able to do that kind of thing." Silence was the reply
and Jacobs became uncomfortable. "Of course, if it's important—"

Eight minutes later, the doorbell rang. Anton Bloch was there, looking impatient and flanked by two of Jacobs' security men.

Irene Jacobs, the former First Lady of Israel, had answered the
chime as well. Her husband reintroduced her to the old Director of
Mossad, the two having met once before. She was practiced and proper as
she greeted their guest, the years of social diplomacy still fresh. The men
then retired to the study, closing the doors discreetly behind. When they
emerged minutes later, Benjamin Jacobs addressed his wife.

"I'm so sorry darling, but I won't be able to keep our arrangement
tonight. I promise to make it up to you soon." He kissed his wife on the
cheek and she beamed, a paragon of understanding.

"That's all right dear. Some other time." Her stone smile told him there would be hell to pay later.

"And I may be late," he warned, "please don't wait up." Jacobs collected his coat and murmured instructions to one of the security men outside the front door. Then, he and Bloch disappeared.

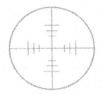

Chapter Twenty-Four

The firemen were walking down the stairs as Chatham was going up. All the hotel's guests and most of the staff had been evacuated, and the only people now on the third floor were police. The forensics team Chatham had put on alert was already busy sifting, scraping, and searching. The woman in charge, Jane Grimm, met Chatham in the hall outside Number 36.

"Good afternoon, Inspector."

Competent and thorough, Grimm was a favorite of Chatham's. Today, however, there was no time for pleasantries.

"What have you found?"

Grimm led Chatham into Number 36.

"The patrolman thought it was another false alarm. He came up to 37 and knocked on the door figuring he could clear things up right away. Nobody answered, so he went back downstairs to talk to the manager. Clearly our friend was home after all. His room was connected to 36 by a door. It was bolted closed, but I doubt it took more than one kick."

"There was no one in this room?" Chatham asked.

"No, it was vacant. I'm not sure how he knew."

"That's what he does. He knows things like that."

Chatham could only see a thin veil of smoke in the room, but the smell, a particularly acrid variety, lingered heavily. They went to the bathroom and Grimm pointed to a pile of ashes and charred debris in the bathtub.

"He started it with a newspaper and some hotel stationery, then threw in a couple of blankets."

"What's that on top?" Chatham wondered, pointing to a pair of melted lumps.

"Jogging shoes. A good choice," she admitted, "gives you a lot of thick, dark smoke, sort of like an old tire. Gets everyone's attention."

"Exactly what time did the alarm go off?"

"The desk clerk called the fire department within a minute of the alarm going off. The fire department dispatcher logged that call at 1:39."

"Damn!" Chatham said in frustration. He had ordered a special watch on all transportation out of the area when he'd gotten the news, but that had been two o'clock. Still a twenty minute gap. "He's gotten a head start again."

They left the bathroom and walked through the shattered door frame that connected to Number 37. A man was poking around the room with a probe of some sort, connected by a wire to a machine on his back. The machine bore markings that identified it as property of the U.S. government. The man wore civilian clothes but had a short haircut, and Chatham decided he was likely a part of this American NEST team he'd been hearing about.

"There's not much here," Grimm said. "A few items of clothing, some food wrappings." She presented a plastic bag that held a collection of tiny, curled scraps. "Wood shavings. We found them on the floor. Of course, no telling how long they've been here. Then there was this . . ." Grimm led to a table where a window blind sat. "We found it up on the shelf, there, pushed all the way to the back." Chatham looked at the closet. He raised up on his toes, barely able to see the top of the now-empty shelf.

Someone called Grimm into the other room and she excused herself, leaving Chatham in silence with the American fellow. He was waving his sensor rhythmically in one corner of the room, looking like a badly dressed orchestra conductor. Chatham studied the window blind. His first train of thought was simple — the last person before Slaton to stay in the room was a decorator who had left it behind by accident. His second train of thought was ridiculous — Slaton was going to take it to Greenwich, put it up on a window for cover, then at the last minute, turn it open and shoot. At least that plot was foiled. He nearly laughed out loud. If it could only be so easy.

He took a closer look. The blind seemed brand new, and the cord used to raise and lower the thing had been cut short, two loose pieces of string dangling from the casing. He stood straight with his hands on his hips, both mystified and intrigued. "What are you up to?" he whispered harshly.

Grimm came back in and Chatham said, "Have you got a . . . ah, a cell phone?"

Grimm pulled a phone from her pocket. "They haven't given you one?"

Chatham frowned. He fumbled and punched at buttons until the display announced that it was READY to do his bidding. He then managed to dial his office. Moments later, Ian Dark was taking instructions.

"—Continental Visions, model number 201048. It's forty-eight inches in length. He may also have bought some wood—"

"Spruce four-by-fours," Grimm prompted.

"Spruce four-by-fours."

Dark acknowledged that he was keeping up and Chatham continued, "I want you to start at this hotel and take a five-mile radius. Any store that might sell something like that, get their transaction records. Go back three, make it four days. That should cover things. We want someone who purchased one, perhaps two of these. Any more and you can toss it out. I want the full transaction record of any sale, Ian. I want to know what else he might have bought."

"You know it *is* Sunday, sir. Any place likely to sell something like this will probably be closed by the time—"

"I don't care!" Chatham yelled at a volume that might not have needed the phone's assistance to reach the Yard. "Call in the store manager, call in the owner! If they don't cooperate, throw them in for obstruction and find the next in line! Get it done now!"

Chatham handed the phone back to Grimm, not remembering to end the call. The Yank in the corner with the funny wand was staring at Chatham, but turned back to his business when the Englishman caught his look. Chatham glared seethingly at the window blind laying on the table. It was key. Key to something. But *what*?

The night was calm, light winds driving a mild two-foot chop on the southern Mediterranean. This was a blessing, since most of the men on board had never been to sea. Mohammed Al-Quatan could see the lights of Malta to the north, flickering yellow in a distant haze. He thought they were getting too close. Twelve miles was the limit. Colonel Al-Quatan strode purposely toward the boat's captain, who stood at the helm.

"We must be there," he insisted.

The captain, a crusty old sort, looked at a GPS receiver mounted above the steering console. He bobbed his head indifferently. "A few more miles."

Al-Quatan spat, "A few more miles and we are in Italian waters!"

The captain snickered. "I am going to the spot you gave me, and that is fourteen miles off the coast of Malta. If you wish, I can turn around now, but the price is the same."

A fuming Al-Quatan turned away. His own men would never speak in such a way. But the old beggar had probably spent his life on the high seas battling Mother Nature. He would not be easily cowed. Al-Quatan wished he had a real boat, not this tired old fishing scow. The Libyan Navy had big patrol boats, fast ones with real sailors. Unfortunately, Moustafa Khalif had not permitted it. He wanted the satisfaction of delivering their prize personally to the Great One. They would ask no help.

The first mate, who was standing at the bow, suddenly gave a shout. The captain leaned forward, peering through the salt-encrusted windshield.

"What is it?" Al-Quatan wondered.

"A boat."

"Is it the one?"

"It is possible," the captain said with a shrug, "but we must get closer."

Al-Quatan gave a signal to his men down in the cabin. There were ten altogether, his best men, and they clambered up the stairs with weapons ranging from submachine guns to rocket-propelled grenades. They assembled unsteadily on deck, many still not accustomed to the movement of the sea.

A few minutes later Al-Quatan saw the outline of the boat, a hundred yards off. It was completely dark. "Get close," he ordered, "and use your light."

The captain maneuvered alongside the drifting boat. "It's an old Hatteras 32 or 34," he announced, "a good craft in its day."

Al-Quatan didn't care if it was Noah's holy Christian Ark. "The light!" he demanded.

The captain obliged, putting his spotlight on the vessel thirty yards to port. There was no sign of anyone aboard.

Al-Quatan wondered where Roth was. He wanted the treacherous Israeli almost as much as what he was selling. The weasel had already squandered away one of the weapons — left it sitting in an English port. Al-Quatan had prayed he'd be more careful with the other. His men spread across the boat and fixed their weapons on the Hatteras, ten gun barrels oscillating against the deck's rise and fall. Al-Quatan took over the spotlight as the captain edged closer. He illuminated the hatches and portholes, but there was no sign of anyone. In the partially covered wheelhouse, Al-Quatan spotted an object covered by a sheet of plastic. His heart skipped a beat.

"Now!" he shouted. "My men will go now!"

The captain inched closer until the two boats were only a few feet apart. Even with light seas, they rocked incongruously, like two drunks trying to waltz.

"That is all," the captain said, "I can get no closer."

One of Al-Quatan's men jumped over to the smaller boat. Landing in a heap, he lost grip of his AK-47 and it clattered to the deck, unleashing a wild round. Everyone instinctively ducked at the sound of the weapon discharging, and Al-Quatan swore he heard the bullet whiz by his ear. Two more men leapt across uneventfully, but then the fourth mistimed his effort badly. He smacked squarely into the side of the Hatteras, with a hollow clunk, and fell helplessly into the wet chasm between the boats.

"Idiot!" the captain yelled. He gunned his motors into reverse to keep the fool from being crushed. The three men already aboard the Hatteras managed to pull their stunned comrade from the sea, minus his Uzi.

The boarding party quickly collected themselves and disappeared into the bowels of the drifting vessel. A minute later, one man stuck his head out of a hatch and waved an all clear signal.

"Get closer," Al-Quatan ordered. Waiting for the right moment, he jumped across, two members of the team grabbing his forearms as he landed.

"There is no one below," one of them announced.

Al-Quatan nodded, then went straight to the wheelhouse and ripped the plastic cover off what he hoped was his prize.

What he saw surprised him at first. It was shiny, silver, and not terribly long. He had expected it to be bigger, more sinister looking. But then he smiled. This was it. He knew this was it! Khalif had been right. After so much effort, so many years of suffering defeat and indignity at the hands of the Zionists, they had finally succeeded. Mohammed Al-Quatan was suddenly overwhelmed, realizing the power that lay before him. He felt almost God-like.

Someone whispered a sharp, "Allah akbar!"

Al-Quatan turned and looked at his men. He saw the same amazement and pride in their eyes as they regarded the seed of victory that lay before them. When the Great One saw what they offered, he would provide anything in return. They would live in proper houses, eat proper food. And soon, certainly soon, the Great One would use this gift from Allah to rid Palestine of the infidels once and for all.

"We have done it, my brothers," Al-Quatan said, offering an unusual moment of fraternity to his underlings. "We have done it!"

Pytor Roth exited the cab by the DEPARTURES sign at Malta International Airport in Luqa. With no luggage involved, the driver stayed in his seat as Roth paid the fare. It was two minutes after nine in the morning here, but more importantly to Roth, two minutes after nine in Zurich. He went immediately into the small, run-down building that passed for a terminal, and found the lone pay telephone. His call was answered immediately. The Swiss were always so efficient. He spoke in English and, after one switch, was talking to the person he wanted.

"Herr Junger, it's Pytor Roth."

Junger's English was decent, if a little hard on the consonants. "Gut morning, Mr. Roth. You are calling about the new account, yes?"

"That's right."

"One moment, I will check."

He was put on hold for what seemed like an eternity. Finally, Junger picked up again, "Ya, Mr. Roth. The funds are on deposit, as we discussed."

Roth exhaled. His lips curled into a smile.

"Thank you, Herr Junger. I'll see you this afternoon with further instructions. You've been most helpful."

"Two o'clock, sir. It is on my agenda."

Roth hung up, still grinning. He might actually sneak out of this predicament after all. For months he'd been stuck between that proverbial rock and a hard place, ending with his journey deep into the godforsaken Libyan desert, to barter with the devil himself. But now there was an end, an escape. And maybe even a profit. He was a man on top of the world.

As he turned away from the phone, Roth swore he heard someone call his name. At first it merely struck him as odd. Only when he saw the stern, heavy-set man closing in from his right did the alarms go off. Roth instinctively veered away, but then a hand gripped his arm on the other side, a grip that made him feel like an animal whose limb had just been caught in a steel trap. The second man was not as big as the first, but he was smiling in a most congenial, discomforting fashion. Roth hoped for a moment they might be some sort of airport security, but then the one with the smile opened his jacket lapel slightly to reveal an ugly handgun. He spoke in Hebrew and said simply, "Come with us, Mr. Roth, or we will kill you."

Roth was stunned. He was so close. So close to wealth and freedom. He felt himself being shoved along, back outside the terminal, one brute on each elbow.

"Who are you?" he asked desperately. "What do you want?"

Neither answered. The men steered him toward a car, a big sedan, and the back door swung open as they approached. Roth panicked. He saw a policeman directing traffic some distance up the curb. He tried to cry out, but at that moment there was a crushing blow to his solar plexus. He doubled over in pain, and nearly did a somersault as he was thrown into the back of the car.

Face down on the floorboard, he tried to catch his breath as the car lurched forward. Heavy boots stomped on his back and legs, holding him down. The car surged ahead, winding through a series of turns. He tried to talk again, but the only response was a quick kick to the back of his head. His hands were tied behind his back, and then a black cloth hood was wrestled over his head. He was frantic now, wondering who these people were. There were a number of possibilities. None of them good.

The car stopped suddenly and he heard a loud noise, like a jet engine nearby. Roth was hoisted out of the car to a standing position. He could see nothing through the hood, but now the noise was excruciatingly loud. He was shoved and guided a few yards, then literally lifted off his feet and pulled upward, his legs bashing over a short set of stairs. Someone yanked him again to a standing position and shoved him back until he fell into a soft chair. He felt bindings being secured around his legs and chest. Seconds later came the unmistakable whine of jet engines rising to full power. The acceleration pressed him back into the soft leather seat. He was on a plane. But going where? And with who?

For a few minutes there were no new sensations. The drone of the engines, the draft from an air vent overhead. But he could tell someone was there, watching him. Without warning, the hood was yanked roughly off his head. Involuntarily, Roth's eyes shut tight, but then he opened them slowly and all became clear. Two men sat staring at him. Two instantly recognizable faces. The former Prime Minister of Israel and the former Head of Mossad glared with daggers of contempt. Pytor Roth knew he was in deep *hara*.

Christine arrived at the cafeteria to find a madhouse. If Scotland Yard was weathering a typhoon of an investigation, this was the eye of the maelstrom. A narrow refuge where the harried staff could find nourishment, companionship and, if they were really fortunate, a few moments peace.

Her escort, this one a grim, brooding type, parked himself at the door while she lined up at the coffee stand. They'd been granting her more freedom, and Dark confided earlier that she'd be released "soon." Christine suspected that meant after this morning. The clock on the wall read 9:09. An hour to go. If only she could quit looking.

She took her fix in a Styrofoam cup, black, and searched for an empty table. Nothing was open, but then a familiar face emerged on the far side of the room, waving her over. It was Big Red. His real name, she'd found out, was Simon Masters. Until today, he'd worked the morning shift as her guard. And he was unquestionably her favorite. Yesterday they'd chatted for much of the morning. He was an affable fellow, with a wife and three small children at home. It had been a pleasant diversion to hear how his kids attacked him every time he came in the door. She could easily envision him falling to his knees while three preschoolers climbed onto his wide shoulders, turning Daddy into a sturdy, yet malleable piece of playground equipment.

As she weaved toward him, Christine noted one disturbing difference from the previous day. Masters was wearing some kind of combat uniform. A heavy vest, a belt bristling with gear, and a radio with a wire that ran to one ear. All of it was black.

"Hello, miss." He insisted on calling her "miss."

"Good morning, Simon."

"Sleep well?"

She shrugged.

"Today's the big day, is it?"

"Yes. What's with all the armor?"

Masters looked uncomfortable. "Listen, this place is crazy. Me and my mates have a private room in back. It's much quieter. Would you like to join us?"

"It has to be better than this," she reasoned.

He signaled to her escort at the door. The man gave a thumbs up and moved to the coffee line himself. Masters then led Christine into an adjoining room, which was indeed quieter. The only occupants were five other men dressed identically to him. They noted her arrival, a few nodding, then went back to their conversations. A wide window at the back gave a panoramic view of a large helicopter outside, settled on a rooftop pad. The pilots were in place, standing by.

"What is all this, Simon?"

He sighed. "It's the Rapid Response Team. I've been put in charge."

"Response? Response to what?" Christine suspected the helicopter was loaded down with weapons. "Is this about David?"

He nodded. "We're on standby. If anything . . . happens, we'll be called in to find him."

"Find him? You mean kill him!"

Masters said nothing.

She sat at a table, set down her coffee, and closed her eyes. "Oh, Simon. I'm sorry," she recanted. "This isn't your fault."

He pulled a chair next to hers, and put a hand on her shoulder. "I know this is difficult for you, miss. I truly do. If anything happens and we get called in, I promise to do all I can."

She nodded. "I know you will. I'm glad it's you, Simon. I just wish that I could talk to him once more." She studied her coffee cup. "Do you remember the other day, what happened between me and that Israeli man in the hallway?"

He nodded.

"He told me something. Something that could change David's outlook entirely. But there's no way for me to tell him."

"Would you like to tell me? In case I run across him?"

She smiled forlornly, "Thanks, Simon. But honestly, I don't think he'd believe it unless it came from that fellow or me."

Christine spotted another clock on the wall. Did every room in this damned building have one? she wondered. It was 9:20.

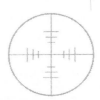

Chapter Twenty-Five

Moustafa Khalif could see it in Mohammed Al-Quatan's face. He felt it himself. Awe. Sheer amazement. It had been that kind of day.

To begin, Al-Quatan had pulled into the fishing docks of Tripoli with a 10 kiloton fission device (arriving well in advance of morning prayers, he'd noted, as if it were an omen). At that same moment, Khalif had been in a private meeting with the Great One himself, who was speechless when told what this small group of state guests had managed to do. From there, the Great One had taken over. He agreed with Khalif. There was only one place to keep such a thing, and arrangements were made immediately to transport it by military helicopter.

Now, hours later, Khalif had caught up with his prize. He was at the Sebha facility, isolated in the far southern reaches of the Libyan Desert. Or rather beneath it. He and Al-Quatan were presently underground, riding an electric golf cart through a tunnel that seemed to have no end. This was the place they had heard about, where important work was done and great secrets kept. It was bigger than Khalif had imagined. Above ground lay a small city — buildings and machinery, all encircled by fences and concertina wire, with guard towers every hundred meters. And then there were the soldiers. Everywhere soldiers. To get this far they'd gone through three security checkpoints. Al-Quatan had been forced to surrender his sidearm at the first. The last had included a full-body scan by some type of walk-through machine, like those in the airports, only bigger.

Then the elevator had taken them down. When it opened, the first thing Khalif noticed was the air. It was stagnant and damp, smelling of sulfur like the water that came from the very deep drinking wells back in Palestine. Then they were guided through a maze of corridors. There were offices, laboratories, and more elevators. Strangest of all was the tunnel through which they now passed. It was big, both wide and tall enough that a good-sized truck could make use of it. Overhead was a continuous, neatly carved arch of rock with a string of lights at the crest. Occasionally, the earthen ceiling above glistened as the naked bulbs illuminated damp areas where moisture somehow seeped into the long cavern. This concerned Khalif, who thought it unnatural and certainly unsafe, but he kept the thought to himself.

The golf cart made a whirring noise as it scooted ahead, the sound accentuated by a constant echo. At the wheel was Dr. Aseem, the Director of the facility. Next to him was a pock-marked man with a submachine gun in his lap. The two visitors sat on a padded bench at the back. The ride had so far lasted ten minutes, probably over a mile.

"Are we getting close?" Khalif asked.

Dr. Aseem smiled. "We are nearly there."

"The tunnel is so long," Al-Quatan remarked.

"I know what you are wondering," Dr. Aseem said. "In fact, I cannot even tell you how long. Not exactly. No one knows. It is a matter of great secrecy. I also cannot tell you what direction it is from the main complex. You see, the Americans have bombs that can go very deep, so the most sensitive parts of Sebha are some distance from the main buildings. And of course, the main facility itself has been largely deactivated. We had to convince our western friends that we are a peace-loving people."

Khalif smiled, encouraged to see that the infidel Americans could be outsmarted. The tunnel came to a curve, then passed through a formidable set of steel doors. There, they entered a wide chamber full of equipment, including a small Toyota pickup and a forklift. Dr. Aseem stopped the cart and led his little group to a well-lit door.

Passing through, Khalif was immediately struck by the brightness of the lights. It was clearly a type of laboratory. There were pipes and flasks, workers in white coats, all of it very antiseptic in appearance. He also noticed how much fresher the air seemed here. Dr. Aseem led them down a hallway and eventually stopped in front of a long window. There, slightly below, and behind a thick pane of glass, was the weapon. It sat still and cold, resting on a metal cart as two men presided over it. They looked like surgeons dressed in scrubs, and each had a mask covering his nose and mouth. Something similar to a dentist's X-ray machine hovered over the shiny steel cylinder.

Khalif felt pride well up from within. It was the first time he had seen it. He now remembered what Al-Quatan had said, about his surprise that it was not bigger or more complex in appearance. But as the truth of what lay before him settled in, he decided that the polished steel cylinder was made even more menacing by its outward simplicity.

"What are they doing?" he asked.

"Seeing what we have," Aseem replied.

"But it is real!" Al Quatan insisted.

"Oh yes, we have already determined that. It contains nuclear material. But we must learn how the rest of it works. There are many ways to design such a thing."

The two technicians were pulling fasteners from a plate near the back of the device.

Khalif said, "I am sorry we did not provide you with the technical data. It was promised us, but the devil who sold us this thing did not complete his end of the bargain." Khalif made no mention of the fact that he himself had only paid half the agreed upon price. He wondered briefly if Roth might be holding back the technical information in order to get full price. Watching the two men work, slowly and deliberately, he realized it wouldn't matter. It would only take a little longer. These were true scientists, the sort of people who could build a place like this underground city.

Aseem beamed toward his guests, "The Great One himself will be here this afternoon. He is very pleased. You have done a great service to your Arab brothers."

The two engineers gently removed the metal plate from the device.

Khalif and Al-Quatan looked proudly through the window, two parents in the maternity ward admiring their offspring. Suddenly, the technicians seemed immobile. The men's faces were largely obscured by the masks, yet their eyes were not. They stared into the thing, at the place where they had just removed the metal cover. Khalif thought they must be in awe, struck to inaction by the magnificent power within. But then one of the men stood back. He ripped off his mask, and it was not amazement encompassing his every feature — it was fear. He yelled, but Khalif could hear nothing through the heavy glass. The man threw his mask down and hurtled through the door that connected to the viewing area.

Without a word, he bolted toward the laboratory.

"What?" Aseem demanded. "What is wrong?"

The man was gone. His partner came through moments later, and Aseem grabbed him by the arm. "Tell me!"

"Run!" the engineer screamed, tearing free and racing after his friend. There was shouting from the technicians and scientists in the laboratory. Feet scrambled and doors slammed. Khalif heard an engine start — the small pickup truck out in the tunnel.

Dr. Aseem looked through the window at the silvery object, regarding it as though it held all the world's evil.

Khalif whirled to face him, "What is happening?"

Aseem began backing slowly toward the door, then turned and ran to join the others.

Only Khalif and Al-Quatan remained. It was the colonel who succumbed. He ran.

"Wait!" Khalif ordered.

Al-Quatan paused at the command, but with a desperate glance at his superior, he disappeared as well.

Moustafa Khalif felt more rage than fear. After a lifetime of struggle, victory was his. But *what?* Suppressing his anger, he pushed through the door and into the working area. At the entrance, he kicked aside the mask that had been dropped by the engineer. When the door closed behind him, all the noise and commotion outside disappeared. His world was enveloped by an overwhelming silence.

He went to it and slowly put out a hand as he approached. Khalif was not a man of science, but he knew such things were dangerous, in silent, hidden ways. They held invisible energy that could destroy a man. His fingertips made contact and he drew a quick gasp — the shiny steel case was cold to his touch. Khalif moved around to where the scientists had been and he saw the opening, no bigger than a man's open hand. He looked inside and saw what they had, now understanding.

"Allah," he pleaded in a hoarse whisper, "could thy be so cruel?"

Among a group of wires and circuitry was a clock with small, red digital numbers. Only time was going the wrong way.

"00:00:17 . . . 00:00:16 . . . 00:00:15 . . ."

Khalif was overcome. In a fit of wrath he banged his fists on the steel case. "No! No! No!"

"00:00:11 . . . 00:00:10 . . ."

He found a wrench on the workbench behind him and threw it at
the horrid object.

"00:00:06 . . . 00:00:05 . . . 00:00:04 . . ."

Khalif lost all control, his eyes crazed and murderous. He lunged to
the bench and found a heavy hammer. Holding it high and wildly over his
head, he swung down with the weight of all the heavens.

The Americans were the first to see it.

"NUDET!"

Lieutenant General Mark Carlson, the three-star in charge of the
National Military Command Center outside Washington D.C., choked
on his coffee and stared at the big screen. He'd heard the word before
a hundred times, but never here. It had always been in the "sim," the
identical-right-down-to-the-water-cooler training room three stories up.
He saw the event designator fall onto a map, which automatically scaled
down to show most of North Africa. The general recovered.

"Say confidence," he barked.

A slightly built master sergeant at a console replied, "Confidence
medium. One gamma detection. Interrogating KH-12."

"Seismic?"

A female lieutenant answered professionally, "Seismic from initial
fix . . . southern Libya . . . sixty to eighty seconds."

"Zoom two-by," Carlson ordered. The big screen's scale shifted, and
Libya got bigger. "KH visible when it's up and locked."

"Yes sir," the sergeant confirmed. Then moments later, "KH confirms. 09:21:14 Zulu. Location matches, near Sebha, 380 nautical south-
southeast of Tripoli."

The commander muttered under his breath, "What the hell have
you done, you crazy goat herder?"

"KH-12 now locked."

The big screen changed to a visual picture of the area in question
from 113 miles up. Carlson thought it seemed out of focus, but then his
training kicked in and he realized they were looking at a huge cloud of
dust. He needed radar to look for a crater.

"How long for a Lacrosse image?"

A man wearing very thick glasses and civilian clothes studied a real-
time computer display of orbital data. "Two hours and seven minutes," he
announced weakly.

"Damn!" the general cursed. "Never there when you need it." He watched seconds tick by on the digital wall clock and waited for the female lieutenant. The CIA had recently completed installation of a covert network of seismic sensors across the Middle East, Northern Africa, and parts of Asia. If anything had happened, the data would be automatically sent by way of a satellite relay. The only problem was that the speed of sound lagged the speed of light by a considerable margin.

"Here it is," the lieutenant said eagerly, knowing all eyes were on her. "Four point two single spike event. Initial filters analysis estimate subterranean nine megaton device, position concurs."

The word "subterranean" raised some eyebrows, but Carlson would have to deal with that later.

"Confidence level now high," the master sergeant added, telling the commander what he already knew.

"That's it then." The general moved two steps to his right, cleared his voice, and picked up the blue phone. On the third ring, the President of the United States answered.

Christine and Masters had been chatting for half an hour. He was just returning with a refill on her coffee when he stopped dead. Two fingers pressed to his earpiece.

"All right lads, we're on!" he shouted.

Chairs flew back and the Rapid Response Team scrambled to the helicopter. Masters smacked Christine's coffee cup down on the table and sprinted away.

"Simon! What is it?"

He turned. "They want us on airborne alert, miss. Seems something is imminent. But we still don't know where he is." He paused for a moment, as if not sure what to say next, then ran for the door that led outside.

Christine sat paralyzed. This was it. They were going after David. She watched the six policemen scramble onto the helicopter, its rotor already starting to spin. She had no choice. She ran.

When she got outside, the noise was deafening and the big blades whooshed violently overhead. She rushed for the side door, and as she got to the runner Masters' hulking figure filled the opening.

His voice boomed, "Get back, miss! It's bloody dangerous out here!"

"Simon, I can help you find him!"

He looked at her as if she was mad. "We've no time for this."

"I can stop him! You know I can!"

She looked up pleadingly against the rotor's downwash.

"Let's go!" came a shout from one of the pilots.

Masters reached down and grabbed a mittful of shirt at the scruff of her neck. There was no hope of moving as he stared at her, his face only inches away. He bristled with an anger she'd never seen, his eyes narrow, the veins bulging in his neck. Just when Christine thought he was going to drag her back inside, she felt herself being yanked off the ground and into the chopper.

At precisely 9:52, Greenwich Mean Time, the heads of state arrived. Limousine convoys stopped twenty meters behind the stage and disgorged their entourages — advisors, security types, and eventually the principals, who quickly disappeared into a large tent behind the stage. From there, final preparations would be made, and at ten o'clock sharp the actors, thirty-one diplomats in all, would climb up to the platform in a strict sequence that had, in and of itself, taken weeks to negotiate. Once on stage, each would walk to his or her chair at a dignified speed and sit — after those who were less important, but before the more important. There would be no nods, winks nor smiles that had not received official sanction and preapproval. When the national anthems began, each would rise and stand respectfully through the course, no yawning or slouching for enemy and neutral music, no particular enthusiasm for one's own. Then the speeches would begin, the order of these set in stone. In fact, the speeches themselves were designated word-for-word, each having been precisely drafted and redrafted to appease all parties. The choreography was absolute. Nothing left to chance.

Chatham and Dark stood inside the tent. They were the only regular law enforcement types present, the rest being politicians, diplomats, and their respective state security details. Chatham noted how they had all dispersed to the four corners of the place. The Arab and the Israeli delegations were separated diagonally, giving the most distance between the two. Their security men eyed one another continuously and with great suspicion. In another corner were the British, acting as hosts and chief negotiators. The British Prime Minister, today's key speaker, was presently surrounded by Foreign Office lackeys who were no doubt pressing in for face time. The fourth corner was station to the largest group, made up of diplomats from all the other countries. Some had aided in the negotiations, while others were simply self-important enough to have sent an "emissary" or "special counsel." They all chatted and mingled casually, as though it were cocktail hour at a state dinner, and a few sipped non-alcoholic refreshments, a prohibition driven more by the time of day than the soberness of the occasion.

Chatham paid particular attention to the Israeli delegation. Zak was in the center, intermittently visible amongst an encirclement of body-guards and aids. He seemed casual enough.

"Do you think Slaton's right about him?" Dark asked in a hushed voice.

Chatham was having the same thoughts. "We'll find out soon enough."

Someone called out, "Three minutes!"

"What did the Assistant Commissioner say when you told him Slaton's version of this mess?"

"Shearer? What makes you think I told him?"

Dark looked mortified until Chatham winked and gave him a pat on the shoulder. "He thought I was stark mad."

Chatham took Dark in tow. They left the tent to take up their position, a small platform at the back of the stage, off to one side. It had been placed specifically on Chatham's instructions. High enough to take in the crowd and surrounding grounds, yet far enough off center to not draw attention. It would also be out of view from any of the three camera angles to be broadcast.

Dark said, "Oh, I think we found out where Slaton purchased that window blind. It was a home improvement store near the hotel where he was staying. He also bought a couple of screwdrivers and some hardware."

"Hardware?"

"Nuts and bolts, that sort of thing. Their records weren't the best, so we're still working on it."

Chatham frowned and scanned the crowd from his perch. Thankfully, it wasn't the kind of event to attract a huge gathering. People everywhere were interested in peace, but they weren't going to stand out in the cold to watch it happen. The skies had been a dull gray all morning and there was rain in the afternoon forecast. A steady wind swept in from the northwest and Chatham found himself wondering what effect it would have on the ballistics of an L96A1, 7.62mm sniper's rifle.

The crowd was an interesting mix. Probably half consisted of diplomatic staff who'd been ordered to attend and applaud enthusiastically at the right times. There were some business types, who apparently thought it smart to be seen at a function like this, and the inevitable smattering of activists. They were students, mostly, here to see the realization of their efforts. Pro-peace, human rights, anti-globalization — they all imagined a degree of victory. Then there were simply the curious, the socially conscientious and, finally, the passers-by with nothing better to do.

Chatham knew there were over a hundred police milling about the area, many of them plainclothes. In retrospect, he regretted it. There was no way they could all recognize one another, which might lead to more harm than good.

Cued by a blast of martial music, the cast began filing onto the stage.

"Inspector!" someone called from below. "Message for you from Headquarters. It's marked URGENT."

Chatham recognized the man from the mobile command post that was tucked away on a nearby sidestreet. He took the paper. Ignoring the gibberish on top, he read the clear text message.

A NUCLEAR DETONATION HAS BEEN CONFIRMED
IN LIBYA. POSITION COINCIDES WITH LIBYAN
WEAPONS DEVELOPMENT FACILITY. LOOKS LIKE
YOUR FRIEND SLATON HAS GOT IT RIGHT, NATHAN.
RAPID RESPONSE TEAM IS ON AIRBORNE STANDBY.
HEADS UP. SHEARER

Chatham showed the message to Dark, then crumpled it and shoved it in his pocket. They watched as Zak came into view, stepping with smooth decorum alongside the head of the Palestinian Council. They took their respective seats behind the podium at center stage.

"He's not going to sign it," Dark remarked. "But he doesn't look worried, does he?"

"No," Chatham agreed.

The British Prime Minister began his remarks. He was notorious as a speaker who could drone for hours, but today's remarks had been strictly limited to three minutes. Zak would be next.

A well-dressed man appeared at the back of the stage. He walked over to Zak and bent down low, almost theatrical in his effort to be discreet. He whispered at length into Zak's ear.

"There it is," Chatham said.

"Can't we just stop it? Stop the whole thing right now? If Slaton is out there, the minute Zak steps up to that podium—"

"No, Ian. I wish we could, but we can't be sure. Speculation doesn't give us that kind of authority."

"No," Dark said in frustration, "not until the first shot is fired. And I doubt there will be more than one."

The British Prime Minister's speech was coming in for a landing as Chatham turned and gave Dark the most peculiar look.

"What did you just say?"

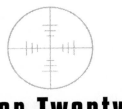

Chapter Twenty-Six

Slaton watched the British Prime Minister closely, and considered what the wind would do to his shot. He couldn't hear what the man was saying, but that wasn't important. The important thing was the visual picture, recognizing the moment that Zak took the podium. The little battery-powered Casio television got good reception. Slaton had checked it at ground level, but here, up higher, the picture quality was even better. Finally, the British Prime Minister backed away from the podium. The view on the screen suddenly switched to a scene of the crowd applauding politely. Slaton hadn't anticipated that. He picked up the cell phone.

Elizabeth Merrill was standing at the window on Dhalal's third floor, watching the ceremonies in the park. She couldn't see it very well from this far away. On the street immediately below she noticed two uniformed policeman who were not watching the proceedings, but instead staring straight at her. *How odd*, she thought, turning away uncomfortably. Mr. Dhalal told her the police had already taken a brief look through the apartment this morning, with his consent. He was clearly annoyed, but more so that the big crowds he'd anticipated had not materialized. Business was suffering.

   She milled about the empty flat and looked at her watch. It was 10:06. She'd been twenty minutes early. Parking had not been a problem, but she'd gotten bogged down at a security checkpoint that restricted access onto Crooms Hill Road. She suspected that was where Mr. Linstrom was now. Her cell phone rang.

"Elizabeth Merrill," she announced glibly.

"Good morning, Miss Merrill. This is Nils Linstrom."

"Ah, Mr. Linstrom. Good morning. Have you been held up in all the security outside?"

"Unfortunately, no. I'm afraid I've had a family crisis. I apologize for not calling sooner."

Elizabeth Merrill's face tightened, but her voice quickly filled with concern, "Oh, dear. I hope it's nothing serious."

"Probably not, but something I must see to. I'm at the airport right now." Linstrom paused. "But I do have some good news. My banker was very enthusiastic about the property and my plans for it. I think we have a very attractive offer for you."

She liked how he used the word we with respect to his banker. This was a big fish. "I'm sure Mr. Dhalal will be glad to hear it. When can we expect you back?"

"Well, I hadn't planned on returning for a couple of weeks, but I might be able to get back this Thursday afternoon. Would that work?"

"Absolutely."

"Good. I'll call tomorrow, once I get my flight information. Again, I'm sorry to have wasted your morning."

"Oh, please don't worry. I've got other business just up the street," she added, hoping her tone was convincing.

"Ah, there is one other thing . . ."

Linstrom's hesitation seemed extended. "Yes?"

"It's rather embarrassing, but it has to do with that silly fall I took the other day."

"You're not hurt, are you?" Her concern was legitimate. Dhalal would be livid.

"Oh, no. Nothing like that. You see, I've lost my wristwatch. It's not really valuable. More of an heirloom, I suppose. My father gave it to me. I looked around all weekend and couldn't find it. Then it dawned on me. When I had my hand up in that small attic I must have hooked it on something. Lost my balance and fell, even ended up with a good scratch on my wrist. I suspect the watch is still up there and I'd very much like to know, one way or the other. Would it be too much to ask to have you take a look? Or perhaps Mr. Dhalal could do it."

Elizabeth Merrill pooh-poohed the idea, "No, that's no problem at all. Mr. Dhalal is busy in his shop, but I can do it."

"Oh, thank you, Miss Merrill. And please be more careful than I was."

"Give me a minute." She put the phone on the kitchen counter. As a property agent for sixteen years she'd been asked to do a lot of strange things. This didn't even make the top ten. She looked around and wondered aloud, "Now where was that ladder?"

Zak had almost laughed. When his aide came on stage and whispered into his ear, he'd managed a terrifically filthy joke. It was all Zak could do to hold a serious expression. He couldn't be angry, though. They'd all have a good laugh about it on the flight home. Zak watched the British Prime Minister back away from the podium. Now it was his turn.

Normally he would have negotiated hard and fast to make the Arab go first. It was always preferable to have the last word. But on this day, Zak would go first — and still have the last word. When he was done speaking, he would turn to see a stage full of tight-lipped starched shirts whose jaws would be resting on their two hundred dollar shoes. And then he would walk away.

He moved to the podium slowly, his face a precise combination — astonishment, but well under control. His words would come in measured bursts, as if extemporaneous, and they would be steel, no doubt to be published verbatim tomorrow in all the world's papers.

"Ladies and gentlemen . . . I had come here today in the name of peace. Unfortunately, information I've just received tells me that not everyone on this stage has the same vision . . ."

Elizabeth Merrill found the ladder in the hall. She got it to the middle of the room and then took off her shoes, which had a substantial heel. She climbed four rungs to reach the small attic door, hoping to find the watch by feel. She didn't want to go any higher. The property agent pulled on the small knob that was the door's handle, but it didn't budge. She reasserted her balance on the ladder and gave a good, sharp tug.

The string ran from the door, through a single pulley, and terminated in a very secure knot at the trigger of the well-mounted rifle. The physical forces involved were undeniable, and could supply only one result. The rifle's recoil caused a cloud of dust to bounce in the attic as the bullet exited the flat, quite cleanly, through a single, meticulously broken slat in the louvered vent.

The only random outcome was of no consequence — the crack of the shot startled Elizabeth Merrill. So much so, that she fell off the ladder.

The audience had no idea what had happened. The report of the rifle was distant enough to be lost in the cacophony of man-made sounds that polluted all big cities. A few did notice a tiny explosion of some kind on the backdrop — shards of debris popping out of a small hole in the curtain.

The multitude of security teams were another story. They were elite units, all having trained for years to recognize exactly such sights and sounds. Zak was tackled hard to the wooden planks. The British Prime Minister was surrounded within seconds. The Arabs and others on stage far outnumbered their protectors, so in line with the instinct of self-preservation, those who realized what was happening simply hit the deck with varying degrees of emphasis. There was shouting and chairs fell over in a wild scramble of bodies. The audience began to catch on that something had gone very wrong, particularly when they recognized that some of the men on stage were now holding weapons and pointing them outward. Slowly, the people on the grass began to react — some fell to the ground, others ran.

Within seconds, the random flailing on stage began to organize. Security men clustered around those who were deemed important and, in amoebic masses, they shuffled backstage and out of sight.

Ian Dark desperately scanned outward, trying to see where the shot had come from.

"Where do you think he is, Inspector?"

There was no answer. Dark turned to see that Chatham was gone. He looked down behind the stage. People were running in every direction, including at least a dozen men with guns drawn. Two big limousines, sporting Israeli flags on the front fenders, spun grass and mud as they fishtailed toward the asphalt. Then he spotted Chatham, running as fast as his lanky old legs would carry him.

Dark, a practiced distance runner, scrambled after him and caught up within a hundred yards. "Where are you going?" he shouted as he ran alongside his boss. "Didn't the shot come from the front?"

Chatham strained for breath. "The helicopter!" he croaked.

The carte blanche of resources had not been squandered. There were two police boats on the river, idling at the docks, an assortment of cars, and a helicopter sat waiting in a clearing on the park's southeast corner.

Chatham waved for Dark to go on ahead. "Tell the pilot to start the thing!"

Dark held his questions and sprinted ahead.

Three minutes later they were airborne, looking down on the remains of what had minutes ago been a world-wide focus of the hope for peace.

Chatham yelled to the pilot in short bullets, trying to get his breath. "Gatwick Airport — get word to Headquarters — the Rapid Response Team — to the airport now!"

Dark was bewildered. His boss took a few more gasps before explaining.

"The *string*, Ian."

"String?"

Chatham eyed the contraption they were riding in suspiciously. "Never been in one of these," he said over the engine noise. "Do they all shake like this?"

"Yes," Dark assured him. "What do you mean about the string?"

Chatham's breath came more evenly now. "Do you remember his hotel room? We found a window blind."

Dark nodded.

"The string, the one that operates the thing. It had been cut off. Didn't that bother you as being strange?"

"I've seen stranger things lately."

"Add in the hardware he bought. Don't you see?"

Dark sat perplexed.

"A spring gun, Ian! He set up a gun somewhere and fired it remotely."

"Of course!" Dark exclaimed. "But he missed so badly. How could he expect a hit on a day as windy as—" He stopped in mid-thought and said simply, "Two rifles!"

Chatham tapped his nose with an index finger. "He's a hunter, Ian. And right now he's flushing his prey."

"But why the airport?"

"Think about the schedule," Chatham prodded.

Dark knew it by heart. "After the ceremony was a luncheon and reception at the Camberly. Eleven in the morning until two in the after-noon. Then Zak was scheduled to leave. Gatwick back to Israel."

"Right. And if someone tried to assassinate Zak, what do you think the Israelis would do?"

"Straight to the airport," Dark said. "But how would Slaton know the schedule?"

"He might still have friends at the embassy. Then again, he might have guessed. He suspected Zak was about to rebut this whole peace process. No need for a reception then, eh? And he knows exactly how the Israelis work their security. Throw in an assassination attempt, and it's a safe bet as to where Zak is headed right now."

"Can't we call the Israelis and tell them not to go to the airport?"

"I'm afraid not. They won't listen to anyone at the moment. That's how these special security teams work. In a crisis they have a plan to get their subject safe and nothing's going to alter it. In ten minutes they'll be at the airport, shoving Zak on his jet. And Slaton will be lining up his crosshairs."

Dark felt a shiver go down his back. "He's thought of everything, hasn't he? Slaton's always two steps ahead," he said dejectedly.

"One step right now," Chatham countered, "and we're gaining."

Chapter Twenty-Seven

The Rapid Response Team had been the first to arrive. Christine sat alone in the helicopter, even the pilots having gone to aid the search. Masters' orders for her had been strict — stay put. Far in the distance she saw a runway where a regular stream of airliners lumbered to either smooth levitation or a noisy stop. Beyond the runway lay the huge passenger terminal, where tens of thousands of people came and went on a daily schedule.

Here, however, set off in a remote corner of the airport, the Gatwick Executive Terminal was a very different kind of place. It was smaller in scale, less busy. There were buildings behind a fenceline, modest in size, yet tastefully appointed. These were the terminals and offices of the private jet operators. Limousines sat discreetly tucked into niches, lying in wait for the occasional Duke or scion of industry. One building had a strip of red carpet extending out across the concrete, ending near one of the neat rows of business jets that were arrayed across the ramp. This was the elite corner of Gatwick, a place reserved for those endowed with either extreme wealth or importance. It was a blatant display of image that Christine completely ignored. Her attention riveted on what loomed a hundred yards farther back on the tarmac — a big jetliner with the Star of David on its tail.

Christine was on edge as she watched the show. Masters was presently at the Executive Terminal gate, the only passage she could see through the perimeter fence, arguing with a pair of serious men. They wore business formal, and each sported the unusual accessory of an automatic weapon. He was joined by two of his team and a pair of uniformed policemen. All were flashing identification cards back and forth, shouting, and pointing in different directions. The rest of Masters' team were already busy, scouring buildings and hangars. And Zak's aircraft was surrounded by two dozen men and women, most showing weapons of their own.

Christine wished David was far from here, far from all these people and their guns. But she knew better. He was here somewhere. Here to assassinate Zak, who might arrive at any minute. And as long as she sat in the helicopter, there was nothing she could do about it.

Another police car arrived and two more officers joined the grand debate. Christine could take it no more. She got out of the helicopter, Masters too engrossed to notice, and headed away from the crowd, along the fenceline. She'd follow it around hoping to see something, anything that could tell her where David was.

As she ran, the big jets gave way to rows of smaller planes. She tried to see into their front and side windows, wondering if David might be hiding in one. She remembered The Excelsior, what David had told her about getting elevation. The higher you were, the better you could see things. There were hangers back by the main gate, but they didn't seem very big. As she looked around, there was only one thing that really stuck out — the control tower. It was a hundred yards away, a big column, square all the way up, then topped by a bulbous cap of windows and antennae. Christine saw people milling around up in the control cab. Some of them were certainly air traffic controllers, and today others might be security, staking out the high ground. There was no way David could be up there. Then something else caught her eye, something she hadn't noticed at first. Halfway up the control tower, a narrow metal walkway was barely visible at the back of the structure. In the front, at the same level, was a single window. But the window had been thoroughly painted over to match the color of the tower. No one inside could ever see through it.

She looked around frantically, realizing time was growing short. *Where are you?* she thought. Farther away from the airport was a big grassy hill. It was high, but too open, with nowhere to hide. And besides, it seemed awfully far away. She kept moving. There was more commotion back at the entrance, and now Christine heard another helicopter in the distance. Almost directly beneath the control tower, she looked up through the angled glass at the top. She could see fingers pointing toward the horizon. But then there was something else. It didn't register at first, but when it did Christine stopped dead in her tracks. *The small window halfway up was open now — only a few inches, but definitely open!*

She yelled, "David!" but her voice was drowned out by the roar of the helicopter passing overhead.

From his perch in the tower the kidon leveled his rifle. He used the telescopic sight to scan the area where his target would be any moment — reconnaissance through a soda straw. Everything was as he expected. The pilots had the big jet ready to go. The number two engine was running, and on the port side a dozen men and women buzzed around the tarmac where a wheeled stairway was up against the airplane's entry door.

He shifted his sight and monitored the gate. A wild ruckus had been going on for the last few minutes. A handful of patrolmen joined the special tactics team that had just landed. They'd begun searching the hangars and buildings at ground level. Chatham had figured it out. But a check of his watch told Slaton that Zak would be arriving in the next two to three minutes. The inspector was too late.

The thought came to mind that so many police would make a clean escape difficult. But then Slaton realized that, for the first time ever, he had not even planned an escape. Every moment had been carefully crafted and designed up until the pull of the trigger. There, he had stopped, disregarding what would happen afterward. Or perhaps not caring. He thought about Christine and briefly imagined what might happen if he could get out of this alive. The equipment room was halfway up the control tower, a tactically commanding position, but there was only one way up. And one way down. The room was full of electronic equipment, racks of radios, and telephone circuitry. A generator, obviously an emergency backup, lay idle in one corner. None of it would help. The only item of possible use was a long rope he'd spotted. If the police came up after him, he might manage to secure it and rappel out the window to — to what?

Slaton forced the desperate thoughts away. He would not allow himself to lose concentration. Not now.

Next to the runway, mounted on a pole, was a big orange windsock. It registered not only the wind direction, but also the wind speed, measured as the angle of rise. Presently, it showed a nearly dead crosswind of eight knots, down from what it had been twenty minutes ago. The kidon figured the mil correction for his sight picture, then applied it, training his weapon on the head of a woman standing at the base of the airplane's boarding stairs. He heard the sound of another helicopter overhead.

If Zak was on the chopper, Christine only had seconds. She ran to the base of the control tower. It was surrounded by a secondary fence, but surprisingly, the gate was wide open. Then she saw why. The heavy door at the bottom, the one that must have accessed the elevator or stairs to the top, had a cipher lock and card-swipe device. There was also a telephone, no doubt to contact the people up above. She ran around to the back of the tower and found an iron ladder attached to the wall, rising straight up to where David had to be. A sign was strung across the base of the ladder on a chain. It read: WARNING : HIGH VOLTAGE : RESTRICTED TO AUTHORISED PERSONS.

Christine ducked under the chain and started climbing. The ladder had been painted time and again, and white flakes came off on her hands. When she got to the top, Christine mounted the narrow catwalk. There was a single door, labeled EQUIPMENT ROOM. She pushed on it and the door moved slightly, then stopped. It had been blocked from within.

Slaton had heard the metallic clanging as someone climbed the ladder. He cursed and watched the gate, willing Zak's entourage of vehicles to appear. Whoever was outside pushed on the door, but he'd already barricaded it with everything he could find. It could probably be shoved open, but it would take a few men to do it. Whoever was out there now was alone. He could barely believe the next sound he heard.

"David!"

There was no mistaking the voice. He hesitated, then shouted, "What are you doing here?"

"David, don't do this! It's wrong!"

He tried to block out her words as she struggled against the door.

"I talked to Anton Bloch, David. You've got to listen to what he told me."

Slaton gave no response as two limousines flew into view, careening through the quickly opened gate. Zak had arrived.

❖   ❖   ❖

Chatham's helicopter touched down near the base of the tower. He immediately spotted Christine Palmer, of all people, banging on a door from a catwalk halfway up the structure. It didn't take much thought to figure out why. He pointed up to show Ian Dark and they ran off, Dark grabbing a machine pistol from the helicopter. Circumnavigating the fence, they were joined by two of Masters' team. All raced for the ladder.

"Zak wasn't the one who killed your wife and daughter!"

Slaton tried to ignore it.

"I know more about it than you or Anton Bloch. Zak was there! He killed everyone on that bus." He tracked the two big Mercedes as they skidded to a halt near the airstairs.

"Yes, David, but there's a part you've never known! Your wife and daughter weren't even on that bus in Netanya. They were killed by a drunk driver, in an accident miles away. Don't you see? The Mossad wanted you to hate, David! Hate so you would kill, just as you're doing now. Zak didn't do it, David! Not your family!"

Slaton locked sight on the rear door of the front car. It opened. He felt for the trigger, but his finger seemed slow to react. Slaton squeezed his eyes shut, then reopened them. It couldn't possibly be true, he thought. Not after all these years. Not after all the pain.

Zak's distinctive balding head appeared. Security men surrounded him, but he was tall enough, and Slaton had a good look angle. The man appeared smug, seeming in no hurry as he moved to the stairs. Slaton tracked him and began the trigger pressure. At that moment, he heard reinforcements clanging up the ladder outside. Too late. He only needed one shot.

Zak was climbing as well, now in clear view as he ascended the boarding stairs. He stopped halfway up, ignoring his ushers, and turned. Through the rifle scope Slaton could clearly see a victorious expression as Zak looked back on the scene.

Her lovely voice pleaded. "David! David, I love you. Don't let them win!"

The kidon's finger quivered.

She screamed, "No! No!"

The crack of the rifle shot was muffled as the equipment room door crashed in. Slaton's shoulder brunted the gun's recoil, but in the next instant he made no move to confront the police, instead retraining his weapon on the distant target. Two machine pistols opened fire. Bullets raked across his side and he was thrown back against a bloodsplattered wall. There, the kidon slumped into a sitting position, silent and still.

Epilogue

When Zak's jet landed in Tel Aviv it was early evening. The Prime Minister was whisked straight to the War Room. There were no public appearances, but a communiqué was released to the press in his name. Firm in tone, it reaffirmed Israel's grave concern over recent events, yet assured the world that the state would persevere in its efforts for a lasting peace. It also expressed thanks to Israel's own Prime Ministerial security detail, and to the security professionals of Great Britain, who had together foiled the assassination plot. The communiqué promised to get to the bottom of the conspiracy, while hinting it might be a long and arduous investigation, given that the assassin was dead and had apparently acted alone.

At ten o'clock the next morning, a second official communiqué was issued, this one short and terse.

AT APPROXIMATELY 8:15 THIS MORNING PRIME MINISTER EHUD ZAK SUFFERED FROM SEVERE CHEST PAIN AND WAS TAKEN TO JERUSALEM'S HERZOG HOSPITAL. THERE, THE PRIME MINISTER WENT INTO CARDIAC ARREST. DOCTORS AND STAFF WERE ABLE TO REVIVE HIM, AND HE IS NOW RESTING UNDER SEDATION. FURTHER TESTS WILL FOLLOW. AT THIS TIME THE DEPUTY PRIME MINISTER, ELIJAH PEER, HAS ASSUMED ALL DUTIES OF THE PRIME MINISTER, AND WILL ADDRESS THE FULL KNESSETT AT NOON.

❖   ❖   ❖

Benjamin Jacobs and Anton Bloch, both exhausted, gathered in Jacobs'
study shortly before noon to watch the speech on television. They had
spent half of yesterday convincing the power brokers of Israeli politics, the
same ones who had ousted Jacobs only days ago, that their new Prime
Minister was at least a criminal, and possibly a traitorous madman. In the
end, their case — the evidence Bloch had acquired along with Pytor
Roth's confession (in person) — had been very convincing. The leaders of
Israel were convinced that Zak had to go. The question was, how?

The man had no political support, but getting rid of him that way
would take time, and they all shuddered to think what damage he could
do in the interim. A not insignificant contingent thought that another,
more successful assassination attempt should greet Zak when he arrived
back in Israel. Cooler heads finally settled on Bloch's idea, which kept the
risk at a minimum.

"How long do we keep him in the hospital?" Jacobs asked.

"A week, maybe two. We'll find somewhere nice and isolated. In a
few days we're going to announce that there's been another cardiac event,
just to make certain."

"You're sure we can keep it secret that there's nothing wrong with
him?"

"Not many people know," Bloch reasoned. "The men and women
on the Cabinet certainly won't ever breathe a word of it. They'd be killing
their own careers, maybe risking jail. There are only four people on the
medical team, two doctors and two nurses. We screened carefully and
they all know the importance of what's happening. The test results and
medical records will be locked down tight."

"What about Zak and his group?" Jacobs wondered.

"Thanks to Slaton, not many of his group are left. Pytor Roth was
never one of them, of course. Just a low-level Aman grunt who'd been
compromised. Zak knew about it and used him. I think we've been able
to put the fear of God in Mr. Roth. That and a few dollars will keep him
quiet. As for Zak himself," Bloch shook his head, "he's a lot of things, but
he's not stupid. He'd be up against treason charges, and when we talked
to him yesterday we made it very clear that if it came to that, life in prison
would be his best outcome. This way he spends a few weeks in the hospital, then fades away."

"Do you think he will? Fade away?"

"The people in that room yesterday were very powerful and very scared. They gave Zak his pension and his life, but if he sets a foot wrong they can take either one back."

Jacobs didn't even flinch. He wondered if he could be getting used to such things. "He almost did it, didn't he? Zak used that first weapon to get himself appointed Prime Minister. The second to destroy a Libyan weapons facility. And he nearly killed the peace process. It all would have worked perfectly if it hadn't been for David Slaton."

Jacobs went glumly to the wet bar and, without bothering to offer, grabbed two round crystal goblets. He filled them both to the midpoint with port from a carafe and gave one to his friend.

"It's not right," he insisted, "Zak getting off the hook while others paid so dearly. You and I only lost our careers. But Slaton . . ."

Bloch lifted his glass, "To David Slaton. May he finally be at peace."

Jacobs touched his glass to his comrade's.

"Peace."

Christine sat on the porch with the mail in her lap. It had been there for fifteen minutes, but April was a beautiful time of year in the White Mountains of New Hampshire. The mornings were still cold, yet when the sun came up it spread a warmth that seemed to bring everything to life. Today the wind was strong, as it often was, but the tall trees bursting with fresh foliage took the brunt of it. Up here you didn't feel the breeze, you heard it. Better yet, that was all you heard.

It would all change in a month or two. There were other cabins nearby, and soon the masses of summer would ascend from Boston. For now, though, it was heaven. And when the crowds eventually did show up, Christine would be gone, back to England to pick up Windsom and cross before hurricane season. Then, finally, back to work. She was already hitting the books every night. Upper Downey had been more than understanding, and Christine was determined to not let him down. When she went back to the hospital, she'd be ready.

She shuffled through the mail and found a letter from her mother. Christine had been e-mailing daily, but mom liked to write back the old-fashioned way. That was okay, although it made for some disjointed conversations. She had brought her up to the cabin last month for a short stay. They talked about things that hadn't come up in years, and it was a salve to both their souls.

The second letter was from Clive Batty. She opened it and was pleased to read that Windsom would be ready in a week — repaired, rigged, and provisioned for the crossing. Good old Bats, she thought. Nothing less than a case of his favorite Scotch.

The last two letters were credit card offers, both promising incredible introductory rates to consolidate Christine's debt. Both had her name spelled wrong. She tore them in half and chuckled, "Welcome back to the real world."

Christine stood up and checked her ugly little watch. The gravel road leading up to the cabin was straight for the last hundred yards and she spotted Edmund Deadmarsh as he came around the bend heading toward her. He was running at a decent clip and then sped up slightly as he closed in. He ended right in front of the cabin, pacing back and forth, and completely out of wind.

She eyed him critically. "Get to the top today, Deadmarsh?"

He shook his head, still pacing with his hands on his hips.

"We don't have forever, you know."

He bent over and put his hands on his knees, then pointed off in the distance. "Mountain—" he croaked, "big mountain."

"All right, Deadmarsh, maybe tomorrow."

He climbed the steps up to the porch and got right in her face, "Would you stop calling me that."

She smiled mischievously, "Okay . . . Eddie."

He tackled her onto the old couch that had become porch furniture. They landed in a tangle. She giggled, he groaned.

"Ow!"

"What is it?" she asked, her humor instantly gone.

Slaton struggled to a sitting position and cocked his head to his shoulder. "That kevlar vest I swiped from the Royal Engineers — it saved my life, but I wish they'd made a long sleeve version."

Her face tightened in worry.

"It's all right," he assured. "And I suppose what really saved my life was having a doctor five seconds away when I took seven rounds."

Christine sighed. He put his good arm around her and they settled back into the big, worn cushions.

"So they wouldn't let you choose a name?" she asked.

"No. It came as a package. The passport, birth certificate, bank account — all the rest. The guy who briefed me on the legend, he was

CIA, I think. Never said where they got it, but it was very thorough."

"And Anton Bloch was the one who made it happen?"

"Yeah. He came to see me while I was still in the hospital. Asked me what I wanted to do. I said I wanted out, the States. He made it happen. Officially, David Slaton is dead."

"David Slaton, the assassin, is dead." She put her head on his good shoulder. "You've been through so much."

"I guess. But . . ."

"What?"

"It's just that I've done a lot over the years," Slaton hesitated, "things that are hard to justify. You could call it patriotism, an undeclared war, or maybe revenge for what I thought happened to my family. But still . . ." his voice faded away.

Christine spoke quietly. "Would you like to talk about it?"

"Yeah, I would," he said. They settled farther back into the couch and he added, "But not right now."

In the months after the debacle at Greenwich, things slowly reverted to normal at Scotland Yard. In fact, with all nuclear weapons accounted for and no assassins running amok, the staff had blithely fallen to old ways and become consumed by the trivial.

Chatham was eying a second helping of the cafeteria's chocolate cake when Ian Dark came bustling in.

"There you are, sir. Did you forget about the briefing? It starts in three minutes."

Chatham was reluctant, eyeing the short queue at the cash register. "What is it they're demonstrating?"

"A biometric hand scanner. It's like fingerprinting, you see, but rather looks at your entire hand. By the end of summer, no one will be able to enter the building without using it."

Chatham raised an eyebrow and wondered about not being able to get into the building. Inconvenience or blessing? He shook his head.

"No, Ian. There's something much more important on the agenda. And I'd like you to come along."

He put a hand on Dark's shoulder and guided him down the hall. They left the building and walked toward Victoria Station. Along the way, Chatham turned serious as he told Dark where they were headed.

"The Israeli Embassy? What for?" Dark asked.

"Ian, since that day in Greenwich we've found out a great deal. Slaton explained much of it himself when I interviewed him afterward in the hospital. We know where he stayed, what he bought, where he ate. We found the spring gun, figured out who set it off. We know exactly how he did it. But there's still one thing, Ian. One thing that bothers me immensely."

"What?"

"He missed, Ian. *He bloody missed!*"

They stood on the tube platform as a car noisily presented itself. Taking a seat to the rear, Chatham carried on, clearly bothered.

"He led us a merry chase all over the country. He killed people, stole cars and weapons, half the time with a complete amateur in tow, and we never got close to him. He planned the assassination perfectly, if you overlook the escape, which I suspect was done intentionally. This man got around the tightest security I've ever seen. Flawless! And then he goes and misses."

Dark didn't seem troubled, "He was at three hundred and ninety yards, Inspector, on a windy day. To hit a target the size of a person from that far off — it's no easy shot."

"But by every account he was an unusually gifted marksman. And everything else was so perfect."

Dark looked at his boss, "You'll never rest, will you? Not until everything makes sense. I thought the months might have made a difference."

Chatham rambled on, "We've searched the tarmac inch by inch. The bullet is nowhere to be found. I've talked to Anton Bloch back in Tel Aviv and he says they've gone over the airplane time and again. No hole, no bullet lodged in a tire. Nothing." He wrung his hands together. "We all heard that shot!"

Chatham had completed a jigsaw puzzle, only to find the last piece missing.

"And this is why we're going to see the Israelis today?" Dark asked.

"I met a chap yesterday in my office, an Israeli from the embassy. I think he might be the new Mossad chief here in London. Nice enough bloke. Had a few questions about what had gone on. We decided a little more cooperation might serve us both better next time. Before he left, I told him what bothered me, what I've just told you."

"Did he have any ideas?"

"Didn't say a thing. But he invited me over this afternoon. So there you are."

Fifteen minutes later they were standing in front of the Israeli Embassy on Palace Green. The man Chatham had spoken with met them at the gate. A congenial fellow, dressed in suit and tie, he looked nothing like the spy he certainly was. Chatham introduced his associate, and the Israeli shook Dark's hand. If he had any qualms about an extra guest, he wasn't letting on. He led the two Englishmen onto the grounds and then inside the embassy building.

"Gentlemen," he said as he guided his guests, "I've heard from a number of sources, both here and back in Israel, that you've been a great help to us in the past few months. I also understand that my government was, at the time, not always . . . forthcoming? Is that the right word?"

Chatham agreed, "It is, sir."

The Israeli smiled. "You told me of your frustration yesterday, Inspector. I think we at least owe you this."

He paused, reached into a pocket, then held out his hand. In his open palm was a smashed blob of metal that would have fit in a thimble.

"Is that it?" Dark wondered.

The Israeli held it closer to Chatham. "You may have it," he said.

The Inspector took it and held it to the light.

"Ballistics can tell us if that's the one," Dark guaranteed.

Chatham didn't need ballistics. Somehow he knew. "Where did you get it?" he asked.

The Israeli beckoned them to follow. They walked further back into the building, through doors and hallways where strangers didn't normally venture — at least that was how it seemed based on the looks they got from the embassy workers. Still, no one challenged them, which meant their escort had plenty of clout. They ended up in a parking garage where a few dozen cars were crammed into tight spaces. Their friend led them to a row of limousines and he gestured to one in particular, which had been backed into its parking spot. Chatham and Dark stood staring at the hood for a moment. Then it registered.

"Good God!" Dark whispered. "Do you mean he—"

"Yes," Chatham said, the weight now gone from his shoulders.

On the hood of the car was a small jagged hole, the metal torn where the bullet had ripped through and probably lodged in the engine below. Just in front of the hole was an upright hood ornament, the trade-mark emblem of Mercedes-Benz. Except all that remained was the ring. The three spokes of the symbol were gone, removed by one round from an L96A1. From three hundred and ninety yards.

Chatham fingered the slug in his hand.

"He didn't miss after all, did he?"

ACKNOWLEDGMENTS

A work of this nature is never complete without suffering under the critical eye of knowledgeable professionals. Thanks to Stan Zimmerman and Dr. Kevin Kremer for their help early on. And to Martha Powers and Susan Hayes — together, your fresh eyes proved invaluable. Bob and Patricia Gussin of Oceanview Publishing, whose support and enthusiasm have been uplifting. And thanks to Susan Greger and her entire staff. You have been, and will remain, essential.

Finally, all appreciation to my wife, Rose, for her enduring patience with the entire affair.

STEALING TRINITY

A NOVEL

WARD LARSEN

Oceanview Publishing
LONGBOAT KEY, FLORIDA

ISBN 978-1-933515-17-5 (cl)
ISBN 978-1-933515-98-4 (pb)

Published in the United States of America by Oceanview Publishing,
Longboat Key, Florida
Visit our Web site at oceanviewpub.com

10 9 8 7 6 5 4 3 2

PRINTED IN THE UNITED STATES OF AMERICA

FOREWORD

For most, it was another day in a long war. Yet as a precursor to human tragedy, July 16, 1945, was a day without parallel.

The leading event came shortly before dawn, in the sparse desert of central New Mexico. In an instant that would irretrievably change the course of the world, a brilliant, searing explosion tore through the sky, turning night into day, sand into glass, and skeptics into believers. It was the world's first atomic blast, code named Trinity.

On that very same morning, two ships slipped from port and headed into the vast Pacific Ocean. To the east, the heavy cruiser USS *Indianapolis* steamed under San Francisco's Golden Gate Bridge, her task to deliver vital components of another atomic weapon — code named Little Boy — to the tiny island of Tinian in the South Pacific. To the west, a Japanese Imperial Navy submarine, designated I-58, also set sail. Her mission, ostensibly, was that of routine patrol, if there could be such a thing in time of war.

In a fashion, both ships would find success. Crossing the Pacific in record time, *Indianapolis* made her critical delivery, then steamed off to rejoin the fleet. And at the stroke of midnight on July 29, I-58 surfaced to find *Indianapolis* dead in her sights.

I-58's captain later claimed to have been astonished at his good fortune. Fortune or not, the results of the encounter have

been well documented. *Indianapolis* took two torpedoes, and
went down in twelve minutes. Of the ship's complement of 1,196,
only 316 delirious seamen were eventually rescued.

At the end of the war, a court of inquiry investigated the disaster. Questions outnumbered answers, but a few were notably
confounding. With the U.S. Navy swarming around the Japanese
mainland, why had I-58 traveled over a thousand miles south in
search of targets? Was it merely a cruel stroke of fate that *Indianapolis* was lost in the vicinity of Challenger Deep, the deepest
abyss in all the world's oceans?

But perhaps the most vexing question arose from the testimony of one group of survivors. They asserted, to a man, that a
short time after *Indianapolis's* demise, the silhouette of a ship
appeared on the near horizon. One sailor went so far as to fire his
sidearm in an effort to attract attention. On studying all evidence,
the court strongly doubted that they had seen I-58 — she had
remained submerged for nearly an hour after the attack. In the
end, the court was entirely unable to account for the presence of
a third vessel, and the matter was summarily dumped into the
"unexplainable" category.

This much is known.

PART I

CHAPTER 1

Colonel Hans Gruber stood facing the stone wall at the back of his office, drawing heavily on a cigarette, a thick French wrap that filled the air around him with fetid gray smoke. On another day, in another place, he might have wondered if the acrid swill would bother the officers about to join him. But deep in an unventilated Berlin bunker, in April 1945, it was pointless. The bombing was mostly at fault, the Americans by day and the British by night, stirring the dust, bouncing the rubble, and creating more of each. Always more. Then there were the constant fires. Ash swirled in the air, at times indistinguishable from the snow, and subject to the whims of a bitter wind that somehow redistributed the mess without ever driving it away.

Gruber remained motionless, his tall, cadaverous frame hunched in thought, as fixed as the stony gargoyles that had once held watch over the building above. He stared blankly at the wall, glad there was no window. The Berlin outside was no longer worth looking at, a place unrelated to that of his youth. Even two years ago there had been hope. From his old office, he had looked down Berkaerstrasse on sunny mornings to see vestiges of the old city. Mothers pushing prams, stores still stocked with vegetables and thick sausage. Now he sat in a hole in the ground, praying for rain to dampen the ash, quell the fires and, most importantly, to hide the city from the next squadron of bombardiers.

A knock on the door interrupted Gruber's miserable thoughts. He turned and stabbed the butt of his smoke into a worn ashtray on his desk.

"*Kommen!*"

A corporal ushered in two guests. In front, Gruber noted without surprise, was SS Major Rudolf Becker. He strode with purpose and was in full regalia — black overcoat, shining jackboots, skull insignia, and a wheel hat tucked tightly under one arm. Behind him came General Freiderich Rode, the acting number two of the Abwehr, the intelligence network that answered to Germany's Armed Forces High Command. Rode's appearance and carriage were very different, a thick-necked jackal to Becker's strutting peacock. He was a working soldier, boots scuffed and trousers wrinkled, a square face carved from granite. His bulldog neck was shaved close, disappearing into the thick collar of his jacket, and the eyes were wide-set and squinting — eyes that might be looking anywhere.

"Gentlemen," Gruber said formally, "please have a seat. Corporal Klein, that will be all."

Both men sat, and the corporal struggled to shut the solid door — something had shifted in the bunker's earthen support structure and it hadn't closed normally in weeks. With privacy established, Gruber sat at his desk facing two men who looked very tired. The room fell silent as he reached into the bottom drawer and pulled out a half-empty bottle of vodka, then three tumblers.

"It's Polish. They cook it in spent radiators, I'm told."

Gruber's guests showed no amusement. They were no doubt wondering why he had called them here. If they hadn't been good friends, they probably wouldn't have come. Rank was becoming less relevant with each passing day, and an unexpected summons to the headquarters of the Sicherheitsdienst, or SD, was enough to make anyone nervous. It was the Nazi party's own intelligence service, run by some of the most desperate men in an increasingly desperate regime.

Gruber poured stout bracers and issued them around. No

one bothered to toast anything — for three German officers a certain sign of lost hope — and three heads snapped back. Gruber set his glass gingerly on the desk and studied it before beginning.

"Have either of you made plans?" There was no need to be more specific.

Behind closed doors, Major Becker of the SS softened, his tone weary. "I have access to a boat, up north. But it will have to be soon. Ivan has crossed the Oder."

Rode said, "There is talk among the general staff of a convoy to the south. But I do not think big groups are good. Those who make it out will be alone, or in very small parties."

"I agree," said Gruber. He had his own escape, but wasn't going to share it, even with his most trusted peers. "How is our Führer holding together?" he asked, addressing Rode, who still attended the occasional staff meeting in the Führerbunker.

Rode shrugged. "The same."

Gruber knew, as did all who had seen Hitler in the last weeks, that their leader's mental health was deteriorating rapidly. He was despondent one minute, then bubbling with optimism the next as he ordered nonexistent divisions into battle against the advancing pincer. His field commanders were no help, making empty promises to avoid the Führer's wrath, each hoping to buy enough time to escape his own last-minute firing squad. Lies to feed the lunacy — and yet another multiplicand in the calculus of Germany's misery.

A rough, wet cough erupted as Gruber reached into his pocket. He extracted a silver cigarette case and plucked out another of the harsh French Gauloises. His doctor had advised him to stop, but Gruber decided it would be an improbable fate at this point to die at the hand of tobacco. The others sat in silence as he lit up, stagnant gray smoke curling up toward a ceiling stained black.

"Gentlemen, our immediate future is as clear as it is untenable. Within certain obvious constraints, it is up to us to plan for the future of the Reich." Gruber let that hang in the air for an appropriate amount of time. "Of course, the first priority is to establish ourselves in a safe place. This will require patience. The world will be in a state of confusion and recovery for many months, perhaps years, and this we must take advantage of."

"Our network in Italy remains strong," Rode suggested. "And Spain is possible."

"No, no. These might be good staging points for our departure, but Europe is out of the question for the near term. We will need a great deal of time to reorganize."

Becker added, "And a great deal of money."

"Yes, indeed. But here we are fortunate. Our Swiss friends are competent and extremely discreet in these matters. Considerable funds will be at our disposal. We will have the money, and we will take our time. But there is one particularly pressing matter."

Gruber stood and flicked his cigarette's spent ashes carelessly on the stone floor. "It concerns an agent of yours, General. Die Wespe."

Rode's eyes narrowed to mere slits. It was his signature stare, the mannerism that combined with his physical presence to wilt peers and underlings alike. Gruber, however, ignored it freely, in the same fashion that he ignored the flag-grade insignia on the man's collar. The structure of command was becoming increasingly fluid as a new order emerged.

"How do you know about Die Wespe?"

Gruber waved a languid hand in the air to dismiss the question as immaterial.

Becker asked, "Who is this Wespe?"

"He is a very special spy," Gruber said, "a fat little German scientist who works with the Americans." He shook his head derisively, still amazed that they could allow such a stupid breach. "He holds information that is vital to our future."

"Vital?" Rode scoffed. "I suspect it will be worthless." He turned to Becker. "The Americans have spent years and an incredible amount of money pursuing wild ideas. We explored the concept ourselves. Heisenberg, our top physicist, headed the effort. It came to nothing."

"We undertook a token project," Gruber agreed, "and it *was* a failure. However these academic types are a difficult breed. They consider themselves above the world, and some have a reputation for — conscience."

"Sabotage is what you mean," Rode countered.

"There were rumors. At any rate, our own work in the area has been feeble."

Becker asked, "What does it involve?"

Rode took a minute to explain the incredible details. He then added, "But it is only a whim on the chalkboards of certain scientists, a paper theory. Nothing has been proven."

The SS man, who knew his weapons, agreed, "I cannot imagine such a thing."

Gruber hedged, "Indeed, the concept has not yet been tested. But Wespe tells us this will come soon. Within months, if not weeks. Is this not true, Freiderich?"

Rode nodded.

"And if it should work?" Becker asked.

"There lies the significance. If it should work, my friend, those with the knowledge will control the future of our world."

Becker said, "And you think we should strive to acquire this knowledge?"

"We must have it!" Gruber paced with his hands behind his back, his angular frame leaning forward. "And it is still within our grasp."

"But are you not aware?" Rode warned, "Our agent in America, the only contact with Wespe, has been lost. He was uncovered, killed when the Americans tried to arrest him."

"Precisely," Gruber said, "which is why I have called you both here today. We must reestablish contact with Wespe, at any cost."

Rode blew a snort in exasperation, "Our networks are finished. Most of our agents have been captured or killed, and some have certainly talked under interrogation. Everything must be considered compromised."

"Agreed. Which is why we must start from the beginning." Gruber took a seat at his desk, coughing again, his lungs heaving to rid the spoiled subterranean air from his body. Recovering, he made every effort to sit erect and display strength, not the weariness that pulled straight from the marrow of his bones. Four thin file folders sat neatly stacked on the desk in front of him. Gruber split them, handing two to each of his compatriots. They were numbered for reference, simply one through four.

"We need someone fresh, someone unknown to your service, Freiderich. But, of course, there are requirements. This person must be absolutely fluent in English, and preferably has lived in America." Rode and Becker began to study the dossiers as Gruber continued. "These necessities limit our options, especially given that this person must be absolutely committed to our cause."

Gruber let that hang. He fell silent, allowing Rode and Becker a chance to take in the information. After a few minutes, they swapped files.

"There must be more information than this," Becker insisted. "Here there are only a few pages."

Gruber shrugged. "We are Germans, so of course volumes exist on each. I have taken the liberty of condensing the information."

Rode finished, and said, "You suggest that only one of these men be dispatched. If the matter is truly so urgent, why not enlist them all?"

"An intriguing thought, Freiderich. One which I entertained myself. But consider. Whoever we send must have enough information to contact Wespe." Gruber set his elbows on the desk and steepled his hands thoughtfully, as if in prayer. "Let me put forward a bit of wisdom from a friend of mine, a pilot in the Luftwaffe. One day, relating his flying experiences, he told me that he would prefer to fly an aircraft with one engine as opposed to two. He thought it safer. This seemed strange to me until he explained — an aircraft with two engines has twice the chance of a powerplant failure." He gestured toward the folders. "Sending them all would increase the probability of making contact with Wespe. But a single failure ruins everything."

The two men facing Gruber gave no argument to the logic.

"So the question becomes, which?"

Becker, the major, looked at Rode, perhaps deferring to rank, even though it held little substance here.

"Number two, without question," Rode said.

Becker nodded in agreement. "Number three is in the hospital, with injuries that might take time to heal. Four has been in Germany for a very long time. I suspect he might be too far removed from America. And number one, the Gestapo sergeant —he sounds like a killer, but perhaps more an animal."

"This one I know personally, and I would be inclined to agree," Gruber said. "But at least he would be true to our cause."

"Do you have reason to doubt number two?" Rode asked.

"No. His record is clear, although . . . something about it bothers me."

"I did not think anyone escaped the Cauldron on foot," Becker said, referring to the siege of Stalingrad, where Paulus's entire 6th Army was lost.

"Yes. I double-checked that. He is, as far as I know, the only one. He walked into a field hospital nearly a week after the surrender—von Manstein's relief Group. It was over fifty miles from the city. And in the middle of winter."

Rode said, "He is highly intelligent, and has fought for the Fatherland time and again. His performance reports are adequate. So what is it that you don't like about him?"

Gruber hedged, "I can't say, exactly. He grew up in America, but his father brought him to our cause at the outset of the war. Yes, he was brilliant academically, having studied architecture at the American's elite university called Harvard. But given that, his military ratings have been something less. Adequate, as you say, but nothing more. He has seen some of the fiercest fighting of the war, yet only recently found the rank of captain."

Becker said, "But any man who could walk out of the Cauldron—he is a survivor. This we need more than anything."

A distant rumble announced the arrival of another wave of American B-17s, and Gruber heard the plaintive wail of the air-raid siren.

"Where is he now?" Rode asked.

"He is assigned as a sniper, attached to the 56th Regiment."

"If this mission is as critical as you say, we must make the right choice. Let's send for him. Then we can decide."

"Yes," Gruber nodded thoughtfully. "But perhaps I will go find him myself." He gave a shout of summons, and Corporal Klein shouldered his way in against the warped door.

"When the raid has ended I will require a staff car."

The corporal shrugged. "We have none of our own, Herr Oberst. The last was taken this morning by a group of Gestapo officers. I can get on the phone —"

"Find something, you idiot!" Gruber shoved the files across his desk. "And secure these back in the safe."

Corporal Klein took the folders and headed out.